LIME STREET BLUES

A wonderful new Liverpool saga

Three Liverpool families, the Flowers, the Baileys and the McDowds, are inextricably linked by music. The youngsters revel in the heady scene of the 1960s, and three of the girls form a successful group – only splitting to go their separate ways. Rita becomes a singer, Marcia a mother and Jeannie deceives the husband she loves in order to have the family she longs for.

LIME STREET BLUES

LIME STREET BLUES

by

Maureen Lee

Magna Large Print Books
Long Preston, North Yorkshire,
BD23 4ND, England.

British Library Cataloguing in Publication Data.

Lee, Maureen
    Lime Street blues.

    A catalogue record of this book is
    available from the British Library

    ISBN   0-7505-2010-8

First published in Great Britain in 2002 by Orion,
an imprint of The Orion Publishing Group Ltd.

Copyright © Maureen Lee 2002

Cover illustration © Angelo Rinaldi by arrangement with
Orion Publishing Group Ltd.

Published in Large Print 2002 by arrangement with
Orion Publishing Group Ltd.

Magna Large Print is an imprint of Library Magna Books Ltd.

Printed and bound in Great Britain by
T.J. (International) Ltd., Cornwall, PL28 8RW

For Richard
with all my love

Part One

3

Chapter 1

1939–1940

'Rose!' Mrs Corbett bellowed. 'Where are you?'

'Up here, madam.' Rose appeared, breathless, at the top of the stairs. 'Making the beds.'

'I'd have thought you'd be finished by now.'

'I've only just started, madam.'

'Huh!' Mrs Corbett said contemptuously. She always seemed to expect her maid to have begun the next job, or even the one after that, leaving Rose with the constant feeling that she was way behind. 'Well, get a move on, girl. I want you in uniform by eleven o'clock. The vicar and his wife are coming for coffee.'

'Yes, madam.' It was exceptionally warm for June and there were beads of perspiration on Rose's brow when she returned to the colonel's room and began to plump up pillows, straighten sheets and tuck them firmly under the mattress. Colonel Max was Mrs Corbett's son, a professional soldier, presently home on leave. He was a much nicer person than his mother, very kind. She was always sorry when he had to return to his regiment.

Mrs Corbett, on the other hand, was never kind. She apparently thought the more Rose was harried, the harder she would work. But Rose already laboured as hard as she could. That

13

morning, she'd been up at six, as she was every morning, to light the Aga. On the dot of seven, Mrs Corbett had been taken up a cup of tea, two slices of bread and butter, and *The Times*. The colonel had been given his tea on the dot of eight, by which time his mother was having a bath, the coal scuttle had been filled, the washing had been hung on the line, the numerous clocks had been wound, and Mrs Denning, the cook who lived in the village, had arrived to make breakfast.

While the Corbetts ate, Rose sat down to her own breakfast, although, more often than not, the bell would ring and she would scurry into the dining room to be met with complaints that the eggs were overdone, the kippers not cooked enough, or there wasn't enough toast, none of which was Rose's fault, but Mrs Corbett behaved as if it was.

Breakfast over, she'd start on the housework; shake mats and brush carpets, dust and polish the furniture, which had to be done every day, apart from Sunday, Rose's day off, but only after ten o'clock, when the Aga had been lit and, if it was winter, fires made in the breakfast and drawing rooms, the morning tea had been served and the beds made.

Today, the housework would be interrupted because the Reverend, and Mrs Conway were coming for coffee and she would have to change out of her green overall into her maid's outfit; a black frock with long sleeves, a tiny, white, lace-trimmed apron and white cap. Thus attired, Rose would answer the door and show the visitors into the drawing room where coffee and biscuits were waiting on a silver tray and Mrs Corbett would rise to greet them, her big, over-powdered face twisted in a charming smile.

Rose wasn't required to show the visitors out. She would change back into the overall and get on with other things; cleaning the silver, for instance, or ironing, the job she disliked most. Mrs Corbett examined the finished work with a hawk's eye, looking for creases in her fine, silk underwear and expensive *crêpe de chine* blouses. Even the bedding had to be as smooth as freshly fallen snow. Rose would be bitterly scolded if one of the pure Irish linen pillow slips hadn't been ironed on both sides, something she was apt to overlook.

'You'll make some man a fine wife one day,' Mrs Denning had said more than once.

'I can't imagine getting married,' Rose usually replied. She did so again today. Both women were in the kitchen, where the windows had been flung wide open in the hope a breath of fresh air might penetrate the sweltering heat. A red-faced Mrs Denning was preparing lunch and Rose was sorting out yesterday's washing, putting it into different piles ready to be ironed. Mrs Corbett was still entertaining the Conways in the drawing room.

She picked up the iron off the Aga and spat on it. The spit sizzled to nothing straight away and she reckoned it was just about right. She put another iron in its place.

'You'll get married,' Mrs Denning assured her. 'You'll not be left on the shelf, not with those big blue eyes. How old are you now, Rose?'

15

'Fifteen,' Rose sighed. She'd been working for Mrs Corbett and keeping The Limes spick and span for over two years, ever since her thirteenth birthday. Holmwood House, the orphanage where she'd been raised, wasn't prepared to keep the children a day longer than necessary and Mrs Corbett had been to examine her, assess her fitness for the job, which for some reason involved looking inside her ears and down her throat.

'I want someone strong and healthy,' she'd said in her loud, sergeant major voice. She was a widow in her sixties, a large, majestic woman with enormous breasts that hung over the belt of her outsize brown frock. She wore a fox fur and a tiny fur hat with a spotted veil that cast little black shadows on her dour, autocratic face.

'Apart from the usual childhood illnesses, I've never known Rose be sick,' Mr Hillyard, the Governor of Holmwood House had smoothly assured her.

'But she doesn't look particularly strong In fact, I'd describe her as delicate.'

'We have another girl that might do. Would you care to see her?'

'Why not.'

Rose was sent to wait outside Mr Hillyard's office and Ann Parker was fetched for Mrs Corbett to examine, but rejected on the spot. 'She's too coarse; at least the other one has a bit of refinement about her.' Every word was audible in the corridor outside. 'What's her name again?'

'Rose Sullivan.'

'She'll just have to do. When can I have her?'

'She'll be thirteen in a fortnight. You can have her then.'

Two weeks later, at the beginning of May, a car had arrived to take Rose away from Holmwood House, a place where she had never been happy and where the word 'love' had never once been mentioned or felt. The driver got out to open the door and take the parcel containing all her worldly possessions. He was a handsome man, old enough to be her father, with broad shoulders and dark wavy hair. His skin was burnt nutmeg brown from the sun. She learnt later that his name was Tom Flowers and he was, rather appropriately, the gardener who doubled as a chauffeur when Mrs Corbett needed to be driven anywhere.

He hardly spoke on the way to The Limes, merely muttering that if she was good and behaved herself she'd get on fine with her new employer. 'She's a hard taskmaster, but her bark's worse than her bite.'

Rose was soon to discover the truth of the first part of this remark, but never the second.

The Limes was a square, grey brick building with eight bedrooms set in five acres of well-tended grounds. Inside was comfortably furnished, though on her first day she didn't see the rooms she would soon come to know well, as Tom Flowers took her round to a side entrance, through a long, narrow room with a deep brown sink, a dolly tub, and a mangle. A sturdy clothes rack was suspended from the ceiling.

He opened another door and they entered a

vast kitchen with a red tiled floor and white walls, from which hung an assortment of copper-bottomed pans, from the very small to the very large. Waves of heat were coming from a giant stove. The shelves of an enormous dresser were filled with pretty blue and white china and there was a bowl of brightly coloured flowers on the pine table that could easily have seated a dozen.

'Mrs Corbett's out for the day,' Tom Flowers informed her, 'and Mrs Denning, the cook, won't be back for a while. I'll show you your room. Once you've unpacked, perhaps you'd like to go for a walk around the village. Ailsham's a nice place, you'll like it. Just turn right when you leave the gates and you'll come to the shops about a mile away.'

'Ta,' Rose whispered.

'Come on then, girl,' he said brusquely. 'You're on the second floor.'

He marched out of the kitchen, up a wide staircase, then a narrower one, Rose having to run to keep up. The door to her room was already open, her things on the bed. Tom Flowers said something that she presumed was 'goodbye', closed the door, and Rose was left alone.

She sat on the bed. It was quite a pleasant room with a sloping ceiling. The distempered walls, the curtains on the small window, and the cotton coverlet on the bed were white. There was a rag rug on the otherwise bare wooden floor, a little chest of drawers, and a single wardrobe. Later, when she opened the wardrobe to hang her too short winter coat, she found a black frock that was much too long and a green overall that

18

would have fitted someone twice her size.

Rose felt too miserable to unpack then. Unhappiness rose like a ball in her throat. Tom Flowers's footsteps could be heard, getting further and further away and, with each step, the unhappiness grew until she could hardly breathe. She lay on the bed and began to cry into the soft, white pillow. She wanted her mother. That could never be because her mother was dead, but she wanted her all the same. All she could remember was a blurred face, a soft voice, soft music, arms reaching for her as she toddled across the room, being cuddled by someone who could only have been her mother. Then one day the soft voice stopped and the music was no more. She had never been cuddled again. The voices since had been harsh, even when she was told that her mother had died. The birth certificate she'd been given with her things stated 'Father Unknown'. She had no one. Now she didn't even have the orphanage, where at least she'd felt safe. She was completely alone in the world.

More than two years later, Rose was still not happy, but she had settled into The Limes. Mrs Denning was a cheerful soul and they got on well. She had two sons, one a year older than Rose the other a year younger, who kept her amused with their escapades. She would never grow used to Mrs Corbett's sharp tongue and being told she was lazy and stupid, but it didn't upset her as much as when she'd first arrived. Her favourite time was evening when she enjoyed the solitude of her room, her head buried in one of the books she'd borrowed from the library van that parked by Ailsham Green for two hours every Wednesday afternoon. She was supposed to have time off when lunch was over and before the afternoon visitors were due to arrive. It was wise to escape from the house, otherwise Mrs Corbett was liable to forget it was her free time and demand she get on with some work. Discovering the library van had been a blessing. She liked romances best, stories about men and women falling in love. Rose wanted someone to love her more than anything in the world.

She had just finished the ironing when Tom Flowers tramped into the kitchen for his midday meal, followed by Colonel Max. Neither men was married and they were the best of friends. The same age, thirty-nine, they had played together as children. Tom's father, grandfather, and great-grandfather before him, had tended the gardens of The Limes since the middle of the last century.

The colonel was delighted to see her. 'I swear this young lady grows prettier by the day,' he exclaimed. 'What do you say, Tom?'

Tom glanced at her briefly. 'Aye,' he muttered. He was a taciturn man, though always polite. Rose found it strange that the gardener, with his tall, strong frame and square shoulders, looked far more the military man than Colonel Max, who was small, almost bald, and rather endearingly ugly.

'One of the pleasures of coming home on leave is having my morning tea brought by the best-looking girl in Ailsham,' the colonel enthused.

'I was just saying, she'll make someone a fine wife one of these days,' Mrs Denning put in.

'If I were twenty years younger, the someone would be me.'

Mrs Denning grinned. She knew, they all knew, including the colonel himself that Mrs Corbett would sooner be dead than allow her son to marry a servant.

Rose's cheeks were already burning and they burnt even more when she noticed Tom Flowers was looking at her again, not so briefly this time. There was an expression on his face, almost of surprise, as if he'd never seen her properly before. She caught his eye and he quickly turned away.

'Lunch will be ready in ten minutes, Colonel,' Mrs Denning sang. 'C'mon, Tom, sit down and take the weight off your feet.' She and Tom were also friends, having gone to the village school together, though Mrs Denning had been in a lower class. In fact, everyone in Ailsham seemed to be connected in one way or another. Rose felt as if she was living in a foreign country and would never belong.

'I suppose I'd better get changed.' The colonel left the room with a sigh, from which she assumed he would much prefer to eat in the kitchen with the servants than with his autocratic mother, but that would have been almost as terrible a crime as wanting to marry one.

Was she really all that pretty? Rose examined her reflection in the mirror behind the wardrobe door before setting out on her afternoon walk.

She had brown hair, very thick and wavy, a bit wild, framing her face like a halo. It seemed a very common or garden face, she thought, with two eyes, a nose, and a mouth. She smiled at herself to see if it made any difference and several dimples appeared in her cheeks, still pink as a result of the colonel's comments. She shrugged and supposed she wasn't so bad.

The shrug reminded her that her brassiere was too tight and she needed a bigger one, size thirty-six. The black frock that had been too big when she first arrived would soon fit perfectly.

The countryside surrounding Ailsham was too lonely to wander around on her own and a bit dull. Rose had got into the habit of walking as far as the village where she usually treated herself to a bar of toffee or chocolate, or a quarter of dolly mixtures.

Ailsham was pleasantly ordinary, not the sort of village that often featured in the books Rose so avidly read. There wasn't a thatched cottage to be seen, nor an ancient stone church with a steeple. She had yet to find a gurgling stream, a hump-backed bridge, or a pretty copse. There were no gently sloping hills, this part of Lancashire being very flat. There was a brook somewhere off Holly Lane, but to get there meant walking along the edge of two ploughed fields and perhaps getting lost.

The village was served by a tiny station, from which trains ran hourly to Liverpool, fifteen miles away, and Ormskirk, only four. The Ribble bus ran twice a day to the same places, early morning and late afternoon, though not on Sundays.

The shops were still closed for lunch when Rose arrived on this particular day; the butchers, where one of Mrs Denning's sons, Luke, worked, the bakers, Dorothy's Hairdressers and Beryl's Fashions where Rose bought all her clothes, including the pink and white gingham frock she had on now and the blue silky one she wore on Sundays. Beryl also sold ladies' underwear, wool, and sewing things. The biggest shop was Harker's, which was actually five shops in one; a general store, a greengrocers, newsagents, tobacconists, and post office.

She sat on a bench at the edge of the green and waited for the shops to open. The pub, the Oak Tree, which got its name from the huge tree on the green directly opposite, was busy and customers, all men, were sitting at the tables outside. The pub, the shops, and most of the houses that she'd passed, had posters in the windows advertising the Midsummer Fête to be held on the village green a week on Saturday. It was being organised by the Women's Institute of which Mrs Corbett was a founding member and chairman of the committee. For weeks now, groups of women had been meeting in the drawing room of The Limes to make final arrangements for the fete. There was a perfectly good Women's Institute hall between the school and the Oak Tree that would have been far more convenient, but the chairman preferred the committee came to her house. Rose wasn't the only person Mrs Corbett bossed around.

The butchers threw open its doors, followed by the bakers. Soon, all five shops were open, but Rose didn't move from the bench. She was watching two girls of about her own age, both vaguely familiar, walking along the path that encircled the green, arms linked companionably.

'Oh, look,' one remarked as they drew nearer. 'The door's open. which means I'm late. Mrs Harker will have my guts for garters.' She abandoned her companion and began to run. 'See you tonight at quarter to six by the station,' she shouted. 'I'm really looking forward to that Clark Gable picture.'

'Me too.' The other girl sauntered into Beryl's Fashions and Rose recognised her as Heather, Beryl's assistant. Beryl mustn't mind her being late.

Rose would have liked to work in a shop and quite fancied going to the pictures, but what she would have liked most of all was to have a friend, someone to link arms with. She rarely met anyone her own age except in the shops. If say she went into Beryl's and bought the brassiere she obviously needed and Heather invited her to the pictures – a most unlikely event – she couldn't possibly go. At quarter to six, she would be setting the table for dinner, which would be served at precisely six o'clock. It would be well past seven when her duties were finished. By then, she would be too weary to walk as far as the station. Anyway, the picture would be half over by the time she got there.

She jumped to her feet, bought a whole half pound of dolly mixtures, and ate them on the way back to The Limes.

Music was coming from the barn that Colonel Max's father had turned into a games room for his sons – the colonel's elder brother had been killed in the Great War. It had a billiard table, a dart board, and a badminton court. The music was jazz, which the colonel only played out of earshot of his mother, who couldn't stand it. Rose loved any sort of music. She danced a few steps on the gravel path, hut stopped immediately, embarrassed, when she saw Tom Flowers regarding her with amusement from the rose garden.

'You look happy,' he said.

'Oh, I am,' she said, but only because it seemed churlish to say that she wasn't.

She went through the laundry room into the kitchen, which should have been empty as Mrs Denning went home as soon as lunch was over and didn't return until half four to make dinner. Rose was surprised to find a cross Mrs Corbett waiting for her, demanding to know why she hadn't answered the bell she'd been ringing for ages.

'It was my time off madam. I've been for a walk,' Rose stammered.

'Oh!' Mrs Corbett looked slightly nonplussed. 'Well, you're late back. I'm having a bridge party this afternoon. I want you in uniform immediately. My guests will be arriving very soon.'

In fact, Rose was five minutes early, but Mrs Corbett would only have got crosser if she'd pointed it out.

A week later, the colonel's leave ended and he left for France. Lots of people telephoned or called personally to wish him luck, which had never happened before.

'Look after yourself Max, old boy.'

'Take care, Colonel. Keep your head down, if only for your mother's sake.'

War between Great Britain and Germany was imminent. Once it started, the colonel's regiment would be on the front line. Mrs Corbett, who'd lost one son in the 'war to end all wars', retired to her room after Colonel Max had gone, and stayed there all morning, emerging as steely-eyed as ever at lunch-time and complaining bitterly that the lamb was tough.

War, when it came, made little difference to Rose's life. It just became busier. Mrs Corbett joined the Women's Voluntary Service and held coffee mornings and garden parties to raise funds. Rose was required to make gallons of coffee and tea, and carry it round to the guests. Mrs Denning had to bake mountains of sausage rolls and fairy cakes, yet was still expected to have the meals ready on time.

'Does she think I'm a miracle worker or something?' she asked Rose in an injured voice.

It came as an unpleasant shock when, after Christmas. Mrs Denning announced she was leaving to work in a munitions factory in Kirkby at four times her present wage. A special bus came through Ailsham to pick the workers up. Mrs Corbett would just have to find another cook.

26

'But I don't like leaving you behind, love,' Mrs Denning said. 'There'll be no one for you to talk to once I'm gone. Look, why don't you leave, get another job? There's loads of work going, what with all the men being called up. You could earn more money and mix with young people for a change.'

'Yes, but where would I live?' Rose wanted to know.

'You'd have to find digs. It shouldn't be too difficult.'

'I'll think about it.' She was too scared. She felt safe in The Limes, just as she'd done in the orphanage. There was a saying, something about sticking with the devil you know. Mrs Corbett was the devil, and Rose would stick with her, for the forseeable future at least.

Mrs Corbett had found it impossible to hire another cook. She wasn't alone. Her friends were having the same problem. Not only cooks, but housemaids, nursemaids, parlourmaids, even charwomen, were abandoning their employers to take up war work. Mrs Conway's maid had become a WREN. Some women regarded it as unpatriotic. How could they be expected to run their own households without servants?

'Of course, it's not unpatriotic,' Mrs Corbett said sternly. 'We've all got to do our bit.' But she hadn't been near the kitchen except to give orders since her own cook had left. A stunned Rose had discovered she was expected to do the cooking in Mrs Denning's place.

'But I can't,' she gasped when the additional

27

duties were explained to her. 'Can't cook, that is.'

'Did you learn nothing from Mrs Denning in all the time you've been here?' Mrs Corbett asked cuttingly.

'No, madam.' There'd been too many other things to do than watch the meals being made. She could fry things, boil things, but when it came to roasting meat, baking bread, making cakes, she was lost. The Aga had four ovens that each did different things, she had no idea what.

She coped for a week. Mrs Corbett was invited out to dine several times, but when she ate at home, the complaints increased with every meal. The chops were burnt, the potatoes soggy, the jelly hadn't properly set. She was a foolish girl for not realising it should have been made the day before.

On Sunday, two old school friends arrived to stay, the Misses Dolly and Daisy Clayburn, who lived in Poplar and were convinced Hitler was about to bomb the place out of existence. On their first morning, Rose found the laundry basket in the bathroom overflowing with dirty clothes they'd brought with them. She took them downstairs and was putting them to soak in the sink in the laundry room, when Luke Denning arrived on his bike bringing a huge piece of meat. It was a horrible morning, very stormy, and the rain ran in rivulets from the brim of his sou'wester and the hem of his oilskin cape.

'We're lucky, living in the country while there's a war on,' he said cheerfully. 'Town folk'd give their eye teeth for a leg of lamb that size.'

'Lucky!' Rose said weakly.

28

'Well, I'll be off.' Luke got back on his bike. 'Oh, by the way. You'll have to collect your own meat as from next week. I'm leaving Friday. Ma's got me a job in her factory. 'Bye, Rose.'

''Bye.'

Rose carried the meat inside and put it on the draining board. It looked much too big to be part of the little woolly lambs she'd seen frolicking over the fields. What was she supposed to do with it? Should it go in the oven covered with greaseproof paper? If so, for how long? Did it have to be cut into bits and stewed – or was that steak, the cheap sort? Maybe it had to be boiled?

She made the morning tea and took Mrs Corbett's up first, then returned for the Misses Clayburns'. They were both sitting up in the double bed when she went into their room.

'We heard the rattle of dishes and were expecting you,' said one. 'Oh, this is nice, isn't it, Dolly? Just listen to that rain! Could we have marmalade with our bread and butter, dear?'

Rose raced downstairs for the marmalade. She was hurrying down a second time, the marmalade delivered, when Mrs Corbett called.

'Was that Luke with the lamb I heard earlier?' she asked. When Rose confirmed that was the case, she said, 'I'd like it roasted for lunch, the potatoes too, served with cauliflower and peas. And don't forget the gravy. For afters, we'll have suet pudding and custard. And kindly stop running everywhere, Rose. There's no need for it. It sounded as if a cart horse was galloping up and down the stairs.'

There was a tight, panicky feeling in her chest

29

as Rose ran through the rain to the coalhouse with the scuttles, filled them, and brought them back one at a time. She was already way behind this morning. The fires had refused to light, the strong wind had whistled down the chimneys and blown the paper out before the flames had caught. She'd had to reset them twice. She wound the clocks, cut the rind off the bacon, and prayed she wouldn't break the yolks when she fried the eggs, something Mrs Corbett found extremely irritating. Then she remembered she'd used the last of the bread to take upstairs, there was none left for toast and the baker hadn't yet arrived with a fresh supply – even Mrs Corbett accepted she couldn't expect her to make home-baked bread.

Her hands were shaking when she set the dining room table. It was quarter to nine, almost time for breakfast. The food had to be served on covered platters on a side table so people could help themselves. She returned to the kitchen and put the strips of bacon in a frying pan on the simmering plate of the Aga, then fried the eggs on the hot plate. All the time, the leg of lamb stared at her balefully from the draining board.

At nine o'clock promptly, Mrs Corbett and her friends came down for breakfast. The bell rang almost immediately, as Rose knew it would. The yolks had broken on five of the six eggs and she was in for a scolding.

'You seem to have forgotten something, Rose,' Mrs Corbett said cuttingly when she went in. 'Although you have provided us with butter, jam and marmalade, there's no toast to put it on. And why is your hair all wet, girl? You look very untidy.'

'It must've got wet when I fetched the coal, madam.'

'Did you not think to wear a scarf? You're obviously having trouble waking up this morning.'

'I'm afraid the bread still hasn't been delivered.' It wasn't her fault, but she felt as if it was and the panicky feeling spread to her entire body. Her legs were threatening to give way.

Mrs Corbett rolled her eyes. 'Please hurry. We'll just have to do without toast, though it isn't very satisfactory. My previous cook wasn't exactly cordon bleu,' she remarked as Rose went out the door, 'but she was vastly superior to this one.'

Rose didn't have time to eat. She hastily cleaned the drawing room, while waiting for the bell to ring when the eggs with the broken yolks were discovered and she'd be subjected to another dressing down. But Mrs Corbett must have decided she'd had enough that morning and the bell didn't ring again.

She was in the laundry, stirring the washing with the dolly when the bread arrived, delivered by the baker himself in his van. 'Won't be doing this much longer,' he said. 'You'll have to get it from the shop. Petrol's being rationed soon. I say, you look moidered. I reckon they're working you too hard. 'Bye, love.'

She hardly heard a word he'd said. She transferred the washing to the sink and rinsed it, then fed each garment twice through the mangle. It was no use hanging the things outside today, so

31

she let down the rack. When everything had been spread as neatly as possible to minimise the ironing, she pulled it back up, something she always found difficult, but it had only gone halfway when she found she could pull it no further. All the strength had gone from her arms. She tried frantically to cling to the rope, but could feel it slipping through her hands, burning the flesh, and the next minute the rack, full of clean clothes, was on the floor.

Rose fainted.

When she came to, she was on the bed in her room and Tom Flowers was bending over her.

'Just found you lying on the floor, so I carried you up here,' he said gruffly, his brown eyes puckered with concern. 'Are you all right?'

'I don't know.' Her body felt as light as air and her head was swimming. She remembered the washing and tried to sit up, but Tom pushed her down again.

'Stay there,' he commanded. 'You need to rest. You've been looking fair worn out lately. Mrs Corbett's a good woman, but she's expecting too much. There was a time when someone came in to do the laundry and all the maid had to do was clean. Now Mrs Denning's gone and you're doing the cooking an' all. I'll have a word with the mistress later.'

'Please don't,' Rose implored. 'She might give me the sack.'

'Never in a million years, young lady,' he assured her with a smile. 'She'd never find a more willing worker than you.'

Rose burst into tears. 'But I don't know what to

do with the lamb,' she sobbed. 'And how do you make suet pudding?'

'You'll learn eventually. All women should know how to cook.' He patted her hand. 'I'll get someone to fetch tea.'

The Clayburn sisters brought the tea, full of sympathy and apologies. 'We're sorry about the washing,' Dolly said, 'but we were so busy packing and shutting down the house, that we hadn't done the laundry for days. Evelyn, Mrs Corbett, said to put it in the basket and you'd do it.'

'And I'm sorry I asked for marmalade this morning,' Daisy put in. 'When you brought it, you looked rushed off your feet. It's just that it made such a lovely change, being waited on in bed. We don't have a maid at home. As from tomorrow, me and Dolly will do the cooking in return for our keep.'

'Thank you,' Rose whispered.

'Evelyn's quite a kind person, but she's a bit of a bully – she was at school. Remember, Daise?'

'I do indeed,' Daisy said in a heartfelt voice. 'A terrible bully.'

Later in the day, Mrs Corbett put her head around the door. 'You should have said you were over-worked,' she said sourly. 'It was foolish to just try keep on until you dropped. From now on, I'll send the washing to the laundry and the Clayburns will take over the cooking. I've just had a phone call from Harker's. They won't be delivering groceries any more, so you can start doing the shopping. There's a bike in the garage. I'll ask Tom to do it up and get a basket for the front.'

At first, she was rather wobbly on the bike, but soon got the hang of it. It was lovely cycling along the country lanes early in the morning, whatever the weather, a shopping list in her pocket, always hoping Mrs Corbett had forgotten something, which happened occasionally and she'd be asked to go again.

Dolly and Daisy Clayburn were without side and had no qualms about being friendly with a servant. Rose was almost glad she'd fainted. Since then, everything had changed out of all proportion for the better. In May, when she turned sixteen, the sisters made her first birthday cake, a chocolate sponge with her name on in white icing. It tasted wonderful.

Nowadays, there were only the two of them when Tom Flowers came in for lunch. She couldn't remember being carried upstairs but, knowing that she had lain in his arms, made her think of Tom as someone she could always rely on if ever she was in trouble again. He was the first person to show her any tenderness and she felt grateful.

Sometimes he came bearing a letter from Colonel Max, who was still in France and always asked after her. She'd give Tom a message to send back. For a long while, the colonel had had little to do except drink wine in the local cafés until the awful day came when Hitler invaded and he was caught up in the vicious fighting. Mrs Corbett was bad-tempered with everyone until, in June, the colonel arrived home to convalesce, having been rescued with a bullet in his shoulder in the great evacuation of Dunkirk.

'Ah, this is what kept me going during the worst of the fighting, the thought of an angel bringing my tea,' the colonel sighed blissfully when Rose entered his room on his first morning back. 'I've missed you, Rose.'

'I've missed you, Colonel. We all have.'

'Yes, but you're the only one that matters, my dear.' He sighed again. 'If only I were younger or you were older! God can be very cruel, Rose.'

'He can indeed, Colonel.' She had no idea what he was talking about.

A few weeks later, Mrs Corbett threw a party to celebrate her son's safe return. Tom Flowers was invited. He was the only man present not wearing a dinner jacket, just a dark suit and tie, and a dazzling white shirt. Rose, whose job it was to take the drinks around the crowded room, thought he looked incredibly handsome, if a trifle uncomfortable, in such exalted company. She stopped in front of him. 'Would you like something to drink?'

'No, ta. I only drink beer.'

'There's some in the kitchen. Shall I fetch it?'

'They'll start dancing any minute. I'll come and help myself.'

The tray quickly emptied and she returned to the kitchen for more. Minutes later, Nelson Eddy began to sing 'Lover Come Back to Me'. It was one of the records the Clayburns had brought with them and she knew the words off by heart. She sang along at the top of her voice, knowing she would never be heard above the din in the drawing room.

'You have a lovely voice, Rose. Though I should have known. Everything about you is lovely.' Colonel Max was standing in the doorway, watching her with a sober expression on his plain little face that always reminded Rose of a loveable monkey. He looked just a little bit drunk. The gay atmosphere had made her feel a tiny bit drunk herself though not a drop of wine had passed her lips. 'Dance with me,' the colonel pleaded. 'It's something else I dreamed about in France when things got unbearably bad.' He seized her about the waist and began whirl her around the table.

'I can't dance,' she gasped.

'Neither can I, my dear, and this shoulder doesn't help.'

She laughed out loud as she attempted to keep in step. 'You're mad, Colonel.'

'Mad about you, Rose. Mad about you.'

There was a loud cough and a voice said stiffly, 'Excuse me.' Tom Flowers entered the room.

'Go away, Tom,' the colonel cried. 'Can't you see Rose and I are busy?'

'Your mother is asking for you, sir. There's someone she'd like you to dance with.'

'He only calls me "sir" when he's annoyed,' the colonel said gaily. 'What's the matter, Tom? Are you jealous? Tell my mother I'm otherwise engaged.'

Rose stopped dancing and pushed him away. 'If you don't mind, Colonel, I think it'd be best if you went.' Mrs Corbett's anger would be directed at her, not her son, if she discovered what he was up to.

Sniffing tragically, the dejected colonel went to do his mother's bidding. For a long while, Tom Flowers stayed where he was, just inside the door, not speaking. Rose was uncomfortably aware of his dark, brooding face and burning eyes.

'It wasn't my fault,' she said when the silence had gone on for too long.

'What wasn't?' Tom growled.

'That Colonel Max asked me to dance.'

'I know that.'

There was another silence, then Tom said in a strained voice. 'You've never seen my house, have you?'

It was the last thing she'd expected him to say. 'Yes. I have. I've passed it loads of times.'

'I'd like you to see it proper.'

'That'd be nice,' she said politely.

'Come tomorrow, after lunch. About two o'clock.'

'All right, Tom. Thank you.'

Disraeli Terrace consisted of ten whitewashed houses with gardens front and back, the only properties in long, winding Holly Lane, about a mile from Ailsham. The houses had been built a hundred years before by the Corbett family for their farmworkers, Tom informed Rose the next day. Anthony Corbett had been a Conservative Member of Parliament and a friend of Benjamin Disraeli, the Prime Minister, hence the name of the terrace.

At the turn of the century, Tom said, the farm land was sold to a local farmer, along with the houses – all except one. When Anthony Corbett died, he had bequeathed the end property, number ten, to his gardener, Ernest Flowers, as a reward for a lifetime of loyal service. The land had been extended, so that the plot of number ten was three times as big as the other nine. Two years before his death. when Colonel Max's father had had electricity installed in The Limes, he had insisted his gardener's house be in receipt of the same facility.

'It's the only one in the row,' Tom said proudly.

'And it's actually *yours*.' Rose was greatly impressed.

A glorious sun shone out of a clear blue sky, exactly the same shade as her best frock, as he showed her around the garden; a velvety lawn surrounded by a wide border of magically scented bushes, flowers and small trees comprising every colour of the rainbow. He told her the names. 'Them's hydrangeas, that's broom, the tree in the corner's lilac and that one's cherry. They're begonias, my favourite. They last till the summer's almost out.'

'It's a nicer garden than The Limes,' Rose said admiringly. 'More colourful, more...' She searched for the right word. 'More haphazard.'

Tom looked pleased. 'Mrs Corbett likes things to be neat and regular. I prefer them a bit wild, haphazard, like you said. I used to grow all my own vegetables until Mother passed away five years ago. The vegetable patch has been lying fallow ever since, but there's still plenty of fruit. Do you like strawberries?'

'Yes,' Rose breathed.

'Well, you can eat the lot come next June.'

'Those flowers around the back door are very pretty.'

'Them's clematis.' He pointed to a sturdy garden shed. 'That's where my dad used to smoke his pipe – Mother wouldn't allow it in the house. Let's go indoors, see what you think about the kitchen.'

Children were playing in the other gardens, their cries and laughter oddly muted in the heat and stillness of the afternoon air. She couldn't remember a child having been near The Limes and the sounds made her smile. 'I love it here,' she cried.

Tom was watching her delighted face. 'It's lovely having you.'

They went inside and she said she much preferred his kitchen to the one in The Limes. It had the same red tiled floor, but was only a fraction of the size, as was the table and the dresser with its flower patterned china.

'It's just right,' she said. 'Not too big and not too small.' The electric stove had four hotplates and an oven and appeared much easier to use than the Aga. A long window over the sink looked out on to the garden. It needed lacy curtains and a bowl of flowers on the sill, she thought.

'The parlour's through here.' He showed her into a cosy room full of dark furniture and a comfortable leatherette three piece. The wallpaper was patterned with swirling red roses. There was an attractive maroon tiled fireplace with a matching rug in front.

'You've got a wireless,' Rose exclaimed. 'And a

piano. I've always wanted to play.' She sometimes played the piano in her dreams.

'It's never too late to learn,' Tom said gruffly.

'Chance'd be a fine thing.' She laughed. 'Mrs Corbett wouldn't let me near her piano.'

'You can play that one whenever you like.'

'Thank you, but I wouldn't know where to start.' She thought it a very peculiar offer. She touched the gleaming lid, which had recently been polished, and couldn't, for the life of her, imagine him with a duster. 'Who keeps everywhere clean?'

'A woman along the way, a widder, does it in return for me doing her garden. She makes my meals an' all. Come on, Rose.' He ushered her through another door into a narrow hall with narrow stairs, apparently determined to show her every inch of his house. Although she felt flattered, she couldn't help but wonder why.

'Have you got any brothers and sisters?' she asked as she climbed after him.

'Two brothers, both younger than me. They left Ailsham for Canada in nineteen twenty-three, not long after Dad died. They send cards at Christmas, but they've never been back. This is the main bedroom.'

They entered a large square room with a low ceiling, more highly polished furniture, and a bed with a brass head and foot.

'It's very nice,' Rose said truthfully. She would have preferred lighter wallpaper everywhere, but it seemed rude to say so.

The two other bedrooms were smaller, but a perfectly adequate size. Tom remembered he hadn't shown her the bathroom. 'It was just an outhouse next to the kitchen, but I had it converted. You can see it later. Would you like a glass of lemonade?'

'Yes, please.'

They returned to the kitchen. Tom's hands shook as he poured the lemonade. He seemed unusually agitated. 'Rose,' he began, then paused, his face glowing a bright, beetroot red.

'Yes?' she said encouragingly.

'Rose, will you...' He paused again. 'Lord Almighty!' he groaned in an anguished voice. 'I never thought this'd happen to me at my age.' He stood and went to the window, looking out, not at her. 'Rose, I want to marry you. I want you to be my wife.' He turned and said huskily, 'I love you, girl. You're on my mind every minute of every day. It's driving me insane.' He fell on his knees in front of her. 'What do you say, Rose? The house, everything I have is yours. I'll look after you, worship you, for the rest of my life.'

Rose bent and put her cheek against his hot one. When she thought about it later, it seemed incredible that she didn't feel in the least surprised. Tom sighed and slid his big arms around her waist. They stayed like that for a long time, both perfectly content. She had given him his answer. More than anything in the world Rose wanted to be loved.

'Are you sure you know what you're doing, girl?' Mrs Corbett asked worriedly when Rose took in her morning tea a few days later.

'Yes, madam.'

'Tom's a fine man, the best, but he's more than twice your age, very old-fashioned and set in his ways. You've had no experience of life. There'll be plenty of young men after you when you're older.'

'I want to marry Tom,' Rose said stubbornly. All Mrs Corbett cared about was losing her maid, knowing she'd never find another while there was a war on. That was the only reason she looked so worried.

Three months later, on a golden day in September, when the leaves were just beginning to fall, Rose Sullivan became Mrs Thomas Flowers. Colonel Max was Tom's best man. There were only three other guests; the Clayburn sisters, who dressed identically and pretended to be bridesmaids, and Mrs Denning.

'The luckiest chap in the world has just married the prettiest woman,' the colonel said soberly when he kissed the bride. 'Are you happy, Rose?'

'I've never been happier, Colonel.'

'Then I hope you stay that way, my dearest girl.'

Rose couldn't understand why there were tears in his eyes.

Part Two

Chapter 2

1957

Jeannie Flowers lay face down on the grass. The hot sun beat down on her back through her school frock, and she liked the way the dry grass tickled her nose and chin, and the palms of her hands.

'Would you like a strawberry?' her mother enquired.

'In a minute, Mum.' She didn't want to move. She felt as if she was part of the garden, connected to the earth itself, as she listened to the birds chirrupping fussily away in the hawthorn hedge and the humming of a bee that was probably nestled in one of the buttercups or daisies that sprang up minutes after the grass was cut – or so her dad claimed.

'Mind you don't get grass stains on your frock, and don't forget your piano practice!'

'I'll get changed in a minute and practise after tea.' Any other day but Friday, she would have taken off the frock as soon as she got home to wear for school next day. She lay where she was until the bee sounded dangerously close, then sat up.

Her mother was sitting on a cane chair with the bowl of strawberries she'd just picked on her knee. Rose Flowers – 'the prettiest name in the world for the world's prettiest woman', according to Jeannie's Dad – had spent the day preparing food for the weekend; pies, savoury and sweet, a large slab of bunloaf, dozens of scones and fairy cakes, and three crusty loaves. The strawberries were for jam. Rose gave one to her daughter. There was a film of flour on her arms and a dab on the end of her little straight nose. 'This looks the biggest.'

'Ta, Mum.'

Mother and daughter, one a smaller version of the other, didn't speak for a while, both thinking about the weekend ahead.

Tomorrow, Ailsham Womens Institute was holding its regular Midsummer Fête on the village green. Rose was in charge of the white elephant stall and the garden shed was full of bric–a–brac that people had been bringing for weeks. Jeannie had offered to help, mainly because she had her eye on a pretty manicure set and an enamelled compact, which Mum had refused to let her buy until the day because it wouldn't be fair.

'And anyway, love, I'm not sure if you're old enough to have a compact at eleven.'

'Oh, *Mum*. There won't be powder in it, will there?' Jeannie had snorted.

'Not if I've got anything to do with it,' her father had said grimly. Women only used cosmetics to disguise the fact they were plain, he claimed, and most didn't manage it successfully. Jeannie's mother had been forbidden to wear make-up – she'd never owned a lipstick in her life.

Dad was entering his marrows and tomatoes in the vegetable show and would almost certainly win again. Some people said this was unfair, Tom Flowers being a gardener by trade, to which Tom would reply that he could have entered a dozen varieties of vegetables and swept the board, not to mention a host of blooms. He had roses in his garden as big as cabbages.

Jeannie could smell the roses now. Their sweet scent, mixed with the quite different smells emanating from the kitchen, made her even more aware of how utterly perfect life was. If she'd had more energy, she would have leapt to her feet, done a little dance, and sung a little song to express her happiness.

Instead, she uttered a long, contented sigh. Her mother looked up and their blue eyes met. They understood each other. Rose smiled. 'Lovely, isn't it,' she breathed.

'Mm!' Jeannie nodded. They were the luckiest, most fortunate family in the world. On Sunday, her younger brother, Gerald, would be nine. Instead of a party, Gerald had asked to go to New Brighton on the ferry, which involved catching the train from Ailsham to Liverpool, then the boat from the Pier Head.

Weekends were always enjoyable, but this was going to be one of the best.

Her elder brother, Max, came into the garden, looking cross. He threw his royal blue blazer, his satchel, and then himself on to the grass. 'Bloody teachers!' he groaned.

'Max!' his mother gasped.

'They damn well are. Well, some are.'

47

'What did you do wrong?' enquired Jeannie.

'Nothing.' Max's tone was hurt. 'Not a damn, bloody thing, yet I still got the strap.'

'I'm sure you must have done something to deserve it, son.'

'You always say that,' Max said hotly. 'You and Dad are never on my side. It so happens that, in the dinner hour, some lousy idiot saw two grammar school boys smoking in Orrell cemetery and reported them to the Head. When they refused to own up, Mr Francis decided to punish everyone who'd been out. Me and Chris Beatty only went to buy lolly ices and ended up getting walloped.'

'That seems awfully unfair, Mum.' Jeannie was anxious that the happy atmosphere not be spoilt. The normally easy-going, if excitable, Max had become quite tetchy lately. He was fourteen, a handsome boy, proud of his good looks, but worried he was growing no taller, while the other boys in his class were shooting skywards. Far more worrying for Jeannie was that he had begun to have violent arguments with their father, whose word until then had been law. Max was named after Colonel Max Corbett, their father's employer and best friend.

'Where's your cap?' Rose enquired.

'In my pocket.'

'And your tie?'

'In the other pocket.'

'Would you like a strawberry? And there's lemonade in the larder.'

Jeannie got to her feet. 'I'll get the lemonade.'

'Ta, sis.'

48

Max came into the kitchen with her, claiming he was hungry. He helped himself to two of the fairy cakes that were for tomorrow's fête. 'Where's our Gerald?' he asked with his mouth full.

'Gone looking for frog spawn in Holly Brook.'

'Lucky sod. I wish I were eight again. One thing I'd never do is pass the bloody eleven-Plus. If I'd failed, I'd have gone to an ordinary school like every other boy in Ailsham. I'd be learning useful things, like woodwork, not stupid Latin.'

'I quite hope I pass the eleven-Plus.' Jeannie had sat the exam a few weeks before.

'Then you must be mad.'

Gerald arrived with a jam jar full of frog spawn, which he emptied into the garden pond. Rose came indoors to prepare vegetables for the tea; home-grown potatoes, runner beans, and carrots. She turned on the oven to heat up a steak and kidney pie she'd made earlier. Jeannie stayed to help, while Max went into the parlour to do his homework, and Gerald disappeared into the lavatory with that week's *Beano*.

On Fridays, Rose always waited for Tom to come home so the family could have tea together. At exactly ten past six, the latch clicked on the gate, and Jeannie looked up to see the tall figure of Tom Flowers wheel his bike into the shed.

Seconds later, he came into the kitchen, his darkly sunburnt face moist with perspiration, clasped his wife in his broad arms, and kissed her. It was a full minute before he noticed Jeannie. 'Hello, luv.' He chucked her under the chin. 'Shouldn't you have changed out of that frock by now?'

'I was just about to, Dad. I've been helping Mum.'

'And have you done your piano practice yet?'

'I'll do it later,' Jeannie said patiently. She liked playing the piano, practising regularly every day, and couldn't understand why people found it necessary to remind her.

'Where are the lads?'

'Around somewhere. Jeannie, set the table, there's a good girl. Tea will be ready in a minute.'

Jeannie threw a yellow and white check cloth over the big, pine table, and began to put out the knives, forks, and placemats with a hunting scene that Dad had bought her mother last Christmas, along with a jug of cream and a bowl of cold, stewed apple for afters. She quickly changed her school frock for an old one, and five minutes later, the Flowers family sat down to tea.

Outside, the sun continued to shine and the birds to sing. A cool, welcome breeze sprang up, blowing gently through the open door and windows, and Spencer, the cat, returned from one of his adventures. Spencer was a great, black tom, with a white vest and three white paws. He jumped on to the dresser and, with calm dignity, watched them eat.

It was the perfect beginning to what would be a perfect weekend, Jeannie thought, and a thrill of pure happiness coursed through her.

Later though, the evening was rather spoilt by yet another row between her father and Max over why the Flowers didn't have a television. Everyone at school had one, why not them?

'If we can't afford it, I'll get a job; do a paper round, work in the fields at weekends,' Max said desperately when everyone transferred to the parlour, a dark, bleak room where the piano was. It was full of big, old-fashioned furniture that had belonged to their grandmother who had died long before the children were born. The wireless was switched on – her mother wanted to listen to a play.

'There's no way you're getting a job,' Tom said bluntly. 'You've got enough to do with your school work, so you can get plenty of O and A levels and go to university. Anyway, whether we could afford it or not, I don't hold with all these new-fangled devices. We didn't have washing machines and refrigerators in my day, and we're not having a television either. We're quite happy as we are.'

'*I'm* not.' Max scowled. 'There's sport on Saturday afternoons and right now there's tennis from Wimbledon. And I'm sure Mum would prefer to watch a play rather than just listen.'

'I'm perfectly happy with the wireless,' Rose cried.

Gerald glanced up from his comic. 'You told Marlene Gray's Mum you'd love a telly.'

'No, I didn't, love.' Rose looked flustered. 'You must have misheard me.' It was rare she disagreed with anything her husband said.

Tom folded his arms. 'Your mother's play's just started and she'd appreciate some quiet. From now on, there'll be no more talk of televisions. That's my final word on the matter.'

'The oracle has spoken,' Max said sarcastically,

51

though he flinched when his father turned angrily on him.

'For that, there's no fête for you tomorrow. You can just stay in and get on with your homework.'

'I'd no intention of going to the stupid fête,' Max muttered.

Jeannie gasped. The fête would be ruined if Max wasn't there. Then her father proceeded to ruin Sunday as well, telling Max, if that was the way he felt, he needn't come with them to New Brighton, either.

Max replied that was fine with him, he didn't care.

Rita McDowd always felt as if she lived at the other end of the world, not just the other end of Disraeli Terrace, when she compared Jeannie Flowers' life to her own. Jeannie was everything Rita longed to be herself; pretty, clever, liked by everybody, with a proper mam and dad, and two very presentable brothers.

They were the same age, Rita and Jeannie, and in the same class at school, but there the similarity ended. Rita was plain, anything but clever and, although she had a dad somewhere, he'd left home ten years before, leaving behind a two-year-old son, a baby daughter, and a wife who'd been only half-alive ever since.

Sadie McDowd managed to keep body and soul together, and her children fed with a combination of state benefits and a job as a kitchen assistant in the village school. There was a time when the family would have been have thrown out of their house when Kevin McDowd, a ploughman, left, but modern technology meant that nowadays farms could manage with only a fraction of the old workforce. The farmer no longer needed so many houses for his employees and a few were rented out. Sadie and her children were allowed to stay, though she was often behind with the rent.

The McDowds were Catholics, the only Irish family in the small, self-contained village where everyone knew everyone else's business, including the fact that Sadie's house was a tip and Sean, her son, was bound to end up in jail one day soon. As for Rita, she was a peculiar little thing, not exactly appealing, with curtains of mousey brown hair and enormous, soulful eyes.

On Friday night, Rita stood with her hand on the gate of number ten and tried to pluck up the courage to go in. If Jeannie or her mother came to the door, it would be all right, but Mr Flowers would turn her away, and Max would look at her as if she were a piece of dirt.

She wanted to ask Jeannie, the only person she regarded as a friend, if she could help on the stall she was manning with her mother at tomorrow's fête, otherwise there was no point in going. She hadn't any money.

Rita stared for ages at the Flowers' front window, with its neat curtains and bowl of pink and cream roses, but in the end her nerve failed her. She returned home, wretchedly miserable, dragging her feet along the dusty road. The sun was setting behind the white houses, and the air was heavy with the fragrant scent of roses. Everyone in Disraeli Terrace took great pride in

53

their gardens – except the occupants of number one. The McDowds' land, front and back, was an expanse of coarse grass. Every month or so, their farmer-landlord sent a man with a scythe to keep it down.

When Rita went in, the kitchen was fuggy with smoke and her mam was sitting at the table with a cigarette in her mouth, which was how she'd been when Rita went out, and how she was most of the time when she was home. Sadie McDowd was lost in dreams of the past and had long ago given up on the present. The house looked as if a hurricane had swept through it, tipping everything out of place, leaving it to gather dust.

Sadie's frequently expressed wish was to return to County Clare where she was born. She'd been happy in Ireland, but the effort required in getting back was quite beyond her. It took her all her time to get as far as the school where she worked. As for Mass, no buses ran through Ailsham on Sundays and, the station was too far to walk to, so neither Sadie or her children had been for years. The feeling of guilt only made her feel worse. She'd turned her back on God. He was no longer watching out for her.

'Would you like a cup of tea, Mam?' Rita enquired.

'I wouldn't mind, luv,' Sadie replied listlessly.

Rita put water to boil in a pan on the ancient electric stove. When she looked for cups, she discovered every dish they owned was dirty, heaped in a pile in the sink, smelling horribly.

'I'm nearly out of fags,' her mother announced in a flat voice.

'You can't have smoked a hundred since Tuesday, Mam!' Rita gasped. On Tuesday, Sadie collected the Family Allowance from the Post Office and bought a week's supply of ciggies.

'I must've, mustn't I, if they've nearly all gone?'

Being Friday, there'd be no money left – the school paid wages monthly – and none expected till the Family Allowance was due again. The weekend would be worse than most, Rita thought gloomily, with her mother hardly speaking, her nerves in rags, fingers twitching endlessly for a cigarette.

The water boiled. Rita washed two cups, made the tea, poured it, and sat at the table opposite her mother.

It was hard to believe that Sadie wasn't much older than Rose Flowers, ten houses and a whole world away. There were photographs around of Sadie, taken before she left Ireland, showing a sparkling young woman with fine, dark eyes, a cascade of black, wavy hair, and a lovely smile. Nowadays, Sadie hardly ever smiled, her black hair was thin and greasy, and the sparkle had long gone. All that remained were the fine eyes, the same colour as Sean's, the blue so dark they were almost navy, dull and listless in her ravaged face.

'Why did me dad leave home?' Rita enquired. It was a question she asked regularly. She liked to be told exactly why her life had gone the opposite way to Jeannie's, veered so wildly off course.

Sadie blinked tiredly. 'Aren't you always asking me that? And haven't I told you a million times already? He didn't want to be stuck in Ailsham

55

working for an Englishman, did he?'

'Why not?' Rita persisted. It seemed a poor excuse for leaving your wife and children.

'Because your dad was a musician, that's why,' her mother replied, as Rita knew she would. 'He could play the fiddle like a dream and sing like an angel, though he'd never had a single lesson in his life. He was a natural and the handsomest man that ever lived. We only came to Liverpool on our way to America – Hollywood – where he was going to make his fortune in the pictures.' She sighed and reached for the Woodbines. 'Ships still sailed, despite there being a war on, but they weren't exactly regular. While we were waiting, the money began to run out. Then I found I was expecting our Sean and your dad had to find a job. All he knew was music and farmwork, so we ended up here, though it was only supposed to be temporary.

'You still haven't said why he left,' Rita pointed out.

'Indeed, I have.'

'No, you haven't, Mam. Why did he leave *us* – you and me and our Sean?'

'You already know, girl. He took off a second time to make his fortune and promised to come back a rich man. Instead, he never came back at all.' The dark eyes glittered with anguish. 'He broke me heart, did Kevin McDowd.'

The mention of riches and fortunes always cheered Rita up a little, reminding her that had things gone differently, she might be living in a Hollywood mansion and not be envious of a soul – certainly not Jeannie Flowers in her little house at the other end of Disraeli Terrace.

The stalls were on three sides of the green, the trestle tables gaily decorated with bunting. Hoop-la, a coconut shy, and a treasure hunt were just a few of the many attractions on offer, and there was a fortune teller with a crystal ball in her own little tent. Among the events shown on the duplicated programme, on sale for threepence, were field sports for children and adults, a baby show, an exhibition of country dancing, and a battle between the scouts and guides as to who would be the first to light a camp fire and boil a kettle. An all-girl accordion band from Ormskirk would provide the grand finale.

The flowers and vegetables were on show in a marquee and, by the time the fête began, Tom Flowers' tomatoes and marrows bore blue rosettes indicating they'd each won a first prize. He marched around the green in the brilliant sunshine, looking for his wife, hands clasped importantly behind his back accompanied by Colonel Max, who had retired from the Army at the end of the war.

Both men were in their fifties, but Tom, with his straight back and dignified bearing, looked much younger. He had strong, weatherbeaten features, a full head of brown, wavy hair, and wore a brown tweed suit and an impeccably ironed cream shirt with a striped tie.

In contrast, the colonel was untidily dressed in a linen suit as crumpled as his cheerful, smiling face. A frayed straw hat with a tartan band covered his completely bald head.

'Ah! Here's your good lady, Tom!' The colonel stopped in front of the white elephant stall, where a wide assortment of interesting items were for sale. 'Busy, I see.'

'I like to see the wife kept occupied, sir.' Tom grinned while they waited for several customers to make their purchases and depart.

Rose blushed. She looked lovely in her next-to-best frock, which was pale green, with a broderie anglaise collar. 'Good afternoon, Colonel. Would you like to buy something? It's all in a good cause.' The proceeds of the fête went to a different charity every year.

'Don't moider the colonel, Rose,' Tom said brusquely. 'He doesn't want to be bothered with other people's rubbish.'

'It's not rubbish, Dad! Some of the things are quite smart. Look at this! Mum said it's a smoking jacket. It's in perfect condition.' Jeannie held up a maroon velvet jacket with frogging down the front. 'And there's some lovely handbags and loads of jewellery, though I don't suppose it's real. I'd buy this bead bangle, 'cept I need the rest of my money to have my fortune told.' The compact and manicure set she'd hankered after had been bought and were safely in Rose's shopping bag.

'That's exactly what I wanted,' Colonel Corbett boomed.

'What, the bangle?'

'No, Jeannie, the jacket. And I'll have the bangle too. Why not!' He winked. 'I'll wear it next time I go dancing. How much do I owe you, Rose?'

'A florin for the jacket, threepence for the bangle. But are you sure, Colonel...'

'Quite sure, Rose, though, on reflection, I think the bangle would suit a narrower wrist than mine – your Jeannie's, for instance. Here's half a crown. It doesn't matter about the change.'

'Thank you, Colonel!' Jeannie breathed when he handed her the bangle with a little, courteous bow. She slipped it on to her wrist. 'Isn't he lovely?' she said when the two men walked away.

Rose laughed. 'You'll never guess where that smoking jacket came from! Mrs Denning, the colonel's housekeeper brought it round. She said he never wore it.'

'Perhaps we'll get it back next year! Oh, hello, Rita!'

Rita McDowd stood in front of the stall in the grubby, washed-out summer frock she always wore that was much too short. There was a look of longing on her peaky face as she stared at the biscuit tin full of cheap jewellery. 'Hello,' she muttered. 'I thought you might like a hand.'

'No, thank you, Rita. Mum and I can manage on our own, but thank you for asking.'

'Actually,' Rose said kindly. 'I wouldn't mind a cup of tea and one of my own fairy cakes, even though I'll have to pay for it. Rita can stand in my place, can't you, dear?'

'If you like, Mrs Flowers.'

'I'd like it very much, Rita. I'd love a little break.'

Rose left and Rita came behind the stall. She always felt very conscious of how insignificant she was next to Jeannie, who was tall for eleven

59

and outstandingly pretty. She had thick, wavy, light brown hair – like the Jeannie in the song – creamy skin with a sheen of pearl, a straight nose, and wide pink lips that always seemed to be curved in a slight smile. Her eyes were the colour of bluebells and they regarded people calmly and directly, full of trust, as if she couldn't conceive of anyone being horrid. It meant that people never were. No one would dream of saying anything unpleasant to Jeannie Flowers and seeing a feeling of hurt cloud those innocent blue eyes. She seemed wise beyond her years, never giggly or silly like some girls.

'Have you been busy?' Rita asked.

'Very, but it's gone off a bit now.' Jeannie turned away when a customer approached. 'Good afternoon, Mrs Bonnington. Yes, they're lovely handbags, aren't they? Only sixpence each. Most are real leather, so Mum says. No, I don't know where they came from, but I'm sure it was somewhere respectable.'

'It's not that, dear. I just don't want to come face to face with someone I know when I'm carrying their old bag. I don't think I'll bother, but I'll take that gold evening purse for my little granddaughter. She'll enjoy playing with it.'

'That'll be threepence, Mrs Bonnington.'

Rita's eyes grew round when Jeannie put the threepenny-bit in a bowl full of coins, most of them silver. There were also a few folded ten shilling and pound notes. She'd never seen so much money before.

The white elephant stall was one of the most popular, being the source of some remarkable

60

bargains. Over the next hour, the girls were besieged with customers, many of them strangers with Liverpool accents, very different to the soft Lancashire burr of Ailsham.

One Liverpool couple bought two handbags, a blue teddy bear, a pile of comics, and a pair of glass candlesticks.

'How much is that lot, luv?' The man had kind eyes and a warm smile.

'Three and sixpence.'

'That's cheap at the price. Have you got change of a pound?'

'Yes.' Rita carefully counted out the change and the couple went away, well satisfied with their purchases.

Jeannie was busy serving someone else and Rita felt herself go hot, then cold, as she crumpled the note in her hand into a tight ball. She'd never stolen anything in her life before, but when she thought of what she could do with a whole pound, the temptation was too hard to resist.

Mam would love some jewellery, a string of pearls, even if they weren't real, and that long white scarf with a fringe was the sort of thing that would appeal to Sean. There was a handbag that Jeannie said had been made out of a real crocodile she wouldn't mind for herself. Most importantly, she'd buy cigarettes, forty, to see Mam through the weekend, and say she'd won the treasure hunt to explain where the money had come from.

First, she'd have to change the note. It would look suspicious, handing Jeannie a pound.

'I promised to buy Mam some ciggies,' she

said. 'I'd better get them now, in case the shop shuts. I won't be a minute.'

'OK, Rita, but hurry. The baby show will soon be over and there'll be a rush. I wonder why Mum's taking so long?'

Rita sped towards the shops on the far side of the green. The Oak Tree pub was doing a roaring trade, the tables outside packed and drinkers lounging on the grass.

'I don't sell cigarettes to under-eighteens,' Mrs Harker said curtly when Rita asked for forty Woodbines.

'Oh, let her have them,' Mr Harker put in. 'We know who they're for, and it's not Rita, is it, girl?'

Rita mutely shook her head. Minutes later, she raced back to the stall, perspiration pouring down the inside of her arms, and felt horribly guilty when she found Mrs Flowers had bought the girls a cup of tea and a fairy cake each.

'It's by way of an apology,' she said. 'I should have come back ages ago, but I could see you both coping admirably. I've had a lovely afternoon lazing in the marquee with my friends.'

'I'd like to buy some things to take home,' Rita mumbled.

'Help yourself, dear.'

The crocodile handbag had been sold in her absence, but there was a big red plastic shoulder bag that Rita liked almost as much and it had its own purse. She put the pearls and the scarf inside, and the remainder of the money, nearly seventeen shillings, in the purse.

For the rest of the afternoon, Rita felt unusually happy. She kept imagining the way Mam's face would light up when she saw her present, not to mention the money and the ciggies. Sean's reaction to the scarf was more doubtful. It depended what sort of mood he was in.

When the Flowers arrived home, Max was in the garden with Spencer curled up on his knee, studying a history book. His father gave him a curt nod and Rose wanted to know if he'd had anything to eat.

'Not a bite,' Max said with an injured air. Rose went indoors to make him a sandwich, and Gerald ran to the pond to see if his frog spawn had developed.

When only he and his sister were left, Max grinned and showed her a science fiction novel hidden inside the text book.

'You haven't been studying at all!' she cried.

'I haven't been reading long, either. I've been to the fête, though stayed well out the way.' He smacked his lips. 'I went to the Oak Tree and drank a whole pint of scrumpy. The landlord was too busy to notice who he was serving. I feel a bit drunk.'

'I hope no one saw you. If Dad finds out, he'll have a fit.'

'I don't care if he has ten fits,' Max said belligerently. 'Did you notice the way he walked round the field with Colonel Max, one step respectfully behind? I bet he never disagrees or says a word out of place, yet at home he's nothing but a bully. I'd tell him what I thought of him, 'cept it would only upset Mum.'

'Oh, Max, don't...' Jeannie paused.

'Don't what?'

'Spoil things. Everything's so nice...' Her voice trailed away.

'It's only nice because we all kowtow to dad, let him boss us around. Even Mum does as she's told. I didn't notice when I was young, but now I'm older, it really pisses me off,' Max said with all the wisdom of a fourteen-year-old.

Jeannie sighed. 'It's only because he loves us.'

'No, it's not. It's because he's a bully and he has to have his own way all the time.' Max thankfully changed the subject. 'Did you have a nice time?'

'Sort of.' She wrinkled her nose. 'Mam deserted us and I was stuck with Rita McDowd all afternoon.'

'You should have told her to sod off.'

'I couldn't, Max. The poor girl thinks she's my friend. I'd feel awful if I hurt her. The thing is, she smells and she's got no conversation. She's got a lovely voice, though. I hadn't realised. She sang "Greensleeves" with the accordion band. She didn't know I was listening.'

'You're too nice, sis. Still, you'll get your reward in heaven.'

It was funny, but Mam seemed more pleased with the pearls than the more important ciggies. Perhaps it was because, as she said, she couldn't remember when she was last bought a present.

'They're not real,' Rita warned.

'Ah, but don't they *look* real?' Sadie cried. 'Fancy you thinking about me! And our Sean too. He'll love that scarf when he gets in. You're a good girl, Rita.' She bestowed an unaccustomed kiss on her daughter's cheek, and became quite animated, demanding more details of the afternoon that had turned out so fortunately.

Rita described how pleased she'd been when the guides, not the scouts, were first to boil a kettle, and what a wonderful surprise it had been when she'd stuck a flag in the ground with her name on and it had turned out to be the very spot where the treasure was buried.

'D'you like me bag, Mam?' she enquired. 'There's a purse to match inside. It's where I put the money that's over. You can buy hundreds of ciggies on Monday.'

'Did you not just say the Flowers are spending tomorrow in New Brighton?' her mother asked thoughtfully.

'Yes, it's Gerald's birthday.'

'Well, us McDowds aren't due a birthday, but I'd like to spend the money on a day out too. What about Southport? It's a far grander place than New Brighton and easier to get to. What do you say, girl?'

'*Yes*, Mam,' Rita breathed.

'In that case, let's start getting ready now. Take your frock off and I'll give it a rub through. It'll be dry in no time in this weather. Then we'll wash our hair, but first of all I'll get rid of these dirty dishes.' Sadie jumped to her feet with a rare show of energy. 'I'll wear me pearls and Sean his scarf, and you can take your new bag. We'll have a fine day out in Southport, so we will.'

Sean McDowd was tall for thirteen, as thin as a lath, with hair as black as soot, and smouldering

65

good looks – the spitting image of his father, according to Sadie. Unlike his sister, he had many friends, mainly boys older than himself over whom Sean was able to exert an extraordinary amount of influence. There was something magnetic about his dark blue eyes, his scowling face, that made his friends want to please him, change the scowl into one of his rare, heart-stopping smiles.

Small gangs of lads, led by Sean, were the scourge of local farmers. At dead of night, they raided their hen coops, stealing not just eggs, but the occasional chicken. Rows of strawberry plants were stripped of fruit, trees denuded of their apples, potatoes and other vegetables dug up from the corners of fields, and sold for coppers to Frank Beggerow's brother who ran a fruit and veg stall in Ormskirk market.

The victims of these atrocities didn't bother with the law; they applied their own. If caught, the culprits were given a good hiding and warned never to do it again, though they usually did, egged on by Sean McDowd, who was rarely caught, and had the makings of a master criminal, the way he could warp minds and bend people to his will.

Nobody realised that Sean made not a penny from his life of crime. He did it for fun, to bring excitement into his deadly dull life and the lives of a few other lads in Ailsham, where no one cared that there was nothing for young people to do and nowhere for them to go. Sean only attended school, the Philip Wallace Secondary Modern in Maghull, in order to pass the time. If something more appealing came up, he didn't go. It was no use the authorities complaining to his mother. Sadie had lost control over her son. He went his own way and there was nothing she could do about it.

On the day of the fête, Sean and his mates were sprawled on the green at the furthest edge of the festivities. They wouldn't be seen dead on the stalls, throwing coconuts and shoving ha'-pennies. Besides which, everyone was broke apart from Jimmy Lowe who'd started work at Easter and bought them a pint of scrumpy each.

Max Flowers was sitting not far away also drinking a pint of the brutally alcoholic Oak Tree scrumpy. Sean nudged one of his mates. 'See over there, the scholarship boy. Letting the side down a bit, eh?' Max had been in the class above him at the village school, an ultra-respectable teacher's pet, perfectly dressed, never in trouble. It came as no surprise when he'd gone to grammar school. Max turned and caught his eye; Sean gave him a look of utter contempt.

Later, he saw the tiny, hunched figure of his sister rush across the green towards the shops. She ran unevenly, like a wounded sparrow, and Sean's hard heart contracted. He loved his family, yet at the same time regarded them with deep resentment. He didn't *want* to care, but couldn't help it. His mother, with her melancholy ways and endless cigarettes, got on his nerves, and Rita was pathetic. As the man of the house, Sean felt there was something he should do to put things right, but had no idea what. He found it best to stay away from Disraeli Terrace as much as possible, not think about it.

They watched the activities on the green from afar, laughing like drains at the frantic attempts of the scouts and guides to light fires, hooting and whistling at the accordion band, trying to decide which of the girls in their brief yellow frocks had the best legs.

The fête ended, the visitors departed, but still they lingered, the scrumpy long gone, wondering how they were supposed to occupy themselves on a Saturday night without a penny between them. They idly watched the stalls being dismantled, boxes packed, tables folded.

Sean suddenly sat bolt upright when he spied his sister again. She was helping pack up a stall – with Jeannie Flowers! His hot, sullen eyes narrowed. He normally had no time for girls, although at school they threw themselves at him all the time. Girls were trouble; clinging, demanding, difficult to get rid of when you'd had enough. Jeannie Flowers, though, was different and often featured in his dreams. She was gentle, ladylike, always polite when they met. Yet Sean always had the feeling she considered him way beneath her, that he meant no more to her than one of the slugs in her father's show-piece garden. The feeling made him burn with rage, until he would remember that Jeannie was still a child with a woman's beauty.

But one day, she would no longer be a child and Sean was determined that when that day came, he would make her his. He desired Jeannie Flowers more than anything else on earth.

It was nine o'clock when Sean arrived home, driven there by hunger, though doubted if there'd be anything much to eat – he could have murdered a plate of egg and chips. To his surprise, he found his mother in an unusually happy mood and his sister quite excited. The sun was still warm and they were sitting on the rough grass at the back of the house, running their fingers through their damp hair, tossing their heads this way and that to dry it. Washing hung on the line.

'Sean!' Rita jumped to her feet. 'See what I've got for you.' She ran into the house and returned with a long white scarf that she threw around his neck, then stood back to admire the effect. 'It makes you look desperately elegant.'

'Where'd it come from?'

'The white elephant stall. Jeannie said it once belonged to Colonel Corbett. It's an evening scarf, but you can wear in the daytime.'

Sean's first thought was that he didn't want the colonel's cast–offs, thanks all the same, but it seemed cruel when Rita had bought it especially for him. 'It's nice,' he said grudgingly. He examined his reflection in the kitchen window and it *did* look smart; elegant, like Rita said.

'And guess what! Tomorrow, we're going to Southport for the day. You'll come, won't you?' she added anxiously. 'I won the treasure hunt, so we've got the money.'

'I suppose so.' He might as well. Tomorrow was Sunday and there'd be even less to do in Ailshain than usual.

Even Sean had to agree the day in Southport went exceptionally well. The small town was crowded with holidaymakers and the sun shone as gloriously as it had done the day before.

Their first port of call was the fairground. Sean scorned the likes of the waltzer and the merry-go-round, and made for the rifle range. He discovered he was a fine shot and, after winning a giant, multicoloured ball straight off, then a jazzy vase with his second go, the irate stallholder gave him his money back and refused to let him have another turn.

An hour later, when Rita judged they'd spent enough money, they wandered along the flat, glistening sand to where the Irish Sea rippled gently in the distance. Rita and Sean kicked the ball to each other; Sadie examined the vase and wished there were flowers in her garden to put in it when she got home.

They strolled along the promenade and admired the pretty, neat gardens, then sat on a bench for a while so Sadie could have a Wood-bine. Sean was dispatched to buy candy floss.

Rita was in her element. She'd only been to Southport once before, on a day trip with the school. The girls had been told to walk in pairs, but she'd been the odd one out, without a partner, trailing behind all day, feeling sad and alone.

Today was different. It was the best day of her life, and she doubted if the Flowers were having a better time in New Brighton. Mam was in a great mood and even Sean, usually so sour, had joined in the fun. Later, they were going to Lord

Street for a sit down meal. Mam said a fish and chip restaurant would be cheapest.

To think that so much happiness was the result of stealing a pound! It made Rita aware of the power of money. She felt quite awed by it. If she could steal a pound every day, their entire lives would change for ever. She knew it was a mad idea. She would never steal again, but she prayed that one day Mam would wear real pearls around her neck and Sean would have an evening suit to go with the evening scarf.

Max's presence was sorely missed in New Brighton. It didn't feel the same with only four of them when there should have been five. Gerald complained his birthday treat had been spoilt and Rose remarked more than once how concerned she was, leaving Max on his own for a whole day. Jeannie longed to have a go on the dodgems, but only with Max, who drove with fiendish abandon, bumping into every car in sight, making her scream with a mixture of delight and fear. She felt the same about the big wheel and the ghost train, but went on both for Gerald's sake, not wanting to spoil his birthday even more.

Her father had been grumpy all day. Perhaps he was also missing Max's company, or it could be he was still cross with Mum. Last night, he had expressed his annoyance with the fact the colonel had been sold his own smoking jacket.

'But it was me that sold it,' Jeannie pointed out.

'Yes, but it was your mother's idea he buy something.'

'I don't see anything wrong with that, Tom,' Rose said mildly. 'It was just his way of giving to charity.'

'Maybe so, but next year I'd be obliged if you'd leave him to make up his own mind how he gives to charity.'

'I'm sorry, Tom.'

Tom made a harrumphing noise and had seemed satisfied with the apology. Jeannie was glad Max had gone to bed early and avoided the incident. He was bound to have said something to inflame things.

She climbed down the steps of the ghost train, which hadn't seemed nearly so frightening without a terrifying commentary from Max.

'Is it time for dinner yet?' she asked her mother.

'I want to stay longer in the fairground,' Gerald whined, though he was normally an exceptionally serene little boy.

'Maybe Jeannie and I could have a cup of tea and you stay with your dad, love,' Rose suggested.

Gerald burst into tears. 'I don't want to stay with Dad. He won't go on things with me.'

Tom's face, which had been tight all day, grew tighter. 'You'll do what your mother says, lad.'

'It's all right, Tom. We'll have a cup of tea later.'

'No,' Tom said authoritatively. 'You'll have one now. I'll see you back here in half an hour.'

'Ten minutes will be long enough.' Rose threw a worried glance at her tearful son.

'Ten minutes will be fine,' Jeannie concurred.

'I said half an hour.' Her father turned away dismissively.

What was happening to them? Jeannie wondered over the tea that she didn't enjoy a bit. Her mother looked upset and hardly spoke during the half hour that seemed to take for ever. Perhaps she was also at a loss to understand why the day they'd been so much looking forward to had turned out so horribly.

Tom Flowers was a confused man. He stalked around the fairground, pointing out the various attractions to Gerald. 'Do you want a ride on this?' he barked when they reached the caterpillar.

Gerald had refused to hold his hand. He lagged behind, sullen-faced, still tearful. 'Not on my own,' he sniffed. He wanted to ride with Jeannie or Max, but Jeannie wouldn't be back for ages and Max wasn't even there.

Max! What was a father supposed to do with a son who treated him with a complete lack of respect? Tom's own father had ruled his family with a rod of iron. Tom had never once disputed a word he'd said. He hadn't particularly wanted to follow the tradition of the eldest son becoming the Corbett's gardener, but it was what his father had expected and Tom wouldn't have dreamt of disappointing him.

Yet Tom's own son disappointed him all the time. It bothered him that the rest of his family didn't approve of the punishment he'd meted out to Max. Instead of understanding, even his dear Rose appeared sorry Max had been left behind.

But a man wasn't a man if he didn't play first fiddle in his own home. In future, Tom vowed he'd come down even harder on his rebellious son. It was time he made a stand – and he'd start now. He turned angrily on his other son. The caterpillar had stopped and he picked up Gerald and put him none too gently in the coach.

'You wanted to come to New Brighton, so stop whinging and enjoy yourself,' he commanded.

They returned to Ailsham two hours earlier than planned. No one felt like going to the shore to built sandcastles or paddle. The swimming gear was unused, the sandwiches uneaten.

Rose loyally linked her husband's arm on the long walk from the station. Jeannie and Gerald ran ahead, anxious to see their brother, but Max wasn't there. He hadn't been expecting them so early. He'd spent the day with a friend, he explained when he eventually turned up. There was another row that night. He didn't give a damn about going to New Brighton, Max declared frostily, but his father had no right to confine him to the house.

Tom, driven to distraction by such flagrant insubordination, slapped his son's face hard. It was the first time he'd ever laid a hand on one of his children. Jeannie realised sadly that their perfect life had come to an end.

Dusk was falling when the McDowds got off the train, sunburnt and content. They'd had a wonderful time in Southport and Sadie couldn't remember them having felt so close as a family before. It was as if they'd turned a corner. She resolved never to let the feeling go.

Chapter 3

In August, a letter arrived to say that Jeannie had passed the Eleven-Plus. She had been accepted at Orrell Park Grammar School for Girls, only a stone's throw from the boys' school that Max attended. A coach passed through the village each morning to take pupils to Philip Wallace in Maghull, dropping off others at the station to make their way by train to their various schools. Two boys from her class had also passed, but Jeannie was the only girl. It didn't bother her. She was confident she would quickly get to know the other girls.

Colonel Corbett sent ten pounds and his congratulations, not that Jeannie saw the money. It went towards her uniform and other necessary items such as a hockey stick and a tennis racket. Three years ago, a similar sum had been sent to Max who, now that he was reminded of it, launched an indignant tirade against his father.

'He didn't even *discuss* it with us, did he, sis? It was *our* money, but he just kept it. I bet the colonel meant for us to buy ourselves presents; a bike, for instance. We *had* to have uniforms, so you and me got nothing out of it. Instead, Dad saved himself ten pounds – *two* lots of ten pounds.'

'My uniform is terribly expensive, Max,' Jeannie said reasonably. 'Dad's not made of money.'

'He's not short of money, either. He earns far more than an ordinary gardener. And we don't pay rent like most people.' Max was determined not to give an inch.

The long summer break passed by dreamily. Jeannie was very much aware that an important part of her life had ended and a new one was about to begin. It was almost like the end of childhood. Groups of girls, who would always be her friends, but no longer the most important ones, gathered in each others' houses or gardens, went swimming in Holly Brook, played cricket with the boys on the green. There was no sign of Rita McDowd, who normally tagged along. She and her mother were picking vegetables on the local farms, someone said.

'Thank the Lord!' said another. 'At least, you'll be rid of her, Jeannie. She had a thing about you.'

'That's because Jeannie was the only one prepared to put up with the evil-smelling little bitch.'

'Don't say that!' Jeannie protested. She felt sorry for Rita, about to start Philip Wallace without a single ally.

She managed to stay calm during her first chaotic day at her new school. She was allocated a peg in the cloakroom to hang her royal blue blazer, and a space in which to keep her outdoor shoes – the girls had to wear special, lightweight shoes inside.

The new intake was addressed by the Headmistress, Dr Farthing, a tall, regal woman, who welcomed them to her highly regarded establishment. Afterwards, the girls' names were called out and they were separated into three forms; IA, IB, and I-remove. Jeannie was in I-remove along with about thirty others.

A young, red-haired teacher introduced herself as Miss Appleton, their form mistress, who would also take them for Art and History. She led them along a corridor, up two flights of stairs, and into a classroom where she stationed herself behind the desk at the front.

'Stay!' she yelled when the girls streamed in after her and made for the desks. Everyone froze. 'Before you grab a desk, this will be your form room for the next year. Wherever you sit, it's where you'll stay. I want no chopping and changing in the months ahead. If you fall out with the girl next to you, then it's just too bad.'

There was a chorus of urgent whisperings. 'Can I sit by you? *Please!*'

As Jeannie knew no one, it didn't matter where she sat. She chose a desk in the middle and not long afterwards was joined by a pretty girl, healthily tanned, with warm brown eyes and dark hair plaited in a thick pigtail halfway down her back.

'Hello, I'm Elaine Bailey. Do you mind if I sit by you?'

'I'm Jeannie Flowers and I don't mind a bit.'

'That's a pretty name!' The girl threw a shabby leather satchel on to the desk. Her gymslip wasn't new and looked like a hand-me-down, as did her blouse, which had a frayed collar.

'Elaine's pretty too,' said Jeannie. She reckoned her new companion must be very poor, but when they remained together in the dinner hour, eating their sandwiches together in the canteen, it turned out Elaine's father was a doctor and she was the third of six children – four brothers and a sister called Marcia. Elaine's uniform had belonged to Marcia, who was in the fifth form of the same school, and she didn't mind that the gymslip was too short.

'Mine's too long.' Jeannie grimaced. 'My mother wanted to take it up a few inches, but Dad wouldn't let her. He said there'd be a mark when it was let down.'

'And she let him *stop* her,' Elaine gasped. 'My mum doesn't take a blind bit of notice of Dad. Mind you, gymslips are the last thing on his mind. It takes him all his time to remember our names, let alone notice what we're wearing. Oh, gosh!' She clapped her hand over her mouth. 'Did that sound rude? I'm sorry. I didn't mean to criticise your mum and dad.'

'That's all right,' Jeannie said stiffly.

'Oh, look! I've hurt your feelings. I'm terribly sorry, Jeannie.' Elaine was genuinely upset. 'In fact, your gymslip looks very smart, almost the New Look.'

'The New Look went out years ago.' Nevertheless, she smiled. She liked Elaine and had already made up her mind she would make a very good friend.

At her old school, Jeannie had always been top of the class, but she quickly discovered she was nothing out of the ordinary when compared to Elaine Bailey whose brain power was prodigious.

She only had to scan the pages of a book and be able to remember every relevant detail, whereas Jeannie had to read it over and over, making notes, then study the notes before she felt she knew it properly.

Elaine wanted to be a doctor, like her father, but specialising in psychiatry. She was quietly studious and didn't show off by always putting up her hand when the teacher asked a question, as some girls did, though Jeannie didn't doubt she knew the answer.

Despite her phenomenal memory, Elaine was terribly absentminded. She consistently forgot to bring the right books to school or the homework that was due to be handed in that day. Fortunately, the Baileys only lived a few minutes away in Walton Vale, so there was usually time to rush home for whatever Elaine had forgotten.

The two girls formed an unspoken partnership. Jeannie, who arrived early at school, waited by the gate for Elaine and checked she'd brought everything, while Elaine explained to her the more obscure points of algebra and geometry.

At the end of the second week Elaine invited Jeannie to tea after school the following Wednesday.

'I'd love to, but I'll have to ask my dad first.'

'What's her name again?' Tom wanted to know when Jeannie told him about the invitation.

'Elaine Bailey. She lives in Walton Vale, only a little walk from Orrell Park. She's terribly clever.'

'I'm sure they're a very respectable family, Tom, if their daughter goes to Orrell Park Grammar.' Rose was watching the proceedings anxiously.

'Hmm! What time will you be home on Wednesday?'

'I dunno. About half past six, I suppose.'

Tom Flowers regarded his own daughter sternly. 'I hope you didn't learn *that* off this Elaine Bailey.'

'What, Dad?' Jeannie asked, mystified.

'"Dunno". It should be two separate words, if I remember rightly.'

'She probably got it from Max.' Max was so often in trouble, it didn't matter if he was blamed for something he might not have done.

'All right, you can go. But enjoy it while you can, girl, because you'll not be having tea with anyone once winter comes. I'm not having you walking home from the station by yourself in the dark.'

'Thank you, Dad!' Jeannie noticed her mother's look of relief.

The Baileys' big, four-storey house was behind a cinema in Walton Vale. It had a brass plate on the front door and the two front rooms had been turned into a surgery and a waiting room that was half full of patients when Elaine and Jeannie arrived. Mrs Bailey acted as her husband's secretary and receptionist, as well as looking after their six children. She was a jolly, surprisingly placid woman, considering the hectic life she led.

The three younger boys – Elaine referred to them as 'the terrible trio' – had already eaten by the time the girls arrived and could be heard creating bedlam in the handkerchief-sized back yard. Jeannie was taken into a large kitchen where the worn wooden cupboards and old-fashioned brown sink contrasted oddly with a tall fridge, a washing machine, and a spin dryer. A big pan of stew simmered on the stove and Jeannie was given a plate and told to help herself

Elaine explained her mum and dad wouldn't eat till later. 'Come on, the dining room's in here. Our Lachlan will be home in about half an hour. He has a violin lesson after school.' Lachlan's name was pronounced 'Loklan', though the spelling made it look quite different, Elaine said. He was fourteen and hadn't passed the Eleven-Plus due to the fact that, as far as anyone knew, he had never read a book in his life. All he thought about was music.

Marcia, the oldest member of the family, was seated at the table when the two girls went into the dining room. Jeannie had already met Marcia, fifteen, and bearing no resemblance to Elaine, being fair-haired, tall, and slim. She seemed to hold strong opinions about every subject under the sun, which she expressed in a loud, grating voice, oblivious to whether someone's feelings might be hurt. She and Lachlan were going to the pictures later that night to see Marilyn Monroe and Joseph Cotton in *Niagara*.

'Have you seen it, Jeannie?' she enquired.

Jeannie was forced to confess she'd been to the pictures only once in her life, to see *The Wizard of Oz* one Christmas.

Marcia looked astounded. 'Only *once*. But you've seen films on telly, haven't you?' she insisted. 'Alfred Hitchcock's *The Man Who Knew Too Much* was on the other night. They say it's not

81

as good as the remake with Doris Day and James Stewart, but we haven't seen that yet?

'We haven't got a television.'

'It sounds like it's still the nineteenth century in your village,' Marcia sniffed disdainfully.

'Oh, no! Loads of people have televisions, it's just that my father doesn't believe in them.'

'What about your mother?'

'She doesn't either.' Jeannie wasn't convinced if this were true. Mum had lately been finding an excuse to call on the Taylors, who lived next door but one, for half an hour or so during the evening. It was Max's theory she was watching their telly.

'She only goes the nights *Hancock's Half Hour* is on, and *I Love Lucy*,' he pointed out.

Elaine was annoyed with Marcia's attitude towards her friend. 'Jeannie can play the piano really well,' she boasted. 'That's a proper achievement, not like watching telly and going to the pictures night after night. One of these days, you'll get square eyes.'

'I can't play all *that* well,' Jeannie said bashfully.

'Let's see how well you can. You've nearly finished tea, so play something for us. There's a piano in the upstairs parlour.'

'She's not here to entertain you, Marcia!' Elaine was even more irritated. 'I don't ask *your* friends to put on a show, not that you've got many.'

'I don't mind.' Jeannie was anxious to avoid a row. She'd play *Minuet in G*, one of the first real pieces she'd learned. Nowadays, she was able to include several of her own little flourishes. She ate the remainder of the meal and asked to be shown the piano. Despite her bashfulness, she could play well and was keen to impress Marcia.

The parlour was large and shabby, and the piano had been sadly neglected. She ran her fingers along the yellowing keys; it urgently needed tuning.

'Don't you need music?' Elaine asked.

'Not for this. I know it by heart.' Her father often asked her to play for visitors. Jeannie had no ambition to become a professional pianist. She enjoyed playing, but it wasn't a passion. Even so, if she was in the mood, she was able to put real feeling into a tune. She did so now, playing the gentle melody with the image in her head of crinolined ladies and men with powdered wigs bowing and curtseying to each other before beginning their minuet.

To her astonishment, she was halfway through, when she found herself being accompanied on a violin. A boy, very like Elaine, appeared beside her, grinning, a violin tucked under his chin, wielding the bow with great enthusiasm. It could only be Lachlan, who'd never read a book. She grinned back, and they managed to finish together, at exactly the same time.

Elaine and Marcia laughed and clapped their hands, and Marcia demanded they play something else.

'Do you know this?' Lachlan closed his eyes and began to play a haunting tune she'd never heard before. Jeannie watched. The sleeves of his grey shirt were rolled up, revealing slight, suntanned arms. Taller than Max by at least six inches, his face was slightly leaner than his sister's, his mouth thinner and wider, curled in a slight smile. He was quite clearly lost in the music. She soon realised guiltily that she'd been watching for far too long and hoped no one had noticed. With one hand, she began to pick out the notes then, gaining confidence, added the bass. She thought she'd made an adequate job of things by the time they'd finished.

'What was that?' she asked.

'"Love Me Tender".' Lachlan's brown eyes sparkled with amusement. 'It's an Elvis Presley song.'

When Jeannie said she'd never heard of Elvis Presley, Marcia screamed, 'Honestly, Jeannie! You can't be real. *Everyone's* heard of Elvis Presley.'

'*I* haven't, but I love his song.'

'It's from a film of the same name,' Lachlan said. 'It's on at the Plaza the week after next. Why don't you come to see it with me and Marcia?'

'Only if Elaine comes too.'

'I'll go if you go, Jeannie.'

'I would have loved to hear you and Lachlan play together,' Rose said wistfully when Jeannie told her what had happened. 'It would be like having a little concert in our own home.'

Jeannie had an idea. 'Why not ask Elaine and Lachlan to tea, and Marcia, I suppose, though I don't like her much. They could come next Sunday, while the weather's still nice. I can meet them at the station.'

'I'll see what your dad has to say.'

84

At first, Tom regarded the request with suspicion. 'How old is Lachlan?' he enquired of his daughter.

'Fourteen.'

'Hmm!' His eyes narrowed. 'I don't like the idea of you being involved with lads at your age. You're only eleven.'

'Oh, *Dad!* We played a duet, that's all. And I'll be twelve in December.' It would be best not to admit she felt quite enthusiastic about seeing Lachlan again. He was the first boy she'd ever *noticed* out of the scores of boys she'd known.

'Your mother said something about going to the pictures. I'm not sure if I can allow that. These people are strangers. I know nothing about them.'

Jeannie knew he was only being protective, but it would be highly embarrassing to have to tell Elaine that her father had forbidden her to go to the pictures, endorsing Marcia's belief that life in Ailsham was positively Victorian.

'Why don't we at least ask them to tea, Tom?' Rose suggested. 'We can see what they're like? I'd love to hear Jeannie and Lachlan play.'

'I don't suppose there'd be much harm in that,' Tom said grudgingly.

'I doubt if our Lachlan will come,' Elaine said. 'Marcia will, because she's dead nosy and she hasn't many friends of her own, but Lachlan always goes to the Cavern on Sundays.'

'What's the Cavern?' Jeannie enquired.

'A club in town, Matthew Street, where they play music – jazz and skiffle. I'm dying to go, but Lachlan won't take me. He goes with a crowd of boys from school and says I'm much too young.'

'Oh, well.' Jeannie didn't show her disappointment. 'It'll be nice to have you and Marcia.'

Elaine returned to school next day with the surprising news that Lachlan had accepted the invitation. 'It's not like him; he's not usually the sort of person who goes to tea. I don't quite know what's got into him.'

Jeannie hoped it was because Lachlan wanted to see her again as much as she did him.

There was no need to meet the Baileys at the station as their father was bringing them in the car – perhaps he felt the need to see what sort of family *his* children were associating with. They arrived on the dot of three in the big, black, pre-war Humber that was its owner's pride and joy, according to Marcia. 'Dad thinks more of that car than he does of us,' she grumbled.

Dr Bailey was a tall, prepossessing man with a luxurious moustache and a warm, bedside manner even with people who weren't his patients. Jeannie had neglected to mention that her friend's father was a doctor, and Tom Flowers was quite bowled over by their distinguished visitor. He humbly showed him around the impressive garden and picked a bunch of chrysanthemums for him to take to 'your good wife.' The doctor left, promising to return at half past six.

Earlier, Max had announced he was going out, having no desire to meet a couple of girls and a boy who played the violin and was bound to be a cissy. Jeannie had pleaded with him to stay and be introduced at least. 'It would look rude, otherwise.' To her chagrin, Max and Lachlan liked each other on the spot, and disappeared into Max's bedroom to talk about football.

The girls went for a walk through the village. It always looked particularly pretty in autumn, even though today was rather dull, without a glimmer of sun. The gardens were bulging with russet flowers and the numerous trees had started to shed their golden leaves, providing a crisp carpet for them to walk on. But Marcia wasn't remotely impressed and loudly proclaimed her astonishment that people were able to *breathe* in such a deadly dull atmosphere.

'There's no one around, only us. I'm convinced nothing but corpses live here.'

'Corpses don't *live*, Marcia,' Elaine said scathingly.

Marcia ignored her sister's intervention. 'It's like that film, *Invasion of the Body Snatchers*. It was about a village, just like this, 'cept it was in America, where the people were gradually being taken over by aliens and weren't human any more.'

'What about Jeannie's family?' Elaine enquired. 'Aren't they human any more?'

'Yes, but only because the aliens haven't reached the part where they live yet.'

'Don't be silly, Marcia.' Jeannie burst out laughing. Yet in a way, although she wouldn't have admitted it, she knew what Marcia meant. Today, Ailsham was silent and deserted. It *did* look dead, and she gave a little shiver, wondering what people were doing behind their front doors and blank windows.

It would be nice to live somewhere like Walton Vale, with a cinema around the corner, loads of shops, and trains running to Liverpool every few minutes. It would also be nice, she thought traitorously, to have a dad like Dr Bailey, instead of one who raised a hundred objections every time his children wanted to go out. Perhaps it was because he was old; he'd forgotten how to enjoy himself and didn't realise she and Max wanted a good time. She kicked at a pile of leaves. There was nothing she could do about it. She loved her father and, if she said anything, it would only upset her mother, whom she loved most of all.

'Are you sure the aliens haven't taken you over?' Marcia quipped. 'You've been quiet an awfully long time.'

'I was just thinking.'

'Could you stop thinking and take us back? I'm starving.'

Elaine gasped. 'I'd like to apologise for my sister's non-existent manners, Jeannie. It'd be nice to say she's not always this rude, except she is. She badly needs her head examining.' She glared at Marcia's head. 'I might do it once I'm a qualified psychiatrist.'

Marcia was unperturbed by this remark and Jeannie explained they were at the other end of Holly Lane and already going back.

As they approached Disraeli Terrace, two boys emerged from the first house; one tall and dark, the other small and fair.

'I spy other human beings!' Marcia remarked with pretend amazement.

'Hello, Jeannie,' the blond boy shouted as they

passed. 'What's it like at your posh school?'

'All right.' Jeannie shrugged.

Marcia turned and looked at the boys with interest. 'I quite fancy the tall one.'

'Sean McDowd? He's only thirteen, far too young for you.'

'Only thirteen! He looks more like twenty. Did you notice the way he looked at me? He's got dead sexy eyes.'

'He was looking at Jeannie, not you,' Elaine pointed out. 'I think he quite fancies you, Jeannie.'

'Well, he needn't bother.' She wouldn't look twice at Sean McDowd.

Tea was cold chicken with tomatoes freshly picked from the garden, potato salad, and chunks of home-made bread, thickly spread with butter. For afters, they had damson pie and cream.

Marcia, as liberal with praise as she was with criticism, declared it quite the nicest meal she'd ever eaten.

'It was delicious, Mrs Flowers,' Lachlan said courteously. 'I really enjoyed everything.'

'Me too,' concurred Elaine.

Rose glanced at the clock. 'It's almost six. Your father will be here at half past and I'm dying to hear Jeannie and Lachlan play.'

Everyone went into the parlour; even Gerald seemed interested.

'Shall we start off with *Minuet in G* again,' Jeannie whispered to Lachlan, who condescended to look at her properly for the first time.

'Why not!'

'And then what about a Strauss waltz and some Chopin? The music's on the stand. We could finish with "Love Me Tender". I've been practising all week.'

Lachlan grinned. 'I couldn't have chosen a better programme myself.' He bowed at the small audience, tucked the violin under his chin, raised his eyebrows at his accompanist, and they began to play.

Dr Bailey arrived when they'd just started their final piece. Rose crept out to let him in, and the doctor enthusiastically joined in the applause at the end of the little concert.

'Well done, son, and you too, Jeannie,' he said. 'That was most enjoyable.'

'I won't be playing this for much longer.' Lachlan waved the violin. 'I'm getting a guitar for Christmas. I want to play rock 'n' roll, like Chuck Berry and Bill Haley and the Comets.'

'That's a shame!' Rose cried. 'You're very good.'

'Well, if it's what the boy wants...' Dr Bailey didn't seem the tiniest bit bothered by his son's intentions.

'Dad,' Lachlan said eagerly, 'if Max comes with us to the Cavern tonight, would you mind driving him home? The Merseysippi Jazz Band and the Ron McKay Skiffle Group are playing.'

Max glanced warily at his own father. Tom was frowning, stuck for words, obviously wanting to protest, but unwilling to do so in front of the doctor. The boys had almost certainly set it up between them, knowing neither man was likely to refuse.

'You can't expect your father to go so much out of his way,' Tom stuttered.

'I don't mind,' the other man said easily.

Jeannie's heart sank at the idea of being left behind, but help came from an unexpected quarter.

'In that case, why doesn't Jeannie come back too? Dad can bring her home with Max.' Marcia suggested in her foghorn voice. 'We can go to the pictures. They only show old films on Sundays. *Frenchman's Creek* is on the Plaza with Joan Fontaine. I saw it ages ago, but I wouldn't mind sitting through it again.'

'Please come, Jeannie,' Elaine implored, as if Jeannie was likely to have any say in the matter.

'That's a good idea, isn't it, Tom?' Rose said before her husband could open his mouth. 'We'll have a quiet evening for a change. There's a good play on the wireless. Gerald will be in bed by then.'

And so it was that fifteen minutes later, Jeannie found herself squashed beside Lachlan Bailey in his father's car and being driven to Walton Vale.

Frenchman's Creek was really exciting. Jeannie was on the edge of her seat the whole way through. When it was over, they went to the Baileys' and Elaine made bacon sandwiches, which they ate in the kitchen. They were still there, talking, when Dr Bailey popped his head around the door to say he was off to collect Lachlan and Max, and would Jeannie like to keep him company?

She went like a shot. It was a new experience to see such brightly illuminated streets and the lights still on in shop windows at such a late hour. There were lots of people about for a Sunday night, but that was because the pubs were letting out, Dr Bailey explained.

As had been arranged, Lachlan was waiting in Whitechapel, outside the Post Office, when his father arrived. There was no sign of Max. He came a few minutes later, staggering slightly, causing the alarmed doctor to ask if he was drunk. 'I thought they didn't sell alcohol in the Cavern!'

Lachlan chuckled. 'They don't. He's not drunk. It's the music, it's made him delirious.'

Max collapsed into the car. 'That was magic,' he gasped. 'I've never heard anything like it in my life before. I didn't know music like that *existed*. All we hear at school is hymns and stupid folk songs and Mum only ever has classical stuff on the wireless. Skiffle's okay, but jazz! Jazz is the best sound in the world! Oh, Jeannie! It made me go all funny inside.'

'If jazz makes you go all funny, wait till you hear rock 'n' roll,' Lachlan advised him. '"See You Later Alligator" will send you round the bend.'

'It sends *me* round the bend,' the doctor remarked mildly.

'Max, why don't you come with us to see Elvis Presley in *Love Me Tender* on Wednesday?' Lachlan suggested. 'Your Jeannie's coming.'

'My father hasn't said yet if I can go,' Jeannie reminded him.

Max banged the seat with his fist. 'I'll *make* him let us go. I'll bloody *strangle* him if he won't let us go. If he won't, I'll kill myself'

Dr Bailey asked if that wasn't putting it a bit strongly? 'I can't see any reason why he won't allow you to visit the cinema. Tell him he's lucky his children bother to ask. Mine do as they please and I have no say in the matter.'

Max snorted. 'You don't know our father. If me or Jeannie did as we pleased, he'd burst a blood vessel.'

'Tell him I'll bring you home, seeing as this Elvis Presley character is involved,' the doctor said good-naturedly. 'But don't expect me to make a habit of it. I'm not prepared to go to and from Ailsham like a yo-yo.'

Outside the walls of number ten Disraeli Terrace, Tom Flowers was very much aware of his place in the world, which was pretty close to the bottom of the social scale. He was keenly respectful of members of the professional classes. Having met Dr Bailey, he considered it would reflect on him badly if he refused to let his children visit the cinema when they'd been offered a lift home.

'But once and no more,' he warned them. The idea of the good doctor providing a taxi service made him uncomfortable. After a furious argument, a wild-eyed Max was told he could attend lunchtime concerts at the Cavern and on Saturday and Sunday evenings, but that was all. Jeannie could go to tea with her friend but, now that the nights were drawing in, it had to be when Max was meeting one of *his* friends, and they could come home together. They must be back by half past seven, otherwise there'd be hell to play, Tom said threateningly.

Benedicta Lucas was very tall and desperately thin; so thin, that the bones in her wrists and elbows showed through her delicate white skin like ping-pong balls. Her face was long and narrow, her pale blue eyes perfectly round, the two contrasting shapes giving a bizarre impression. She had lank, creamy hair, and the quietest voice anyone had ever heard – or not heard, as it was very difficult to know what Benedicta was saying in her timid whisper. She had the unfortunate habit of turning bright crimson if attention was drawn to her, so just answering the register caused her some embarrassment – the mention of her unusual name was inclined to raise a few giggles – and poor Benedicta, with her weird appearance and equally weird name, had become a figure of fun.

It was therefore a little surprising when, one day just before Christmas, as I-remove were in the middle of a history lesson, Benedicta raised her hand for the very first time and asked Miss Appleton in a whisper if she could please be excused.

Miss Appleton, who was describing the victories and exploits of her favourite historical character, the Black Prince, nodded irritably, and the ghostly figure of Benedicta got up and left the room.

A good fifteen minutes had passed before the form mistress realised the girl hadn't come back. She scanned the rows of bored, interested, or uncomprehending faces in front of her for someone she could trust to send in search of her missing pupil. Her eyes lighted on Jeannie Flowers, the most sensible girl in the class, popular with everybody.

'Jeannie, will you see what's happened to Benedicta, please? She might be feeling sick or something. Let me know if anything's wrong.'

'Yes, Miss.'

Benedicta was found within minutes. Although the lavatories appeared empty, one door was closed. Jeannie bent down and saw a pair of feet underneath. She knocked. 'Is that you, Benedicta?'

There was a muffled, 'Yes.'

'Are you all right? Miss Appleton sent me to find you.'

'I'm not all right. I want to die.'

Used as she was to dealing with Max's histrionics, Jeannie wasn't as thrown by this statement as some girls might have been.

'Why?' she enquired calmly.

'No one likes me,' Benedicta replied in a hoarse whisper that contained more than a touch of hysteria. 'Everyone hates me. I can't stand sitting next to Edna Fellows. All she does is ignore me. She wanted to sit by some other girl, who preferred to sit by some other girl, and she's fed up being stuck with me. No one talks to me. If I speak to Edna, she just tells me to shut up. She told me again this morning and I decided I couldn't stand it any longer. I'd sooner die.'

'Come out and I'll talk to you.'

'You're only doing it because I'm crying.'

'I didn't know you were crying.'

'Who are you?'

'Jeannie Flowers.'

There was a long pause before the catch clicked on the door and a hunched, red-faced, red-eyed Benedicta shuffled out. 'I suppose you'll tell everyone what a show I've made of meself,' she sniffed.

'I won't tell a soul, except Elaine Bailey, who's my friend.'

'*I* haven't got a friend. And I've no brothers and sisters, or a dad. He died when I was two. If it wasn't for me mam, I'd think I was invisible.'

'You're anything but invisible,' Jeannie said generously. Benedicta Lucas was merely the sort of person you looked at once, but not twice. The only memorable thing about her was her awful name.

'I'm not very clever either,' she whispered. 'I don't always understand the lessons and I daren't ask Edna to explain.'

'You must be clever if you passed the Eleven-Plus.'

Benedicta sighed miserably. 'I didn't pass, I failed. Me mam pays, five guineas a term. She had to take on an extra cleaning job to pay the fees and buy the uniform, which cost a small fortune. She ses I'm her "investment in the future", though I'm not sure what that means.'

Jeannie wasn't sure either. It was getting a bit too complicated for her. 'I tell you what,' she said, 'do you have school dinners or bring sandwiches?'

'I bring sarnies. I'm eligible for free school dinners, but Mam doesn't want anyone to know we're that poor.'

'Me and Elaine bring sandwiches, so why don't you eat with us?'

The girl squirmed. 'Elaine mightn't want me.'

'She'll want you as much as I do.' Jeannie hoped this was true. She and Elaine had reached the stage where they shared quite intimate secrets, which they couldn't do with Benedicta present. But she felt the same obligation to take Benedicta under her wing as she'd done with Rita McDowd, despite her so often being a nuisance.

'Will you do us a favour?' Benedicta pleaded.

'If I can.'

'Don't call me Benedicta. I hate it. It puts people off. They might like me if I was called Jeannie or Elaine.'

'What shall I call you then?'

'Benny. It's a boy's name, but I prefer it any day to Benedicta.'

'It's not really a boy's name if it's short for your own. There was a Charlotte at my old school, but everyone called her Charlie. Look, we'd better be getting back – Benny – else Miss Appleton's likely to send someone in search of us both.'

Benny Lucas turned out to be a bigger nuisance than Rita McDowd. She stuck to the girls like a clam and became sulkily jealous if she discovered they'd been out together and she hadn't been asked. She was invited to tea at both their houses. Marcia ignored her existence and Max considered her a pain.

On one icily cold day in February they went to tea in Benny's house in Grenville Street, Bootle on the clear understanding they didn't mention they knew her mother was a cleaner.

'She tells people she works for the council, which she does, except she says she's in the office, though I bet no one believes her. Saturday afternoons, she cleans some bank.'

Mrs Lucas was as small as her daughter was tall, just as thin, and even more knobbly. She wore a neatly darned jumper and a skirt beginning to fray at the hem. Her hands were unnaturally large, the knuckles swollen and red from years of hard work. The house was a tiny terrace, poorly furnished, though the old furniture sparkled and there wasn't a speck of dust to be seen. A small fire burnt in the grate and the room was cold. Jeannie had to stop herself from shivering, which would have looked rude. Mrs Lucas kept glancing at the grate, as if weighing up whether or not to throw on a few lumps of coal.

Great pains had been taken with the food; lamb chops, roast potatoes, and peas, followed by a massive trifle decorated with cherries and hundreds and thousands. The dishes were mostly chipped, but the tablecloth looked new, as if it had been bought especially for the occasion.

Benny was clearly the apple of her mother's eye, her 'investment in the future', and the sole topic of conversation throughout the meal. Apparently, there wasn't a single talent that Benedicta didn't possess. Her mother's small, tired face became alive and her eyes glowed when she described how well she could dance, sing, write poetry, sew, knit, embroider, draw the prettiest pictures. She could walk at eleven months.

Elaine raised her eyebrows at her friend, and she and Jeannie shared a smile. They hadn't noticed Benny being capable of any of these things, apart from walking.

By the time they reached the trifle stage, Benny was cringing with embarrassment. 'Oh, Mam, you're not half laying it on thick. Jeannie and Elaine can do things too, you know. Jeannie's dead good at playing the piano – she sometimes plays at assembly – and Elaine's going to be a doctor when she grows up.'

Mrs Lucas went on to remark that her Benedicta was going to join the Civil Service when she left school. What's more, she didn't doubt she would have learned to play the piano brilliantly if only they'd had one.

'She wasn't the least bit interested in us,' Elaine remarked later when she and Jeannie walked through the chilling wind to the bus stop. 'She didn't ask us a single question about ourselves. Her own life is so dead miserable that she's living through her daughter, like a leech. Stage mothers are like that, pushing their children to do things they weren't able to do themselves. I read about it in a book on psychiatry.'

'Gosh! The things you read!' As ever, Jeannie was awed by her friend's knowledge. 'I thought my dad watched over us too much, but he's not nearly so bad as Mrs Lucas.' She sighed. 'Poor Benny.'

'My dad doesn't watch over us at all. He just trusts us not to do anything stupid.'

'Does that mean my dad doesn't trust me and Max?'

'I'm not sure,' the budding psychiatrist said thoughtfully. 'It could be that, or he's got a power complex. I'd need to know him better before making a prognosis.'

'I wonder if Mrs Lucas knows Benny came next to bottom of the class? I bet she hasn't seen her end of term report.'

'Benny probably didn't show it her.' Elaine linked her friend's arm and squeezed it. 'Oh, Jeannie! I'm so glad we're us.'

'So'm I,' Jeannie replied with a sober nod. 'I'll never complain about my dad again.'

'You will.'

'I suppose. I'm still trying to talk him into letting me go to the ice rink on Saturday.'

'If Benny comes, Mrs Lucas will expect her to be another Sonja Henie.'

'Who's Sonja Henie?'

'A Norwegian ice skater. She won the Olympics and became a Hollywood film star.'

A cheerful fire, much bigger than the Lucas's, blazed in the grate of the waiting room on Orrell Park station when Jeannie arrived to find Max staring gloomily into the flames. He'd been to see Lachlan. They no longer talked about football; it had been replaced by a feverish interest in rock 'n' roll. The Baileys had a gramophone and Lachlan earned enough from a paper round to buy records; Little Richard, Jerry Lee Lewis, Buddy Holly, and the one and only Elvis Presley.

'You're late,' Max grumbled.

Jeannie glanced at the clock. 'I'm not. I'm dead on time. What's the matter? You don't half look

100

miserable.' Max rarely looked anything else these days. He was growing, but only slowly, and was still shorter than most boys in his class. But that wasn't his only problem.

'It's Dad,' Max grumbled inevitably. 'He won't buy me a guitar. He said he couldn't afford it, but I know he can.'

Just as the topic of football had been discarded, so had the longing for a television. Now Max wanted a guitar. Not just wanted one, *needed* one. It was vital for his continued existence. Lachlan had one, why not him? It wasn't as if *he* could do a paper round and save up for one himself It wasn't allowed. Nothing was allowed. He had no control over his destiny and might as well be in Walton Jail, or even dead.

'You can't possibly know what Dad can or can't afford,' Jeannie told him severely.

'It so happens that I do.' Max blushed slightly. 'How?'

'The other day, I was in Mum and Dad's bedroom and the door to the wardrobe wasn't shut properly. When I went to close it, I noticed a shoe box inside, behind the clothes. I wondered what was in it, that's all. I wasn't being nosy.' Max paused and continued in a dramatic voice. 'It was full of ten bob and pound notes. I didn't count them, but there must have been hundreds.'

Jeannie didn't ask what he'd been doing in their parents' room. She often found him peering into the wardrobe mirror to see if he'd grown any taller. 'That's hardly any of our business, Max,' she said.

Max flew into a temper. 'Honestly, sis! You can

101

be a little prig sometimes. Of course it's our business when we want things and he's hoarding money like Silas Marner.'

As with Sonja Henie, she had no idea who Silas Marner was. If the truth be known, she was slightly shocked herself, thinking how easier life would be for Mum if she had a washing machine and a fridge like lots of other women. As for a television, after watching the Baileys', she wouldn't have minded one herself. It was like having your very own little cinema in the house.

Spring, and the trees in Ailsham were sprinkled with little green buds, like confetti. Tiny shoots thrust their way through the damp black soil and Tom Flowers began to spend more time in his garden. Not that he ever neglected it. Even in winter there was always something that had to be done, but in the spring his heart lifted when he saw familiar plants bursting into life, greeting him like old friends. He turned over the earth in the vegetable patch with a young man's vigour.

'Where's Dad?' Max enquired of his mother one Saturday morning when his father was nowhere to be seen. He intended to go on the attack again about the longed for guitar that he wanted more than life itself.

'Out.' Rose was furiously kneading bread in the kitchen, flour up to her elbows.

'Out where?'

'Never you mind.' His mother smiled mysteriously.

Max lounged around the house, sulking. Without a guitar, he had no idea what to do with himself. Almost two hours later, he heard a car come along Holly Lane. He ignored the sound until he realised that instead of passing the house, the car had stopped outside. It was unlikely to be Dr Bailey bringing Lachlan on an unexpected visit, the engine wasn't smooth enough. Nevertheless, Max went outside for a look. The car, small and grey, wasn't just outside the house, but had turned into the drive – and his father was behind the wheel.

Rose appeared, still smiling, wiping her hands on a tea towel, followed by an astounded Jeannie and an excited Gerald. Spencer the cat strolled behind, only faintly interested.

'Is this *ours?*' Gerald squealed.

Tom climbed out of the car and carefully closed the door. 'Yes, it's ours,' he said gruffly. 'I just bought it. It's a Morris Minor, brand new.'

'I didn't know you could drive, Dad,' Jeannie exclaimed.

'I used to take Mrs Corbett, the colonel's mother, shopping before the war. Mind you, that was in a Rolls.' He fondly patted the bonnet of his own car, just like Dr Bailey. Jeannie wondered if all men looked upon their cars as if they were human.

'Can we go for a ride, Dad?' Gerald was kicking the tyres until told firmly to stop.

'In a minute. I'd like a cup of tea first.' Tom's hands were shaking. Not only had he not driven since Mrs Corbett's death twelve years ago, but handing over his life's savings had caused a certain amount of turmoil. He needed to sit down for a while.

In the warm kitchen, he said, 'Now I can collect you from the station, but you, Jeannie, must be home by eight and Max by nine. But only two nights a week, mind you. The other nights you must concentrate on your homework.'

'Oh, Dad!' Jeannie flung her arms around her father's neck. If she went to the pictures straight from school, she could see the whole programme before catching the train.

With the car, Tom felt he was retaining control of his children's lives. Now they were dependent on him for lifts and everyone knew where they stood. There would be no more fights. Also, he quite liked the idea, next time the Baileys came, of saying to the doctor, 'There's no need to come and fetch the children. *I'll* bring them home.'

Max was scornful of the new arrangements. He considered them pitiful, just as the car was pitiful beside the Baileys' Humber Hawk. He would have much preferred a guitar.

Chapter 4

While Sean McDowd's reputation in Ailsham couldn't have been lower, he was looked upon in an entirely different light at Philip Wallace Secondary Modern. Rita quickly discovered being Sean's sister was a distinct advantage. Not only that, the McDowds were no longer the only Catholics, and there were plenty of other Irish names; Reillys, Murphys, McThis and O'That.

Unless somebody from Ailsham bothered to inform them, no one knew that Rita lived in a hovel with a mam who'd let herself go. Not that this was true nowadays anyway. The excursion to Southport had turned out to be something of a tonic for Sadie. She'd begun to take a pride in herself and her surroundings. The house was clean and there were dried leaves – white, like flattened pearls – in the vase Sean had won at the fairground. As well as working as a kitchen assistant at the village school, Sadie also washed dishes in the Oak Tree four nights a week, and the extra money made all the difference, especially as she'd cut down on the ciggies. Along with what they'd earned picking fruit, it enabled Rita to begin her new school with a perfectly adequate uniform, even if it wasn't new.

Sadie had found a magazine in the pub with a photograph of a film star called Audrey Hepburn. 'You'd suit your hair short like that,' she told Rita. 'You've got a pixie-ish sort of face like her. Would you like me to cut it?'

'Oh, I dunno, Mam. I'll think about it.' Later, Rita had examined her very ordinary reflection in the mirror. She gathered her brown hair in one hand and pulled it to the back of her neck. Without hair, her face found its shape – a small, quite perfect oval. She decided to let Mam cut it.

Once the hair had been cut, washed and dried, Sadie ran her fingers through it. 'It almost looks a different colour,' she marvelled. 'And it feels lovely and thick.'

Rita had acquired a fringe. Her eyes looked bigger, her neck longer. She was very pleased with her new hair, and even more pleased when, while waiting in Holly Lane for the coach to Philip Wallace on her first day, Jeannie Flowers remarked how nice she looked. Jeannie and Max got off at the station to catch the train to Orrell Park. Sometimes, Sean also got off at the station to go who knew where? A place more interesting than school, Rita supposed.

For all his truanting, total disinterest in learning anything whatsoever, and his indifference to homework, Sean was one of the most popular boys at Philip Wallace. When a teacher railed at him, somehow it was always the teacher who came off worse, his or her voice rising higher and higher with frustration, while Sean looked bored out of his mind, the words having no effect, and his stock rising even more with the rest of the class.

School uniform was encouraged, but not compulsory, and Sean set a bad example, always dressing in black, adding to his image as a rebel, a hero, the sort of person the other boys would have liked to be, but hadn't the nerve. As for the girls, they were crazy about the slim young man with dark good looks and smokey blue eyes that gazed sardonically on all around him. Even one or two of the teaching staff nursed a secret, unwilling admiration for Sean McDowd.

As the sister of this remarkable young man, Rita found herself very much in demand, particularly by girls. They linked her arm in the playground and questioned her about her brother. What sort of food did he like? What was his favourite colour? Had he already got a girlfriend? Did he prefer blondes, brunettes, or redheads? Rita answered the questions as best as she could, wondering why they wanted such useless information.

At going home time, a few girls often waited with her for the coach to Ailsham. They didn't get on, but it gave them a reason for being in the vicinity of Sean McDowd, that is if he'd condescended to grace school with his presence that day. They talked to Rita in loud voices, hoping Sean would notice and give them one of his rare smiles. But Sean was as indifferent to the girls as he was to homework or anything else to do with school.

In Rita's second term, she wasn't the only one who was surprised to find there was a subject in which her brother professed an interest.

Philip Wallace was a new school, built only four years ago. So far, it wasn't particularly well thought of. No one went out of their way to send their children there, and the Headmaster, Mr Catchpole, was always looking for ways in which his establishment could acquire a good reputation.

At assembly one morning, he announced his intention of starting a school orchestra, presuming there were sufficient pupils who could play instruments. Anyone interested should give their name to their class teacher. There would be auditions during the dinner hour on Friday.

Before commencing the first lesson, the teacher asked for names and, as she said later in the staff room, 'I nearly died when Sean McDowd put up his hand. Apparently, he can play the drums.'

Sean had never been near a drum kit in his life, but he knew there was one behind the stage in Ailsham Women's Institute Hall, where concerts and dances were sometimes held.

On the way home, instead of getting off in Holly Lane, he waited until the coach reached the village, then made his way to the hall, which was in between the Oak Tree where his mother worked at night and the school where she worked by day. It was January and pitch dark. No one noticed the tall, slight figure slope to the rear of the building.

He entered by simply breaking a window in the gents' toilet, leaving it open for a quick escape when someone came, which they inevitably would after a time. At first, people might not take much notice, but as soon as a member of the Women's Institute heard the noise he was about to make and realised the sound was coming from their hall, they'd be there like a shot.

The kit was full of dust, which didn't matter, but there were no sticks. Sean cursed and searched for something, anything, that would do in their place. He found a small Union Jack on a thin pole, ripped off the flag, and broke the pole into two over his knee. Better than nothing.

He sat on a stool behind the array of drums, took a deep breath, and lightly eased his foot down on the bass pedal, then tapped the snare and the tom toms, flicked the cymbals, assessing their individual sounds. Although he'd never touched a set of drums, Sean had played them hundreds of times before inside his head. He smiled in a way no one, not even his mother, had ever witnessed, a slow, dreamy, rapturous smile. At last he was making music.

Sean had never revealed to a soul that he had his own personal wireless lodged in his brain. He switched it on and off at will. Entire orchestras played just for Sean McDowd. Violins soared, drums thundered, fingers flew over the keys of a grand piano. The sound was magnificent, soul-shattering, triumphant.

This wasn't all that Sean listened to while he travelled on the bus to school, sat in class as a teacher's voice intruded irritatingly in the background, lay in bed at night, wanting to sleep, but unable to resist the Ceilidh band thumping out a jaunty jig or a woman singing a haunting Irish lament. The sound of a lonely flute might wake him next morning, sweet yet sad. Then there were the love songs, plucking at his heart-strings, making him think of Jeannie Flowers.

Whenever this happened, his heart would quicken, his pulse would race. One day...

Sometimes, Sean himself was the source of the imaginary music. His own hands wielded the sticks over a set of drums much grander than the one in Ailsham Women's Institute hall. His fingers plucked the strings of a guitar, a double base, caressed a piano's ivory teeth, and his arm wielded the bow on many a violin or cello.

He took after his father. 'He lived and breathed music, did Kevin McDowd. It was in his blood,' his mother had said on numerous occasions.

Once he had checked the tone of the drums, Sean began to hum 'Twelfth Street Rag'. He struck the drums lightly in rhythm with the tune. He did this another half a dozen times, getting the hang of things.

He could do it! Now it was time to play it properly. Pressing his foot on the pedal, he let rip, as he had done so many times before in his imagination. Sean pounded the drums, tapped them politely, coaxed them, whispered encouragement, bent his head and cocked his ear, half expecting the drum he was beating to talk back and tell him what a grand job he was doing. He felt as if his arms had grown and he no longer had merely two as the sticks thrashed wildly, gently, subtly, slyly over the cheap set of drums that had never known anything like it before.

People came, as Sean had expected, though the outraged voices in the hall came as a shock. He dropped the sticks, made for the gents, and was halfway across the field behind the hall by the time the secretary of the Women's Institute and her husband burst into the room behind the stage, to find the cymbals still trembling, a Union Jack destroyed and, later, a window broken in the gents' toilet.

'Guess who I saw in the Cavern last night?'

Jeannie shrugged. 'I dunno, Max. The Queen? Marilyn Monroe? The Archbishop of Canterbury?'

'No, idiot. It was Sean McDowd, of all people.'

'I don't know why you should sound so surprised. Sean's just as much right to be there as you.'

Max had no idea why the sight of Sean had made him feel so uneasy. Perhaps it was because Sean, who was there alone, didn't dance, didn't talk, didn't move from the side of the stage, where he stood very still, unsmiling, watching the Acker Bilk Jazz Band, watching every single movement the musicians made, taking everything in. After a while, Max noticed Sean wasn't still any more. He had closed his eyes and his foot was tapping, his head nodding slightly. Even the thumbs on his long hands were twitching. Sean *was* the music. It had taken him over.

In view of what happened a few weeks later, Max was right to have felt uneasy when he saw Sean McDowd in the Cavern – he'd been there several times since and *he* didn't have to leave early to catch a train so his father could pick him up from the station.

The Flowers and the Baileys had formed their own group, the Merseysiders, with Lachlan on

111

guitar, Jeannie on piano, Elaine wielding a tamborine, and Max playing the mouth organ. At first, Max had thought this dead pathetic, but having practised every spare minute, he'd become quite capable – and it was only till he got a guitar.

They played in the Baileys' parlour until the neighbours complained, then in the Flowers' until *their* neighbours complained, and transferred to the Flowers' garden shed, where they were surrounded by seed boxes, tins of paint, and garden tools. Tom's bike had to be removed to make room. Deprived of a piano, Jeannie lost interest in the music side of things, but not the close proximity of Lachlan Bailey, who was growing taller, broader, and more attractive by the minute. She made do with an old toy xylophone and stayed with the group in the hope that Lachlan would continue to throw her the odd smile, though both girls considered the whole thing a huge joke, while the boys took it very seriously indeed.

Lachlan often sang while he played. 'I ain't nothing but a hound dog,' he would holler, doing his best to sound like Elvis Presley, or 'Love me tender, love me do,' making odd faces and swivelling his hips around like his idol. The girls found it hard to keep their faces straight, particularly when Lachlan's voice began to break, covering several octaves, or they were ordered to join in with a 'tra, la, la'.

Rose said she thought they sounded very professional. She liked Saturday mornings when Elaine and Lachlan arrived early so they could 'rehearse' – for what, she had no idea. She toiled away in the kitchen, a smile on her face, wishing she'd had the opportunity to have such fun when she'd been young.

Tom Flowers listened while he worked in the garden, wincing every now and then. Still, the youngsters weren't doing any harm, except to his ears. Spencer, the cat, kept well out of the way.

It was on such a Saturday morning in May, the Merseysiders were playing and Lachlan was singing 'Rock Around the Clock' when the shed door opened and Sean McDowd stepped inside, dressed from head to toe in sinister black.

'Greetings, scholarship boy.' He nodded at Max. 'I was passing and wondered what was going on.'

'You've got a nerve,' Max spluttered, but Sean ignored him and addressed Lachlan. 'You play that thing dead good,' he said.

'It's a guitar,' Lachlan explained, adding, though he wasn't sure why, 'I'm not a scholarship boy.'

'I know it's a guitar. Meself, I play the drums in the school orchestra.'

'Do you now!' Lachlan looked excited. 'We could do with a drummer, except we haven't got a drum kit.'

'Drums are shit to play. All that comes out is a noise. It's not proper music. Can I have a go on your guitar?'

'If you like.' Again, Lachlan wasn't sure why he so willingly handed the instrument over. Normally a generous, good-natured boy, he was reluctant to let even Max, his friend, touch his

113

precious guitar. But there was something magnetic about this young man that made Lachlan want to please him. 'Have you ever played before?'

'No.' Sean held the guitar against his thin chest and looked down at it tenderly, as if a beautiful woman was clasped in his arms.

'What you do,' Lachlan explained, 'is press the strings against the fret...'

'I know what you do.' Sean's long fingers plucked nimbly at the guitar, moving them quickly up and down the fret, gauging the tone, playing one note over and over, then another, and another, watched by an astonished Lachlan and an outraged Max.

Jeannie, still reeling from the swear word, realised Sean was finding the scale. Within five minutes he had found all eight notes. He played them an octave higher, an octave lower. It wasn't long before he was able to strum a passable version of 'Jerusalem', which they used to sing at Friday assembly in Ailsham Junior School.

When he'd finished, he handed the guitar back to Lachlan. 'How much did it cost?' he enquired.

'Five pounds or thereabouts. It was a Christmas present, so I'm not exactly sure. This is an acoustic guitar; electric ones are much dearer. My dad got it from Crane's in Hanover Street.'

'If I get one, can I come and play too?'

'Yes, yes, of course,' Lachlan said eagerly. 'You're a natural. I can't believe you've never played before. I used to play the violin, but it still took a while to get as far on the guitar as you just did.'

114

'What sort of music were you playing when I came in?'

'Rock 'n' roll. It's the best music in the world.'

'I think so too. See you in a few weeks' time then.' Sean disappeared as quickly as he'd come.

'Who was that?' Lachlan asked excitedly. 'Whoever he is, he's a genius.'

'His name's Sean McDowd,' Jeannie supplied.

'He's the chap our Marcia fancied,' said Elaine. 'She'll be sorry she didn't join the group when I tell her.' Marcia had refused to have anything to do with the Merseysiders, a decision everyone had greeted with relief Elaine decided aloud not to mention Sean McDowd in case Marcia changed her mind.

Max didn't speak. He thought it best not to, because all that would have come out was a stream of invective. He never thought he could hate Lachlan, but he did now for saying Sean McDowd could come back. And when he returned – Max had no doubt that he would – he'd have a guitar and be able to play as well as Lachlan, possibly better. Max would be left behind, with only a stupid mouth organ. He knew he was jealous, but didn't care. He recalled his friend's face as he'd watched Sean find the notes so easily and naturally, as if he'd been born to play. Lachlan had been full of admiration. When Max tried, his fingers were everywhere, stumbling and awkward. Perhaps he would never be able to play. Perhaps he would never grow any taller. Max let out a groan. He was doomed.

'I wonder,' Jeannie said, 'where Sean expects to get the money from for a guitar? They're awfully

115

poor, the McDowds,' she explained to Lachlan and Elaine.

Max glowered and wondered too.

Sean rang Peter Beggerow, the owner of the fruit and veg stall in Ormskirk market, from the phone box at the end of Holly Lane. 'Will you be needing a hand over the next few weeks, Pete?' he enquired.

'I wouldn't mind some help with shifting crates and stuff on Sat'days, mate. By the way,' he added slyly, 'is there any veg going?'

Vegetables were hardly worth the trouble stealing – bulky and you got only a pittance for them. Sean wasn't interested. 'How about chickens?' he asked.

'Chickens are always welcome.'

'How much will I get each?'

'Sixpence, mate.'

'What about a bob?'

'What about eightpence?'

'Let's say ten.'

'Let's say ninepence each. That's me limit, Sean.'

'Ninepence, then. I'll take them round your Frank's house.'

'Give us a call when you do.'

Over the next few weeks, a few farmers noticed their stock of poultry had been reduced by two or three the night before. They kept a careful lookout, but it didn't happen again. Sean was careful never to hit the same farm twice, otherwise he'd find the owner lying in wait, ready to give the thief a good hiding.

He went to school two days a week in the hope of keeping officialdom off his back; the rest of the time he went round the village, knocking on doors, asking if there were any odd jobs he could do. For sixpence or a shilling a time, he cleared gardens, cut down trees, mowed lawns, cleaned windows, washed cars, all the time listening to the in-built wireless in his head, hearing himself playing the guitar.

Saturdays, he worked on Pete's stall in Ormskirk, where several fat chickens were usually for sale as a result of Sean's night work.

Two months later, he had acquired five pounds, eight and sixpence, not all of it come by honestly and, early one glorious July morning, with a brilliant sun shining out of a perfectly blue sky, he caught the train to Liverpool and presented himself at Crane's in Hanover Street, with the intention of purchasing a guitar.

The assistant was a middle-aged man with tired eyes behind a pair of thick glasses. 'So, you're after one of the lowest range models?' he remarked, curling his lip.

'I'm just after a guitar,' Sean said in a surly voice.

'You won't get an electric one for that much.'

'I don't want an electric one, thanks.'

'We only have three in that price range. They're on the wall over there.'

The cheap guitars looked the same as those costing ten times as much, but Sean knew the expensive ones would be made from superior materials, have a better tone, be the product of a more skilled craftsman. But the time for such an instrument had not yet come.

A five-pound guitar – four pounds, nineteen and elevenpence, to be exact – was taken off the wall and laid on the counter. It made an echoey, booming sound that was music in itself to Sean's ears. He caught his breath, picked it up, and cradled it in his arms, then ran his hand over the hard curves. All he had to do was hand over the money and it would be his.

He looks as if he's just been given a million quid, the assistant marvelled, watching Sean's face as he nursed the five-pound guitar. 'Do you want to look at the others?' he asked, more kindly now.

'No, this one'll do.'

'Would you like a tutor?'

'What's that?'

'A book with instructions on how to play.'

'I'll be teaching meself, thanks.'

'How about a plectrum? Some people use a plectrum rather than their fingers. They're only a penny ha'penny each.'

'I prefer me fingers.' Sean plucked a few strings. He couldn't imagine using anything else. He stood the guitar carefully on the floor, took a paper bag out of his jacket pocket, and emptied the contents – hundreds of coins, both copper and silver – on to the counter.

'Have you been robbing the collection box?' the assistant joked, as he began the painstaking task of counting the coins. Initially, he hadn't taken to the taciturn, arrogant young man, but he'd looked at the guitar in the same daft way as he himself had once looked upon a clarinet. *His*

118

talent had been such, he'd ended up selling them, rather than playing them. But he had a feeling it would be different with this customer.

'All present and correct,' he asserted when the money had been counted. 'I suggest you buy a spare set of strings. It'd be a nuisance if one broke when you weren't in a position to buy another.' He hoped the lad had enough money.

'OK, I'll have a set.' Sean gave an abrupt nod. He still had eight and sixpence in his pocket.

'Will you be wanting a strap?'

'I'll have the cheapest. How much is that?'

'Webbing's one and six; blue, red or black.'

'Give us the black.' He was getting the strap in return for a couple of chickens.

'Well, good luck,' the assistant said when business had been completed and his customer was ready to leave. 'What's your name, son?'

'Sean McDowd. Why?'

'I just wondered. I'll keep me eye open for your first concert.' He watched the lad walk out into the dazzling sunshine and felt sure that one day he would hear the name of Sean McDowd again.

'Is that you, Sean?' his mother screamed when he opened the back door.

'Yes, Mam.' He was halfway upstairs when she appeared, hands poised angrily on her hips.

'There's been a man here today from school, Mr Something-or-other. He said you've hardly been in for weeks...' Sadie gasped. 'What's that you're holding, Sean, lad?'

'A guitar, Mam,' he said proudly.

'Oh, son! You haven't pinched it!'

119

'No, Mam. I earned the money to buy it. That's why I haven't been at school. I've been working, doing odd jobs like.'

She was probably the only mother in the world who understood that owning a musical instrument was more important than school. Her visitor had already been forgotten. 'Let's have a look?'

Sean returned downstairs and Sadie ran her hands over the polished wood. 'It's lovely,' she breathed. 'Can you play anything yet?'

'Not yet,' Sean conceded. 'Not properly. I was just going up to me room to practise.'

'Go ahead, luv. I'll bring you up a cup of tea in a minute.'

When Sadie went up with the tea, Sean was holding the guitar, softly strumming the strings. He had his back to her and, for a moment, she had a feeling of déjà vu. He looked so much like his father. Kevin McDowd will never be dead while his son's alive, she told herself.

Rita insisted on nursing the guitar while Sean ate his tea, though it meant her own got cold. 'I like the feel of it,' she commented. 'It's so big, yet it's not heavy.'

'That's because it's hollow,' Sean said good-naturedly. He had rarely felt in such a good mood.

'I'm not stupid, Sean. I can see it's hollow. Does this mean you won't be playing the drums no more in the school orchestra? They've asked me twice this week where you were. You were needed for a rehearsal or something.'

'What did you tell them?'

'That I didn't know, which is the truth. Elsa Graham on the coach said you'd pruned their oak tree and got sixpence for it, but I didn't know that till later. Not that I'd have told them at school,' she added hastily, 'if I'd known before.'

She hadn't bothered to tell her mother, either, Sadie noted, but didn't complain. She'd rather the children stuck together than told tales.

'Can I have me guitar back now, Rita? I'm going up to practise in me room.'

Not long afterwards, Sean was interrupted by a ferocious banging on the wall that adjoined the next door house. 'Will you stop that bloody racket,' their neighbour yelled. So, he took his guitar outside into what was now a perfect evening to end a perfect day.

He wandered along the edge of the cornfield at the back of Disraeli Terrace, the small, waif–like figure of his sister following a few steps behind, picking out all the Irish songs he knew. 'In Dublin's fair city...' He whispered the words as he played, disturbing the birds that rustled impatiently in the hedge, arid the small creatures that lived close to the roots.

Rita began to sing with him, the words soaring up to the sky and disappearing into the deepening blueness.

...Where the girls are so pretty,
I first set my eyes on sweet Molly Malone,
As she wheeled her wheelbarrow,
Through streets broad and narrow,
Crying cockles and mussels, alive, alive-o.

Sean turned to face his sister, threw back his head, and laughed. He had never felt this happy before.

They finished the song together.

Alive, alive-o-o,
Alive, alive-o-o,
Crying cockles, and mussels,
Alive, alive-o.

Sadie stopped washing the dishes to listen to the sound of her children singing in the distance, accompanied by the faint strum of a guitar. 'What a voice our Rita's got,' she marvelled. 'I never realised it was quite so powerful. If only their dad was around, he'd be desperately proud.'

Chapter 5

1960

In September, the Merseysiders played their first gig and were paid five pounds. They now had five members: Lachlan Bailey, Sean McDowd and Max Flowers on guitar – having worn his father down, Max had been bought a bass guitar for Christmas two years before – Frank – known as 'Fly' – Fleming on drums, and Ronnie Connors on keyboard. Elaine and Jeannie had dropped out. They had better things to do with their time.

It had been no one's idea to have a keyboard player until Ronnie Connors' Dad heard about the group and asked if his son could join. Mr Connors owned a factory making sanitary ware on Kirkby Industrial Estate. A keen music fan himself, he was willing to let the Merseysiders practise in his factory once the workers had gone home. Not only that, Ronnie was eighteen and could drive. His father was equally willing to let him use the firm's van. The group were not only being offered a place to play where there would be no neighbours to complain, but transport for them and their equipment. Under the circumstances, a keyboard player seemed an excellent idea. The instrument was called a Rickenbacker, and had been imported from America. It was electric, easily carried, and made a sound that was half piano, half organ.

The morning after their first gig – Fly Fleming's sister had got married and they played at the reception – Jeannie, anxious to know how they'd got on, woke her brother early, simply by dragging the clothes off his bed. 'How did it go?' she demanded.

'Flippin' hell, Jeannie,' Max growled. 'I didn't get in till all hours. I'm exhausted.'

'Did people clap and cheer? Or did they boo and jeer?'

'Huh! Very funny. The young ones liked us; the old ones didn't. The old ones wanted war songs like "We'll Meet Again", not "Great Balls of Fire".' Max gave a nonchalant yawn. 'We've got another gig.'

'You haven't!'

'It's a wedding again. One of the bridesmaids is getting married next month.'

Rose popped her head around the door. 'How did it go, son?'

'They got another booking, Mum,' Jeannie told her.

'That's marvellous, Max.' Rose flushed with pleasure. 'I'll go and tell your dad. He'll be pleased.'

'Will he hell,' Max said cynically when their mother had gone. 'As far as Dad's concerned, rock 'n' roll is the music of the devil.' For the first time, he noticed the empty bed on the other side of the room. 'Where's our Gerald? He's up early.'

'Gone out to escape the frosty atmosphere. You've been too wrapped up in other things to notice, but he's still in Dad's bad books for failing the Eleven-Plus. Tomorrow, he's starting at Philip Wallace.' Jeannie picked up the bedclothes and threw them back. 'Would you like a cup of tea? Or would you prefer to go back to sleep?'

'Both, please, the tea first.'

'I'll bring it up in a minute.'

Jeannie left, and Max sat up and tucked the clothes around him. Last night had been fantastically exciting. He'd never known a night like it before, the way the girls had yelled and screamed and the boys had roared their approval, demanding more. It was the first time most had heard rock 'n' roll, and they'd loved it. Over the last few months, similar groups had started to play at the Cavern in place of jazz and skiffle; Rory Storm and the Hurricanes, Cass and the Cassanovas.

Closing his eyes, Max lived through the night again, visualising the eager, manic faces, feeling the same sensation of power. *He* was one of the people responsible for this frenzy of emotion. He felt exactly the same when he listened to rock 'n' roll.

Remembering, Max gave a blissful sigh, though the more he thought about it, he couldn't recall many of the faces being directed at *him*. At least half were watching Lachlan, and the other half Sean McDowd; soppy, stupid, idolising faces. He wondered if there'd been *anyone* looking at Max Flowers?

Perhaps it was because he didn't stand centre stage, but over to one side so the difference in height between him and the other guitarists wasn't so apparent – Lachlan was six foot, Sean

125

slightly more, but Max had stopped growing at five and a half feet and, now that he was seventeen, was likely to stay that way for ever.

How could God have been so cruel? Everyone remarked how like his father he was, with his thick, brown hair, brown eyes, evenly spaced features. He even had the same broad shoulders. In fact, he had everything except his father's height. Yet Jeannie, who was so much like their mother, was already inches taller than her. Any day now, she'd be taller than *him*.

Jeannie came in with the tea and Max said bitterly, 'Is Dad dancing for joy because we've got another gig?'

'He's in the garden. He might be dancing for joy out there.'

'Oh yeah!'

Tom wasn't dancing, but staring moodily, hands in pockets, at a tub of begonias coming to the end of their lives, wondering whether to pull them up or leave them for another week or two – they still provided a patch of colour. It was a decision that would have normally taken him a mere second, but today Tom had an unaccustomed feeling of lethargy.

To tell the truth, he didn't give a damn about the begonias. He was concerned only with the fact that his sons were letting him down. Jeannie had never given him a moment of concern. She studied hard and was doing well with her lessons, which was ironic in a way, for what point was there in a girl getting O levels? It was nothing but a waste of time and taxpayers' money. He'd soon put Rose right when she suggested letting their daughter stay at school till eighteen like her friend Elaine, take A levels, possibly go to university.

'You finished learning at thirteen, love,' he pointed out. 'And it hasn't done you any harm. What need have you ever had for education?'

'None,' Rose had agreed. 'None whatsoever.'

From anyone else, the 'none whatsoever' might have sounded cynical, but not when it came from his dear Rose.

The world was becoming a difficult place for Tom to understand. He felt left behind. Animals were being sent into space, Ireland was erupting, H-bombs were being exploded all over the place and, perhaps the worst thing of all, sons no longer respected their fathers. They went their own way; hang the opinion of their elders and betters. No matter how many times he impressed upon Max the importance of education and the futility of spending so much time on that damn guitar, Max refused to listen. He came and went whenever he pleased, shutting his ears to anything his father might have to say.

Now, according to Rose, who seemed quite pleased about it, he'd got another 'gig', which meant that instead of studying for his A levels, his final year at school would be overshadowed by this group he belonged to. It didn't matter with the other lads, they were all at work. The Mc-Dowd lad worked in the local garage, and Lachlan was a dispatch clerk in some factory. The situation would have been just as intolerable had the music been even vaguely decent, but the jarring, discordant sounds only set Tom's teeth on edge.

Then Gerald, despite the headmistress insisting confidently that he was bound to pass the Eleven-Plus, had failed. What's more, he didn't seem to care he'd let his dad down. Tom even had the strangest feeling that Gerald had failed deliberately, that he set more store by sticking with his friends than attending a decent school.

'Breakfast's ready, Tom,' Rose called.

'Coming, love.' Sniffling disconsolately – all he'd ever wanted was for his lads to do better than himself – he went into the kitchen where bacon, eggs, and tomatoes awaited him. There was a rack of toast and a dish of home-made marmalade. He noticed the table was only set for two. 'Where is everyone?' he asked.

'Our Jeannie's just left for Elaine's. She decided to walk to the station rather than ask for a lift. It's a lovely morning.'

'She's off early.'

'Dr Bailey and his wife are spending the day in Chester. They're taking Jeannie and Elaine and the three little boys. I thought I told you, Tom.'

He remembered that she had. Nowadays, he was told what his children were up to. They didn't ask, not even Jeannie. 'What about Gerald?'

'He had breakfast early and went to Holly Brook. Max is still in bed. He didn't get in till past midnight.'

'Sundays, we always had breakfast together,' Tom mumbled, aware there was a tremor in his voice.

Rose put a cup of tea in front of him. 'Things change, Tom. The children are growing up. They'd sooner be with their friends than us.'

It seemed all wrong to Tom. Surely, he should be the one to decide when to let his children go, not the other way round? He didn't like the way his wife had spoken to him, either, as if he was a confused old man.

Gerald came in. 'I found a frog, a lovely mottled one. I've put it in the pond.'

'That's just what we needed, Gerald, another frog.' Rose fondly ruffled her baby's hair. 'Are you looking forward to your new school tomorrow?'

'Oh, *yes*, Mum.' The boy's eyes shone. 'The first thing I'm going to do is put my name down for the orchestra. Sam Hughes said they give you lessons. I want to learn to play the guitar like our Max.'

Tom stifled a groan.

Marcia Bailey had refused to countenance university. She left school in July, aged eighteen, and went to work behind the counter in Woolworth's. Even Dr and Mrs Bailey, who didn't believe in interfering in their children's lives, considered this an extraordinary thing for a girl with numerous O and A levels to do.

'She says she wants to experience all aspects of life,' Elaine told Jeannie on Sunday morning as they strolled, arm in arm, through the heart of Chester with its Tudor streets and expensive shops. The others had gone to the zoo, but the girls had decided they'd sooner window shop and meet up later for lunch. They'd discovered an interest in fashion and pestered their mothers for new clothes. 'After a few months, she's going to work in a factory, then an office, then on the trains, and after that a hospital. Then she might join the forces or become a policewoman.'

'Or she might get married,' Jeannie suggested. 'It seems serious with that Graham chap.'

'*He* thinks it's serious, but Marcia's only playing with him.'

'That's cruel.'

'Yes, but you know our Marcia. She never does things by halves.' Marcia was all over Graham when they were together. 'What do you think of that nightie, the black one?' Elaine stopped and pointed to a window displaying glamorous nightwear. 'You can see right through it.'

Jeannie contemplated the black, diaphanous garment. 'It's pretty, but what are you supposed to wear underneath?'

'Nothing, least I don't think so.'

'It can't possibly be nothing,' Jeannie said practically. 'It would never keep you warm. Perhaps it's worn over pyjamas.'

They decided that, or some other explanation, must be the case, as the nightie couldn't possibly be worn as it was.

'Look at those brassieres,' Elaine gasped. 'They're all pink lace. All Mum ever buys for me is plain white cotton.'

'Same here. See, there's blue and yellow ones too. I never knew you could get yellow brassieres.'

'And yellow knickers to match.'

For some reason, at the very same time, the girls felt the urge to laugh. They staggered along the pavement, holding each other up, until they reached a café and decided a cup of tea would calm them down. They went inside and ordered a pot for two and buttered scones.

After a few moments, feeling calmer, Jeannie said, 'That nightdress would look daft over pyjamas.'

They contemplated the shocking, hardly credible notion, of wearing the sheer black nightie and nothing else.

'It wouldn't hide a single inch. Everything you've got would be on show.' Elaine wrinkled her nose. She was only fourteen, but had developed what she considered was an enormous and grossly obscene bust. 'I mean, you couldn't let a man see you in it, not even if he was your husband.'

'What point is there letting a woman see you?'

Elaine sighed. 'Or wearing it by yourself?'

'So, it can only be a man,' Jeannie deduced. Both girls shivered delicately. 'I think,' Jeannie said slowly, 'only think, mind, that when I got older, I might possibly wear it in front of Steve McQueen.'

Elaine thought hard for a long time. 'I might with Jack Lemmon,' she said eventually. 'But I'd have to be awfully old, at least twenty-one, and I'd still wear a bra and pants. What about our Lachlan? Would you wear it in front of him?'

'Good Lord, no!' Jeannie had told Elaine some time ago that she had feelings for her brother. She was unable to describe exactly what the feelings were, just that she wished Lachlan would pay her some attention from time to time. More than that, and she would have felt embarrassed.

'Actually,' Elaine said, dropping a bombshell, 'Lachlan said we can go to the Cavern with them a week on Wednesday. There's a rock 'n' roll group playing – Vince McLoughlin and the Vulcans.'

'My dad will never let me.'

'Ronnie Connors will pick everyone up in the van. We'll have to ask Benny, but she can make her own way from Bootle.'

'He still won't let me,' Jeannie said gloomily.

'Doesn't your mum ever have a say in what you do?'

'Dad wouldn't let *her* go to the Cavern if she wanted.'

'No,' Tom said firmly that night. 'Absolutely not. No daughter of mine is going to set foot inside the Cavern, I'll tell you that for nothing. It's not a place for young girls.'

'But, Dad,' Jeannie argued desperately, 'all the girls who go are only young. Max went when he was my age.'

'That's got nothing to do with it. What time would you be home? There's school next morning and you'd be half asleep instead of concentrating on your lessons.'

'It's not fair. Elaine's going and Benny's Mum is bound to let her.' Jeannie was near to tears. She had felt certain he would refuse, but now that he had, there was a finality about it. It was no use pleading. A week on Wednesday, her friends

132

would be at the Cavern and she would have to stay at home and imagine the wonderful time they would be having. She'd always wanted to see the place her brother and Lachlan went on and on about, saying how lucky they were, that people from all over the country came to visit the Cavern, yet they had it on their very own doorstep.

'I'm going to bed,' she said sullenly.

Rose looked at her daughter with concern. 'But, love, it's only half past seven.'

'I don't care.'

'What about your homework?' Tom enquired.

'I've done it.'

Jeannie ran upstairs, leaving Tom with the satisfaction of knowing at least one of his children was prepared to do as she was told. 'Would you like the wireless on, love?' he asked his wife. She looked exceptionally pretty tonight, his Rose. Having caught the sun throughout the long, hot summer, her slim arms and bare legs were tanned and, although she wore only a simple white blouse and a cotton skirt, she couldn't possibly have looked more lovely. The sun had added streaks of gold to her brown curly hair, which needed cutting – he'd prefer it didn't hide her slender neck. Tomorrow, he'd tell her to get it trimmed.

'No, thank you, Tom.' Rose clasped her hands together on her lap. 'You know what you said the other week, about girls' education not mattering?'

'Yes, love.'

'Then it won't matter, will it, if Jeannie can't

concentrate at school? It'd only be for one morning, and as she's only a girl, what difference would it make?'

Tom stared into his wife's innocent blue eyes, unable to fault her simple logic.

'Poor Jeannie,' Rose continued with a sigh. 'She's such a good girl, never makes a fuss, not like Max. That's the first time I've known her to go to bed in a huff.' Her hands were clasped so tight that the knuckles showed white as she struggled to contain her anger. 'On second thoughts, you can turn the wireless on. There's a concert on the Third Programme.'

'As you wish, love.'

Rose sat back in the chair and closed her eyes as the strains of Rimsky-Korsakov's *Scheherazade* crept gently into the parlour, filled with the big, gloomy furniture that she hated, but which Tom refused to get rid of because it had belonged to his mother.

He was a bully! The way he'd spoken to Jeannie had made her stomach turn. For a moment, she'd wanted to leap up and scratch his eyes out. It wasn't that Jeannie was weak, she just didn't like to cause trouble. She was a kind, thoughtful girl and Tom took advantage. With Max, he'd given in, the way bullies did once they realised bullying would no longer work. Max had just forged ahead, got on with his life, hang the consequences. There was nothing his father could do to stop him.

Rose's resentment had taken a long time building up. She was used to doing as she was told. For a long time after they were married, it had seemed quite natural to do exactly what Tom wanted, *be* what he wanted; a willing, docile wife, who agreed with everything he said, never argued because she couldn't bear to hear his raised voice in reply, or see his face crumple into a scowl. In the orphanage, children who'd wanted a quiet life kept their heads down, never caused trouble. Rose had continued this way, blissfully content in her nice house at the end of Disraeli Terrace with her adoring husband and three beautiful children.

She couldn't quite put her finger on when things had started to change – when *she* had started to change. It might have been when Max began to badger his father for a television and she'd begun to wonder why only Tom's opinion mattered. She would have loved a television, but didn't dare say, just as she didn't say how much she'd like a fridge and a washing machine when she knew Tom was dead against them. Not for any real reason, it was just the way he felt. Nor did it seem proper when he came down so hard on his children – he seemed to forget that they were hers too – because they wanted to spread their wings. There was no real reason for that, either, only that he enjoyed having power over people who were younger, smaller, and weaker than himself.

'Where are you off to?' Tom asked when she stood up.

'I thought I'd take our Jeannie up a cup of cocoa.'

'You're not to bother. It was her decision to go to bed without any supper.'

Rose nearly sat down again, like a trained dog, she thought. 'I'll make us some tea then,' she said.

'Don't forget, no cocoa,' Tom called as she left the room.

She made the cocoa and took it upstairs, her heart throbbing painfully in her breast. She'd disobeyed him! It was her first act of defiance. She'd been meaning to do it for ages, opening her mouth to say something that refused to be said because she felt frightened. Everything would change; the atmosphere in the house, their relationship with each other. Everything. He would look upon her differently. She would no longer be his dear little Rose.

'Are you awake, love?'

Jeannie's head was hidden under the clothes. The curtains were drawn, although it was still light outside. 'Yes,' she whispered.

'I've brought you some cocoa. You'd better sit up.'

'Thanks, Mum.'

In the dim light, Rose saw that Jeannie's eyes were swollen with crying. Everything's a battle, she thought. Every move forward they want to make ends up a battle. She sat on the edge of the bed and gave her daughter a little pat. 'Tomorrow, love, tell Elaine you can go to the Cavern.'

Jeannie gasped incredulously. 'Did you talk Dad into letting me go?'

'Not yet, but I will. In the meantime, it'd be best if you didn't bring the subject up while he's around.'

'Are you sure, Mum?'

'Absolutely sure, Jeannie. Now, drink your cocoa, and you'd better have a little read before you go asleep, otherwise you'll wake up in the early hours and find you can't drop off again.'

'You sound funny, Mum.'

'I can't think why, Jeannie. I'm exactly the same as I've always been.'

She checked Gerald was asleep. His new clothes were laid on a chair, ready for school tomorrow. Max was out, the van having called for him at midday. It would be hours before he came back.

Downstairs again, Rose made the tea and tried to prepare herself for the accusation that would meet her when she took it into the parlour.

Did you make cocoa for our Jeannie when I specifically told you not to?

Such a petty, stupid thing to say. What sort of man would make an issue out of something so trivial?

She tiptoed in – as if less noise would make Tom less angry. But Tom was fast asleep, snoring slightly, and hadn't heard her go upstairs. Rose put his tea on the hearth and returned to the chair with her own. She watched her husband as he slept. With his chin tucked in his neck, his mouth slightly open, he looked very old, older than sixty.

That was another thing. Rose placed her own tea on the hearth and put her hands to her cheeks. She was thirty-six and Tom was the only man she'd known intimately. Lately, she'd wondered what it would be like to be made love to by a younger man, a man who didn't fall asleep in the chair every night and wanted to go to bed earlier and earlier so he could fall asleep again, always insisting she went with him, when she would prefer to stay and listen to a concert or a Book at Bedtime, a man who would take her dancing or to the pictures, buy her jewellery and scent, not things for the house, as Tom did, expecting her to be pleased, which she had been, once.

In the afternoons, after she'd done the house-work and was waiting for the children to come home, Rose would sit in her meticulously clean kitchen and, in her mind, she would lie with this mysterious, faceless man, let him touch her, kiss her, do the things that until now only Tom had done.

Then Gerald would come in, and she would come to her senses, ashamed, though it didn't stop her from doing the same thing the next day, and the next.

Tom gave an extra-loud snore that turned into a grunt and woke him. For a second, he looked at her vacantly, then noticed the tea. 'You should've given us a nudge, love,' he said, stretching his arms. 'You know, I wouldn't mind us getting to bed early tonight.'

'It's only just gone eight o'clock, Tom.'

'It wouldn't hurt to have a few extra hours.'

'I'm listening to this concert. It doesn't finish for another hour.'

He looked slightly surprised. Reaching over, he turned the wireless off. 'It's finished now, my love,' he said, eyes twinkling, as if it were a joke.

Rose wanted to kill him. He wasn't being nasty,

just assumed she would automatically do as he wished. She considered turning the wireless on again, but hadn't the stomach for the inevitable row, their first. He would be hurt, deeply hurt and, in a way, she supposed she still cared for him. After all, he adored her, but the woman he adored no longer existed. She'd become someone he might not even like. She'd leave hurting him until it became unavoidable, until a week on Wednesday when Jeannie went to the Cavern.

The girls wore slacks for the first time. Jeannie and Benny's were black, Elaine's dark green. On top, they had on loose fitting blouses with short sleeves. Benny had tied a chiffon scarf around her head and it hung over her shoulder like a tail. Elaine's dark hair had been released from its sensible plait and flowed down her back like a cloak. They felt very grown up and sophisticated.

Going down the Cavern steps for the first time was probably more momentous than entering Tutankhamun's tomb, Elaine remarked in an awed voice. They paid the entry fee, signed in, and were met by a bombardment of noise and a curious smell, a mixture of cigarettes, soot, damp, and perspiration. The bare, brick walls glistened with moisture.

They entered what appeared to be a dimly lit railway tunnel, long and narrow with a curved ceiling. Smoke drifted in layers underneath, like a gently moving canopy. They explored, and discovered two more tunnels connected by a series of arches. The first was furnished with rows of seats, mostly occupied, for those who'd come for the music. Another had been set aside for dancing, and the third was packed with people who just appeared to be talking very loudly in an effort to be heard above the tremendous, pounding music.

'Let's dance,' Jeannie suggested, unable to keep still another minute – her body seemed to be twitching in rhythm with the beat. The boys, who seemed to know everyone, had disappeared.

They danced self-consciously at first, hopping from one foot to the other, though quickly got used to the liberated feeling of being able to twist their bodies and wave their arms about without people thinking they were mad. They did this till exhausted, then went to look for a cold drink.

Lachlan was by the bar talking to a couple of girls. Jeannie was too exhilarated to care. This was turning into the best night of her life. It wasn't just the Cavern, but the people there. They seemed far more alive and animated than other young people she'd known. Elaine and Benny looked unusually vivacious and she supposed she must do herself. Even the drink, Coca Cola, was different to anything she'd had before; it tasted peppery and tickled her nose.

Elaine came up with the bright idea of buying a lipstick between them before they came again. 'We're the only girls here who aren't wearing make-up. We'd all suit pink. We'll come again, won't we?' she said anxiously.

'Deffo,' Benny concurred. 'This place is the gear. But I couldn't afford to come more than once a week. I can't ask Mam for more pocket money. What about you, Jeannie?'

'I dunno.' Jeannie chewed her lip. 'I'm not even sure if I'll be allowed to come again. My mum acted very strangely this morning. She insisted I take these clothes with me to school and get changed at Elaine's. She said it'd be best if I didn't come home for tea. I've got a feeling Dad doesn't know I was coming. He doesn't even know I've got slacks. Mum bought them the other day and said I wasn't to mention it.'

Elaine said she hoped there wouldn't be hell to play when Jeannie got home.

'I hope so too.' Jeannie would prefer not to think about it. It would only spoil things. 'Let's sit and listen to the music for a while.'

They sat behind Max who had his eyes glued to the small stage where Vince McLoughlin and his Vulcans, three guitarists and a drummer about the same age as himself, were performing 'Shakin' All Over' with wild, intimidating exuberance. The small space was entirely filled with the raw sound and the hoarse voices of the four, scruffily dressed young men. Jeannie caught her breath and grabbed the sides of her chair with both hands. The urgent, thumping beat was doing something to her head and her heart. Her lungs were threatening to burst, her feet unable to keep still. She noticed a small, unused piano on the stage, and wished she could play it. At least it would give her fingers something to do.

The music stopped suddenly and she relaxed and let out a long, slow breath. Leaning forward, she tapped Max on the shoulder. He looked surprised to see her when he turned round. 'The guitars sound different to yours,' she said.

141

'They're electric, that's why.'

The rest of the unreal, never to be forgotten night passed far too quickly. Benny was the first to leave. 'Mam won't go to bed till I'm home and she has to be up at five for work in the morning. Next time, perhaps we can come at the weekend and stay as late as we like.'

Elaine agreed. 'I'll be half dead in the morning and we've got double science.'

Jeannie laughed and said she was quite likely to fall asleep during double science, but didn't care.

Her mother must have been listening for the van. She was standing in the doorway when, at almost midnight, Ronnie Connors drew up in front of Disraeli Terrace. His three remaining passengers got out. Sean McDowd, who had hardly exchanged a word with any of them all night, didn't speak, just shrugged his shoulders as he trudged away, which she supposed was his way of saying goodnight.

'Surly bugger,' Max muttered, but proved just as surly when they went indoors, refusing the offer of a hot drink and going straight to bed.

'He's in a mood,' Jeannie announced as she followed her mother into the kitchen.

'Our Max seems to have been in a mood for the last five years. What's the reason this time?'

'They were talking about it in the van on the way home. Lachlan has decided they have to have electric guitars – all rock 'n' roll groups have them – and they're buying Vox amplifiers too. The others are going to club together to buy Max a guitar because he can't afford it. It makes him feel like a sponger. Poor Max,' Jeannie said with feeling.

'I'm not surprised he's in a mood. I'd be too in the same position.' Her mother looked annoyed. 'I'm sure we can manage to buy Max a guitar on hire purchase. I'll have a word with him tomorrow. What about you? Did you enjoy yourself, love?'

'Oh, *Mum*, it was...' Jeannie searched for words to describe the last few hours. '...*wonderful!*' she gasped. 'My head's still buzzing. Where's Dad?' She glanced around the kitchen, as if expecting the stern figure of her father to appear out of the pantry or from under the table.

'In bed,' her mother said lightly. 'He went ages ago.'

Jeannie was slowly coming down to earth. She vaguely remembered she'd been expecting a scene, the sort there'd been when Max had started to come home late, an angry, shouting scene. Why was Mum still up, but not Dad? And why did Mum look so calmly cheerful? Perhaps Dad hadn't minded, after all, when he discovered she'd had gone to the Cavern?

'Is everything OK, Mum?'

'Everything's fine, Jeannie. Now, tell me about tonight, first things first. What's it like, this Cavern? I wouldn't mind going there myself one of these days...'

Tom had been having his tea when he'd noticed Jeannie wasn't present. He was thinking there'd been a time when his children used to run and greet him when he came in from work. Nowadays, he merely got a casual 'Hello, Dad,' when they condescended to appear.

'She's gone to Elaine's,' Rose told him. She'd been hoping he'd have finished the meal by the time they had this conversation.

'I suppose she'll want a lift from the station later,' he grumbled.

'There's a lift already arranged. Ronnie Connors is bringing her home in the van.'

It took a while for the meaning of this to sink in. Rose watched his brow crease and his eyes glaze over as he tried to make sense of the words. Eventually, she took pity on him. 'She's gone to the Cavern, Tom. I told her she could. Her friends were going and it didn't seem fair for her to be left out. She won't come to any harm, believe me.'

'*You* told her!'

'Yes, Tom, I did.' She felt nervous, but not frightened as she'd expected. Her prime feeling was one of impatience. The whole thing was excessively silly. She wanted the argument over and done with in as few words as possible.

'Without discussing it with me first?'

'I don't recall you discussing it with me before you refused to let her go. Would you like more custard on your pudding?'

He pushed the dish away and she just caught it before it shot off the end of the table. 'How dare you, Rose! How dare you go against my wishes!'

'I'm your wife, Tom. I can go against your wishes whenever I please.' But she should have done it earlier, and done it gradually, she realised when she saw his stricken face. It was unfair to

144

spring this on him right out of the blue. She said, gently, 'Marriage should be a partnership, not a dictatorship.'

He blinked. 'Where did you get that from?'

'Out of my own head, Tom. It's only common sense.'

'How long have you been thinking things like that?'

'I've no idea,' Rose conceded truthfully.

'And you've never said anything before?'

'I think you'd have noticed if I had.' She laughed. It was a mistake. Tom's face darkened.

'Don't use that tone of voice with me, my girl,' he snapped.

'Oh, Tom. I'm not your girl, I'm your wife,' she reminded him again. 'You seem to have finished your tea. I'm going to listen to the wireless.' She wanted to get away from his ridiculously angry face. She'd wash the dishes later. 'By the way,' she added, stopping by the door, 'I went to Ormskirk this afternoon and arranged to buy a television on hire purchase. It's being delivered the day after tomorrow.'

'You'll not get an extra penny off me to pay for it.' He looked triumphant. 'When it arrives, you'd better tell them to take it back.'

'We'll see, Tom.' She'd tell him another time that she'd got a part-time job. He'd had enough shocks for one night. The Post Office needed someone behind the counter five mornings a week. Rose was starting on Monday. She'd always been good with figures, not that Tom had noticed.

Later, she heard him go into the garden, and shortly afterwards, Gerald came home. He'd

145

joined the Scouts, something that clearly met with his father's approval, as he hadn't objected.

'What did you do tonight, love?' she asked.

'Knots. Shall I show you how to do a reef knot?'

'I'd like that, Gerald. You never know when a reef knot might come in handy.'

Gerald went to bed, shortly followed by Tom when it was barely dark. He didn't bid her goodnight.

Rose stayed in the parlour, the wireless turned on low, only half listening to the soft music, the murmuring voices like friends in the night. She watched the moon rise in the dark sky, before getting up to close the curtains and turn on the light, and deciding she felt like a drink.

The dishes were still unwashed when she went into the kitchen, and she was about to run water in the kettle when she thought about another sort of drink. There was still sherry in the larder from last Christmas. She poured a glass, feeling daring, and took it back to the parlour.

'This is the life,' she whispered. Come Friday, she'd have a television to watch when she stayed up late – she resolved never to go to bed early again. After she'd paid for the TV, she'd get a washing machine or a fridge. She tried to decide which was the most important, but one seemed just as necessary as the other. When the time came, she'd toss a coin.

And so Rose passed the time while she listened for the sound of the van bringing her children home. For the first time in her life, she felt like a proper human being. She felt like herself.

The Merseysiders auditioned for a man named Billy Kidd, who owned a club, the Taj Mahal in Toxteth. He came to the Connors' factory in Kirkby to hear them play amidst the baths, lavatories, and cisterns in the store room.

'Now, remember lads, no swearing,' Lachlan said while they waited for Billy to arrive, glancing sternly at Fly Fleming, the main culprit in this department. Lachlan was the undoubted leader of the group, expecting the same dedication from the others as he gave himself. Max, Sean and Fly were just as anxious to set the world alight with their music and didn't protest when they rehearsed well into the early hours and all day Sunday, leaving only Saturday night free. Ronnie Connors didn't say anything, but they suspected his heart wasn't in it. He did his best, but he was only there because of his father and gave the impression he'd sooner be somewhere else.

'Me, swear?' Fly's look of injured innocence would have shattered a dozen hearts. 'Have youse lot ever heard me swear?'

'Never,' the others chorused.

'You're getting me mixed up with some other bugger, Lachlan, me old mate. I don't hold with bad language, me.'

'I could do with a drink,' Ronnie complained. 'Me nerves are in tatters.'

'You know we never drink before we play,' Lachlan told him.

'This group has a strictly no drinking, no swearing policy,' Fly said in a deep, sepulchral voice. 'What about girls, Lachlan? Can we at least look at them?'

'You can look, but don't touch.' Lachlan grinned.

'We'd have had more fun joining a seminary,' Max complained.

'Perhaps we should change our name to something religious,' suggested Fly. 'The Boppin' Bishops, or the Holy Ghosts.'

Even Sean, who rarely joined in the banter, choked over this remark.

'The Jumpin' Jesuits,' Fly continued, 'Hey! What about the Dixie Deans?'

'You're getting boring, Fly,' Lachlan snapped. They heard a car draw up outside. 'Billy Kidd's arrived. Come on, lads, shoulders back. This is it.' He went to open the door.

'Shoulders back!' Fly hooted. 'He'll have us doing PT next. We'd have had even more fun if we'd joined the fuckin' Army.'

Billy Kidd didn't want his club left behind when the new phenomenon, rock 'n' roll, took hold, which he was convinced it would one day soon. These five young lads were the best he'd heard so far. The keyboard player wasn't so hot, but the two tall guitarists played and sang as if inspired, easily making up for the weak link. He booked them to appear every Wednesday at the Taj Mahal for the next six weeks. The fee he offered was derisive, but the group were too busy congratulating each other – it involved a great deal of punching, slapping, and shoving – to notice. Either that, or they didn't care. Billy reckoned he could have got them for nothing and wished he hadn't mentioned money at all.

Without telling a soul except his sister, Max left school and got a job as a clerk in Lachlan's factory. His studies were getting in the way of music, he explained. The teachers kept expecting essays and stuff, and he couldn't spare the time.

For two weeks, he and Jeannie had left the house together, but instead of getting off at Orrell Park, Max went on to Sandhills Station, where he changed his blazer for a sports jacket and went to work instead of school.

'You'll have to tell Dad soon,' Jeannie warned. 'The longer you leave it, the worse it'll be.'

'No, it won't,' Max replied laconically. 'If Dad finds out tomorrow, it won't be any worse than if he'd found out last week. Anyway, there's nothing he can do except rant and rave, and since Mum got a job and bought a television, he's lost some of his steam. I suspect there's been a major power shift.' He laughed, as if he thought it extremely funny.

Jeannie didn't laugh. She had also noticed the way her mother had suddenly started to take decisions, while her father seemed to shrink into the background. She felt sorry for him, and also guilty that the situation could possibly be her fault for going to the Cavern when it had been expressly forbidden. What's more, she'd been every week since, which only made her feel more guilty, but not guilty enough to stop.

The truth about Max emerged when Tom Flowers received a letter from the headmaster of Orrell Park Grammar wanting to know if Max was ill.

'Perhaps you could do me the courtesy,' the Headmaster wrote stiffly, 'of letting me know the reason for your son's long absence from school.'

'What the hell's going on?' Tom roared at his wife, but Rose was equally mystified and just as annoyed. It was left to Jeannie to tell them what Max had done. Rose ran to fetch a glass of water when Tom's face turned so red he looked about to explode.

His anger was further inflamed when Max didn't come home that night. 'What is this, a lodging house?' he demanded of his wife the next morning.

Rose's answer only made him angrier still. 'We need a telephone, Tom. Max would have been able to tell us why he couldn't come home if we had a phone. The van might have had a puncture and you could have picked him up. He probably spent the night at the Baileys'. Do calm down, dear. It's not the end of the world.'

'What? That he didn't come home or that he left school without permission?' Tom stomped out of the house. A few minutes later, Rose saw him wobbling along the road on his bike. If he wasn't careful, he'd have a heart attack, she thought worriedly.

She would have much preferred it if Max had stayed at school and got his A levels, then put his mind to other things. But young people were only concerned with the here and now. The future was the last of their worries.

There was, of course, the inevitable row when Tom and Max came face to face, but Tom's heart wasn't in it. No one took notice of him any more.

In vain did Rose lecture him on the need to change to accommodate their growing children. 'We can't treat them like babies for ever, Tom. Max is almost an adult, old enough to fight for his country or get married. He can't be forced to stay at school if he doesn't want to.'

Tom couldn't see why not. He was Max's father and, until he was dead or had lost his reason, what he said should be law, as it had been with his own father. What's more, he didn't take kindly to being lectured by a woman who, in his eyes, wasn't much less than a child herself. These days, Rose was coming out with all sorts of claptrap. He suspected she got it off that damn television, which he refused to watch. He wasn't even prepared to sit in the same room when it was on and, as no one seemed prepared to accommodate *him* and turn it off, Tom was left to feel that there was no place for him in his own home with his own family.

Chapter 6

'Is that coat warm enough, luv?'

'It's fine, Mam.' The brown jacket was much too thin for December. Once outside, the cold wind would whip right through it, but if Benny so much as hinted at this, a warm coat would be acquired from a cheque shop in a matter of days and extra hours of cleaning would have to be done to pay for it.

'Why don't you wear your school coat. It's got a nice, thick lining,' Mrs Lucas suggested.

'People don't go to clubs in gaberdine macks, Mam. I'd look daft. Does me hair look all right?'

'It looks lovely, Benedicta.' Her daughter's pale hair was tied in bunches with red ribbon, which she thought a little odd on an almost fifteen-year-old, but Benedicta assured her that it wouldn't appear out of place in the Cavern. 'You look lovely altogether,' she said admiringly. 'You could do with another jumper.'

'This one's perfectly all right. White goes well with me black slacks.'

'I meant for a change. Every time you go to the Cavern you wear the same thing.'

'I'm sure no one's noticed,' Benny said stoutly. 'Anyroad, I'm not going to the Cavern tonight, am I, Mam? We're going somewhere called the Taj Mahal. The Merseysiders are playing their first proper gig.'

Gig! It all sounded very strange and foreign. Mrs Lucas boasted endlessly to her fellow cleaners about the exciting life her Benedicta led, off every week to the Cavern with the daughter of a doctor and a very polite girl from around Ormskirk way who played the piano.

'I'll just take a last look at meself in the upstairs mirror.'

The low-wattage bulb in her mother's bedroom, together with the heavily spotted wardrobe mirror, combined to produce a somewhat ghostly apparition, but Benny was more or less satisfied with her appearance. Despite what her mother said, she knew she wasn't even faintly lovely, but managed to make herself noticed by twisting her hair into unusual styles and drawing around her eyes with black crayon – her mother didn't know about the crayon, which she did on the train. Loads of girls did it, but it suited Benny Lucas, with her long narrow face and perfectly round eyes, more than most. It made her look outlandish, though perhaps 'exotic' would be a better word. She attracted the boys just as much as Jeannie, who genuinely *was* lovely, and Elaine, with her long dark hair and Venus de Milo figure. Neither wore make-up, apart from a little smear of the lipstick they shared.

They were such goody-goodies, Benny thought contemptuously. She'd be glad when she went to work, made friends of her own, and didn't need Jeannie or Elaine any more. They were useful at school, particularly Elaine, who helped explain the subjects that Benny found difficult, so that her position in class improved with each term.

153

She gave her blurred reflection an approving nod and ran downstairs. 'Will you be all right?' she asked her mother.

'Of course, luv. Have you got enough money?'

'Yes, Mam.' They went through the same ritual every time Benny went out. 'Shall I throw another lump of coal on the fire before I go.'

'No, ta, luv. I'll do it in a minute.'

'Don't wait up.'

'I always wait up, don't I? I'd never sleep until I knew you were home.'

Benny paused at the door. 'I love you, Mam.'

'I know you do, girl. Off you go now, and have a good time. Be careful crossing the road, won't you?'

The door slammed. Mrs Lucas listened to her daughter's footsteps hurry along the street. She waited until the sound had stopped altogether, before fetching down a blanket from upstairs, which she wrapped around her tiny figure, including her feet. It saved the coal. She'd keep the fire going for as long as she could with bits of wood until Benedicta came home. Then, she'd add more coal, and they'd both sit warming themselves over a cup of tea, while Benedicta described the events of the evening in detail.

There probably wasn't a happier mother in the whole of Bootle, thought Mrs Lucas as she snuggled into the chair inside her blanket. She closed her eyes and imagined Benedicta just approaching Marsh Lane Station. The mother waited with her daughter, sat beside her on the train, walked with her to the club, which she thought would look something like Buckingham Palace.

Everyone gasped when Benedicta went in because she was so beautiful. At this point, the mother's imagination faltered. Instead, she contented herself with the knowledge that Benedicta was having a lovely time. It was with this thought in her mind that Mrs Lucas fell asleep.

They all decided that the Taj Mahal wasn't a patch on the Cavern. Firstly, it wasn't in a basement, a black mark against it straight away, but over a furniture shop in Upper Parliament Street. The interior walls had been knocked down to make a large room that had been painted purple. The purple didn't go with the ceiling that was dark blue and scattered with silver stars. Mirrors had been fitted over the windows, so it appeared as if half a dozen similarly coloured rooms led from the main one.

Jeannie thought the effect very ominous, but Elaine preferred tawdry.

'At least it's warm.' Benny was still shivering in her thin coat. 'I think I'll keep it on till I thaw out,' she said when the others went up to the cloakroom on the second floor. 'I'll save you both a speck till you come back.' The rows of chairs were gradually being filled with people much older than the crowd that frequented the Cavern.

Jeannie and Elaine came back to say the Merseysiders were in the bar – the group had arrived earlier to set up their equipment, which was already on a small stage at the end of the long room, their name on the big drum in black and gold.

'There's a licensed bar up there,' Jeannie said tersely, 'and no one noticed Ronnie Connors getting as drunk as a lord. He said he only did it to calm his nerves, but Lachlan's worried he'll make a mess of things.'

A few minutes later, the lights went out, leaving the only illumination over the stage. A small plump man in evening dress appeared and introduced himself as George Kidd, the club's owner, 'But folks calls me Billy – Billy the Kid, geddit!'

A few people groaned, 'Come on, Billy. We've heard all that before.' Tonight, Billy announced in an accent that was half Scouse, half American, was the debut performance of an exciting new group, five talented Liverpool lads, who were about to set the world on fire. 'Put your hands together for the Merseysiders,' he cried.

There was only a smattering of applause from the crowd. The girls and a few others in the audience made up for the lack of enthusiasm by clapping as hard as they could. A good-looking man in the row in front, dressed like a gangster in a pale suit, black shirt, and white tie, whooped loudly when Lachlan led the group into the room, Ronnie Connors following unsteadily at the rear.

The last time Jeannie had heard the boys play together was in their garden shed, long before they'd acquired a drummer and a keyboard player. She remembered thinking it a bit of a joke, that they'd merely been fooling about, although the boys had taken themselves very seriously.

And it had paid off, she thought proudly, when the Merseysiders let rip with 'Jailhouse Rock', followed by 'Wake up Little Susie' and 'Great Balls of Fire', the sound booming from the amplifiers, rolling round the walls, making the room vibrate.

That was her brother, Max, strumming his new electric guitar, and singing away, a microphone to himself on the side of the stage. This was the end result of the battles he'd had with their father, his fixation with the Cavern, his abandonment of school at the most crucial point in his education. Jeannie felt tears come to her eyes and wished her dad was there to see his happy, shiny-eyed son fulfil his most cherished ambition. Max was a real musician at last, showing a face to the world that was rarely seen at home.

Lachlan and Sean shared a microphone centre stage, their heads almost touching. Lachlan stood with his feet wide apart, his entire body twisting and turning as he flung his hands over the strings of his red guitar, unlike the tightly controlled Sean McDowd, who hardly moved, apart from the slight sway of his slim hips.

After a while, she realised that Lachlan was playing for the audience, but Sean was playing for himself. Lachlan wanted to entertain; Sean didn't care if he entertained or not. But he *must* care, Jeannie reasoned, otherwise he wouldn't be here, playing to a crowded room.

Fly Fleming was having a great time on the drums. He was a bulky, tough-looking young man, with laughing eyes, a mountain of red hair, and an infectious sense of humour. Everyone liked Fly. Even the inscrutable Sean had been known to double up with laughter at one of Fly's dry, off the cuff remarks. Now Fly beamed happily at everyone from the back of the stage.

After a while, Jeannie became aware that Fly and the others were covering for Ronnie Connors whose fingers seemed to have lost their way on the keyboard. What should have been Ronnie's solo pieces were buried beneath some inspired but unexpected drum-playing or the thunderous twang of three guitars. She hoped she was the only one to notice, because otherwise the group's performance was electrifying. Not that Jeannie enjoyed it. She was too concerned that something might go wrong – Ronnie might fall off his stool, for instance, or off the stage altogether.

By the time the group's allotted hour was nearing its end, Jeannie had become aware of something else, something far more worrying than Ronnie's fumbling antics on the keyboard. Compared with Lachlan and Sean, Max wasn't a great performer. He played in a plodding, mechanical way, and his voice was slightly harsh, whereas Lachlan's was a lilting baritone and Sean's husky whisper, with its slight Irish accent, was very appealing, even sexy, though she'd never considered Sean McDowd remotely sexy. Sean and Lachlan carried the group, they were the stars, over-shadowing the others.

Perhaps, because she was Max's sister, she was being over-critical. To everyone else, he might seem perfectly all right – and he could always improve with time. Jeannie prayed this would be the case. Playing the guitar meant everything in the world to Max. It was his life.

The applause at the end of the final number was light to say the least, with only a few showing their appreciation of an hour of spectacular rock 'n' roll. The man who'd whooped earlier jumped to his feet, gave a standing ovation, then hurried out of the room after the group – except for Fly, who stayed behind to dismantle the drums.

'I've never heard such a tuneless racket,' a voice behind said disdainfully. 'It'll never catch on, that rock 'n' roll.'

'Give me jazz, any day,' said someone else. 'Preferably traditional or New Orleans.'

'I prefer modern meself, but any sort's better than that rubbish.'

'They could do without that keyboard player. He was pissed out of his mind.'

'Never mind, mate. There's jazz after the interval. I'd have come just for that, but I'd never have got a seat.'

Jeannie had nothing against jazz, but she wasn't in the mood for it right now. 'I don't know about you,' she said to Elaine, 'but I'd sooner not stay for the second half.'

'Me, neither. Let's find the boys. C'mon, Benny.'

Benny got up, her face impassive, and followed them. She also preferred not to stay, but it would have been nice to be asked.

The Merseysiders looked pale and exhausted. They were in the bar where they were being delivered a stern lecture by Billy Kidd. 'They're a backward lot out there,' Billy waved a dismissive arm. 'They still wipe their arses on the *Liverpool Echo*. I hope they didn't put you off, kids, 'cos you're booked for five more weeks. Rock 'n' roll is gonna be the biggest phenomenon ever to hit the music industry in this country, and I wanna be part of it. It's already taken off in America and before long it'll take off here. I've got some press adverts lined up for next week, and word'll soon get around that the Merseysiders are a great group. There's just one thing.' Billy's plump, smiling face grew hard. 'You'd probably do even better without having to cover for a screwed-up keyboard player. Three guitars and a drummer, that's a great combination. I'd drop the keyboard if I were you.'

'He's not screwed up, he's drunk, the idiot.' The man in the pale suit had been eavesdropping on the lecture. To the girls' surprise, he leapt forward, seized Ronnie's ear, and twisted it. Ronnie yelped.

'Lay off, Dad. Me nerves were in tatters. I needed a drink.'

Jeannie and Elaine looked at each other, impressed; fancy having such an attractive dad!

'You nearly spoiled everything.' Mr Connors twisted his son's ear even harder. 'I feel like kicking you from here to Timbuctoo for letting the other lads down.'

'I won't do it again, Dad. Promise.' Ronnie didn't look nearly as ashamed as he should.

'I should hope not,' Mr Connors snorted. 'When you lads are ready, I'll take you and your stuff home in the van and come back later for my car. This idiot can't be trusted behind the wheel, not in his condition. He's been given every encouragement,' he said complainingly to Billy. 'When I was a lad, I'd have given anything for a career in music, but my dad wouldn't hear of it. According to him, the best job in the world was plumbing. "A plumber's never out of work," he used to say. So that's what I became, a plumber. Did well, too, like my dad said. But I wanted better than that for my own son, yet this is how he repays me.'

Four middle-aged men in identical loud check suits had come into the bar. 'See them,' Billy Kidd hissed. 'That's the Clive Merry Jazz Quartet, a dying breed. They're on next, but by this time next year, they'll have a job finding anyone to listen to them. Well, lads, I'll see you all next week.' He fixed a false smile on his face and went over to effusively greet the men he'd just pronounced a dying breed.

'I think he's what you'd call "two-faced",' Mr Connors said with a wry grin.

As Billy Kidd had predicted, the group's reputation grew by dint of advertising and word of mouth. The weeks passed and the audiences became younger and less inhibited, cheering wildly after every number. The Merseysiders were booked for six more weeks and were offered twenty-five pounds, a monumental figure, so they thought. From now on, Billy decreed Friday would be rock 'n' roll night at the Taj Mahal. He suggested the group acquire a manager.

'You kids have got a great career ahead of you and you'll need your interests looking after. A manager can arrange gigs, make sure you're paid and receive any expenses you're entitled to.'

'Where do we find a manager?' Lachlan asked.

'You're already looking at him, lad. Me! If you're agreeable, I'll draw up a contract and all you have to do is sign on the bottom line.'

'I'd like to read the contract first,' said Sean.

'Naturally. I wouldn't dream of asking you to sign something you haven't read.'

'And I'm not signing anything for longer than five years.'

'Five years it is. But, Sean,' Billy said earnestly, 'if I'm going to be your manager, you've got to learn to trust me.'

'So, did they sign?' Jeannie asked Elaine when she was relayed this item of news. Max hadn't mentioned anything about a contract.

'Yes. Dad said they were mad, they might be signing away their future, but Lachlan said all he wanted to do in the future was play the guitar and having a manager would only make that easier. All the group feel the same way, Sean too, but he's a bit more canny than the others.'

June again. Midsummer. Another fête on Ailsham village green, another hot day. Rose Flowers was helping in the refreshment tent where it felt as if the temperature had reached boiling point.

For the very first time, Jeannie wasn't coming; she'd gone into town with Elaine and Benny. All they did was wander round the shops looking at clothes they hadn't the money to buy. Rose sighed. It seemed a pointless exercise, but

Jeannie obviously considered it more exciting than attending the fête.

It might have been a matter of principle or just sheer cussedness, but Max hadn't been since that time four years ago when Tom had made him stay at home. Gerald was around somewhere, a member of the scout troop that would vie with the guides to see who could first light a fire and boil a pan of water. Rose sighed again as she poured tea into a row of plastic cups. In another four years, Gerald would be sixteen and likely to turn up his nose at the fête – Gerald, her baby, would be *working!* She did a quick calculation. By then, she would be forty, Tom sixty-four and on the verge of retirement.

'Oh, my *God!*' she gasped out loud and was glad when no one noticed.

What was she to do with the rest of her life, living with a sullen Tom, her children grown up and no longer at home? Stay in the Post Office, getting older and older, buying more things for the house having paid for the television, she was now getting a washing machine on hire purchase. But she wanted to *do* things, not just buy them. Max and Jeannie had done more in their short lives than she had in her much longer one, mainly because she had missed out on this vital, growing-up period, moving from childhood to adulthood, from the orphanage to employment with Mrs Corbett, within a single day.

Waving away a cloud of steam spurting from a kettle on the stove beside her, she thought that this was no place to be on such a hot day.

It was even beginning to get on her nerves, all

this moaning, even if it was in the privacy of her own head. It was time she pulled herself together. Even so, if she pulled herself together until she tied herself in knots, it didn't disguise the fact that the future looked very bleak.

The summer term was coming to an end. Rita McDowd was fifteen and ready to leave Philip Wallace. She already had a job lined up, as a waitress in Owen Owen's restaurant, right in the heart of Liverpool.

'I'll be giving up both me own jobs soon,' Sadie McDowd told Rose when she went into Harker's for cigarettes – if the Post Office counter had no customers, Rose helped in the other part of the shop. She'd always made a point of acknowledging Sadie during the years when the rest of the village had ignored her. Now they had their sons' musical careers in common.

'I don't know about you, Rose,' Sadie continued chattily, 'but I find Ailsham a bit dead. I thought I'd get a job in town meself. I can look around the big shops in me dinner hour, and me and our Rita can go together on the bus.'

'That'll be nice.' Rose had never thought she'd be envious of Sadie McDowd.

Ailsham was expanding. The Ribble Bus Company had altered the route of its Liverpool–Ormskirk service so that it passed through the village to accommodate the growing number of residents. Behind the school, a large housing estate was in the course of construction and already half occupied. On the outskirts of the village, not far from Holly Lane, an engineering factory was nearing completion on what would eventually become a trading estate. And in Holly Lane itself, two new bungalows had appeared and building plots were being advertised for sale. There was talk of a supermarket, another pub.

Tom Flowers regarded all this as an abomination, but Rose couldn't wait for the outside world to swallow up Ailsham whole.

Jeannie wasn't due to leave school for another year. The day they broke up, she got her end of year report. It was good, but not as good as Elaine's, who was top of the class, as usual. Jeannie was fifth. Last year, she'd been second, but didn't care she'd dropped three places. She'd had more interesting things on her mind than lessons, like the Cavern and the Taj Mahal. And rock 'n' roll.

Benny was pleased to discover she was fourteenth in the class of thirty. 'At least I'm in the top half,' she crowed.

'Are you going to show it to your mother this time?' enquired Elaine.

'Not likely! She doesn't know we get reports. If she did, she'd expect me to be top in every single thing.'

That night, Rose suggested Jeannie remain at school till eighteen and take A levels, possibly go to university. Jeannie declined with a shudder and said it was the last thing she wanted. She would take her O levels – it would be silly to waste the last four years and it would mean she'd get a better job – but then she'd like to start work so she could earn money, buy clothes, and go out

165

whenever she felt like it.

'There's just one thing, Mum. Can I stop having piano lessons? Miss Pritchard doesn't approve of music written in the twentieth century. She won't let me play anything modern.'

'In that case, I'll drop a note in Miss Pritchard's on my way to work tomorrow and tell her you won't be coming any more.'

'Shouldn't we ask Dad first?' Jeannie had been wanting to broach the subject for ages, but was worried she would upset people, never dreaming it would be so easy.

'There's no need to ask your father. You're fifteen. You can't be made to have piano lessons if you don't want them. It would be a shame though, love, if you gave it up altogether. You're very talented.'

'I'll never give up, Mum.' She still practised every day and had no intention of stopping. Whenever the Merseysiders played a new number, she learnt to play it herself picking out the melody with her right hand, adding the bass with her left, sedately at first, then, if the neighbours were out, and with a devil-may-care expression on her normally cautious face, she would press her foot on the loud pedal, and number ten Disraeli Terrace would jump to the stirring beat of rock 'n' roll. She thoroughly enjoyed letting herself go and only wished she could do it in public in front of an audience. She'd never told a soul, not even Elaine, how much she'd like to be part of a group, just like the boys. But female rock groups were unheard of and all Jeannie could do was dream.

The Merseysiders had got used to seeing badly printed posters pasted on the windows of empty shops and on abandoned buildings announcing their next performance at a town hall somewhere, or some other location, like a community or church hall, even a scout hut. Sometimes they had main billing. Other times their name was at the bottom of the poster when they supported a better known act, such as Acker Bilk's Paramount Jazz Band or Humphrey Lyttleton. They still played every Friday at the Taj Mahal.

Lachlan was anxious for them to play at the Cavern where four guys who called themselves the Beatles now appeared regularly, along with Gerry and the Pacemakers, Johnny Sandon and the Searchers, and other beat groups, gradually squeezing out jazz. The place was packed to the gills every night with fans.

The Taj Mahal didn't have the same loyal following, nor as good an atmosphere. It could accommodate an audience of a hundred and fifty at the most, whereas the Cavern could take a thousand – and it opened lunchtimes. There was nowhere to dance in the Taj Mahal, and the bar served alcohol, so a few people came for the drink, not the music, and often fights were only narrowly avoided.

Although Lachlan's sole reason for living was to play the guitar, he wanted to do it in the best place, in front of as big an audience as possible. It was his belief that the Merseysiders were just as good as the Beatles and the other groups that reigned supreme at the Cavern. He demanded, on more than one occasion, that Billy, their manager, book them a gig.

'I'm trying, kid, I'm trying,' Billy would cry, spreading his fat arms and shrugging. 'But no one's interested over there.'

Whenever they played a gig, Billy gave them a pound each. More often than not, they did two gigs a week, sometimes more. The extra money was a bonus, though their ultimate goal was to earn enough to give up their day jobs so they could concentrate on music to the exclusion of everything else.

Sean, the youngest member of the group, wasn't as naive as the others. According to their contract, Billy was entitled to just twenty per cent of the performance fee, yet he never doled out more than a quid each. It seemed unlikely that the organisers of the various gigs they played paid out exactly the same paltry sum. Sean didn't say anything. He couldn't see himself sticking with Billy Kidd for five years and, if he was breaking the contract, it meant he could walk out whenever he pleased.

'It's lovely, Sean. Can I try it on?' Sadie lifted the gold pendant on a slender chain out of its velvet box.

'It's your birthday present, Mam. You can do whatever you like with it.'

'Oh, would you just look at me now!' Sadie was admiring her reflection in the mirror. 'You're a good lad, Sean McDowd.' She stroked her son's lean cheek and Sean shuffled his feet uncomfortably. He didn't like shows of emotion, yet had enjoyed his mother's pleasure at the gift.

'Would you like something to eat, son?'

'I wouldn't mind egg and chips.' He couldn't imagine enjoying anything as much as he did egg and chips. 'Is there any tea on the go?'

'I'll make some before I start on the spuds.'

Sadie sang while she peeled the potatoes. She felt so happy, yet wouldn't have minded a little weep, so touched had she been by Sean's present. He was the best son a mother could have, and Rita was the best daughter. She was ashamed of the way she'd neglected them during the years when they'd been little, but she'd been sunk in misery and despair, pining for Kevin.

She didn't need Kevin any more, not now she had such a good job. Sadie virtually ran a small hotel in Hawke Street in the centre of Liverpool. It had just twelve bedrooms and catered mainly for travelling salesmen. The couple who owned it, Mr and Mrs Lunn, lived in the basement. They were getting on, no longer up to running the place on their own. They could manage weekends when there were only a few guests, or sometimes none at all. Sadie saw to the laundry, answered the phone, bought the groceries, even attended to the post, answering letters in her careful, schoolgirlish handwriting. She was gradually improving the place, buying new curtains, and flowers for the reception area. A woman called Bridget did the cleaning and came in early to make the breakfasts. In effect, Sadie actually had her own staff of one!

The man in the labour exchange who'd sent her

after the job had said, 'You look the sort of person who could handle responsibility.' Sadie's head had been swollen ever since. She'd bought a couple of new frocks with her first week's wages and had her hair set once a fortnight. She was beginning to resemble the pretty teenage girl who'd left County Clare in search of fame and fortune with Kevin McDowd – the louse, Sadie added as an afterthought.

'What's that you're singing, Mam?'

Sadie hadn't realised she'd been singing. She hummed a few more notes to see if she could recognise the tune. 'It's one of your dad's,' she shouted. 'It's one he wrote himself.'

To her surprise, Sean came to the kitchen door. 'What's it called?' It took a few seconds to remember. '"Moon Under Water".'

'Do you know all the words?'

'I'm not sure. I'll have a go.'

'Like the moon under water,' Sadie half-sang, half-spoke. 'I can't touch you.'

Like stars in a mirror, you're not there.
Like a rainbow in the sky,
A shadow flitting by,
A cobweb in the wind, a promise unfulfilled,
Like a dream that's gone by morning,
Or mist when day is dawning.
You're my love,
You're my life,
But you're not there.

'What do you think?' she enquired when she'd finished.

'I like it, Mam.'

'It wouldn't do for your lot, would it, son? It's not your sort of music.'

'It might be. Perhaps you could write the words down. Lachlan wants to include a ballad instead of us doing a whole hour of rock 'n' roll when we play at the Cavern.'

It'd be great if they could do a ballad of their own. Under pressure, Billy had at last booked them a date in December.

The date, a Saturday, happened to coincide with Jeannie's sixteenth birthday. Dr and Mrs Bailey offered to arrange a special birthday-cum-Christmas-cum-celebratory tea party for Jeannie, the Merseysiders, and their relatives, and Benny's mother, of course, if she cared to come.

'It'll only be a buffet meal,' said Elaine. 'There wouldn't be room for everyone to sit down.'

'That doesn't matter,' Jeannie said blissfully. She couldn't think of a better, more satisfactory way of spending her birthday than at the Cavern with a party beforehand.

'It's not my sort of thing,' Tom Flowers growled when Jeannie told him about it.

'But, Dad, it's only a party.' She didn't like the idea of him being left out.

'I told you, it's not my sort of thing,' he said stubbornly.

'Everyone else's Dad will be there.' As far as she knew, there'd only be Dr Bailey, but it didn't hurt to exaggerate.

'I'm sorry, Jeannie.'

Jeannie gave up. 'You don't mind if Mum

171

comes, do you?'

'These days, your mother does as she pleases. She's not likely to ask my permission.' He turned away and went into the garden shed where Mum said his own father had gone to smoke a pipe and where his son now went to sulk.

Rose Flowers conferred with Sadie McDowd next time she came into the Post Office. 'D'you mind if I go with you and your Rita to this tea party thing? To tell the truth, I've hardly been out of Ailsham in the dark. I'd feel odd on the bus on my own.'

'Of course I don't mind, Rose.' Sadie spoke with the confident air of someone who travelled on buses all the time when it was dark. 'I'll be glad of the company. Rita's going straight to the party from work, then she's off to the Cavern with your Jeannie and the others. Are you buying a new frock?'

'Yes,' Rose said impulsively, although, until then, it hadn't crossed her mind.

Mrs Lucas was another who turned the invitation down. 'I've got nothing to wear,' she told Benedicta. 'Anyroad, luv, I don't talk posh enough and I might use the wrong knife and fork.'

'Don't be daft, Mam. It's a buffet meal and there won't be knives and forks. I'd love you to come.'

'I know you would, luv, but I'd feel much happier staying at home and think about you enjoying yourself.' And other things, such as by this time next year, Benedicta would be working for the Civil Service and Mrs Lucas would have given up her cleaning jobs altogether. She couldn't wait.

'Sweet sixteen!' Lachlan remarked when he met Jeannie on the stairs. She was on her way up from the kitchen where she'd been getting something to eat and he was on his way down. 'Old enough to be kissed.' He smiled and kissed Jeannie chastely on her left cheek, stopped smiling and looked at her seriously for a minute, then kissed the other cheek, not quite so chastely this time. Then he groaned and his face seemed to collapse. 'Jeannie! I've been longing to do this for years, but you seemed so young.'

He slid his arms around Jeannie's waist and the plate of miniature sausage rolls and vol-au-vents fell with a clatter and everything rolled to the bottom of the stairs while Jeannie Flowers and Lachlan Bailey enjoyed their first proper kiss.

It was a long, soft, sweet kiss, full of youthful exuberance and delight. Halfway through, Jeannie felt the urge to put her arms around Lachlan. Her hands came to rest on the back of his lean neck, his hair threaded through her fingers, she could feel his heart beating rapidly against her own. A dozen emotions swirled crazily in her breast. She could hardly breathe.

Then a door opened upstairs, there were voices downstairs. The two young people broke away.

'Who's been throwing food all over the place?' Marcia demanded in her piercing voice.

'Jeannie and I bumped into each other and she dropped the plate,' Lachlan explained. He gave Jeannie a shy smile. 'Sit down and I'll bring you

173

something else to eat.'

'Oh, dearie me!' Rose Flowers merely whispered the words to herself when her daughter came into the Baileys' parlour. 'Something's happened. Something extraordinarily nice.'

If the truth be known, Jeannie looked a touch simple, smiling crookedly at nothing at all. Her cheeks were flushed, her eyes starbright. Rose had an inkling of what the reason might be, a feeling confirmed when Lachlan came in with two plates of food, and more or less threw himself at her daughter's feet. She felt like crying. He was a lovely young man who would make Jeannie very happy.

Mrs Bailey nudged her husband and dipped her head in the direction of their son. Dr Bailey followed her gaze and they both smiled. Observing this, Rose wished she had a husband with whom she could do the same, but had Tom been there, the young couple would have been subjected to a thunderous look instead. She was even more glad he hadn't come.

Relations between her and Tom had reached rock bottom. Rose resented being made to feel guilty for going to a party – their own daughter's sixteenth birthday party – to which they'd both been invited. Did he expect her not to go either? Didn't he feel guilty for staying at home?

He hadn't said anything, but she could tell he didn't like her new frock. It was a perfectly ordinary, entirely respectable frock. But it was grey. Until recently, he'd always chosen her clothes and preferred her in light, pastel colours – flowery colours, because she was his flower, his very own rose. Well, now she was a grey flower and he'd just have to like it or lump it. It was up to him.

'You know,' said Mr Connors, the keyboard player's father, 'if Max hadn't told me otherwise, I'd have taken you for his big sister, not his mum.

Rose had no idea how to answer. She'd never flirted in her life and had no small talk. 'I had Max when I was eighteen,' she said eventually. It seemed a very dull, too sensible reply. She was probably supposed to tell him he looked young enough to be Ronnie's brother, which wouldn't exactly have been a lie. He was a handsome man, clean cut, with boyish good looks. His eyes were brown and she thought they looked a trifle sad. He was oddly dressed in a tan shirt and trousers with a yellow tie. She wondered what it would be like to be married to a man the same age as herself

'Are you going to the Cavern later to see Max play?' he enquired.

'Oh, no,' Rose stammered. 'I don't think Max would like that. He'd feel embarrassed. And my husband will be expecting me home long before then.'

Mr Connors gave an impertinent grin. 'I don't blame him. So would I, if I was married to you.' This was an awful thing to say when the rather nice Mrs Connors was only across the room, deep in conversation with Sadie McDowd.

'Are you going, to the Cavern, that is?' she asked.

'Yes. Our Ronnie's dead nervous, playing there for the first time. If he's not watched, he'll have too much to drink. They don't sell alcohol, but he can always buy his own and take it with him.' They both glanced at Ronnie, who was innocently drinking orange squash.

'Oh,' Rose said inadequately. 'I hope my Max doesn't drink too much.'

'I've never seen anything other than Coca Cola pass your son's lips, Mrs Flowers – can I call you Rose? I'm Alex, by the way.'

Rose gulped. 'Er, yes.'

'They're very well-behaved, the group, considering all the temptations that come their way.'

'What sort of temptations?' Rose asked, alarmed.

'Well, drink's one, the other's girls. Girls by the dozen, throwing themselves at the lads whenever they play, hanging round afterwards offering – well, you know.' He winked.

'Excuse me.' Rose stumbled out of the room and made her way to the big, old-fashioned bathroom. She sat on the edge of the bath, breathing deeply. Why, it seemed only yesterday that she'd led Max by the hand to school on his first day. Coupled with the sight of Jeannie, clearly in the throes of first love, it almost made her wish she hadn't come to the party and had stayed at home with Tom.

Almost.

The Merseysiders left at half past six in the van, followed not long afterwards by the girls, who caught the bus, accompanied by Marcia and her boyfriend, Graham. As it was Saturday, there'd be a queue and they wanted to be sure they'd get in. Alex Connors took his wife home, then drove into town.

Rose and Sadie stayed at the Baileys' for another hour. 'So we can drink to our sons' success,' said Dr Bailey, producing a bottle of wine. 'I didn't want to get it out while the boys were here. I understand Ronnie has a weakness for drink.'

'Only because he's scared, poor boy,' Mrs Bailey remarked. 'Did you see the way his hands were shaking? I think his father pushes him too hard.'

'Parents!' Dr Bailey made a face. 'If they're not stopping their kids from doing the things they want, they're forcing them to do the things they don't!'

The Cavern was the same as always – hot, smelly, packed, buzzing with excitement. Three groups were playing that night and the Merseysiders were second on the bill.

'Piggy in the middle,' Marcia shrieked, before thankfully disappearing with the besotted Graham.

'No one knows what he sees in her,' Benny explained to Rita McDowd. 'She's got a voice like a foghorn.' Benny had taken Rita under her wing. It was nice not to be the odd one out for a change. Rita seemed easily impressed, listening wide-eyed while Benny boasted of her previous visits to the club. 'I've been here loads of times, and to other clubs too.'

The first group had come on to the stage. 'This lot aren't very good,' Benny hissed. 'I've seen them before.'

Rita responded with a little nod. It was hard to believe that she was sixteen and actually worked as a waitress in Owen Owen's. She didn't look much more than twelve in her plain brown frock with a Fair Isle cardy over. Her blue eyes were huge in her little, peaked face, and she spoke in just a whisper. All she had going for her, Benny thought disparagingly, was the fact she was the sister of Sean McDowd, with whom Benny had been madly in love since the minute she'd set eyes on him.

It struck her that Jeannie and Lachlan seemed pretty close tonight. She'd noticed at the party the way they had gazed at each other with sickly expressions on their faces. Since they'd arrived at the Cavern, Jeannie had hardly spoken and looked as if she was coming down with the plague or something.

Jeannie definitely wasn't herself that night. She felt as if the contents of a feather pillow had come loose inside her stomach and were being blown crazily about.

Lachlan had kissed her!

And she'd kissed him back!

The Merseysiders were around somewhere, probably guarding their gear while they waited to go on. Every now and then, Lachlan would appear and kneel beside her chair. 'Are you all right, Jeannie?' he would ask in a strange, cracked voice.

'Yes,' Jeannie would reply in a similarly strange voice. Or, 'Yes, Lachlan. I'm fine,' which she undoubtedly was, though it was a pretty peculiar sort of fine. Perhaps tumultuously fine, or turbulently fine would be better.

She couldn't wait for the tall, handsome figure to come on to the stage – Lachlan, with his clean-cut good looks and crisp dark hair. *He's mine*, she would say to herself

People were getting up, moving about. The first part of the programme had come to an end, but she hadn't heard a note. Elaine spoke to her from somewhere very far away.

'Mm,' Jeannie said dreamily.

'I said, would you like a Coke?' Elaine looked amused for some reason.

'Please.'

There was a commotion through one of the arches. A man shouted, 'Oh, God, no!' But Jeannie hardly heard. Nor did she hear when her brother approached and began to gabble something in her ear. It wasn't until Lachlan's name was mentioned that she came to.

'Lachlan's doing what?' she demanded.

'Him and Fly are trying to keep Mr Connors away from Ronnie in case he kills him.'

'Why?'

'Bloody hell, Jeannie, you haven't listened to a word I've said,' groaned a wildly exasperated Max. 'Ronnie's completely plastered. He's been lacing his cordial with gin ever since the party – we found the bottle in his pocket. Now he's gone completely berserk and said he wants no more to do with the group. He claims it was all his dad's idea and he can't take any more. Then he collapsed in a heap, and that's when Mr Connors tried to kill him.'

Jeannie couldn't understand why Max was telling her this and why he was looking at her so pleadingly. 'We're in a hole, Jeannie,' he said tearfully. 'Only for tonight. All our numbers, apart from one, have been arranged around the keyboard. Anywhere else, we'd try and muddle through. We've done it before. It's not the first time Ronnie's had too much to drink. But not tonight, Jeannie, not at the Cavern.'

'Oh, Max! What are you going to do?'

'Jeannie!' Max put his hand on her arm and shook it urgently. *'Please listen!* Time's short and we need you in place of Ronnie. You know all the numbers, you've played them at home. I've heard you. It'll be a piece of cake.'

'What?' Jeannie screamed.

'A piece of cake,' Max insisted.

'I couldn't possibly, Max.' Jeannie was shocked to the core at the idea. 'I'd be too nervous. I've never performed in public before, and please don't say it'll be a piece of cake again, because it won't be.'

Max sighed. 'I told Lachlan you wouldn't do it. He thought you'd never let us down.'

'I'm not letting you down.' She thoroughly disapproved of people who let other people down.

'How else would you describe it, Jeannie? This is our first gig at the Cavern and we'll sound like shit.'

'I've never played an electric piano before.'

'It's exactly the same as a normal piano, 'cept it's plugged in and the keyboard's smaller.'

'My hands are trembling, Max.' So was her voice.

180

'We all feel like that before a gig,' Max said kindly. 'It goes away when you start to play.'

'Honest?'

'Honest.'

'Did Lachlan really believe I wouldn't let you down?'

'Yes. C'mon, Jeannie. We're on in a minute.' He took her hand and led her across the floor of the crowded, sweaty Cavern. The short journey was to change Jeannie's life for ever.

At first, she wasn't just nervous, more like terrified out of her wits. Her hands still shook and she didn't feel confident she was playing the right keys, though it sounded all right so she must be. The first number was a Chubby Checker song, 'Pony Time', followed by 'Travelin' Man' and a rock 'n' roll version of 'Mack the Knife'. From across the stage, Max signalled when she was due to launch into a solo.

Halfway through the fourth number, 'Peggy Sue', Jeannie suddenly got into the swing of things. Knowing hundreds of people were listening no longer made her feel nervous, but spurred her into playing faster and faster, better and better, her fingers dancing over the keys. She was using the piano to tell the audience that she'd fallen in love with them and wanted them to love her back. Her timing was perfect. She found herself able to pause for a dangerously long time, then catch up with incredible speed that earned a short burst of applause. The first time she did this, Lachlan turned and gave her the thumbs up sign. Max smiled proudly and Fly Fleming gave her a huge encouraging grin.

'I could do this for ever,' she cried, but the words were lost in the music.

'And now for a change in rhythm,' Lachlan announced after about half an hour. 'I'd like to introduce Rita McDowd, who's going to sing for us a brand new song, "Moon Under Water".' He gestured towards the audience. 'Rita!'

Max signalled to a surprised Jeannie that she wasn't to play as Rita McDowd rose from her seat and came towards the stage, much to the astonishment of Benny, who'd assumed Rita knew nothing about music and had been giving her the occasional lecture in between numbers.

Sean removed his guitar and put it over his sister's head, adjusting the strap to make it smaller. Then he stepped back. So did Lachlan and Max. Fly lay down his drumsticks; Jeannie put her hands on her lap.

Rita plucked a few notes then, with a shy smile at the waiting crowd, began to sing.

Like the moon under water, I can't touch you.
Like stars in a mirror, you're not there.
Like a rainbow in the sky,
A shadow flitting by...

Silence fell upon the Cavern and all that could be heard was the glorious, amazing voice of Rita McDowd; deep, thrilling, and silkily smooth, without the slightest tremor, and so powerful it was almost impossible to believe it came from such a small, fragile figure.

How did I ever think she was plain? Benny

182

wondered. On stage, under a single spotlight, Rita had become an entirely different person, as if a light had been switched on inside her. Her enormous eyes glowed, her mobile face, like her voice, reflected the emotions about which she sang; the melancholy of the words, the sadness and hopelessness of unrequited love.

At the door of the Cavern, a man, more than twice the age of the usual regulars, had been about to leave when Rita started to sing. He'd missed the announcement and already has his foot halfway into Matthew Street, when he was stopped in his tracks, not by the singer, but the song. *His song!*

Kevin McDowd was on his way to London from Ireland and had called in the Cavern, just to see what the place was like, before catching the train. He was hoping that yet another change of scene would bring him luck. Dublin, New York, California, even Australia for a while – not one of these places had produced an improvement in his fortunes. This would be the third time he'd had a go at London and he'd probably end up doing the same as last time; playing the fiddle in the occasional Irish club, earning real money on building sites. He was beginning to toy with the idea of giving up show business altogether. He'd never got beyond the fringes and perhaps it'd be wise to get a decent job before he was too old. Once, he'd saved up religiously for a year and made a record, but it had sunk without trace.

He returned slowly down the Cavern steps. The girl had a knockout voice and she wasn't a bad guitar player, either. The group that had driven him out had remained on stage, instruments still. It was partly envy that had made him leave, mixed with despair. He was envious of their youth, not their talent, and despairing of himself. These young people had their entire future ahead of them, full of hope and dreams of stardom. They might not make it. Lady Luck was arbitrary and could touch the not-quite-so-good with her capricious finger and ignore the best.

''Tis better to travel than arrive.' He'd read that somewhere. He'd enjoyed the travelling once, but the journey had taken too long. It was well past the time that Kevin McDowd should have arrived.

'Like a dream that's gone by morning, or the mist when day is dawning,' the girl sang hauntingly.

Where had she got the words from? He couldn't remember ever writing them down. He'd sung it numerous times himself, many years ago, in pubs and clubs all over Ireland. Surely someone hadn't remembered the words since then?

The girl finished singing and there was an outburst of applause. She returned the guitar to its owner and hurried modestly back to her seat. Another guitarist, a good-looking lad, stepped towards the mike. 'Thank you, Rita. That was great.'

Rita!

Kevin suddenly felt very hot. Could it possibly be that this girl, who'd been a babe in arms when he left, was his daughter? It would explain where the song had come from. It had been one of

Sadie's favourites. She was always singing it. And if this was his daughter, then his wife and son mightn't be very far away.

He pushed his way through the crowds in every part of the club, heart thumping, expecting any minute to come face to face with Sadie, wondering what he would say if he did, but the girls were all kids. There wasn't a woman there over twenty, nor a lad who looked remotely like his son.

The stage! It was the obvious place to look, not for Sadie, but for Sean. The group was raising the roof with 'Don't Be Cruel' and Kevin edged as near as he could. He hadn't looked properly before, just listened, but now there wasn't a doubt in his mind that the lad who'd loaned the guitar to Rita was his son, Sean.

Sadie didn't recognise him at first. She arrived at the Phoenix Hotel promptly at eight. The guests, all men, were in the middle of breakfast. She was sorting through the post behind the reception desk and mentally counting heads as the dining room emptied. They had ten guests at the moment, and when that number had emerged, she took it for granted breakfast was over, so was surprised when Bridget, the ancient cook-cum-cleaner, hobbled out of the kitchen with a rack of toast.

'Who's that for?' Sadie enquired.

'A guest, of course. Apparently, he arrived late last night. This is his second lot of toast. I don't think he's had a decent meal in quite a while.'

'What's his name?'

'I dunno, do I? It'll be in the register.'

'I'll give him the toast while you get on with the dishes.'

'As you say.' Bridget shrugged.

'Good morning,' Sadie said brightly when she entered the dining room.

'Good morning,' replied the guest, a fortyish man, as thin as a stick, with a heavily lined face and receding hair that rested in little black wisps on his shabby collar.

'Here's your toast now.'

'Thank you, Sadie.'

The fact that the stranger had used her name didn't click until Sadie reached the door. 'How did...' she began, staring at him more closely. *'You!'* she gasped and grabbed the door for support when her legs no longer seemed prepared to hold her upright. 'What are you doing here? How did you know where to find me?'

'Rita told me.'

'Our Rita?'

'How many Ritas do we know? I met her last night at the Cavern. She's got quite a voice on her, that girl. Our Sean's no mean singer either, and he's brilliant on the guitar.'

'You're a sneaky, underhand individual, Kevin McDowd. I bet you didn't let on you were her daddy.'

'Ah, come off it, Sadie. It wouldn't have been right. I just told Rita I knew her mammy and she happened to mention where you worked.' His eyes twinkled in a way that was irritatingly and achingly familiar. He may have lost his looks, but the devilish charm was still there. She was glad she'd worn her favourite dress that morning,

186

bright red, flattering the curves that had re-appeared over the last few years. 'I thought I should introduce meself to me own wife first.'

'Introduce yourself! Introduce! As if I didn't already know you.' Sadie picked up a plate off the nearest table and flung it at him. He caught it easily.

'Good shot, me darlin' girl.'

'Don't darlin' girl me, you eejit.' She staggered slightly. 'Jaysus! I'll have to sit down before I fall down.'

'Are you all right?' There was concern in his voice as he jumped to his feet. He came over and helped her into a chair. She flung his hand away.

'Don't dare touch me,' she spat. 'I've had to do more on me own than just sit on a chair these last fifteen years. And where have you been, I'd like to know? Why didn't you come back like you promised?'

He gave a long, tragic sigh. 'Because I didn't want to come back a failure, Sadie, girl. And that's what you're looking at, a desperate failure. I tried, believe me I tried, but everything I did, everywhere I went, I failed. I'd intended to come back with me pockets stuffed with gold, but all I can show for the last fifteen years is an ould fiddle in me room upstairs, and a bag of clothes that would make a tramp turn up his nose. Instead of gold, there's only a few measly bob in me pocket, and a train ticket to London.'

'London?'

'I should've gone last night. I only landed from Ireland yesterday afternoon, and I thought I'd drop in on this famous Cavern. To me astonishment, weren't me own son and daughter there, giving great performances? I'm only surprised you weren't there as well.'

'I didn't know Rita was going to sing, did I? She didn't tell me till she came home last night, or they couldn't have kept me away. Sean won't let me watch him play; he'd feel uncomfortable, so he ses. He's got your talent, Kevin McDowd, but he hasn't got your neck.'

'Maybe not, Sadie, but he's got presence. Something I never had. The girls couldn't keep their eyes off him.'

'You couldn't keep your eyes off the girls,' Sadie sniffed.

'There was no need to look at other girls when I had you, darlin'.' His eyes narrowed appreciatively. 'And don't you still look wholesome, even after all these years?'

'*You* don't. If the truth be known, you look about ninety-four and you seem desperately short of skin. And hair,' she added, grinning unexpectedly.

He grinned back. 'You're doing me confidence a load of good, darlin'.'

'When are you leaving for London?'

'I'm not. I'm needed here.'

'Needed! What for?' She folded her arms and gave him a dark look, despite being somehow, illogically relieved that he intended to stay. '*I* don't need you, that's for sure. Not any more.'

'To see to the interests of me children, that's what for. They've got a future in show business and they'll be wanting a manager, someone who'll steer them in the right direction, keep them on the right track. And who better to do that than their daddy?'

'You're too late. The Merseysiders already have a manager.'

He looked so disappointed that she felt sorry for him. 'What's the set up?' he asked. 'Is Rita a member of the group or not?'

'She's not. That's the one and only time she's sung in public. Mind you, I've been paying for her to have singing lessons. She goes to Crane Hall every Thursday after work – she works as a waitress not far from here. In case you haven't noticed,' she added scathingly, 'women don't play much of a part in the music scene today.'

'What about the other girl, the one on the keyboard? She was brilliant.'

Sadie looked puzzled for a moment. 'Oh, that was Jeannie Flowers from the other end of Disraeli Terrace. She was just standing in for some fella who got himself pissed rotten beforehand. Jeannie's still at school. According to our Sean, as from now, there'll only be four members in the group; three guitarists and a drummer.'

This news cheered Kevin up somewhat. 'So,' he said thoughtfully, 'there's two show-stopping young women urgently in need of a manager. All I need to do is find is another couple of good-looking wee girls to play the tambourine and sing a bit, and I'll have a group.'

Although Colonel Corbett regarded his gardener as a friend, he wouldn't have dreamed of inviting Tom Flowers to eat in his dining room. It was nothing to do with class. He just didn't want the food ruined by visions of his mother turning in her grave. It meant that when Tom came indoors for something to eat at midday, as he had done for almost fifty years, the colonel dined in the kitchen, though even that was something he could never have done when his mother was alive.

On the Monday after his son had made his first triumphant appearance at the Cavern – so far, no one at home had dared tell him that his daughter had also played a part in the triumph – Tom slouched disconsolately into the kitchen to be met by his employer and a beaming Mrs Denning, now a widow, who'd returned to The Limes some years before to become the colonel's housekeeper.

'You old sly boots,' the colonel cried. 'Why didn't you tell us?'

'Tell you what?' enquired a bewildered Tom.

'That Max belongs to a group that played at the Cavern on Saturday night. I only found out when Mrs Denning here told me.'

'I didn't think you'd be interested.' He hadn't expected the colonel to have even heard of the Cavern. As for Max, he was too ashamed to tell a soul about the lad's infatuation with the guitar. It would have been different had he played anything that could be identified as music, instead of a raucous jumble of sounds.

'It was my nephew told me.' Mrs Denning put two large bowls of soup on the table. 'Martin went to the village school with Max. He's thrilled to bits that one of his old classmates has done so well for himself.'

190

'What's the group called, Tom?'

Tom couldn't for the life of him remember. It was left to Mrs Denning to supply the answer. 'The Merseysiders.'

'Did Martin say what they were like?' Tom asked cautiously.

'I didn't see him over the weekend, but they must have been good. They've played all over Liverpool, so Martin says. He's only just found out your Max belongs.'

'You should have told us before, Tom,' the colonel chided. 'You know how much I like music.'

'But a very different sort of music,' Tom reminded him. He had the uncomfortable feeling he was being subtly told off.

'Rock 'n' roll's only a hop, skip and jump away from swing, Tom.'

Tom gulped. The colonel saying 'rock 'n' roll' was akin to hearing him utter the worst sort of blasphemy.

'Anyway, Tom,' Mrs Denning brought her own soup to the table and sat down, 'you must be feeling very proud.'

He tried very hard to feel proud, but it was impossible.

Chapter 7

'So,' Lachlan grinned, 'what's all this about a girlie group?'

'Don't be so patronising!' Jeannie tapped his nose reprovingly with her finger. 'It's a *girl* group. I didn't know, but there's loads in America – the Supremes, the Ronettes, Martha and the Vandellas, to name a few.'

It was Boxing Day afternoon, ten days since the Merseysiders had played at the Cavern. Jeannie and Lachlan were squashed together in an armchair in Dr Bailey's waiting room, which appeared to be the only place on earth where they could be alone. The rather dull room had a tiny, paper Christmas tree on the table in the middle of some old magazines. The mantelpiece was crammed with cards from the doctor's patients. Elsewhere, the house throbbed with life. Dishes were being washed, the television was on upstairs, the younger Baileys were playing football in the yard despite the freezing weather, and on the top floor Marcia was singing 'Moon Under Water' in a sickly, sugary voice.

Lachlan was still grinning. 'And soon we'll have our own girl group on this side of the Atlantic – the Flower Girls.'

'Mr McDowd – Kevin – got the idea for the name from mine.' She glared at him. 'You're not taking this seriously, are you?'

'Are *you?*' Lachlan raised his perfect, utterly adorable eyebrows.

'Hardly a week goes by without another new group turning up at the Cavern, always boys,' she reasoned, 'so I don't see anything funny about a group of girls.'

'It's not funny, it's just ... weird! Somehow, I can't see you taking off.'

'The world won't end if we don't.' Jeannie shrugged philosophically, unwilling to admit she was desperately hoping the Flower Girls would succeed. 'Me and Benny aren't giving up school or anything. We're staying for O levels. Rita McDowd will still be a waitress and Marcia will continue doing whatever it is she's doing at the moment.'

'Working in Jacob's biscuit factory.' He was grinning again. 'Seriously though, Jeannie – Benny Lucas and our Marcia! It's got to be a joke.'

'I used to think the Merseysiders were a joke at the beginning,' she tartly pointed out. Had she not loved him quite so wholeheartedly, she might have punched him. 'Mr McDowd – I mean, Kevin –just wants two girls to move around a bit, sort of hum in the background, and occasionally shake a tambourine, while I play the piano and Rita sings.'

'I seem to remember our Elaine was an expert tambourine shaker when we first played in your garden shed.'

'Elaine's not interested. She'd sooner study. When Marcia found out, she only drove your dad's car to our house, didn't she, knocking us up in the middle of the night to demand she be a Flower Girl. She was worried Mr – Kevin – might have got someone else by morning. In fact, he's quite pleased, because she's the same type as Benny – tall, fair, and slim.'

'Marcia can't sing,' Lachlan pointed out, suppressing a giggle. He jerked his head skywards, to where his sister was now offering a soulful rendition of 'Strangers in the Night'. 'She sounds like a dying cat.'

'Oh, Lachlan! Don't exaggerate. She doesn't have to sing. Marcia and Benny are just decoration. Kevin doesn't want them to sing. It would detract from Rita.'

'I must admit, Rita's got a fantastic voice.'

'I'm glad you think the Flower Girls have got one thing going for them,' Jeannie sniffed.

'They also have a fantastic keyboard player.'

'Lachlan!'

'Jeannie!'

They sank further into the chair, wrapped tightly in each other's arms, and began to kiss. So far, Jeannie had done nothing in her life that remotely compared with kissing Lachlan Bailey, not even playing the piano. A sweetness rose in her breast and in her throat, there was a ringing in her ears, and she was overcome with a heady sensation of dizziness.

'I love you,' Lachlan said thickly when they came up for air.

Jeannie cradled his face in her hands. She could feel bristles under her thumbs. He needed a shave. This simple evidence of manhood sent a thrill through her body. She recalled the first time they'd met in the upstairs parlour. She'd been playing *Minuet in G*. He'd been wearing a school uniform, only a boy. She'd fallen in love with him then. Now he was a man and she loved him even more.

'And I love you, Lachlan,' she said, clearly and distinctly, so he would have no doubts.

There was a knock on the door. 'Tea's ready,' Mrs Bailey shouted.

'Coming,' they cried together.

Elaine was in the kitchen when Jeannie went in. She'd been helping her mother make the tea. Weeks ago, when Jeannie had been invited to the Baileys' on Boxing Day, she had envisaged helping too; comparing presents with Elaine and laughing together at the television when it wasn't remotely funny. Instead, she'd spent all her time with Lachlan, entirely neglecting her friend.

'Elaine!' She put a contrite hand on her arm.

'Oh, Jeannie!' Elaine understood straight away. 'It doesn't matter. This was bound to happen one day. One of us had to be first and it happened to be you.'

'But we'll always be friends?'

'Always,' Elaine assured her with a smile.

At the same time, in number one Disraeli Terrace, Kevin McDowd was also sitting down to tea with his family. He'd been there since Christmas Eve. The Phoenix Hotel closed over the festive season and he'd scarcely a penny in his pocket, he pathetically informed Sadie. It looked as if he'd be spending Christmas with the Salvation Army.

'That's if there's room, he added darkly. 'Otherwise, I can see meself on the streets.'

'You can stay with us,' Sadie said ungraciously. 'But you're sleeping in the parlour, on the couch. And while you're there, you can keep your hands and your other bits and pieces to yourself. You'll be there as a guest, not me husband.'

'I wouldn't dream of laying a finger on you, Sadie.'

'You'd better not.'

On Christmas Day, after dinner, Sadie burst into involuntary song while she washed the dishes, thrilled to bits that she had her darling Kevin back. She had no intention of letting him have the slightest inkling of how happy she was until he'd been sufficiently punished.

'I've been a wild rover for many a year,' she warbled loudly, thinking this was the best Christmas in a long time, when Kevin gave a whoop, ran into the parlour to fetch his fiddle and began to play. The bow skimmed like wildfire over the strings; he'd lost none of his skill. Sean gave one of his rare smiles and fetched his guitar from upstairs, then Rita brought the old acoustic one on which she'd learnt to play. One Irish tune followed another. Kevin knew them all and his children quickly picked them up.

After an hour, or it might have been two, everyone laid down their instruments, exhausted, and began to talk instead. Kevin told them about his adventures in Hollywood, how he'd once been on the set when Fred Astaire had danced with Judy Garland, and had been an extra in an Alan Ladd film. 'I was a policeman,' he explained. In Australia, he'd merely wandered around, playing in one dusty pub after another. By the end of the day, as far as Sadie was concerned, he might never have been away.

They say it's money that makes the world go round, but it's not, it's music, she reckoned. It was something of a miracle when you thought about it. All the operas, concertos, symphonies, the ballads and the folk songs, jazz, blues, ragtime, swing, and now rock 'n' roll, all from eight little notes.

Sean told his dad he wouldn't stick with the Merseysiders for long. 'The manager's a crook. I don't trust him as far as I could throw him.'

'You mustn't think of leaving yet,' Kevin advised. 'You and that Lachlan lad make a good team. You complement each other. He plays from the heart and you from the soul. He's an extrovert; you're the opposite. Between the pair o'yis, the audience's emotions are wrung dry. That drummer's good, he's got a great personality, pleasing. The other guitarist's just OK. He doesn't turn people off, but he doesn't turn them on, either. That's all right, it means the attention's centred on you and Lachlan. Two stars are better than three, makes life easier.'

'Max is a shit player,' Sean agreed.

'He's not shit, just average. Stick with the group, son, until you've made a name for yourselves. *Then* leave, if you still feel like it.'

'I'd like to go solo.'

'Do it when you're someone and the record companies will come running. If you did it now, there wouldn't be a flicker of interest.'

At this point, Sadie felt bound to point out that

197

he'd used to boast about himself in the same way. 'You were forever on the brink of signing a contract with this company or that. Success, stardom, was always just round the corner. Yet look at you now, Kevin McDowd! You're a failure. You said so yourself. Now you're doing the same with our Sean, raising his expectations beyond all reason. Not only that, you're doing it with Rita and Jeannie and them other two girls, promising them heaven and earth, yet you haven't got a penny to your name. How will they get off the ground? That's what I'd like to know.'

'I don't know, either, not yet. You know, Sadie, darlin', we all need to have dreams.'

'I don't have dreams,' Sean informed them. 'I have plans.' He afforded his father one of his infrequent smiles. 'I'm dead pleased you're back, Dad,' he said warmly.

Alex Connors presented Jeannie with the electric piano that she'd played in a way his son never had and never would.

'You were brilliant, girl. Our Ronnie was never cut out to be a musician, I realise that now. I just wish my father had done for me what I tried to do for my own lad, encouraged me to take up music as a career. But, there you go. I was foisting me own thwarted ambitions on our poor Ronnie. Anyroad,' he sighed, 'he's coming into the business with me, so the piano's surplus to requirements. You may as well have it. Max says you might be starting a group of your own, so good luck, girl. I'm glad the piano's going to a good home.'

'Ah, well, that's something!' Kevin McDowd rubbed his hands together excitedly when informed of this generous act. 'The Flower Girls have got their own wee piano.'

'Now all you need is an electric guitar for Rita,' his wife sneered, 'a place to rehearse, a dozen or so properly arranged numbers – not just the songs, but the music. And will they be wearing costumes or any old rags? Once you've sorted that lot out, where will they play I'd like to know? Or have you already got the gigs lined up? I'm sure every club in Liverpool is panting for a girl group.'

'I'll cross that bridge when I come to it. Sean's buying Rita a guitar, and aren't I already working on the arrangements? You're a real put-downer, Sadie McDowd,' Kevin complained. 'No wonder I left home when I wasn't offered a breath of encouragement.'

'You were offered every encouragement. But that was then; this is now, when you're a self-confessed has-been. Anyroad, aren't I offering the encouragement of the sofa in me parlour and not asking a penny for board and lodgings?'

It was February and Kevin was still living in Disraeli Terrace, not doing a stroke of work apart from poring over scraps of paper, charts and lists and sheets of music, scribbling here and scribbling there, his hair standing on end – what was left of it.

Once or twice a week, without Sadie's knowledge, Kevin slipped along to the Oak Tree at dinner time for a pint of Guinness to stretch his legs and enjoy an hour or so of adult male company for a change.

So far, no one had recognised him as the curly-haired young Irishman who'd left Ailsham almost sixteen years before, not that Kevin would have cared if they had. He still retained the ability to charm the birds off the trees and quite a few of the Oak Tree customers were pleased to see him whenever he breezed in. One was Colonel Corbett, who sometimes treated himself to a couple of whiskies after lunch. As a regular soldier, the colonel had spent much of his youth abroad, in Africa and India. Kevin had also done his share of travelling and they swapped tales of their adventures overseas.

It wasn't until their fourth meeting in March that they discovered a mutual interest in music. The colonel liked swing, big bands such as Stan Kenton, Duke Ellington, Tommy and Jimmy Dorsey. Kevin liked more or less everything, big bands included.

'My gardener's lad belongs to one of these new pop groups; the Merseysiders,' the colonel boasted.

Kevin smiled delightedly. 'And doesn't me own son, Sean, belong to the very same group?'

'Does he now!'

'He does indeed. And aren't I in the very process of setting up another group, the Flower Girls, that includes your gardener's daughter, Jeannie, and me own darlin' girl, our Rita?'

The colonel looked annoyed. 'You'd think Tom would let me know what's happening on my very own doorstep. If they were my children, I'd shout it from the rooftops.'

'Meself, I'm dead proud,' Kevin declared smugly. He went on to explain he already had a programme worked out for his group. 'Twelve numbers in all. I wrote a couple of them meself. Rita's already started practising, Jeannie too. Now all we need is somewhere to rehearse where the neighbours won't be sent berserk. You can hire rooms in town, but they cost an arm and a leg.'

'You can use my barn,' the colonel said instantly.

'Your barn!' Kevin had visions of sharing the barn with half a dozen cows and assorted rats. An imaginative man, he could already smell the manure.

The colonel must have sensed his dismay. 'It hasn't been used as a barn since the turn of the century,' he reassured his new friend. 'My father had it renovated and my brother and I used it as a games room when we were young. It's where we held our regimental dinner a few years back. It has electricity, a lavatory, even a tiny kitchen.'

'It sounds ideal,' Kevin enthused.

Tom Flowers felt even more like a stranger in his own home when he learnt from Miss Pritchard that Jeannie had given up piano lessons. No one had bothered to tell *him*. The music teacher was understandably annoyed.

'After all these years, Mr Flowers, I would have expected more than a brief note informing me my services were no longer required.'

'I'm sorry, Miss Pritchard.'

201

'I didn't say anything because I knew you'd make a fuss,' Rose said when he broached the subject. 'She wouldn't let Jeannie play the sort of music she likes.'

How anybody could like the music Jeannie played these days was beyond him. She didn't even use the family piano, but some tenth-rate miniature instrument she'd been given. The thing had been set up in her bedroom and didn't sound remotely like a proper piano. His ears were regularly assaulted by a noise that bore little resemblance to music as he'd always known it. Now Jeannie was getting involved with some group or other, and Tom daren't say a word, not even the mildest of criticism, otherwise Rose would claim he was being unreasonable. It was all the idea of that McDowd chap from the other end of the terrace. Tom vaguely remembered him walking out years ago and leaving his family in the lurch. Now he was back and interfering in other people's lives.

If it wasn't Jeannie on her perverted piano, Gerald could be heard in the garden shed playing Max's old guitar. He wanted proper lessons, Rose informed him. 'There isn't a teacher in Ailsham. The nearest one I can find is in Spellow Lane. You'll take him in the car, won't you, Tom?'

The unkindest cut of all came when the colonel accused him of being unforthcoming. 'I had to find out about Max from Mrs Denning, and it was a chap in the pub who told me about Jeannie. Really, Tom.' He shook his head sorrowfully. 'I wish you wouldn't keep me in the dark about your children's achievements.'

Achievements! Tom was more confused than ever. People in the village kept stopping to congratulate him on how well Max had done but, in Tom's view, Max had done nothing but disappoint him. If things had gone the way he'd planned, his eldest son would now be at university. *That* was something Tom wouldn't have hesitated to boast about. *That* would have made him proud. And instead of Jeannie finding a nice, safe job in an office, something else that would have pleased him, it looked as if she were following in the footsteps of her brother.

'Gerald's starting guitar lessons soon,' he muttered just in case the colonel found out from someone else.

'Good,' the colonel said approvingly. 'You know, Tom, it's a pity Rose knows nothing about her antecedents. One or other of her parents must have been very musical, because the children certainly don't take after you.'

Tom humbly agreed.

Rita McDowd had always wanted to sing but, except for very rare occasions, had felt inhibited by circumstances and her own withdrawn nature. It was impossible for her to burst into song the way her mother sometimes did. Her body felt too tight, closed up. She felt scared, almost ashamed, of someone hearing. When they sang hymns at school assembly, Rita merely whispered the words, worried she'd draw attention to herself by releasing her voice, knowing it would soar as high as the ceiling, drowning every other voice around her.

The singing lessons at Crane Hall made her feel like a caged bird that had suddenly been set free. For an entire hour, she was able to sing as high and as low and as loud as she liked. Her voice flew, as smooth as velvet, up and down the scales. The instructor, Madame Vera, a retired opera singer, who was never seen without full makeup and adorned with an assortment of colourful silk scarves, was hugely impressed. Rita was taught to relax, breathe more slowly, draw in her stomach, sing for an audience, not just for herself.

'You're holding yourself back, dearie,' Madame Vera advised in her lovely contralto voice. 'You must learn to let go. Imagine yourself being born, being expelled from your mother's womb, wanting to let the whole world know that you're alive and well. Sing, Rita, sing! "I'm alive and well."'

'I'm alive and well,' Rita sang, not in the least embarrassed.

Nor did she mind when Sean asked if she would sing at the Cavern, their father's song, 'Moon Under Water'. She felt as if she had truly been reborn. She could sing any time and anywhere.

It was the song her father had recognised first, not his children. Now he was back amongst them and she'd loved him straight away. They were a family again. For the first time in her life, Rita was properly happy.

Kevin said he'd never known a first rehearsal go so well as the one on Good Friday in Colonel

Corbett's smartly renovated barn. Rita was brilliant, Jeannie was brilliant, Marcia and Benny were almost brilliant, understanding straight away what was expected of them. They had to move in unison, only a simple series of steps; once to the right, clap hands, once to the left and clap again, turn towards each other, step forward, step back, then turn to face the audience and clap. With the slower numbers, they just had to sway to and fro and hum.

'You were great, girls,' said a pleased Kevin when they'd sung the final number, 'Will You Still Love Me Tomorrow'. 'Once you've got the movements off pat, I'll work out a more complicated routine.'

'I've already got them off pat,' Marcia informed him.

'So've I.' Benny was determined not to be outdone.

'I've yet to work the new steps out,' Kevin said sternly.

'Can't we work them out between ourselves?' Marcia demanded.

'Indeed you cannot,' Kevin replied, even more sternly.

'I thought we were supposed to have tambourines?'

'You'll have tambourines when I've got the money to buy them.'

'Well, I think you were all marvellous.' Sadie had come with them, armed with refreshments. 'Who'd like a cup of tea?'

'Me!' everyone chorused.

Sadie left to make it and Jeannie's thoughts

switched to Lachlan, who was rarely far from her mind these days. He thought the whole idea of the Flower Girls daft and she desperately hoped to prove him wrong, even if she didn't have a great deal of faith in the project herself. It didn't stop her from putting all her heart and soul into her playing both for Kevin's sake – and her own.

Marcia thought the whole thing a bit of a giggle, but a highly enjoyable one at that. She was determined to experience every aspect of life, within reason, that is, before marrying Graham and settling down. It didn't matter that it was taking much longer than Graham would have liked.

Benny smiled at everyone agreeably, but inwardly simmered. She had only a competent singing voice and had never touched a piano in her life, yet felt jealous of Rita and Jeannie. They were the stars. It wasn't fair. For Benny, the group was the opportunity of a lifetime. She didn't want to take the Civil Service exam that Mam was always on about. Say she didn't pass? And if she did pass, was she supposed to work at a humdrum job until a husband came along? The Flower Girls were her ticket to a different, exciting world. She was praying like mad they would succeed.

Sadie emerged from the kitchen with a tray of tea things, and they sat around and discussed the future. It was Kevin's opinion they would soon be ready to perform in front of an audience. 'Just a few more rehearsals and you'll be fine. I'd like you all back on Sunday and Easter Monday. Now, when you've finished your tea, we'll go through the whole performance again.'

When Rose Flowers left the Post Office at one o'clock, she was surprised to find it was a beautiful day and quite warm for early April. The sun was a crisp, yellow ball in a perfectly clear blue sky. That morning, it had been raining, and since then she'd been imprisoned in a tiny cubicle at the back of the shop. Several customers had probably remarked on the fact the weather had improved, but she hadn't listened. With a heavy heart, she began to trudge in the direction of Holly Lane. It was Thursday and Gerald was going to tea with a friend straight from school and wouldn't be home till late. The other two could turn up any old time. Tom would arrive on the dot of ten past six, as he always did. Lately, when she heard the catch go, she felt the urge to scream and never stop, knowing his sour face would shortly appear in the kitchen and they would hardly speak to each other for the rest of the evening.

Perhaps if Max and Jeannie weren't having such a wonderful time she wouldn't have felt so discontented. She was ashamed of feeling envious of her children, Jeannie in particular, who literally glowed with love for Lachlan. But she couldn't help it. Rose had never been in love and now it was too late.

She passed the station, paused, retraced her steps for some mysterious reason and went inside. People were waiting on the platform for the Liverpool train. Impulsively, she bought a ticket and joined them. It would be the first time she'd gone into town on her own and she felt guilty, as if, somehow, she was betraying Tom.

The train arrived and her legs felt heavy when she stepped into the carriage. She remembered the dirty breakfast dishes were still on the table at home and there was washing waiting to be hung on the line because it had been raining when she left. There would have been time to hang it out and have it dry by teatime.

Rose felt like an escaping criminal while the train made its way towards Liverpool, stopping frequently to let passengers on and off, many of them women on their own. She wasn't doing anything unusual. It just felt that way.

The train drew into Exchange Station and everyone got off. She walked in the direction of the shops and spent an enjoyable hour wandering around Lewis's department store admiring the latest fashions. Next time she bought a frock, she'd get black, and she'd love a pair of stiletto heeled shoes. Tom would hate both, but she didn't care.

Yes, she did! Well, not exactly *care*. She just didn't want to create more animosity between them, and in order to do that it seemed she would have to spend the rest of her days doing only the things that Tom wanted, dressing the way *he* liked.

Back again on the ground floor, she bought a lipstick, a box of face powder, and a tiny bottle of scent, then retired to the Ladies to experiment. The powder took the country girl shine off her nose and the lipstick accentuated the shape of her already shapely mouth. She dabbed the scent behind her ears and put some on the corner of her handkerchief

Satisfied, Rose left the shop and strolled along Lime Street, looking for more big shops to explore. A small queue had formed outside a cinema on the corner waiting to see a picture called *Some Like It Hot*. Rose chewed her lip. Dare she go? She'd only seen one film in her life before. One Christmas, when the children were small, they'd all gone to see *The Wizard of Oz*. Would it be yet another betrayal? Did Tom disapprove of the cinema as much as he did of television? She couldn't recall him passing an opinion on it.

A hand touched her arm. A voice said, 'It's a great picture.'

Rose jumped. 'I beg your pardon!'

'I said, it's a great picture. I've not seen it, but it got dead good reviews.' A good-looking man in a cream suit, cream tie, and dark green shirt, was smiling at her warmly. 'Remember me, luv? Alex Connors, Ronnie's father. We met at the Baileys'.'

'Of course I remember you.' She recalled he'd paid her some embarrassingly flattering compliments. 'Oh, and thank you for the piano. Jeannie was thrilled to bits.'

'I'm just glad it went to a good home. How's the group coming on, the Flower Girls?'

'I don't get much from Jeannie, she has other things on her mind, but Sadie McDowd says they're very good, though they still haven't played a gig. How's Ronnie?'

His thin lips twisted wryly. 'Happy, according to him. Are you planning on seeing this picture?'

The queue had started to move. 'I don't think so. There's no one going on their own.'

'In that case, why don't we go together?'

'Oh!' Rose blushed scarlet. 'I wasn't dropping a hint.'

'I know you weren't, luv.'

'What about your work?'

'They can manage without me. Anyroad, I've done enough for today. I've just copped a contract fitting bathrooms, materials, and labour on a big estate round Gateacre way. That's what I was doing in town. C'mon, luv.'

Before she could protest, he'd cupped her elbow with his hand and was leading her quite firmly towards the cinema entrance. 'Two at the back,' he said to the woman in a glass cubicle, much bigger than the one Rose occupied five mornings a week. 'Would you like some chocolates, Rose? You said I could call you Rose at the party,' he reminded her.

'No, thank you,' she croaked. What she was doing was terribly wrong, yet there was nothing to stop her from leaving, particularly when Alex Connors said he'd buy chocolates anyway. He crossed to the sweet counter, giving her the opportunity to escape if she wanted. Rose did want, but rather less than she wanted to stay.

Some Like It Hot was hilariously funny. Rose laughed till she cried, conscious all the time of Alex Connors' shoulder pressing lightly against hers.

'I've never known anyone enjoy a film so much,' he said when it was over and they were outside.

'I don't get to the pictures much,' she confessed. 'It was quite a treat.'

'You should go more often. Watching you enjoy yourself was a treat in itself.' He looked at her keenly. 'Would you like something to eat?'

Rose wished she could stop blushing. 'I should be getting back,' she murmured, making absolutely no move to do so. She didn't want to go back. The afternoon in his company had been magic and she wanted it to last.

'Can't you ring your husband and tell him you'll be late?'

'I suppose I could. What time is it?' She noticed the shops had closed. People were making their way home.

'Almost six.'

'Tom doesn't get home till ten past. I'll ring then.' He wouldn't answer, having refused to have anything to do with the phone, but at least she could claim she tried. 'Shouldn't you call your wife?'

'Iris never expects me till she sees me. I often stay late at work, after everyone's gone. It's nice and quiet, and I can think.' He sighed and looked rather sad. 'Mind you, saying that, it's even better the nights the Merseysiders rehearse in the store room.'

'It was awfully nice of you to let them stay when Ronnie's no longer a member.'

'It would have been dead mean to have made them stop.'

'What do you think about when it's quiet?' Rose asked.

'The opportunities I never had, the dreams that

didn't come true, why I'm there, and not some-where else entirely different. I'm a discontented sod, Rose.' He laughed shortly. 'Do you like Chinese food?'

'I've never had it before.'

'Well, there's a first time for everything. There's a place in London Road. If we cut through Lime Street station, you can call your husband from a phone box.'

To her surprise, when Rose dialled, the receiver at the other end was picked up. It was Gerald.

'Mum!' He sounded hurt. 'You're not here and Dad's really angry. The table hasn't been cleared and there's no tea made.'

'I thought you were having tea at your friend's?'

'His mum's ill. I left early without anything to eat.'

'I'm sorry, love.' She wanted to cry for some reason. 'Tell Dad I've been unavoidably de-tained. You'll find a casserole in the fridge. It just needs heating up, and there's fruit cake in the larder. Just heap the dirty dishes in the sink and I'll do them when I get home.'

'All right, Mum. What time will that be?'

'I'm not sure, love. As soon as I can.'

Alex was waiting for her outside the phone box. 'Are you all right?' he asked when she came out. 'You seem a bit upset. Look, if you like, I'll drive you straight home. My car's not far away. I don't want you getting into trouble with your husband.'

'I've never done anything like this before but, no, I don't want to go home, thanks. I'd rather have a meal with you.'

They looked into each other's eyes and Rose saw straight away that he was as lonely and unhappy as she was, and that the afternoon had been as magical for him as it had been for her. She also knew her words had moved their short relationship on to a different plane that he might not find acceptable. She almost hoped he wouldn't, so she could return to the dull safety of Disraeli Terrace and never see him again. But Alex said in a soft voice, 'Come on, Rose. Let's go.'

He held out his hand and Rose took it.

Gerald was still up watching television when she got home – Alex dropped her off at the end of Holly Lane. There was no sign of Tom.

'Where's your dad?' she asked.

'Gone for a drink,' Gerald sniffed. 'He said I was to go to bed.' Tom occasionally went to the Oak Tree for a pint. 'Jeannie rang to say she's staying with Elaine. I've no idea where our Max is. Hardly anybody's in these days, Mum,' he said sulkily, 'not even you.'

'Oh, come off it, Gerald. Today's the first time I haven't been here when you've come home from school.'

'Where have you been?'

'You'll never believe this, but I've been to the pictures!'

'Who with?' he asked suspiciously. He was worse than Tom.

'A woman called Clara Baker,' Rose said promptly, having prepared an explanation on the way home. 'I bumped into her in Liverpool. We used to be friends. She was in the Women's

Institute and we used to do the cake stall together at the Midsummer Fête. She and her husband moved away, ages ago, to Hoylake.'

Gerald blinked. 'What were you doing in Liverpool?'

'Shopping. Honestly, love. I think you're turning into Inspector Maigret.' Rose laughed, hoping he didn't notice how false it sounded. 'Liverpool's only a few miles away, not the other side of the world.'

'You usually go shopping in Ormskirk on Saturdays.'

'Well, today I decided to shop on Thursday and go further afield.' She clapped her hands. 'Bedtime, Gerald, otherwise your dad'll be cross when he gets home and finds you're still up.'

'He's already cross. 'Fact, I've never known him in such a bad temper. I hope you're not going to the pictures again.'

'It so happens that I am. I'm meeting Clara Baker on Thursday next week. And there's no need to pull a face, Gerald Flowers, because you can't exactly claim you've been neglected. Next time, I'll leave the tea on the table, something cold. And I'll tidy up before I go, so you and your dad will have nothing to complain about.' He was thirteen and well old enough to look after himself, while she was thirty-seven and still young enough to...

She daren't even *think* of the things she'd like to do.

Tom came home, his face like thunder. He obviously felt that this time he had a genuine grievance. She told him the same story. His face hadn't changed by the time she'd finished.

'I might have known you wouldn't understand,' she cried. 'You'd think I'd committed murder, not been to the pictures.'

'It's not the sort of thing you've ever done before.'

'More's the pity. But it's the sort of thing I'm going to do again. I'm entitled to something out of life, Tom. I'm bored out of my mind, staying in night after night.'

'You've got the W.I.,' he argued.

'Do you really think that's enough?'

'It is for some women.'

'How would you know?'

He didn't know. How could he? He mumbled something incomprehensible and went to bed. Rose curled herself up in a chair, revelling in the solitude and the silence. Her mysterious, imaginary lover now had a face, and the face was that of Alex Connors.

Tom was still angry with Rose next day, but he'd believed her when she claimed to have met someone called Clara Baker in Liverpool. Hard as he tried, he couldn't remember the woman who'd left Ailsham with her husband to live in Hoylake. He was worried what sort of person she was. Rose had had little experience of the world and the woman might be a bad influence.

'Do you recall a Clara Baker who used to be in the Women's Institute?' he asked Mrs Denning when he went for his midday meal.

'Yes, I do, Tom. Nice young woman, very

pretty, as I recall. Wasn't she friendly with your Rose? She and her husband went to live in Hoylake.'

'I can't quite bring her to mind.'

'She walked with a slight limp. I understand she'd had polio as a child.'

'Ah, I remember now. Yes, she did seem nice.' He felt relieved and was about to mention Rose had bumped into Clara Baker the day before, but Mrs Denning got in first. 'It was terribly sad that she died.'

'Who died?'

'Why, Clara Baker, of course. She died in child-birth. Oh, it must have been a good five years back. It's not the sort of thing that happens much nowadays, but she was always in poor health. Are you all right, Tom? You've gone awfully pale.'

Chapter 8

There'd been a time when Liverpool was the richest city in the country outside London and its docks the second biggest in Europe. It had supplied the world with an abundance of fine actors and comedians, and its people were famous for their wit and good humour. But now Liverpool was on the verge of becoming famous for something else – rock 'n' roll.

The Cavern was already a beacon for everyone who wanted to listen to beat live and they came from all over British Isles. The Merseysiders played regularly, always to an enthusiastic crowd, though they still appeared every Friday at the Taj Mahal. For the first time, Lachlan regretted signing a contract with Billy Kidd when the Beatles acquired a young, enterprising manager, Brian Epstein, who put the four untidy young men through a startling transformation. They had their hair cut, wore suits, tidied up their act, and emerged more charismatic than they'd been before.

'Billy hasn't a clue about presentation or promotion,' Lachlan complained to the others.

They all agreed that Billy wasn't up to handling a rock 'n' roll group. He was lazy, had no imagination, and wouldn't know how to get them on the wireless, as Brian Epstein had done with the Beatles. They also agreed, ruefully, that it was a bit late to realise that now.

In May, a Granada television crew descended on the city to make a programme, *Outside the Cavern*, about the other Liverpool beat clubs. An excited Billy broke the news that the Taj Mahal would be included and the Merseysiders, one of the most popular local groups, would play on the night.

When Kevin McDowd heard, he immediately paid Billy Kidd a visit.

'Not you again!' Billy groaned when Kevin captured him in the bar of the Taj Mahal, his head buried in the *Racing Times*. 'If you've come about your bloody girl group, then you've had it. They're not going on and that's final. Me club would become a laughing stock.'

Kevin glanced at the newspaper. 'Y'know, Billy, I'd never have taken you for a gambling man. It requires nerve and more than a bit of courage to have a wee flutter on the horsies now'n again.'

'I've got nerve, I've got courage,' Billy blustered. 'I have a flutter most days, not a wee one, either.'

'In that case, I bet you twenty-five quid that the Flower Girls won't raise even the suggestion of a giggle if they play at your lovely club.' Kevin's face almost cracked in two as he gave his most charming, ruthlessly persuasive smile. 'And this is a wager you can't lose, Billy, because if some rude, heartless soul dares to take a breath that sounds remotely like a titter, then you'll be up twenty-five quid. And if no one does? Well, I won't want a penny off you. So, you see, Billy, you can't lose, and it shows how much con-fidence I have in my four, wee girls.'

Billy considered this. The mad Irishman was

218

right. He couldn't lose. He was getting an act for free, and all he had to do was persuade one of his regulars to emit a little laugh during the girls' performance and he would be in receipt of twenty-five smackeroos. The club's reputation wouldn't be harmed by a duff act. There'd been duff acts before, all clubs had them occasionally, including the Cavern.

'All right,' he said. 'How about a week Monday?'

'That won't do, Billy boy. I'd prefer me wee girls went on two weeks on Tuesday.'

'But that's the night the television's coming!'

'I know that, Billy, but they're coming for the lads, not the girls. What difference will it make?'

Billy gnawed his fat lips. 'Make it fifty, and you can come two weeks Tuesday.'

'Done!' If someone laughed, and Kevin didn't doubt Billy would make sure someone did, he didn't have fifty bob, let alone fifty quid, to settle the bet. But he'd cross that bridge when he came to it.

The Flower Girls worked themselves up into a state of desperate hysteria when he informed them they had a gig at last, even Rita, usually so calm about everything.

'And isn't it what we've been working towards all these last months?' Kevin said impatiently.

'Yes, but the television will be there,' Marcia cried.

'Don't worry, they won't be interested in youse lot,' Kevin lied. They would if he had anything to do with it.

The Merseysiders couldn't afford to buy suits, but on the night Granada television came to the Taj Mahal, they had their hair cut and wore black trousers and identical dark blue shirts. At the start of the evening, they hung around at the back of the room beside the camera that had been set up earlier – the Granada guys were in the bar having a drink. Normally, they too would have waited in the bar until the first act had finished, but wouldn't have missed tonight's first act for anything.

Apart from Sean, whose trust in his father's judgement was implicit, the others had little faith that the Flower Girls would do well, if only because they were girls. Rock 'n' roll and women didn't go together.

'The world isn't ready for this yet,' Lachlan muttered. He was worried for Jeannie, who would be devastated if she made a show of herself. He wasn't bothered for his sister. Marcia made a show of herself almost every day.

'The world never will be.' Max chewed his nails and wished Kevin McDowd hadn't come back from wherever he'd been and involved Jeannie in a stupid group that was bound to fail.

Fly Fleming expressed the wish he would faint. 'If I do, just leave me on the floor until it's all over.'

Others in the audience were on tenterhooks as they waited for the girls to appear; Elaine, a few pupils from Orrell Park Grammar, Alex Connors, and Marcia's boyfriend, Graham, who rather hoped they'd be dead hopeless and Marcia would at last agree to marry him. All the parents, apart from Kevin McDowd, had been strictly banned and left to worry at home.

The atmosphere in the Taj Mahal was already electric with excitement when the lights went out and, for a while, the room was in total darkness, until the rotund figure of Billy Kidd appeared under a single spotlight. Tonight, Billy announced, his club, not for the first time, was at the forefront of the entertainment scene. Not only was there a television camera present, but the audience was in for a rare treat. 'One of these days you'll tell your grandkids you were there the night this group first played in public. Ladies and Gentleman...' He paused dramatically, '...the Flower Girls.'

The spotlight went out and from the darkness came the sound of a piano, just single notes, playing the first lines of an Elvis Presley number, 'Don't Be Cruel'.

Then the piano stopped and the lights over the stage came on. For a few seconds, the Flower Girls, in their dazzling red frocks remained perfectly still; Rita centre stage, holding her guitar, Benny and Marcia behind, heads bent, legs slightly apart, and Jeannie at the side poised over the piano. Then all four looked up, smiled, and the stage exploded into sound.

'Don't be cruel, to the one you love,' Rita sang, while Jeannie's hands danced over the keys, and the other girls moved together with precise, hypnotic symmetry.

The audience, accustomed to groups being introduced and stumbling in full view on to the stage, tripping over wires, fiddling with their instruments while they talked amongst themselves before deigning to play a note, were stunned by this display of naked professionalism. This was show business for real. They gasped and burst into spontaneous applause.

That'll do me wee girls a load of good, thought Kevin McDowd, watching from the back. They'd all been nervous, but the little show of appreciation would give them the confidence they needed. He glanced sideways. The Merseysiders, even Sean, looked pole-axed, their mouths hanging open in surprise. He hoped Billy, wherever he was, looked the same, and realised that, so far, not a single soul had laughed.

Kevin waited until the girls had delivered another number, 'Here Comes Summer', and were halfway through the next, before making his way upstairs to the bar, where the only occupants were the barman and the two boyos from Granada, one young and red-haired, the other in his forties.

He bought a box of matches and was on the point of leaving, when he stopped, his face a mask of astonishment that only his wife would have recognised was faked. 'Aren't you the fellas from the television?'

The younger man nodded. 'I'm the reporter, Ricky Perry. That's George, he's camera.'

Kevin shook his head in a mixture of sadness and bemusement. He was dealing with fools, the look said. 'Don't you realise history's being made downstairs?'

'I don't get you, mate,' said George.

'You should be down there, recording it for posterity.'

'Recording what?' demanded Ricky Perry.

'The debut performance of the first all-girl rock 'n' roll group in the country, that's what. The press is there, two of 'em, taking notes. I tell you what, fellas, you'll kick yourselves for the rest of your lives if you don't get them girls on film.'

'What are they called?' Ricky got out his notebook.

'The Flower Girls. Anyroad, I'd better be getting back. I only came for these.' He held up the matches. 'I don't want to miss another minute.'

Downstairs again, Kevin threw the matches away and held his breath. Had the boyos swallowed the hook? His girls had done another number for the spellbound audience when the two men strolled in during a rousing version of 'Be-Bop-a-Lula'. A few minutes later, Ricky Perry was scribbling madly in his notebook and the camera was rolling.

The Flower Girls were being filmed and Kevin had no doubt that some discriminating, far-sighted editor would make sure there'd be a few clips of their performance when the programme was aired, though no one seemed to know when that would be.

After the interval, it was the turn of the Merseysiders. The lads played for all their worth and congratulated themselves afterwards. They also had no doubts that their performance would be noticed and stardom awaited.

Over the next few weeks, numerous families

throughout Liverpool scanned the *TV Times* the minute it came out in the hope that *Outside the Cavern* would be shown that week, but found themselves sadly disappointed.

The Flower Girls received a glowing write up in the *Liverpool Echo* but, although Kevin toured the local clubs, waving the review, not a single gig was forthcoming. Even Billy Kidd refused to give the group another booking. He was more than a little annoyed with Kevin McDowd. In some way, he wasn't quite sure how, he'd been outsmarted and done out of fifty quid.

'But they were bloody phenomenal,' Kevin screamed. 'The audience loved them. You're an eejit, Billy?'

'They're a one-off act,' Billy maintained stiffly. 'A novelty. No one'd come to see them a second time. One performance and they've lost their surprise value.'

'The only surprise is women that can play rock 'n' roll as well as men.

In June, Jeannie and Bennie took their O levels and a Careers Officer came to the school to discuss what they intended doing with their lives. They were interviewed separately.

'I'm going into show business,' Benny announced when her turn came.

The smartly dressed woman smiled kindly. 'It's what many young people want to do, but it's not a very secure career, unless you become a star.'

Benny proudly tossed her head. 'I already belong to a group.'

'Really! Does it pay well?'

'Well, no.' The group had cost more than it had made, a simple deduction, because it hadn't made a penny. Sean had bought Rita her guitar, Jeannie had been given the piano, the red, sequinned dresses had been hired and returned to the costumier the next day.

'Perhaps it wouldn't be a bad idea to have a second career in reserve,' the woman suggested tactfully. 'Something you can fall back on if things don't go as planned.'

Benny sighed. Like all the Flower Girls, she'd been sadly disappointed by the lack of response following their performance at the Taj Mahal where they seemed to do so well. The audience had shouted for more and everyone had said they were fantastic.

'That's showbiz, kids,' Kevin had said only the other day. 'It's a case of one step forward and two steps back. You'll have to learn to get used to it.'

The trouble was Benny couldn't afford the time. In a few weeks, she would be leaving school and be obliged to start work. It was the moment her mother had worked towards over the last five years. Mam was due for a rest from her never-ending toil. Working wouldn't prevent Benny from staying with the group, but Kevin often spoke of the day when she and Jeannie left school and he could look for gigs in other places, even London. She couldn't ask for days off from a job she'd only just started. It was different for Rita, who could easily get another waitressing job, and Marcia never worked anywhere for more than five minutes. Jeannie had no idea what she was going to do.

'Me mother's always wanted me to work for the Civil Service,' Benny said listlessly.

'I can arrange for you to sit the exam. I'll submit your name, shall I?

'I suppose so.'

They still rehearsed regularly. Kevin maintained they had to keep fresh, something might turn up any minute, but the spark had gone and even Kevin was beginning to look disheartened. One Sunday afternoon, Marcia didn't come and sent a blunt message, saying she had more important things to do. It was the first time all four girls hadn't turned up.

July came and Jeannie and Benny left school. Benny had already taken the Civil Service exam and passed – she wasn't sure whether to be glad or sorry. She was offered a job as a clerk with the Inland Revenue in Water Street, with the agreement she have one afternoon a week off to learn shorthand and typing.

'It means extra money when I get the qualifications,' she told her ecstatic mother. At least someone's dreams had come true, she thought despondently.

Jeannie's long-term future had already been decided. As soon as the Merseysiders achieved success, she and Lachlan would get married. It was just a matter of filling in time until the longed-for and inevitable day arrived. In September, she was commencing a six-month commercial course.

During the summer holiday, she met Elaine most days. If it was raining, they went to the pictures, or New Brighton or Southport if it was fine. The nights Lachlan wasn't playing, he and Jeannie would shut themselves in Dr Bailey's waiting room, or Lachlan would come to Ailsham and they'd go for a walk through the village that always looked especially lovely because she was linking his arm.

The O level results arrived. Elaine had achieved six A grades, Jeannie a B and four C's, little better than Benny who got five C's, and should have been thrilled to bits, but was the opposite when they met her on Friday in the Taj Mahal.

'I would have been pleased, once, but now I don't care any more,' Benny said bitterly. 'Me job's as dull as ditchwater. I'm so bored, I ache all over. I can't stop thinking about the Flower Girls, how different it would have been if...' She shrugged, unable to go on. Her eyes were as bitter as her voice.

'We're all a bit fed up about it,' Jeannie said.

'I'm more than a bit. I feel like killing meself, if you must know. You've got Lachlan, so what do you care? Marcia's got Graham, and Rita can sing anywhere. It's not over for her, but it is for me.' She got up abruptly. 'I'm going home. I don't want to see any of you ever again.'

'Where are we now?' Rose whispered.

'Paris,' Alex said in her ear. 'We're on the banks of the Seine and there's an orchestra playing 'specially for us.'

'Is it light or dark?'

'Dark. The moon's a little yellow curve, like a slice of lemon.'

'Are there any stars?'

'Millions,' said Alex. 'Millions and millions of stars. If you close your eyes, you can see them.'

'My eyes are closed and I can already see them. I can see everything, even us.'

'What are we doing?'

'Just dancing.'

'Not kissing?'

Rose, eyes still closed, shook her head.

'Well, we are now!' His lips came down on hers, hard and passionate, demanding. They stopped dancing and everything inside her body seemed to melt as she kissed him back, then collapsed against him, helpless with desire. He lifted her up and carried her over to the bed in the rather ordinary Liverpool hotel room and they made love, On the rather crackly wireless, the Everley Brothers were singing 'All I Have to Do is Dream.'

'Is this just a game too?' Rose asked when they'd finished. Now her body felt as light as air, completely empty. They lay flat on their backs, not touching, exhausted.

Alex turned on to his side, resting his chin on her shoulder, his hand on her stomach. 'Is it a game to you?'

'I don't know,' Rose said truthfully. 'I don't know if it's make believe or real.' They always pretended they were somewhere else, never Liverpool: a South Sea Island, dancing on the flat golden sands while palm trees swayed gently in the warm breeze; a night club in New York; a London park; a luxury liner on its way to who knows where? Today it had been Paris, on the banks of the Seine.

'It's real all right.' Alex kissed her. 'So real, I'm not sure if I can stand seeing you only once a week for much longer.'

Neither could Rose. She thought about him every minute of every day, living for Thursdays when they could be together. 'I think we should just go on playing the game,' she said nevertheless. 'I can't see any alternative.'

'You know the alternative,' he said gruffly. 'You're just not prepared to consider it.'

Rose shuddered. 'I couldn't leave Tom and the children.' She'd thought about it though.

'The last thing I want to do is hurt Iris and me lads, but there comes a time when you have to put yourself first.' He had another son, Carl, two years younger than Ronnie.

'Does there? If we were together all the time...' – Had she really said that? – '...the games would have to stop. It would be different,' she said, indicating the bed, 'being able to do this every day.' It would be heaven and she knew it. 'We'd have to live somewhere, an ordinary house. You'd go to work, I'd make the meals, do the washing.' For some inexplicable reason, she began to cry because it was what she wanted more than anything in the world, yet it seemed impossible. Too many people would be hurt.

Alex kissed the tears away. 'I love you.'

'I love you too,' she sobbed. 'But *why* do we love each other?'

'We just do. Do we need to know why?'

'Yes. I think you fell in love with me because you're so unhappy. You're searching for things, a different life. You've always wanted something different. Iris and the boys were never enough. You dress funny and go to clubs, wander round town and pick up women outside cinemas. Having an affair's right up your street – romantic and dramatic and exciting... Oh! How many affairs have you had before?' she demanded, suspicious now. She'd die if she discovered she wasn't the first.

'None,' Alex said flatly. 'And you're the one and only woman I've ever picked up, though you couldn't exactly call it picking up when we'd met before. Now listen while I tell you why you fell in love with me.' Rose curled up against his lean, naked body and listened. 'Because,' he began, 'you married an old man...'

'He wasn't *that* old!' she protested.

'OK, so you married a man much older than yourself. You've never loved him, but he made you more or less happy. Then your kids started growing up, and all of a sudden it dawned on you what you've missed. This!' He ran his hand over the curve of her hip. 'And this!' He kissed her breast. 'Love and sex. Sex and love. So, one day you pick up this gorgeous guy outside a cinema. He fancies you. You fancy him. After a few weeks, you go to bed together and it's bloody marvellous.' His brown eyes creased with wonder. 'More than marvellous,' he gasped. 'Words haven't been invented to describe it. The thing is, Rose, more or less any decent guy would have done.'

'That's not true,' she cried, shocked. 'I love *you!*'

'And I love *you*. We were both ripe for affairs, Rose. But once that fact is put aside, the truth is that we both love each other. I didn't want it to happen. I didn't expect it to. It's a miracle. I want to spend the rest of my life with you.'

Rose was silent. Every word he'd said was true. She had no idea how it had happened that she was able to contemplate leaving her family, her home, everything, for Alex Connors, whom she'd known for only four months, met for merely a few hours every week. As he said, it was a miracle.

'I wish we'd met twenty years ago.' She sighed.

'Twenty years ago I was in Egypt in the Army.'

She clutched him fiercely. 'Thank God you weren't killed!'

'Perhaps He was saving me for you.'

'How was Clara?' Tom asked when she got home. He always asked and it always threw her.

'Not very well. In fact, Tom, I wondered if you'd mind if I went to stay with her one weekend? Her husband's going away soon and he's worried about leaving her on her own. It'd be a little holiday for me. I've never had a holiday,' she reminded him, thinking what a hopeless actress she was. Even to her own ears, it sounded like a lie, but Alex had suggested they try to have a few days away together. They had agreed it would be bliss.

'I wouldn't mind, no, but leave Clara's telephone number when you go, 'case there's an emergency.'

'She isn't on the phone.'

231

Tom's brow creased. 'That's surprising, considering her husband has his own business.'

Rose attempted to get her wits together before answering. 'I never said her husband had his own business,' she said carefully.

'Didn't you, love?' He slapped his knee and she jumped. 'It must have been Mrs Denning, you know, the colonel's housekeeper. She remembers Clara well. I happened to mention you two had met.'

Wings of panic began to beat wildly inside Rose's head. She should have made someone up, not used a real person. Clara Baker might no longer be living in Hoylake. She could be anywhere in the world by now, possibly writing to someone in the village. It hadn't crossed her mind that Tom would check up on her – she had no doubt that's what he'd done. The panic was replaced by anger. Trust him! He still thought he owned her.

'Then Mrs Denning's wrong,' she said in a cool voice. 'Peter Baker might have had his own business once, but now he's a teacher. That's why they moved to Hoylake.' She was sinking deeper and deeper into a mire of lies, but didn't care. Perhaps she was doing it deliberately. The deeper she got, the closer the day would come when she would be found out and feel obliged to leave. Then she and Alex would be together for always.

'I'm still surprised they're not on the phone,' Tom said.

It was mid-August when the *TV Times* announced that *Outside the Cavern* was being

232

screened on Wednesday, next week. The boys were delirious with excitement. Jeannie rang Marcia and asked what they should do about Benny? 'You never know, they might show a glimpse of the Flower Girls. We should tell her the programme's on.'

'To hell with Benny,' Marcia said crisply. 'Elaine told me the way she behaved. Anyroad, I bet she hasn't got a television.'

'She'll know people who do – she could come to your house.'

'Over my dead body. I should forget about Benny if I were you.'

It was decided that everyone connected with the programme should watch it together and the Baileys' was the obvious place. On Wednesday night, the living room was arranged like a cinema, with chairs from the waiting room brought up and arranged in rows. The terrible trio, who were quite big by now, bagged the front row, in front of their mother and father and Sadie and Kevin McDowd. Elaine, Fly, Max, Rita, and Sean sat behind, and Marcia and Graham shared the back row with Lachlan and Jeannie. It was a hot, muggy, airless night and the windows were wide open.

'I should have bought ice creams,' Mrs Bailey remarked. 'I would have done a roaring trade during the interval.'

The programme started with shots of Liverpool; the Liver Buildings, St George's Hall, the Protestant cathedral, still unfinished, then the exterior of the Cavern. Ricky Perry, the young reporter Kevin had spoken to, was outside. 'This isn't the only place in Merseyside where rock 'n' roll thrives, folks. Other clubs are also doing their bit to spread the word. The first club on tonight's schedule is the Mardi Gras.'

The camera switched to the interior of the Mardi Gras where five young men they'd never heard of were playing a strained version of 'Blue Suede Shoes,' followed by a tuneless composition of their own.

'They're useless,' Max shouted.

The group was heard out in disdainful silence until Ricky Perry reappeared and announced they were now about to visit the Iron Door. A well-known local group, Ian and the Zodiacs, belted out their own foot-tapping versions of two Bill Haley numbers.

An interval followed and Mrs Bailey went downstairs to put the kettle on, returning just in time for a visit to the Blue Angel and another Liverpool group.

'We must be last,' Lachlan groaned. He was tightly clutching Jeannie's hand.

'They always save the best for last,' Kevin McDowd remarked sagely.

Ricky Perry was back again. 'Finally, the Taj Mahal, once, like the Cavern, a venue for great jazz, now converted to great rock 'n' roll. I wasn't expecting any surprises when I dropped in at the Taj Mahal, but I certainly got one. A really big, very pleasant surprise.' He winked. 'Just watch, folks. You're in for a treat.'

Everyone gasped when the Flower Girls appeared on screen halfway through 'Be-Bop-a-Lula'.

Kevin jumped to his feet, waving his arms. 'Jaysus! If it isn't me wee girls!'

'Shurrup.' Sadie yanked him back on to the chair.

It was a strange experience, watching herself play the piano. Jeannie hadn't realised that her entire body jiggled in time to the music, that for most of the time she was half off the seat, and her feet, not just her hands, were never still.

Rita's voice seemed too powerful to come from her tiny, waif-like body. There was something fascinating about the way she remained quite still, like Sean, when she sang, even during the fast numbers .

We're good, Jeannie thought. Marcia and Benny moved perfectly together, though Benny was a little bit wooden. Marcia's body was more attuned to the music and it showed. She was clearly enjoying every minute.

The song finished, the audience applauded. Rita began to sing 'Will You still Love Me Tomorrow'. Now the camera zoomed in on Rita's face, Jeannie's hands, someone's feet – Marcia or Benny's. It moved slowly backwards until the four girls filled the screen, until the backs of the rapt audience came into view.

More applause, louder this time. A voice over – Ricky Perry's – 'Now, how does this song grab you, folks?' and the Flower Girls were still there, and Rita was singing 'Moon Under Water'.

Jeannie was getting anxious. The girls had had more exposure than any other group. There wasn't much time left for the Merseysiders.

Ricky Perry came back, saying incredibly

flattering things about the new girl group, wondering if they'd start a trend, while the finishing titles slowly moved up the screen. No one in the Baileys' living room spoke until the producer's name appeared and it became obvious the programme was over.

'They didn't show *us*,' said Lachlan in an appalled voice.

Early next afternoon, Billy Kidd unlocked the door of the Taj Mahal and found Kevin McDowd sitting on his stairs.

'How did you get there?' he gasped. He'd been seriously narked the night before when his group, the Merseysiders, had been sidelined by McDowd's wee girls.

'The cleaner let me in,' Kevin snarled. 'Did it not cross your moronic mind that there'd be a crumb of response from last night's programme and your club's the only place people could contact? The phone in your office has been ringing all morning, but I couldn't answer it because the cleaner refused to leave the key. She'd have thrown me out altogether, except she didn't have the strength.' The phone rang again. 'Answer it, man,' Kevin said curtly. 'It's probably Hollywood, wanting me girls to make a film.'

Billy discovered a sense of urgency and raced up the two flights of stairs. His club would benefit from any subsequent publicity, even if his group didn't, The phone stopped the minute the door was unlocked. Kevin stared at the instrument, willing it to ring again. It did. A club in Manchester wanted to book the Flower Girls for a gig on Saturday.

'We'll be there,' Kevin promised recklessly. He called Jeannie and demanded she alert Marcia and Benny. 'Tell them to come to the barn tonight straight after work.' Rita would have to take tomorrow and Saturday off, pretend to be sick. The girls hadn't performed together for almost a month. They'd need the next few days to get back into shape and learn a couple of the new songs he'd written. He'd scarcely replaced the receiver when the phone rang again, and continued to do so for the remainder of the afternoon. People wanted to book gigs, arrange interviews, take the girls' photos. Most importantly of all, M&M called, a record company, requesting that they come for an audition in London on Monday next. A recording contract might be on the cards.

'Let us know what time you'll be arriving, and there'll be a car waiting at Euston station.'

'I will indeed.' Kevin was beginning to feel more than a little drunk. Never, in his wildest dreams, had he expected such an outcome. It was too bad about the Merseysiders, but he had no doubt they'd make it someday.

Marcia was easily found. She was working in a florists and, when Jeannie called and told her about the urgent need to prepare for the gig on Saturday, she left on the spot.

'The manager will be annoyed, but his breath smells,' she said, as if this was sufficient reason to leave the man in the lurch.

'Is it a personal call?' the woman on the

237

switchboard enquired when Jeannie phoned the Inland Revenue in Water Street and asked to speak to Miss Benedicta Lucas.

'Yes.'

'I'm afraid staff aren't allowed personal calls. Sorry.'

Jeannie went into the garden and found her mother in a deck chair staring into space. She explained she was about to go to Bootle. 'Benny said she wanted nothing to do with us again, but she probably didn't mean it. She'll be thrilled with the news. I'll tell her mum if she's in and I'll leave a note for Benny in case she's not. I'll write it now, just in case. Gosh! I wish it weren't so hot.'

'Tell Benny what, love?' her mother asked absently.

'About the gig on Saturday. Kevin McDowd rang. Remember? It's all because of that programme last night.'

'Oh, yes.' The blue eyes lit up, as if she'd only just become aware her daughter was there. 'You were wonderful, love. I'm ever so proud.'

'Are you all right, Mum?' Jeannie asked worriedly. Her mother might be physically present, but lately her mind seemed to be miles away. She was becoming increasingly forgetful.

'I'm fine, Jeannie. Absolutely fine.' The radiant smile that followed should have been enough to convince anyone that Rose Flowers couldn't possibly have been better. Yet it only worried Jeannie more. She wrote a note for Benny and, while waiting for the bus, wondered what possible reason her mother could have for looking so ecstatically happy?

She decided not to let it bother her. There were enough *un*happy people to worry about at the moment – the Merseysiders. Fly Fleming and Sean McDowd seemed quite laid back about things, but Lachlan and Max were desolate. They'd expected last night to be a turning point in their careers.

'That was a total wash-out,' Max had groaned when his dazed brain was able to accept the fact that *Outside the Cavern* had ended and the Merseysiders hadn't even been given a mention.

'You wouldn't say that if you'd have been on and not us,' a jubilant Marcia pointed out.

'You weren't supposed to be on. It should have been us.'

'Who ses?' Marcia argued. 'That Ricky Perry chap obviously decided we were the best.'

Mrs Bailey thought tempers would be calmed with a cup of tea and insisted Marcia help. 'You're only making things worse, dear.'

Lachlan was gazing moodily at his feet, no longer holding Jeannie's hand.

'I'm sorry,' she whispered.

'Not as sorry as I am,' he said bitterly. 'D'you know what, Jeannie? I'm jealous, jealous of my own girlfriend.'

'That's only natural,' she said soothingly.

'Would you have been jealous if it had been the other way around?'

'No, but only because I didn't expect they'd show us.' If she was Lachlan, she'd be spitting tacks. It had been a tremendous thrill seeing the Flower Girls on national television. She wouldn't have missed it for the world, even though it had made the man she loved intensely miserable. It would have been best if they'd shared the time, then everybody would have been happy.

In Grenville Street, two boys in swimming trunks were playing on their bikes, and an elderly lady sunbathed sleepily on her doorstep. After knocking twice on the Lucas's front door and receiving no response, Jeannie slipped the note through the letter box and made her way home. Her fingers were itching to get back to the piano, sadly neglected during the summer holidays.

Mrs Lucas crept into the hall and picked up the folded piece of paper. She'd recognised her daughter's friend when she peeked through the parlour curtains, but hadn't opened the door. She'd smelt danger. And she'd been right to, she thought, when she read the neatly written message.

Dear Benny,

You may not know this, but the Flower Girls were on television last night. As a result, we've been offered a gig in Manchester on Saturday. We're meeting in the barn tonight; come as soon as you possibly can. We have to rehearse like mad over the next few days.

See you later, Benny.
Jeannie.

Mrs Lucas felt her blood run cold. Benedicta was

nicely settled in her important job, bringing home good money. That singing thing she'd been involved with had terrified her mother. It wasn't what ordinary people did and she'd been too ashamed to mention it to a soul. Now, she told everyone she met that her Benedicta worked for the Civil Service and was studying for qualifications.

She read the letter again. 'We have to rehearse like mad over the next few days.' Tomorrow was Friday, Benedicta was due in work, and Mrs Lucas wasn't quite sure which she would put first – singing or her job!

'It's not fair,' she muttered aloud. Poor Benedicta would be torn in two, wondering which to choose, not wanting to let her friends down, yet knowing her job was more important.

'I'll save her the bother of picking one or the other.' Mrs Lucas felt quite virtuous as she tore the paper into several pieces, took it into the yard, and flushed it down the lavatory.

By nine o'clock that night, it became obvious Benny wasn't coming. Having heard the rest of Kevin's news, the girls were too manic with excitement to care. Marcia flitted to and fro behind Rita, pretending to be two people and making a desperate show of herself 'We'll have to get someone else,' she told Kevin.

'Do you think I don't already know that!' There were theatrical agencies in Liverpool. Tomorrow, early, he'd ring one and ask for a fourth girl straight away. Someone tall and skinny, at least five feet eight, pretty, and an experienced dancer

241

who'd learn the moves in a jiffy.

The girl arrived at midday, having caught a taxi all the way from Allerton to Ailsham, she explained breathlessly. 'I saw that programme last night on the telly, and I said to me ma just before I left, "I'm going to be a Flower Girl, Ma." So she emptied the gas and electricity meters in order to scrape the fare together for a taxi. "You'll melt on public transport," she said. "It's like an oven out there." Me name's Zoe Streeter, by the way. Well, it's not really Zoe. I was christened Doris, but Zoe is me stage name.' She was even more breathless now than when she'd begun. 'Here I am, ready, willing and able, as they say,' she added slightly belligerently in view of the four faces that regarded her with more than a little astonishment.

Zoe Streeter was more beautiful than pretty. Tall and slender, with a dancer's grace, her perfectly shaped head was supported by a long, stem-like neck, and her skin had a marble sheen. Great dark eyes glistened above the elegantly moulded cheekbones that Jeannie, for one, would have given her eye-teeth for.

'You're black!' exclaimed Marcia.

'Thanks for telling me.' Zoe tossed her head. 'I'd already noticed that meself.'

At first, Kevin had wondered how to get rid of the girl and do it kindly, but then he decided a black Flower Girl could only enhance the group, making an attractive, if not startling, contrast to the fair- haired, light-skinned Marcia. 'Have you done much in the way of professional dancing, luv?' he enquired.

'I've danced at the Moulin Rouge in Paris, the London Palladium, the Windmill, only in the chorus up to now.'

As she only looked about eighteen, Kevin was inclined to take this with a pinch of salt. He didn't bother to ask what such an experienced dancer was doing in Liverpool. 'I'll show you what to do in a minute. What I want is someone who can learn fast. Did the agency explain we've got half a dozen gigs lined up, as well as an audition with M&M on Monday? Can you sing?'

'She doesn't have to sing, only hum,' said Marcia.

'I'm great at humming,' the girl said stoutly. 'I'm not too bad at singing, either.'

She picked up the moves in no time, adding a few suggestions of her own. Kevin was relieved that Marcia, normally an awkward customer, didn't seem to mind being taught some fresh steps by the sparkling newcomer, who had a great sense of rhythm and genuine stage presence. When it was time to leave, he rubbed his hands together gleefully, glad Benny hadn't turned up. Until now, he'd considered Rita and Jeannie the only vital members of the group. The two other girls weren't really necessary, just a bit of decoration. Zoe had only been there a few hours, but already he couldn't imagine the group without her. She was the final piece of the jigsaw puzzle, fitting in perfectly, bringing out the best in Marcia.

Now the Flower Girls really were a group of four.

The Manchester gig went like a dream, despite a few catcalls amongst the cheers when the Flower Girls first appeared on the tiny stage. There were tears in Kevin's eyes as he watched his wee girls perform. He'd made it at last, though not quite in the way he'd always imagined. The group were his creation. He knew in his bones that they would become stars and he could stop borrowing off Sadie. The same red sequinned dresses they'd worn at the Taj Mahal had been hired again and it was Sadie, bless her, who'd paid. They'd need proper transport to get them around. Marcia, who could drive, had borrowed her dad's car to bring them to Manchester and Kevin wasn't too sure if she'd asked permission. He just hoped Dr Bailey wasn't called out urgently.

Soon, they'd have a whole wardrobe full of costumes, and one of them vans with seats to cart them around. Kevin would never buy a Burton's suit again. Instead, he'd have them made in Savile Row, shirts an' all, silk ones. As for his darlin' wife, she'd have the biggest, fluffiest, most expensive fur coat money could buy, and the owner of number one Disraeli Terrace could have his disgusting property back. The McDowds would live in a mansion, *two* mansions – one in Liverpool, the other in London – and he'd buy a pretty cottage somewhere in Ireland. Oh, and he'd start going to Mass again, thank the Lord for his good fortune.

On the way home, he gave the exultant girls ten pounds each. 'It's your share of the fifty-quid performance fee. I've kept ten for meself, twenty per cent, for being your manager.'

'Max said Billy only gives them a pound whenever they play a gig,' Jeannie remarked.

Kevin was outraged. 'Our Sean never said anything. It's time the lads had a word with Billy Kidd,' he snorted. 'He spends too much money on the horsies.' He told the girls to be at the barn by ten o'clock sharp next morning to prepare for Monday's audition. 'How you sound will matter more than the way you look. We'll concentrate on the vocals and the music. I want more input from Marcia and Zoe.'

Zoe gave an ecstatic sigh. 'I'm not half glad I lost me digs in London and came back to Liverpool, completely skint. I wouldn't have missed this for anything.'

The car that waited for them at Euston Station was long, black, and luxurious, and the leather seats squeaked expensively. The peak-capped driver leapt out and carefully placed Jeannie's folding piano in the boot. Rita preferred to hold on to her guitar. They glided through streets that Zoe knew well. She pointed out the various sights – the British Museum, Covent Garden, the Strand. Kevin's relationship with London hadn't covered the West End.

They eventually stopped in a quiet side street off the Embankment. The driver helped them out and showed them into a tall plain building with a vast reception area and a female receptionist, dwarfed behind her big, curved desk. Their footsteps were muffled in the velvety thickness of the grey carpet. The doors of a lift opened, a man entered, and the doors closed with scarcely a sound.

'I've an appointment with Murray Stubbs.' Kevin's normally loud, chirpy voice had been reduced to a whisper. 'Please,' he added unnecessarily.

'Sit down,' the receptionist told them in a voice like cut glass, 'and I'll let him know you're here.'

No one spoke while they waited. Although the heat outside remained oppressive, inside it was unnaturally cool – and unnaturally quiet. Jeannie shivered. She'd been looking forward to the audition, but suddenly felt very nervous. Marcia seemed subdued, Zoe less so. Rita, as ever, showed no emotion. She wore one of her little girl frocks and her eyes were hidden behind a fringe of thick, brown hair.

Murray Stubbs arrived, a smooth young man with owlish spectacles, wearing a smart draped suit.

'Did you have a good journey?' he asked, but didn't wait for a reply. 'The studio's on the third floor.'

They followed him towards one of the soundless lifts. Jeannie felt as if she was entering a coffin. The lift soared upwards and her stomach did a sickly somersault.

'Bloody hell!' Marcia gasped, when they emerged into a long, grey corridor. 'I've left me insides on the ground floor.'

The studio was as quiet as a grave. Murray Stubbs went away and a young man in shirt-sleeves came and plugged in Jeannie's piano, then attached Rita's guitar to an amplifier. Rita,

Marcia, and Zoe stationed themselves behind the microphones, and the young man said, 'Whenever you're ready!' He went through a door and reappeared behind a glass panel from where he made a thumbs up sign.

Kevin had managed to take a few steps inside the studio, but ever since had remained frozen to the spot. 'Well, girls, you know what to do,' he mumbled. 'Walk On By', then 'Rock-A-Hula Baby'.

'I think you're supposed to leave, Dad,' Rita told him.

'Oh, yes!' He still didn't move.

'In there.' Rita pointed to the door the young man had used, and seconds later, Kevin's white face was watching them through the glass.

Jeannie stared fixedly at the keyboard and felt total panic. *She couldn't remember where to put her hands!* Which note was C? Where was A? Had she played 'Walk On By' before?

Suddenly, the door was flung open and Kevin stormed in. His sparse hair stood on end and his eyes blazed with feverish excitement. 'I've been in a daze,' he roared. 'But now I'm all right again. You're me wee girls and you're going to take the world by storm. You're going to perform like you've never performed before. In a minute, this whole building's going to rock. The lifts will stop. That Murray boyo's glasses will shatter into a million little pieces. The whole of London will grind to a halt, all due to you four girls. Now, I'm going back in there,' he pointed to the door he'd just sprung out of, 'and I'm going to clap me hands like a maniac.' He clapped his hands three times and everyone jumped. 'You won't hear, but you'll see. When I clap a third time, it's a signal to begin. And remember this, me wee girlies, me body might be behind that piece of old glass, but I'm leaving me heart and soul with youse lot.' He made a quick Sign of the Cross. 'So, good luck to all o'yis. I know you'll do your best.'

And they did!

Chapter 9

'It's not fair.' Max said sulkily. 'It's five years since the Merseysiders first got together. The Flower Girls haven't been around five minutes, yet you've already got a recording contract and do gigs all over the place. Trust you to fall on your feet.'

'Does Lachlan think it's unfair?' Jeannie asked. It was show business, not unfairness, but she didn't bother to point this out when Max was in one of his dark moods.

'He hasn't said anything.' Max kicked the chair with his heels, something he'd done since he was a little boy. They were having breakfast in Disraeli Terrace. Gerald had gone to school, their parents to work. 'It wouldn't be so bad,' Max continued plaintively, 'if it was something you'd really *wanted* to do. You used to think it was all a joke. If I hadn't asked you to play that night in the Cavern, it'd never have happened.'

'How would you know what I wanted to do? Unlike you, I didn't shout it from the rooftops. Perhaps you'd have done better with a manager like Kevin,' she said smugly. 'By the way, there's something I've been meaning to say for ages.' She told him it was Kevin's opinion Billy Kidd wasn't paying them nearly enough. 'I'd have it out with him if I were you.'

The Post Office was particularly busy that morning. A couple wanted forty-eight-hour passports and it took Rose ages to fill in the details. She did her utmost to keep her mind on her work. It was necessary to concentrate to the exclusion of all else when dealing with money. Twice she'd given the wrong change. Fortunately, no one had noticed apart from the customers concerned. She was thankful when the small queue at her cubicle came to a temporary end and it became one of those rare times when the entire shop was empty. Mrs Harker announced she was going to make them a cup of tea and Rose relaxed. But not for long. She drew the envelope that had come that morning out of her pocket. It was postmarked Ailsham, and her name and address had been printed in big, bold letters with a black felt pen, as had the four-word message the envelope held.

CLARA BAKER IS DEAD.

Tom was the only person who could have sent it. On the days she met 'Clara' he would bombard her with questions when she got home. 'How was Clara today?' 'Does Clara work?' 'Has she got children?' 'And what did Clara eat?' he'd ask when she'd say they'd had a meal. She'd found it very odd, almost sinister.

Was Clara dead? How could she find out? Months ago, she'd looked in the telephone book and there'd been two P. Bakers in Hoylake. She had no idea if the 'P' stood for Peter. Should she ring both numbers and ask to speak to Clara? And if she was there, was Clara supposed to write a statement saying they'd been meeting every

Thursday for the last six months – or even come to Ailsham and tell Tom this to his face? She couldn't possibly do either.

Did it *matter* if Clara was dead? It would be terrible, of course, but Rose felt confused. If Clara *was* dead and somehow Tom had found out – through Mrs Denning, for instance – then he'd have known all along she was meeting someone else and the someone could only be a man. He'd been playing with her. Now he'd decided to terrorise her as well.

She comforted herself with the thought that she was meeting Alex later, though when she showed him the note he'd insist it really was time she left home and came to live with him. Rose put the letter back in her pocket. The idea of spending the rest of her life with Tom when there was an alternative life to be had with Alex hardly bore contemplating. But could she bring herself to leave? Despite the note, Rose still wasn't sure.

Benny was rushing across Clayton Square when she saw Jeannie's mother walking towards her. She'd always thought Mrs Flowers extremely nice, but she didn't fancy them coming face to face right now, not when she was in such a desperate hurry to get back to work. To her relieved surprise, Mrs Flowers turned abruptly left and went into the Stork Hotel, which Benny thought slightly odd. She'd never seemed the sort of person to frequent Liverpool hotels on her own. She must be meeting someone, though it was a bit late for lunch.

She wished her own mam would get out more,

251

but she was too nervous to set foot outside Bootle. Benny was sick to death of being dispatched all the way up London Road to T. J. Hughes in her lunch hour to purchase the bargains advertised in the *Liverpool Echo* the night before. Mam didn't realise that London Road was a good mile from Water Street and Benny didn't have the heart to tell her. She got so much pleasure out of the Irish linen pillowcases, tablecloths, the crockery and cutlery, all bought for a song, running her red, swollen hands over them as if they were gold. Today, it was two pairs of flannelette sheets that Benny had never dreamt would be so heavy. She changed the carrier bag to her left hand before the right lost all feeling.

Seeing Mrs Flowers had made her think about Jeannie and Elaine, something she tried to avoid. Benny had realised months ago that she'd cut off her nose to spite her face by parting so acrimoniously with her old friends. She hadn't made any new ones at the Inland Revenue. As far as she knew, no one went to the Cavern or any of the Liverpool beat clubs. She hadn't tied her hair in bunches, drawn lines around her eyes, or worn her slacks since the last time she'd seen Jeannie and Elaine in the Taj Mahal. Life these days was very ordinary and numbingly dull. She couldn't recall when anything even faintly interesting had happened. She felt so utterly wretched, it was hard to appear normal and act pleasantly at work.

Benny arrived at Whitechapel, cursing the sheets, which must weigh a ton. Her shoes had started to hurt and perspiration was running down her arms. She'd have caught a bus back to work, but it was safer to walk in case one didn't arrive on time and she'd be late. Employees who were late received a severe ticking off from the supervisor.

She had a brainwave. If she got a move on, she could go down Matthew Street, only slightly out of her way, and pass the Cavern where there'd be a poster listing future gigs. Next time the Merseysiders were on, Jeannie and Elaine would almost certainly be there, and she'd go and beg them to forgive her. 'I was a pig,' she'd say. 'I don't know what came over me. Perhaps it was starting that horrible job when I'd so much been looking forward to being a Flower Girl.' They were a soppy pair and she had no doubt that forgiveness would be instantly forthcoming.

She experienced a whiff of aching nostalgia when she walked down the narrow street lined with tall, crumbling warehouses, remembering the marvellous times they'd had in the innocuous little building that was the Cavern. As she drew nearer, she saw people emerging from a lunch-time session. 'That was super,' a girl remarked as she linked her boyfriend's arm. 'Don't you dare claim rock 'n' roll is the prerogative of males again.'

The Cavern door was open and a programme had been pasted on the wall just inside. Benny looked for Monday lunchtime, interested to know which group the girl had been talking about.

The Flower Girls!

The bag with the sheets fell from her band. Her head started to buzz and she felt dizzy. It couldn't possibly be *the* Flower Girls. They wouldn't have started up again without *her*. Some other group must have stolen the name.

More people were coming out. The session must be over. Benny had to wait for ages before the flow of people stopped and she was able to go downstairs. She forgot about work, about being late, about everything except the need to establish that *these* Flower Girls weren't *her* Flower Girls, that she hadn't been comprehensively and unbelievably betrayed.

No one took any notice of her. Perhaps they thought she'd forgotten something and had come back to collect it. The stage was empty, but there were still a few stragglers left, including a couple of girls leisurely eating sandwiches. Voices could be heard coming from the middle section. Benny stood perfectly still until, one by one, the owners of the voices appeared through one of the arches – Kevin McDowd first, then Jeannie, Marcia, Rita, and a tall black girl she'd never seen before.

With a feeling of sick horror, Benny realised the black girl had taken her place. For a few seconds, she knew what it must be like to die. People died of shock. Something happened, so awful, that their mind couldn't accept it. They preferred to be dead.

'Benny!' Jeannie was the first to notice her. 'It's lovely to see you. Were you here for the whole performance? What did you think?'

Benny was completely taken aback. How could Jeannie bring herself to sound so normal? Didn't she realise what they'd done? Realise how she'd feel, finding they'd regrouped without telling her?

'Why didn't you tell me you were back together?' she asked hoarsely.

'But, Benny, I did!' Jeannie cried. 'I put a letter through your door the day we heard we were to go for an audition.'

'Audition?'

'It was in London with M&M,' Marcia, who'd never liked her, said boastfully. 'We made a record. It reached seventy-seven in the charts, but the next one will do better. It's out in October.'

'I never got any letter.'

'I definitely put it through your door, Benny. It said to come to the barn that night straight after work. Oh, and I tried to ring your office, but they wouldn't put me through.'

'You could have come round our house again.'

'There wasn't time, girl.' Kevin McDowd had joined in the conversation. Benny noticed he was wearing a dead posh suit. The Flower Girls were identically dressed in black pleated skirts and white blouses. 'We only had a few days to get ready. When you didn't turn up, I had no choice but to get someone else. Zoe's a professional dancer. She's done a great job in your place.'

The black girl, Zoe, gave her a friendly smile, but Benny hated the usurper on the spot. She wanted to suggest, no *demand*, that Zoe be given the push and she be taken back, but knew instinctively this would be a waste of time. The group, with Zoe, had moved on without her.

'We all assumed you didn't come because of

your job, Benny,' Jeannie said kindly. 'It would have meant taking all sorts of days off.'

'I didn't come because I didn't get a letter telling me to,' Benny insisted stubbornly. She loathed her job. If it had meant belonging to the Flower Girls again, going for an audition, she would have given it up like a shot. Her dark thoughts were interrupted by another, even darker. Perhaps they'd deliberately got rid of her. Jeannie was lying about the letter – she must be, otherwise she would have got it. Kevin was lying when he said they'd waited for her to turn up.

'I can't think what happened to that letter. Look, why don't you come back tonight, we're on with the Merseysiders?' Jeannie again, Jeannie the hypocrite, pretending to be ever so kind. 'We can go for a coffee afterwards and talk.'

Talk about what? How successful they were? The exciting things they'd done – the record they'd made in London, the gigs they'd played. The things *she* should have done with them. 'I'm busy tonight.'

Marcia was becoming impatient. 'I'm starving. Who's coming for a meal?'

'Me.' Rita spoke for the first time. Until now, she'd regarded Benny inscrutably through her fringe of brown hair.

'I wouldn't mind a bite to eat.' Zoe shoved her arms into a lovely red mohair coat.

'I'll put the stuff in the van,' Kevin said. 'Where'll we go?'

'The Chanticler?' Marcia suggested.

'The Chanticler it is. I'll see youse girls in a jiffy.'

'They'll want to lock up soon, Benny,' Jeannie said gently.

She was in the way, being dismissed. There would never be a worse moment in her life than this. Benny picked up the sheets and trudged silently up the stairs. At the top, she turned. Jeannie was watching her sympathetically.

'I'll never forgive you for this, Jeannie Flowers,' she hissed. 'Never! Not for as long as I live.'

'But Benny,' Jeannie cried. 'I haven't done anything.'

'Liar!' Benny left, vowing never to enter the Cavern again.

Instead of returning to work, she went straight home, terrifying her mother with her white-as-death face and icy hands.

Mrs Lucas lit the fire and tried to rub some warmth back into her daughter's long, cold fingers. 'Do they know at work that you're sick, luv?' Benedicta shook her head. 'Then don't you think you'd better go back?' she whispered fearfully.

'For Christ's sake, Mam!' Benedicta screamed. 'I'm allowed to be sick. It's only a job, not prison. They don't come round beating us with whips.'

'All right, luv. I was worried you'd get into trouble, that's all.'

'Then stop worrying. If anyone says anything, I'll leave and get another job.'

The afternoon wore on and Benedicta gradually thawed out as more coal was recklessly flung on to the fire. When her mother made yet another cup of tea, she agreed to have a cheese sarnie, having eaten nothing but breakfast all day – the trip to T. J. Hughes at lunchtime hadn't left time for even a snack.

'Mam,' she shouted when Mrs Lucas was in the kitchen, 'did a letter come for me, it must be a couple of months ago now? Not a letter with a stamp, I'm not sure even if it was in an envelope. Jeannie didn't say.'

Mrs Lucas was glad they were in separate rooms. She jumped so violently that the milk she was pouring into a cup went into the saucer. It was a while before she could bring herself to pick up the saucer and pour the milk into the cup where it should have gone. Was this why Benedicta felt so poorly? She must have met that Jeannie girl who'd told her about the letter. Had it really been so important?

'Did you hear me, Mam?'

Benedicta would never forgive her if she knew it had been flushed down the lavatory. She might not understand it had been done for her own good. 'Yes, luv.' She licked her lips nervously. 'There's never been a letter, no. I'd have kept it for you if there had. Perhaps she put it through the wrong door.'

'Oh, yeah! And the neighbours wouldn't have brought it round, like, if she had?'

The cups rattled slightly when the tea was carried into the living room. 'Then perhaps she didn't bring it at all.'

'That's more likely the truth of it,' Benedicta said bitterly. She watched her mother carefully remove the cellophane from the sheets and stroke them lovingly – she'd probably been dying to do it all afternoon. Poor Mam! She'd never know

258

that, if things had gone differently, one of these days it might have been silk sheets she'd be stroking.

Benny tightened her fists until the nails dug painfully into her palms, and vowed that somehow, some day, in some way, she'd get her own back on Jeannie Flowers.

'How was Clara?' Tom asked, as Rose knew he would. She had rehearsed her answer on the way home in Alex's car.

She sat in the armchair, her movements slow and deliberate. It was important she appear to be in control. 'Actually, Tom,' she said easily, 'I know I shouldn't had misled you all this time, but I haven't seen Clara Baker in years, not since she left Ailsham.'

His eyes narrowed suspiciously, though her answer had obviously surprised him. 'So, who've you been seeing then?'

'No one!' Rose laughed. 'I've been treating myself to the pictures and a meal on my own. You'd have only thought me mad if I'd told the truth.'

'But you're gone for hours!'

'I always start with a wander round the shops. Oh, Tom,' she cried, 'I need to get away from Ailsham, from this house.' She gestured around the old-fashioned room. 'I need a bit of time to myself, just one day a week. I've been stuck in the village nearly all my life. I suppose I want a bit of freedom.'

'Why didn't you tell me this before?' he demanded.

259

'I didn't think you'd understand. I thought it sounded more believable to say I was with a friend, so I pretended to meet Clara, until today, when I couldn't bring myself to lie any more. *Do you understand, Tom?* I don't want to stop having just one day a week on my own.' If he proved amenable, it would give her a breathing space before she left for good. That afternoon, she and Alex had made up their minds that that time would inevitably come, but she'd sooner wait until Gerald left school, started work, was virtually a man, before she deserted her youngest child.

'It makes sense, sort of,' he said grudgingly.

'There!' She clapped her hands delightedly, aware it seemed terribly false. 'I saw Gerald's light on when I came up the path. I'll make him some cocoa seeing as he's still awake. Would you like a cup, Tom?'

'No, ta. I'll turn in myself now you're home. By the way, what did the postman bring this morning?'

'Eh?' She felt herself grow cold. She'd been so pleased with her explanation for Clara's non-existence, she'd actually forgotten about the sinister message that had arrived in the post.

'I saw him turn into the house when I was leaving. I just wondered who it was from.'

'It was some sort of circular. I can't remember what it was about. I threw it away.'

'I see. Goodnight, Rose.'

'Goodnight.' As she listened to her husband tramp upstairs, Rose was left to wonder uneasily if she'd made things better or worse.

She didn't bother with cocoa for Gerald, but poured herself a glass of sherry – the bottle had been replaced many times over the last few months. 'Not much longer,' she whispered. 'I won't have to put up with him all that much longer.'

Tom knew he would never sleep. His tormented brain wouldn't let him. She was having an affair, sleeping with another man. His Rose, his dear, precious, lovely Rose was letting another man touch her in the places that belonged solely to him. He could smell the other man on her whenever she came home from her meetings with 'Clara'. Imagining them together was driving him insane. He'd thought the note, CLARA BAKER IS DEAD, would scare her off. If it had, Tom was prepared never to mention the matter again, despite the hurt that would never go away. Instead, she'd just come up with another lie. It was obvious that she had no intention of not seeing this other man again.

He remembered the day he'd collected her from the orphanage, the day he'd proposed. It was her purity and innocence that had drawn him to her. Now she was soiled. Yet this didn't make him love her less, just differently, with a boiling passion he'd never felt before. He beat the pillow with his fist. She was *his*, and another man would never touch her again.

His eyes were closed when she came into the room. He heard the soft slither of her clothes as she took them off, the dull click of her suspenders, the tiny rustle of stockings being removed from her slim, shapely legs, and imagined the other man listening to the same seductive sounds as he waited for her in bed. Where did they do it? he wondered feverishly. Perhaps one day he should have followed her and tortured himself even more.

She slid carefully into bed. He could tell she was doing her best not to disturb him. He opened his eyes. She was lying on the very edge of the bed, as far away from him as possible. For a while, he lay watching the tumble of hair, the curve of her cheek profiled against the dim light that crept through the drawn curtains. His heart was pounding painfully in his chest and his body was racked with raw, primitive jealousy.

He reached out and put his hand on his wife's face and turned it towards him. He could feel a pulse beating in her neck beneath his thumb.

'Rose,' he whispered, 'I love you.'

Perhaps if she'd answered, 'I love you too,' as she'd done so many times in the past, he might still have forgiven her everything, but she didn't say a word and he wanted to weep. He pressed his thumb against the pulse and she wriggled uncomfortably.

'Don't, Tom.'

He pressed harder and she spluttered, 'Tom, that hurts!'

There was nothing he could do that would hurt as much as she'd hurt him. A feeling of madness came over him as he straddled her, both his hands around her neck, and squeezed. It was the only way he could keep her for himself, stop the other man from ever touching her again.

She was gagging now, making hoarse, croaking sounds. Her neck felt as thin and delicate as a bird's in his big, broad hands. 'I love you, Rose,' he said, over and over again. 'I love you.'

At first, he wasn't conscious of the banging on the door, until he heard his son's voice. 'Mum! *Mum!* Are you all right?' The handle turned and Tom collapsed back on the bed, just as Gerald came rushing in. 'What's the matter, Mum?'

Rose was gasping, trying to regain her breath. 'I just had a horrible nightmare,' she said hoarsely.

'Would you like some water, Mum?'

'I'll go down and get it myself. Go back to bed, love. I'll be all right.'

'Are you sure, Mum?' Gerald said anxiously.

'Yes, love. I'm sorry I woke you.'

She was putting on her dressing gown, pushing her feet into slippers. Seconds later, the door closed. Tom heard the bed creak in Gerald's room, then water run in the kitchen. He lay, staring at the ceiling, and wishing he would die.

Rose curled up in a chair and vowed that never again would she sleep in the bed upstairs with Tom. Max and Jeannie came home from the Cavern where they'd both been playing and went straight to their own beds, unaware their mother was in the parlour.

She didn't sleep, too terrified to close her eyes in case Tom appeared, armed this time with a knife, giving her no chance to make a noise and alert the children. If it hadn't been for Gerald, by now she would be dead. She hadn't thought Tom capable of such violence. 'I love you,' he'd kept

263

saying while he was trying to kill her. It was a vile, unnatural way to love someone. She shuddered at the memory.

At seven o'clock, his heavy footsteps sounded on the stairs and she heard him go into the kitchen. She curled even further into the chair, trying to make herself invisible, dreading that he might come in, say something, even apologise for last night. She wouldn't know what to say. She couldn't imagine ever speaking to him again.

Half an hour later, he left. She heard the wheels of the bike creak down the drive and breathed a sigh of relief.

Gerald came down and she went into the kitchen and made his breakfast, though her hands were shaking badly. She broke the yolks on both eggs and recalled how bitterly Mrs Corbett used to complain when she did this. While Gerald ate, she took up tea to Jeannie and Max.

Max looked at the clock and groaned. 'Oh, Mum! It's only quarter to eight. We didn't get home till nearly two.'

'I'd like you to drink this, then come downstairs for a minute. Afterwards, you can go back to bed and sleep for the rest of the day if you want, so there's no need to get dressed. I have to tell you something. It won't take long.'

'Can't you tell us tonight?'

'No, it has to be now.'

Jeannie proved easier to prise out of bed. 'There's no need to get dressed,' Rose said.

'Mum! Where on earth did you get those bruises on your neck?' her daughter asked in a shocked voice.

Rose turned up the collar of her dressing gown and didn't answer. She had forgotten there would be bruises from Tom's big hands.

When the children were sitting expectantly at the kitchen table, Rose took a deep breath. 'The thing is,' she began, 'I've been having an affair and your dad's found out. We haven't been getting on in a long time, and I'm afraid I've got no alternative but to leave.'

There was a long, astounded pause, before all three spoke together.

'Is that why you've got the bruises?' Jeannie demanded angrily.

'An affair!' Max guffawed. 'I don't believe it!'

'You can't leave!' Gerald wailed. 'Who'll cook the food and make our beds?'

There was another pause.

'What bruises?' Max frowned.

'They're on her neck,' Jeannie informed him. 'We'll just have to make our own beds and cook the meals between us,' she added sensibly, before bursting into tears.

Gerald decided to join her. 'I don't want us left on our own with Dad.'

'I'm sorry,' Rose said fervently. 'So very, very sorry.' She decided to be honest with them, but only to a degree. 'I was going to leave, but not for a few years, until Gerald was at least sixteen, but I'm afraid your father's made it impossible for me to stay.'

'He would!' Max hadn't had much time for his father in a long while.

'You can't really blame him, love. After all, I was having an affair. Not many men would forgive their wives something like that.'

'Not many men would beat them black and blue, either.'

'Max! He didn't beat me. The bruises were – an accident.' She wished she'd noticed them first and covered them up. She didn't want to leave with them hating Tom when they had to, somehow, live together from now on.

'Won't we ever see you again?' Gerald sobbed.

'Oh, love!' She put her arm around his heaving shoulders and, for a moment, wished she'd never set eyes on Alex Connors. 'Of course! As soon as I've got an address, I'll ring and let you know. It might be only a few days and you can come and see me – or we can meet in town, have something to eat. That would be nice, wouldn't it?'

Jeannie sniffed and dried her eyes. 'Will you be living with, you know, the man you've been having the affair with?'

Rose felt herself blush. 'Yes.'

'Who is it?' Max asked curiously. He was the least upset of the three. 'Have we met him?'

She blushed again. 'It's Ronnie Connors' father, Alex.'

Gerald appeared bemused, but the other two stared at her and she could tell they were imagining her and Alex together.

'He's very nice,' Jeannie said eventually.

'A decent guy.' Max nodded. 'Does Ronnie know his dad and my mum are about to set up house together?'

'No! You mustn't say anything, Max, until it's all been sorted out.' Alex didn't know she'd decided to leave. He might not be around today

266

to tell, and he mightn't be prepared to leave his family on the spur of the moment. 'Look,' Rose swallowed hard, 'you've all been marvellous about this. I thought you might hate me. But now I'd like Max and Jeannie to go back to bed, and Gerald, please go to school. I don't want to walk out with you all here, watching. I'd only cry myself to death. I've got to write a note for your dad and pack some clothes, and I'd prefer you out of the way.'

Jeannie flung her arms around her mother's neck. 'The house won't be the same without you, Mum.'

'Please don't say things like that, Jeannie. I'm already on the verge of tears.'

''Bye, Mum.' Max hurried out of the kitchen and Rose noticed he was badly in need of bigger pyjamas.

Gerald grabbed his satchel and left without a word.

Rose sighed, went into the hall, and picked up the phone. She sat on the bottom stair, nursing it for a while, wondering if Alex had really meant the things he'd said. Was it only to make the affair more exciting that he'd asked her to live with him, knowing she would refuse, ready to call it off if she didn't? He might be horrified to learn she was about to leave Tom. She visualised him offering a dozen excuses for why they couldn't be together – Iris wasn't well and he couldn't possibly tell her, not just now; the business needed all his attention; he couldn't afford somewhere for them to live; could they wait until after Christmas?

His secretary answered the phone. 'He's busy right now. Could you call back later? Oh, he's just come into my office. Who shall I tell him is calling?'

'Mrs Flowers.'

'Hold on a moment, Mrs Flowers. He's gone into his own office.'

'Darling!' said Alex a few seconds later.

He was coming in an hour to fetch her. Rose raced around the house, throwing things into an ancient suitcase. She packed towels, then returned them to the airing cupboard in case the children needed them. Did the same with the toothpaste, even though there was another tube. In the end, she took only her clothes, her makeup bag, and the few items of jewellery she possessed. As she climbed stairs she had climbed a dozen times a day for more than twenty years, she thought to herself, I will never do this again. She would never again comb her hair in front of the parlour mirror, never wash these particular dishes in this particular sink.

When everything was ready and the suitcase packed, she looked for Spencer to give him a final hug, but the cat had gone for his morning stroll over the fields and couldn't be found. She sat at the table to write to Tom. After last night, she couldn't bring herself to put 'Dear Tom' and just started with 'Tom.'

She sat for ages staring at this one word, unable to think of another. What did you say to a man who'd almost strangled you a matter of hours before? In the end, she merely wrote, 'Goodbye,

Rose.' She tucked the paper behind the clock on the sideboard. It wouldn't matter if the children read it. It told them nothing.

Outside, a horn sounded. Rose picked up the suitcase and opened the door. Alex was there! She caught her breath, knowing she would remember this moment when she was a very old woman, the moment when she walked away from one life and into another. She entirely forgot about her children when Alex got out of the car and came up the path towards her. He wasn't quite as handsome as she'd always thought, not quite so tall, not all that young. But he was the man she loved. His face was soft with love and anticipation. He stopped suddenly, put his hands in his pockets, took a deep breath and rocked back on his heels, as if he couldn't believe that this was really happening.

The woman from the new bungalow opposite was just leaving. She waved and shouted, 'Good morning, Mrs Flowers.'

'Good morning,' Rose called, 'and goodbye,' she added softly so the woman couldn't hear.

'What shall we do?' Fly asked. 'Kill him?'

'Only if we can do it slowly and very painfully,' said Max.

'Leave him to me.' Lachlan looked stern and forbidding.

'Are you going to kill him for us?'

'Shut up, Fly.'

They'd just finished their Friday night gig at the Taj Mahal and were preparing to buttonhole Billy Kidd in his office and demand he hand over

269

the money he owed. They'd asked around and discovered he'd been paid at least ten pounds and sometimes as much as twenty for the gigs they'd played all over Liverpool during the last few years. Yet he'd only given them a quid each! They'd worked it out, added it up, and reckoned they'd been done out of just over a thousand pounds. They'd demand a thousand then tell Billy to get lost.

Lachlan felt he'd let his troops down. He should have noticed before but, like the rest of them, money had always been the last thing on his mind. He thought of the things they could do with a whole thousand; buy their own van, instead of having to borrow the one from the garage where Sean worked which was usually full of dirty engines and spare parts; get better guitars, more powerful amplifiers. The list was endless.

Billy's face was a mask of injured innocence when Lachlan told him what they knew, that he'd been stealing their money for years.

'I didn't *steal* it.' Billy looked outraged. 'I invested it in a special account set up in the group's name. You see,' he said earnestly, 'one of these fine days, you'll want to get married, buy a house, and it means you'll all have a little nest egg saved.'

'We'd sooner save our own little nest eggs, thanks all the same,' Lachlan said coldly. 'How much is in this account?'

'I'm not sure.' Beads of perspiration appeared on Billy's brow when faced with four pairs of accusing eyes. 'A few hundred smackeroos, I reckon.'

'We reckon there should be more than that. Perhaps you could take the money out of the account on Monday. We'll come on Monday night to collect it.'

'It's not the sort of account you can draw money out at the drop of a hat.'

'We don't mind waiting a few days,' Fly said generously.

'Running this club, it's an expensive business.' The suspicion of a tear rolled down Billy's fat cheek. 'Right now, I'm in a bit of a hole. If I had to empty that account, it would break me. I've used it as collateral, see, against a loan. I'd lose the club. *Then* where would you play?'

Max hooted sarcastically. 'Your logic's a bit dodgy. Billy. Are we expected to keep the Taj Mahal going so we can play here once a week? When you signed us up, you promised us the earth. Instead, you haven't done a single thing except pinch our money.'

'Invest,' Billy said weakly.

'Oh, yeah!' Sean didn't believe there'd ever been an account. The money had been lost on the horses, as he'd suspected all along. He was glad the truth had come out. Billy had served his purpose and the group could move on.

'You're supposed to pay us, not us pay you,' Fly growled. 'All you've ever cared about is making enough out of us to keep your head above water.' He looked at the others. 'I still think we should kill him.'

'What are we going to do now?' asked Max, ignoring Billy who, by now, was weeping copiously. 'I don't know about you lot, but I'd sooner not have a manager than be stuck with a crook like him.'

'You signed a contract,' Billy blubbered.

'Which you've broken,' Lachlan snapped. 'Max is right. We'll have to make do without a manager, but we need someone to take phone calls, else we'll end up missing gigs.'

Sean thought about offering his dad as manager, but Kevin was too involved with the Flower Girls to find time for another group.

'My mum's always in,' Lachlan said. 'She won't mind taking messages. We'll get cards printed with our phone number on.'

'What about me?' Billy asked pitifully. 'Won't you be playing at me club again?'

'Not unless you hike up your rates considerably, Billy,' Max told him. 'We'll let you have a card and you can give Lachlan's mum a ring – she'll let you know when we're free.'

Jeannie wasn't prepared to give up her career and take over her mother's role as her father seemed to expect. 'We'll all have to pull together,' she told him. 'I'll do the meals if I'm here but, if I'm not, then someone else will have to do it. The same goes for the washing and the cleaning. We can make our own beds.'

'I've never made a bed in my life and I'm not starting now,' Tom growled. He felt as if he were adrift in a flimsy boat on an angry sea, without bearings. The world had lost all meaning. Nothing was normal any more. He was on a different plane to other people. Their voices sounded very far away. Rose had gone and

272

nothing would ever be the same again. Somehow, he had managed to blank out the fact he'd nearly killed her. It had merely been a dream, and life had been a dream ever since. The only reality was that she had betrayed him with another man.

'Then I'm sorry, Dad, but you'll just have to sleep in an unmade bed.'

He couldn't comprehend his daughter's refusal to look after him and her brothers as good daughters did when their mothers were no longer around. Out of sheer cussedness, he got rid of all the things Rose had bought. The television was sold, the washing machine, the fridge. He arranged for the telephone to be removed.

'So, it's back to the Dark Ages,' Max sneered.

'People used to manage without them things. We'll manage without them now.'

Except they weren't managing. Jeannie refused to do the washing by hand and it was sent to the laundry. They kept running out of food because no one had time to go to the shops. Sometimes, Gerald was provided with a list of things to buy on his way home from school. Without a fridge, the milk went sour and the butter turned rancid. From the other end of Disraeli Terrace, the McDowds kept Jeannie and Max informed of the gigs and other events that concerned them in the music world.

Tom wouldn't lift a finger to help, not even to remove the sheets from his bed to be washed, or carry the used dishes as far as the sink. If Jeannie wasn't around, it fell to Max or Gerald to cobble together an unsatisfactory meal for themselves and their father. For the first time, Spencer ate out of tins now that Rose was no longer around to prepare him choice little meals, occasionally having to do with a ham or sardine sandwich if the cat food ran out.

Gerald was desperately unhappy. His brother and sister could escape from the house, sometimes, in the case of Jeannie, for days if the Flower Girls were playing away from Liverpool. Gerald was hungry and never seemed able to find a clean shirt. He hated school, which he'd always liked, and there was rarely a clear space in the entire house where he could do his homework. To cap it all, he sorely missed the television, particularly the football.

In December, two months after their mother had gone, Jeannie returned from a gig in Newcastle to find the kitchen looking as if it had experienced its own little earthquake. Dirty dishes were piled everywhere, including the dresser, there were tea towels on the floor, a bin overflowing with empty tins. A parcel of clean laundry had been ripped open, a few things roughly removed, leaving the rest in a crumpled heap.

'Oh, *Gawd!*' she groaned.

There was a knock on the door. It was Rita McDowd. 'You dropped your purse in the van. Jaysus!' she gasped, when she saw the mess. It reminded her of the kitchen of her own house many years ago. These days it was spotless and had every conceivable modern device. Dad was talking about buying their own place as soon as they'd made enough money. How things change, Rita marvelled. Life was like a seesaw. One minute you were up, the next down.

'This will have to stop,' Jeannie announced sternly. 'I'm not quite sure what I'm supposed to be – a member of a relatively successful pop group, or a charwoman. We'll have to get a cleaner, though I bet Dad won't agree.'

Tom pretended to be appalled at the idea. He flatly refused to have a stranger in his house, although it wouldn't have been the first time.

'In that case, Dad, I'm leaving,' Jeannie told him curtly. 'I'm not prepared to live in a pig sty and I don't have time to keep this place clean.' Because she was the only female member of the family, she was expected to do everything. She was run off her feet and had no leisure time. It didn't matter that she was earning twice as much as Max and her father put together.

'You do whatever you like,' Tom said.

'Don't worry, I will.' It was possible she still loved her father, but she'd lost all patience with him. At times, she felt pity for him, but then remembered the bruises on her mother's neck. It irritated her the way he refused to muck in, do his share. Max and Gerald did at least try, though weren't much use.

Rose had no idea what was happening in the house she'd left behind. The children met her in town at least once a week and, on Jeannie's instructions, she was told everything was fine. 'You're not to worry her,' Jeannie said. 'She'll only feel guilty if she knows the truth. Let's not spoil her happiness.'

And Rose was happy, no one could doubt that. It was evident in her dazzling blue eyes. Alex had bought a pretty cottage in Lydiate and they were doing it up. Rose was sewing curtains and painting walls, tasks that seemed to give her an inordinate amount of pleasure. Everyone would be invited to tea when the place was finished.

'I'm coming with you,' Max said with alacrity when he found out Jeannie was looking for another place to live.

'What about me?' Gerald said anxiously. 'You can't leave me behind with Dad!'

'You're only fourteen. You've got another year to go at school,' Jeannie reminded him.

'I can change schools, other kids do.'

Her little brother looked on the verge of tears, as he so often did nowadays. He missed Mum far more than she and Max did. She couldn't possibly leave him in this miserable, dirty house, with only their taciturn father for company, even if it did mean him changing schools. 'If you come with us,' she said, 'you'll sometimes be left on your own, and I won't have time to look after you, not the way Mum did. You'll have to learn to do things for yourself.' She turned to Max. 'You too. I'm not having the place a tip, nor am I prepared to be the only one who makes the meals and washes up afterwards. You're to do your share, both of you – which was supposed to happen here, I might add, though I never saw much sign of it.'

At the beginning of January, the three young Flowers moved into the top half of a large furnished house in Toxteth. Tom wasn't all that bothered to see them go. His wife and children had sadly disappointed him. Now there was no one to impress with his masculine disdain of housework, he engaged a woman who came in twice a week and cleaned the place from top to bottom and also did the washing and ironing. When Mrs Denning learnt he was on his own, she offered to come after she'd seen to the colonel and make him an evening meal. Sometimes, she stayed and they played cards.

Tom wouldn't have said he was happy, but he no longer had to put up with four bewildering individuals who wouldn't do as they were told. Life was simpler, easier, his mind at peace, with only a self-reliant cat to keep him company most of the time. It came to him one night that perhaps he'd married too late in life. He wasn't cut out to be a husband and father. He'd been too set in his ways and should have remained a bachelor, like the colonel.

There wasn't a parent in sight in the flat in Toxteth, not a soul to prevent them from having a party every night if they wished and staying up as late as they liked. Whenever the Merseysiders played, Lachlan and Fly would come back with Max and they'd sit talking and drinking coffee into the early hours, Jeannie too and, more often than not, Zoe and Marcia, who couldn't bring themselves to go back to their own homes when it was only midnight. Sean and Rita McDowd rarely took part in this nocturnal socialising. Mornings, the flat would be full of bodies – on the settee, the floors, and occasionally in the bathroom. Elaine would always remain Jeannie's best friend, but she was rarely seen in Toxteth, being too busy studying for her A levels.

Despite his unconventional surroundings, Gerald discovered an ability to sleep through the noise and thrived at his new, inner-city school.

In April, Gerry and the Pacemakers reached number-one in the charts with 'How Do You Do It?', and the following month the Beatles did the same with 'From Me to You'.

The rock 'n' roll phenomenon had begun in earnest and Liverpool groups were at the forefront, dominating the charts. Hordes of eager managers and agents descended on the Cavern in search of groups to sign up. The Merseysiders were taken on by a big London agency, Frith and Ford, that had been established for more than forty years. 'You're our first rock 'n' roll group,' Eddie Ford, grandson of one of the deceased founders, cried jubilantly when they signed the contract.

Three months later, the Merseysiders reached number five in the charts with 'A to Z'. Sean and Lachlan had written the words and music between them, but the Flower Girls had already beaten them to it with their recording of 'Moon Under Water', which had climbed as high as number three the month before. By then, the Beatles had played at the Cavern for the last time.

Lachlan bought Jeannie an engagement ring for her birthday in December. Colonel Corbett had always been fond of his gardener's children and rejoiced in their success. He said he would be honoured if they allowed him to hold an engagement party in his barn.

Their families were invited, their numerous friends and *their* friends, old schoolmates, Billy Kidd who, for all his faults, had helped both groups on their way, Eddie Ford from the agency and his young wife.

Not everyone was pleased to receive an invitation to Jeannie's birthday-cum-engagement party. When Benedicta Lucas received hers, she spat on it and threw it on the fire in disgust. 'Cheek!' she muttered.

Tom Flowers wasn't asked. He wouldn't have come, but Rose and Alex would be there and it was best not to risk a confrontation so soon.

In the years to come, Jeannie often looked back on her party as the best night of her life. She bought a new frock, which was white, almost ankle length, with a silver thread running through the soft, silky material, and silver sandals with high, spiky, heels. She wore a white flower in her brown hair.

'You look like a goddess,' Lachlan said softly when he collected her from the flat in Toxteth, which she was soon to leave. He'd learnt to drive and was now the proud owner of a bright red MG sports car. 'A beautiful, beautiful goddess.' He kissed her gently. 'Or a bride. *My* bride.'

'I will be soon.' They were getting married in the spring, secretly, with only their immediate families and close friends present. Both groups had acquired a multitude of fans. They didn't want their wedding ruined by crowds of hysterical teenagers.

News of the party must have leaked out. When they arrived in Ailsham, there was a policeman at the bottom of the drive leading to The Limes, attempting to control about twenty screaming girls.

'It's Lachlan Bailey and Jeannie Flowers!' The windows of the car were suddenly full of excited faces. Fists thumped against the glass.

'Are they a couple? I didn't know they were a couple?'

'I thought they were brother and sister.'

'No, Jeannie's Max's sister. Lachlan's sister is another Flower Girl.'

'Clear off now,' the policeman said genially. 'Come on, girls, clear off. Let people through.'

Inside the car, Jeannie shivered. 'They frighten me.'

'They *terrify* me!' Lachlan laughed.

It turned out to be a perfect night. The eight young people, the Merseysiders and the Flower Girls, felt as if there was nothing on earth they couldn't do. Eyes followed them everywhere, some filled with pride, some with envy.

The girls hugged and kissed and loudly expressed their love for each other, even the normally tongue-tied Rita. It was genuinely meant and deeply felt. They had shared a unique experience, each making a deep impression on the others' lives.

Colonel Corbett made a speech. The Flowers and the McDowds had put Ailsham on the map, he said. Business at the Oak Tree had increased tenfold with people wanting to know where they lived. Virtually every young person in the village was learning to play the guitar in the hope of following in their idols' footsteps. He finished by saying the party wouldn't be complete without a short performance from the stars. 'I think the proper term is a "gig".'

They were ready for this. The girls had agreed to go first. They started their favourite, 'Be-Bop-A-Lula', then a new number Kevin had just written, never heard before in public, 'Banana Skins', and, to a burst of applause, their hit song, 'Moon Under Water'.

Halfway through, the Merseysiders joined in, Sean's languid sleepy tones like a dusky shadow of Rita's enchanting voice, providing a unique, musical experience for the audience.

The song finished to more applause. For a few seconds, there was silence, then Lachlan began to sing, 'I dream of Jeannie with the light brown hair...'

'Aahh!' sighed the crowd. It was so romantic!

Lachlan strolled across to his fiancée, his bride-to-be, and knelt in front of her. His brown eyes never left her blue ones. She knew he was committing himself to her totally. They would never, never stop loving each other. Then Lachlan finished singing, kissed her, and the crowd sighed again.

Across the room, Rose Flowers laid her head on Alex's shoulder and he gripped her waist. They thought about each other and the child growing in Rose's womb, *their* child.

Kevin McDowd gave his wife a nudge. Sadie nudged him back, a bit harder than necessary, he thought with a grin. Strewth, she was a fine looking woman altogether, a credit to him and to Ireland. Jaysus, Mary and Joseph, wasn't life just great? He'd made it in show business at last and had been allowed back into Sadie's bed. He telegraphed a little message to God, thanking Him for His blessings.

The noise of the party could be heard far away in Holly Lane where a stunned Tom Flowers was beginning to wonder if he might have been wrong about his children. Perhaps there was something to be said for this rock 'n' roll rubbish, after all. The sound of the music, the thought of so many people enjoying themselves, made his own house feel deathly quiet and unnaturally empty. For some reason, the hairs on his neck bristled and he felt himself go very cold as he realised he'd done nothing right and everything wrong. If only he could go back in time, start again, be a better husband to his wife and a different father to his children.

For the first time in his adult life, Tom Flowers wept.

Part Three

Chapter 10

1967

There was something Lachlan wanted to tell her. Every now and again he would open his mouth to say something, then change his mind. As their lives appeared to be proceeding smoothly, without a cloud in sight, Jeannie reckoned it couldn't be all that important and he'd tell her in his own good time.

She swam two lengths of the pool to cool herself down, then climbed back on to the side and dangled her feet in the sparkling blue water. It was mid-June and debilitatingly hot. The sun blazed down on her back and she half expected her wet skin to sizzle. She'd had enough. It was better to be sickly pale than have a tan if it meant suffering such torture.

Indoors was much cooler, with the windows open and a fan whirring on the living room ceiling. She went into the bedroom, changed out of her wet bikini into a loose cotton shift, and returned to the lounge. The sound of the fan, its faint, never-ending hum, got on her nerves. Before flinging her listless body full length on the settee, she switched on the record player to drown the noise. There was already a record without a label on the turntable, the Mersey-siders' latest, shortly to be released.

Apart from Lachlan in the basement studio, the house was empty for a change. The lack of human life, like the fan, also got on her nerves. It must be the oppressive heat that was making her feel so irritable.

The Merseysiders and the Flower Girls – except for Rita who lived with her parents – had bought properties close to each other on the strip of coast that stretched from Crosby to Southport. Jeannie and Lachlan's five-bedroom bungalow, with two acres of grounds and its own pool, was situated between Formby and Ainsdale and was only two hundred yards from the shore. Built ten years ago for an American businessman to his own design, for a reason unknown to the new owners, it had been christened Noah's Ark. All the rooms were large, at least twenty feet square, with floor to ceiling windows. The walls were white, which Jeannie and Lachlan had seen no reason to change. They bought white furniture to match and white rugs to scatter over the polished wooden floors.

Noah's Ark would have been quite unremarkable had it not been for the long, wide hall – the estate agent had described it as a reception area – which had a domed glass ceiling, tinted green, soaring like a blister above the red tiled roof. The established gardens – trees at the front, lawns, flower beds and a pool at the back – were surrounded by a thick, impenetrable hawthorn hedge. A winding drive led to the front door, making the property invisible from the road.

Jeannie thought it the sort of house that needed lots of people in it and would be perfect for when she and Lachlan had a family. Lachlan was impressed with the large basement and its potential as a studio.

The studio had been fitted out and was used by both groups. Fly Fleming usually brought his wife when the Merseysiders rehearsed or made a record, a salt of the earth Liverpool girl called Stella, who'd become a good friend. Jeannie wished she could say the same for Max's wife, Monica. Monica, who would have been pretty if her expression hadn't been so mean, had been a groupie, hanging round after the gigs were over in the hope of being picked up. Max had succumbed, not for the first time, but Monica had turned up two months later and announced tearfully that she was pregnant and the father could only be Max.

Jeannie wasn't sure whether her brother was admirable or an idiot for marrying her. Monica had obviously set out to trap him. Everyone had tried to persuade him to pay the girl off, but Max had seemed quite resigned to becoming a husband and father. Their little boy, Gareth, was a charmer. Jeannie felt quite misty-eyed with longing for a baby of her own whenever she held him in her arms.

The new record drifted to its subdued end. It was very different to anything the Merseysiders had done before. Sean played the flute, Fly's drums sounded as if they'd been covered in thick velvet, bells tinkled in the background, and the accompanying guitars were merely a dull throbbing blur. It was called 'Marzipan Dream', and Lachlan's voice was just a haunting whisper.

The music scene was changing. Rock 'n' roll would never go away, but some groups were producing gentler music for a gentler decade. In America, people sang of wearing flowers in their hair and talked of peace. Record sleeves were covered with psychedelic whirls and chubby angels. Male groups wore loose, flowing clothes, grew their hair long, and had started to sport earrings and rows of beads. Bands called Perfumed Garden, Nazareth, Marble Orchard, and South California Purple played at the Cavern.

The Flower Girls had no need to alter their image. They'd never played solely rock 'n' roll and moved seamlessly in and out of the new scene.

As soon as 'Marzipan Dream' finished, the fan began to hum. Jeannie went down to the basement to unearth Lachlan from the studio. She was only recently back from a month long tour of Australia and before that he'd spent a fortnight in America. They'd hardly seen each other for ages, yet here he was, burying himself beneath the ground for hours on end.

He was sitting in front of a vast desk of switches and knobs, wearing headphones, and didn't hear her come in. She watched him for a moment. He was twenty-five, and the long, wavy hair, tied back with cord, the cream cheesecloth shirt, loose-sleeved and collarless, didn't disguise his broad, muscled masculinity. She slid her arms around his neck and he immediately removed the headphones.

'I'm feeling neglected,' she complained.

'Darling!' He pulled her on to his knee. 'I'm

dead busy, but I don't mind being interrupted by a beautiful woman.' He kissed her chin.

'I'm bored,' she told him. 'I'd like to do something.'

'Well, I can think of something straight away. Lie down on the carpet, it's nice and thick.'

She grinned. 'OK, but after that what shall we do?'

'Eat, swim, paint a wall?' They both found it relaxing to repaint the walls when they began to lose their dazzling whiteness.

'I'm not hungry, it's too hot to paint, and believe it or not, it's too hot to swim. We need an indoor swimming pool, Lachlan,' she added in a whining voice.

They both laughed at her perfect imitation of Monica, who was constantly demanding things. 'Poor Max, though,' Lachlan said soberly. 'He'll end up in the poorhouse if he's not careful.'

'I know, but you can't speak to Max. He takes umbrage.' Max and Fly weren't as wealthy as the others. Sean and Lachlan wrote their own songs and quite a few had been used by other artists, resulting in big royalty cheques arriving twice a year. Fly and Stella didn't mind, they were already rich beyond their wildest dreams, but it was a sore point with Monica that their smart house in Birkdale was smaller than the Baileys' and they didn't have a pool or their own studio or a garage that held three expensive cars, one of which, the Land Rover, Lachlan had bought in a weak moment, but could never find a use for, preferring his Ferrari. Jeannie disliked driving. She never went long distances if she could avoid it, and had a Mini for shopping.

'Why are you still on my knee?' He pretended to look cross.

'Where else am I supposed to be?'

'On the floor, with no clothes on, I might remind you.'

'Oh, all *right*.' She rolled her eyes and gave an extravagant sigh, then yelped when he tickled her waist.

The basement door opened and a voice shouted, 'Is someone being murdered down there?'

Jeannie made a face and got to her feet.

'Who is it?' Lachlan called.

'Fly. I've brought the missus. She came in her cozzie and made straight for the pool. I hope you don't mind.' He came clattering down the stairs, smiling genially, as always. 'When we're away, I'm always dying to get home, but as soon as I'm there, I get bored shitless. Stella swears the Merseysiders are joined at the hip. We can't live without each other and move in a pack. Hi, Jeannie. Was it you who screamed? Jaysus!' He winked lewdly. 'I hope I didn't interrupt anything.'

'Nothing that can't wait, Fly.' Lachlan beckoned him over. 'Listen to this. It's "Marzipan Dream". Those bells are a bit too intrusive. I think we should make them softer.' They both put on earphones and Lachlan flicked a switch. Seconds later, they were totally absorbed in their latest record.

'They've already forgotten they've got wives,' Jeannie said when Stella climbed out of the pool to say hello. She was a lovely, curvaceous young woman, with wide apart grey eyes and beautiful skin. Her black hair was plastered to her scalp like a mermaid's.

'Fly would sooner make love to his drums than me.' She had a loud, deep-throated laugh that made people wanted to join in.

'I'm sure Lachlan would prefer to be married to a guitar.'

They sat companionably together on the edge of the pool. Despite their complaints, they were both perfectly happy with their music-obsessed husbands.

'The Flower Girls don't get all preoccupied with music, not like the men,' Stella remarked. 'It's life or death with them lot.'

'Women have more things to think about, that's why,' Jeannie explained. 'Lachlan wouldn't eat if he wasn't reminded. He doesn't have to worry about the house being cleaned or the washing done. And he hasn't a clue what's happening in the rest of the world. He doesn't know there's been a six-day war in the Middle East or that China exploded a H-bomb the other day. He only knows the Americans are fighting a war in Vietnam because someone wrote a song about it. Us girls are happy to leave the music side of things to Kevin McDowd. He writes the songs, arranges the music, does the recording, organises the publicity, whereas Lachlan and the others have to have their fingers in every pie. Gosh it's hot! Do you mind if I go inside? You stay if you like.'

'I'll come with you. I'll have another dip later. I

need a drink, me throat's as dry as a bone. By the way, we brought some wine, but I bet Fly didn't put it in the fridge like I told him.'

The wine was on top of the fridge, not in, but there were already enough bottles chilled. They were sitting in the lounge beneath the fan, sipping the wine, when Max arrived with Gareth toddling at his side. Monica had gone to Southport to buy another outfit for Marcia's wedding on Saturday, he said. 'She'd bought a costume, but it'll be far too warm if the weather stays like this.'

'That doesn't sound a bad idea,' Stella mused. 'I've got a costume too, lilac grosgrain. The jacket's lined and it's got long sleeves. I'll melt away to nothing on a day like today.'

Jeannie said she also had a costume, pale lemon linen, but instead of a skirt, it had a sleeveless dress, which she could wear without the jacket. 'It's Mary Quant,' she said. 'Incredibly short.'

Max went down to the basement, leaving the adorable Gareth with his only too willing aunt. Not long afterwards, Sean McDowd arrived, having been summoned on the downstairs phone to give his opinion on the bells in 'Marzipan Dream', followed half an hour later by the rest of the McDowds, who'd been out to lunch. 'I've written a new song,' Kevin said excitedly – he was always excited about something. He'd like Jeannie to play it later, see what she thought. Rita liked it. 'Don't you, luv?'

Rita shrugged, which could have meant yes or no, and didn't speak.

The house suited being full. Zoe wasn't coming. She was in London with her boyfriend, an actor, who had a small part in a West End play being premiered that night. Marcia, of course, was involved in preparations for her wedding.

Marcia was marrying the son of a lord, the patient Graham having been dispensed with long ago. There'd been dozens of other boyfriends in between.

Dr and Mrs Bailey didn't mind that their daughter's wedding was being held in the wilds of Wiltshire, not far from Salisbury Plain, rather than in Walton Vale. It meant they wouldn't have the burden of the arrangements. Someone else would be ordering the flowers, the cars, the photographer, organising the reception, and doing the myriad other things necessary for a wedding.

The Elroy-Smythes had lived in the village of Harwood for more than four centuries. Their manor house had been added to several times over the years and now had thirty-eight rooms.

Philip Elroy-Smythe, Marcia's husband-to-be, was better known to the outside world as Phil Smythe, a guitarist with the Awkward Crew, a moderately successful beat group. Six months ago, the Awkward Crew had supported the Flower Girls in a whirlwind tour of the British Isles. Phil would have preferred a quiet wedding in a register office, but Marcia liked the idea of a grand affair and the entire village of Harwood was coming to a dance being held after the reception.

The Flower Girls and the Merseysiders had

been invited, along with their various husbands, wives, and boyfriends and, of course, Kevin and Sadie McDowd. They would stay two nights and travel down the day before.

Jeannie and Lachlan set off on Friday morning, another oppressively hot day, in the two-seater, milky-white Ferrari with matching leather seats. Lachlan loved driving. He said little over the first thirty or forty miles, though once or twice he opened his mouth to speak, but must have thought better of it. Perhaps he was worried about the group. Normally easygoing to a fault, fulsomely good-natured, generous, and exquisitely polite, these attributes could vanish in a flash where the Merseysiders were concerned. He would become a tyrant, as protective as a mother with her new-born child, worrying over the slightest, most insignificant details, such as the volume of the bells in 'Marzipan Dream'.

They left Shropshire and entered Worcester, roughly halfway there. Jeannie asked if they could please stop at the next pub for a drink and something to eat. Lachlan would have driven the entire length of the country and back again without a single break.

'This one looks quite nice,' she said when they were approaching a long, low, thatched building with a hanging sign outside and Lachlan was about to roar right past. The brakes screeched, and, with an air of reluctance, he slowed to turn into the car park.

The garden was full of customers, drinking and baking in the sun. They went inside where it would be cooler and they hoped they could tuck themselves in a quiet corner, out of the way of any eager autograph hunters.

Jeannie found an empty booth where they could hide behind the high, wooden partitions. After a few minutes, Lachlan arrived with two glasses of orange juice and said their chicken salads wouldn't be long. Then he sat, staring into his drink, not speaking.

'What's the matter?' Jeannie asked. She wasn't prepared to wait any longer for him to tell her whatever it was that was bothering him.

'Nothing.'

'Don't lie,' she said sternly. 'You've been worried about something for ages. I'm your wife. You should be able to tell me.'

'You won't like it.'

'Do you want a divorce?'

'Jeannie!' He looked quite horrified. 'What an awful thing to say!'

'Have you got a disgusting sexual disease?'

He laughed then. 'What other terrible things are you going to accuse me of?'

'Everything I can think of that a man would be reluctant to tell his wife.'

'OK, then.' He gave a deep, soulful sigh. 'Sean wants to go solo. He's waiting until "Marzipan Dream" is launched before going public with the news.'

She frowned, puzzled. 'But you always expected that might happen one day. We've talked about it before. You'll just have to get someone else to take his place.'

'That won't exactly be easy. He's a one-off, people like Sean don't grow on trees. But that's

295

not all.' There was something almost furtive about the glance he gave her. 'Eddie Ford wants me to dump Max at the same time.'

'Dump Max! Oh, Lachlan! It would kill him.' Her brother was just as obsessive about music as Lachlan. More than that, he was vulnerable in a way Lachlan had never been. Max was fussily concerned about his image and his size, painfully aware his fame wasn't as great as the others. Egged on by Monica, he constantly complained he was being sidelined, under-exposed. 'Since he met you,' she said, 'all he's ever wanted is to play the guitar.'

'I know,' Lachlan said slowly. He gave her that furtive look again. 'That's why it's going to be so hard.'

'You mean you're going to do it? Dump him?' she gasped.

He began to twist his glass around, one full turn, then back again. 'I've got no choice,' he mumbled.

'Yes, you have, Lachlan. You can tell Eddie Ford to go and jump in the lake.'

'Except that Eddie's right, darling.'

'Don't darling me, Lachlan Bailey,' she said angrily. 'It's my brother we're talking about. I think you should dump Eddie.'

'Eddie's a first-class agent. Max is just an adequate guitarist without an ounce of personality on stage. The Merseysiders get thousands of fan letters. Most are for me and Sean.' He said this matter of factly, without conceit. 'Quite a few come for Fly, but Max gets hardly any. He's become a drag on the group. Eddie thinks it's due to him we've never managed to hit the number one spot in the charts.'

The barmaid came with the food. She said quietly, 'I know who you are. I won't disturb your meal, but if you wouldn't mind signing the menu before you go, it would please my daughter very much. She hasn't been too well lately.'

'We'll do that.' Jeannie gave her a smiling nod, but as soon as the woman had gone she turned on her husband. 'Lachlan, every record you've made has been in the top ten. You earn as much in a week as most people do in a year. Do you have to be so greedy?'

'It's nothing to do with money or greed,' he said coldly. 'It's to do with being the best, being number one. It's what I've always wanted for the Merseysiders. I've carried Max all this time because he was my friend and your brother, but Eddie's just signed up these two kids, only eighteen. They've been playing the northern clubs. I've heard them and they're bloody brilliant. They'll be joining the Merseysiders when Sean and Max leave.'

'You mean, when Sean leaves and Max gets dumped.'

Knowing that her brother was about to have his world fall apart, spoiled what would have otherwise been a very enjoyable weekend. She had never felt so cross with Lachlan before.

Harwood Hall was a lovely place to stay in summer, with its spacious lawns and gardens, its orchard and the lake shaped like a figure of eight surrounded by lush, trailing trees. The other time they'd come it had been March, and the place was desolate, the trees bare, the grass overgrown, and the house icily cold.

There was no sign of Marcia or the occupants of the house when they arrived to find people hurrying purposely in and out of rooms, up and down stairs, along corridors, busy with preparations for tomorrow's wedding. A maid showed them to their extremely grand, but shabby room on the first floor.

Jeannie unpacked their clothes – Lachlan's grey morning suit with flared trousers, her yellow costume, a wispy black semi-evening frock for tonight – and hung them in the wardrobe that was big enough to live in. The yellow cartwheel hat of lacquered straw and Lachlan's grey top hat were placed carefully on the top shelf.

Harwood Hall was woefully short of bathrooms, so she was glad to find the nearest free. After wallowing briefly in the oversized tub, she returned to their room and was pulling on a pair of white jeans and a sky blue T-shirt, when Lachlan announced he was going to look for Sean and Fly. 'Their cars are outside,' he said stiffly.

'See you later,' Jeannie said stiffly back. They'd hardly spoken to each other since they'd left the pub.

The window overlooked the side of the house where the visitors' cars were parked; Sean's black Maserati, Fly's low slung red Jag, the Baileys' Ferrari, Zoe's bright red mini with daffodils painted on the doors. ''Cos I'm a Flower Girl. Geddit?' Zoe said when she first showed it off.

Rita couldn't drive and was coming with Kevin and Sadie in their Rolls. Soon, Max would arrive in the sensible Mercedes, which had a special seat in the back for Gareth. Dr and Mrs Bailey couldn't come till tonight. He still drove the pre-war Humber, refusing to relinquish it for something more modern, though parts were becoming more difficult to obtain.

Three people were standing by the opulent cars; an elderly man and a young couple hand in hand, admiring – or possibly envying – the sleek shapes, the luxurious interiors. Like most people, they probably couldn't afford to buy a set of tyres for the Ferrari, let alone the car itself. She felt disappointed with Lachlan, who had so much, yet still wanted more. He wouldn't rest until he was top of the charts; second or third wouldn't do. Their wealth had been acquired easily from doing what they enjoyed, and they'd quickly got used to buying anything they wanted.

For the first time, Jeannie felt guilty for having so much money when most of the population had so little. She almost wished Marcia was getting married in Walton Vale to someone very ordinary, like Graham, not the son of a lord in a church where the bones of his ancestors rested in their crumbling tombs. Life had been more fun, she thought nostalgically, more lighthearted, in the days when they'd had to pool their money to see if there was enough to get them in the Cavern or pay for the cheapest seats at the pictures.

But things couldn't be expected to stay the same. The Beatles, for instance, were world famous now. Last year, they'd gone to Buckingham Palace to collect their MBE's from the Queen. Lachlan had never said, but she sensed he was jealous of their fame.

Jeannie was about to turn away from the window, when a dusty Morris Traveller drove up, parked badly, and the driver got out, a pretty, rosy-cheeked young woman, dowdily dressed, her dark hair knotted in an untidy bun.

Jeannie hammered on the window. 'Elaine!' she yelled. 'Elaine! Wait there, don't move, I'm coming down.' She raced downstairs. Minutes later, she flung her arms around her friend. 'Oh, Elaine! You look marvellous. The very picture of health. It's ages since I last saw you. How's things?'

'Wearisome. I hate driving, but how else was I supposed to get from London to Wiltshire with loads and loads of luggage. I finished Imperial College today,' she explained. 'My fourth year. Only another two to go.'

'You work so hard, you make me feel ashamed.' They linked arms. 'How's things, medically speaking?'

'Fine. I gave Cordelia an appendectomy the other day.'

Jeannie shuddered. 'I don't want to know anything about Cordelia! I shall definitely not be leaving my body for medical research. I can't stand the thought of people like you mucking about with me, even if I'm dead.'

The cadaver Elaine and her group practised on had been christened Cordelia. She was treated for a variety of medical conditions, then heartlessly shut away at night in a freezing drawer.

They wandered around the grounds, passing the big marquee where trestle tables were being erected, talking animatedly as they brought each other up to date with all that was happening in their busy lives. Elaine was dating a fellow student, but it wasn't serious. 'I've no intention of marrying a doctor. We'd never see each other.'

Jeannie told her about 'Marzipan Dream' – 'it's not like anything the Merseysiders have done before' – and that 'Moon Under Water' had been included on Frank Sinatra's latest LP. 'Kevin's beside himself with joy.'

Elaine declared that news capped anything else she might have to say. 'It would be so trivial by comparison.' She wanted to know if Jeannie had seen Marcia around. 'Last time I came, my bridesmaid's dress wasn't quite finished. I have to try it on and make sure it fits.'

'We're not long here ourselves. Lachlan's gone in search of Fly and Sean. Let's go indoors, though it's a madhouse in there.'

They found a woman who thought Marcia might be upstairs with the bridesmaids who were trying on their dresses. 'The dressmaker arrived about an hour ago.'

After another search they found Marcia in a bedroom along with half a dozen other women, one of whom was Zoe and another Lady Elroy-Smythe, Julia to her friends. Two were brides-maids, cousins of the groom, wearing their cream slipper satin dresses inside out. The dressmaker was kneeling on the floor, her mouth full of pins, making last–minute adjustments to the waist of one. Marcia was standing in the middle of the room ordering everyone about. Her designer wedding gown had been bought in Paris, a magnificent creation comprising yards and yards of lace criss–crossed with pearls. It was suspended like a balloon from the picture rail.

'Elaine!' Marcia screeched. 'You're late. Come and try your frock on immediately. Oh, and look at your hair! It really is disgusting. Just because you're nearly a doctor, it's no excuse to lose all interest in your appearance. Thank goodness there's a hairdresser coming in the morning. Oh, hello, Jeannie. She's another Flower Girl,' she announced to the other women.

Jeannie accepted a glass of sherry from Julia on condition she stayed well away from the dresses. She sat next to Zoe on the bed, wondered where her husband was, and decided she didn't care. It wasn't the first disagreement they'd had, but it seemed the most serious. She'd never felt so disappointed with him before.

After dinner, the young people, about thirty in all, descended en masse on the village pub. Jeannie was glad when the men remained in the saloon and the women went into the lounge. She sat with Elaine and Stella, who'd never met before. An understandably sulky Monica had been forced to remain at Harwood Hall when she could find no one to look after Gareth. Stella listened, occasionally startling the room with her infectious laughter, while Elaine described how she used to play the tambourine in the Flowers' garden shed. 'And Lachlan used to make me and Jeannie sing. That was in the days before Fly joined the group.'

'I don't think my father would have taken lightly to a set of drums in his shed,' Jeannie said drily.

As the night progressed, the crowd in the saloon grew rowdier and rowdier. Someone started to play the piano and the Merseysiders gave an impromptu, drunken concert. Stella tut-tutted and promised to give Fly an earful when she saw him.

'Have you and our Lachlan had a row?' Elaine asked when Stella suddenly had to make a dash for the Ladies. 'You hardly spoke to each other during dinner.'

'Not a row, more a difference of opinion.' She imagined an inebriated Lachlan, who usually drank no more than a single pint or a couple of glasses of wine, with his arm around Max, best mates, when in the very near future he intended stabbing him in the back. She contemplated warning Max what his 'best mate' had in mind, but it would only prolong the agony and do no good at all. What's more, there was always a slight chance Lachlan might change his mind. 'Actually, Elaine, I'm getting a headache. It's the smoke and the noise and this awful heat. I think I'll have an early night.'

'D'you want me to come with you?'

Jeannie wouldn't have minded, but Elaine was obviously enjoying herself. 'No, I'll be all right. Tell Stella I'll see her in the morning.' She impulsively kissed her friend. 'You're going to make the most beautiful bridesmaid the world has ever seen.'

The noise from the pub could still be heard when Jeannie went through the gates of Harwood Hall, where the lights appeared to be on in every room. She didn't feel remotely like an early night. It was too hot to sleep and her head was buzzing rather than aching. What she would have liked was a long talk with a sober Lachlan, an unlikely prospect right now.

To the side of the house, through the trees, the lake was visible, glistening like a mirror in the light of a full moon. Jeannie strolled towards it, disturbing the birds in the trees and other small, earthbound creatures, as she made her way through the rough undergrowth. She arrived at the glassy stretch of water and saw a bench clearly visible on the other side. She tramped around the edge accompanied by faint plopping sounds, as if fish were raising their heads above the water, then diving for cover when they saw her.

She came to the bench and sat down with a thankful sigh. The metal bars felt cool through her thin frock as she cast around in her mind for something to think about other than Lachlan and what would happen to Max when he was no longer a Merseysider. A memory surfaced and she grimaced. They'd forgotten to sign the menu for the barmaid who'd asked so nicely, hadn't interrupted their meal as some people would have done. Her daughter had been ill, she'd said. Jeannie resolved they would return the same way and give the woman the autographs she wanted. She didn't like letting people down.

The moon was reflected in the lake, she hadn't

noticed until now, a shimmering circle of golden light, as still as the real moon, and looking just as solid. Had Kevin been watching a similar sight when he'd written his song?

'Moon under water,' Jeannie sang. She didn't have much of a voice, it was too thin, but Kevin thought it sweet. 'I can't reach you. Like stars in a mirror, you're not there. Like...'

She jumped and stopped singing when, from somewhere within the middle of the trees, came the haunting strains of a mouth organ playing the same song. Her mind immediately went back to the day she'd first met Lachlan. He'd done the same thing, though she'd been playing the piano and he the violin.

A man emerged from the black trees on the bank opposite. She couldn't tell who, only that it wasn't Lachlan, who was probably legless by now, and unable to tell one end of a mouth organ from the other.

The man continued to play as he came round the edge of the pool with long, loping strides, and she recognised Sean McDowd. They rarely spoke to each other. She'd never liked him and sensed he felt the same about her. It seemed strange that he should approach her now. Perhaps he thought she was someone else. Sean had had relation-ships with a string of well-known women. His picture was often in the papers, a grim, unsmiling figure escorting some model or actress to a play, a nightclub, or a film premiere.

He was only a few feet away when he put the mouth organ in his pocket. 'Hi, Jeannie,' he said, so can't have thought she was someone else. 'I saw you leave the pub.'

'I had a headache,' she explained, adding, 'It's gone now,' in case he offered sympathy for something she didn't have.

'Good.' He sat beside her on the bench. 'It's nice here.'

'I was just wondering if it was a scene like this that inspired your dad to write his song.'

'Could be.' He nodded thoughtfully and said no more.

'Lachlan said you're leaving the group,' Jeannie said eventually. 'I hope you do well on your own.'

'I'm looking forward to it. I prefer to make me own decisions, be in charge of me own destiny, as it were.'

'I love being a Flower Girl, but I don't look upon show business as my destiny. I don't care who's in charge.'

'So, what is?' he asked curiously.

'My destiny?' She was surprised he was interested. 'I'd like a family; two children at least, quite soon.'

There was another long silence. Jeannie felt strangely comfortable in his presence. He stretched his arms along the back of the seat, stretched out his long legs and crossed them at the ankles. His chin was sunk into his chest and Jeannie surreptitiously examined his perfect profile. He wore his hair long and tied back, like Lachlan, and was dressed all in black. She recalled that a recent poll had placed him second in a list of Britain's sexiest men – another Sean had come top, the star of the James Bond films, Sean Connery. The man she was sitting next to on the bench by the lake, who people in Ailsham once thought had the makings of a master criminal, had become a famous entertainer instead, a heart throb. Thousands, if not millions, of women would give anything to be in her place.

Jeannie experienced an unexpected and totally unwelcome thrust of something in her chest that could only be described as desire, a sensation that, until now, had been reserved only for Lachlan. She gasped and shifted uneasily on the bench, trying to rid herself of the sensation, think of other things – the moon, the moon under the water, moving now, wobbling a little. The water must have been disturbed.

Then Sean slid his arm further along the bench until it rested on her shoulders. Gently, very gently, he pulled her towards him, put his other hand on her cheek, and kissed her. She didn't respond, but nor did she stop him. She didn't want him to stop. His lips were hard, yet un-demanding. He wanted nothing back, just her acceptance of his long, sweet kiss, that was only interrupted by the voices of people coming home from the pub.

'I love you,' Sean whispered, and was gone.

Lachlan wasn't the slightest bit drunk. He was stone cold sober and walked a straight line to prove it. 'You know I never drink much. I had one beer, that's all.'

'You *sounded* drunk,' Jeannie argued. She'd been pretending to be asleep when he came into the room and tripped over her shoes so she pre-tended he'd woken her. It was then she accused him of being drunk and he accused her of thoughtlessly leaving her shoes in the middle of the room for anyone to fall over.

'I sounded as if I was having a good time, that's all,' he said haughtily. 'We all were. It's not necessary to get plastered in order to enjoy yourself, though Max over-indulged, as usual. He'll have a head on him in the morning. Fly can drink like a fish and it doesn't affect him.'

'Perhaps Max senses his entire world is about to collapse, and that's why he over-indulged.'

'Don't exaggerate, Jeannie. Max is lucky to have got as far as he has. He can join another group or go into management. He must have more than enough in the bank to last till he sorts himself out.'

'Oh, and you think Monica will be happy about that? She'll be as mad as hell and the person she'll be maddest with is Max himself.' Jeannie turned over in the bed with a flounce so she was facing away from Lachlan when he got in. For the first time they slept with backs to each other. Not that Jeannie slept much, and it wasn't thoughts of her brother that kept her awake, but the memory of Sean's kiss, which she could still feel on her lips. Why hadn't she pushed him away, slapped his face, stopped him somehow? It troubled her that she'd let another man touch her when Lachlan was the only man she'd ever wanted. She'd betrayed him, just as he was about to betray Max.

When they woke, the sun was streaming into the room and they were facing each other. Jeannie reached for him at the same time as he reached for her. They made love, savagely, like strangers.

'Perhaps we should row more often,' Lachlan gasped hoarsely when it was over. 'We've been married for four years, but that was the best ever.' He groaned. 'I love you, Jeannie Flowers.'

'And I love you, Lachlan Bailey.' She snuggled into his arms, Sean's kiss forgotten until later in the day when she saw him again. They greeted each other coolly, as if the kiss had never happened.

Rita hunched in the background when the guests followed the newly married couple out of church where they were met by an enormous cheering crowd, a posse of eager photographers, and two television cameras. She hated being filmed or photographed except if she was singing when she didn't care. Other times, it made her uncomfortably aware of her plain looks and her inability to smile naturally. She managed to stay out of sight until there was a call for the other Flower Girls to be photographed with the bride and her dad came looking for her.

'You're wanted, girl.' Kevin took her hand and led her to a shady spot under a tree where Jeannie, Zoe, and a radiant Marcia were waiting. 'I wish you'd taken your Mam's advice and worn something a bit more fashionable, luv,' Kevin said. 'You look like Little Orphan Annie in that get up.' Rita's calf-length frock, bought from C&A, was cream with a pattern of pastel flowers and a sailor collar. She'd bought her hat in the same shop, a little cream straw boater.

Rita clenched her teeth and tried not to wince while the photographers yelled at them to look up, look down, smile, look at the bride, and the television cameras rolled.

The torture continued. The Merseysiders were requested to join the group and positively refused to wear their top hats. It was too hot and they looked daft with long hair. She was grateful when Sean put his arm around her. He was the only one who guessed how she felt. 'It'll be over soon, sis,' he said quietly. She noticed his eyes flicker in the direction of Jeannie, who looked gorgeous in a brief yellow frock and a big hat to match, and wondered if he still had a crush on her after all this time. His girlfriend had arrived this morning, a model called Anita something. She came from somewhere in Latin America and had thick, black, shining hair.

The camera wielders announced they'd had their fill. The guests began to drift towards the line of cars waiting to take them back to the reception. Some preferred to walk. Rita tagged on to the end of a group of walkers.

No one spoke to her, until an elderly man in front turned round, and waited for her to catch up.

'Aren't you a Flower Girl?'

'Yes,' Rita mumbled.

'I've seen you on television. You look very different when you sing. For a minute there, I hardly recognised you.'

'People never do.' When she sang, she came alive.

He held out a hand for her to shake. 'Robert

310

Briggs, the bridegroom's grandfather. How do you do, Flower Girl. I'm afraid I don't know your name.'

'Rita McDowd. Are you a lord?'

'Good gracious me, no. I'm just plain mister. Philip's mother is my daughter. You're very shy, aren't you, Rita McDowd?' he said in a kindly voice.

Rita nodded numbly at this undeniable and clearly obvious fact.

'You shouldn't be. You're a very talented, extremely successful young woman, yet you pretend to be invisible. Would you like to hold my arm?'

'Please.' She linked him and he patted her hand.

'There!' he said comfortably. 'I feel very honoured. What you need is a guardian angel, someone who'll constantly remind you of how wonderful you are, take you out of your shell. I'd offer to do it myself, but I'm getting on in years and it takes me all my time to walk up this hill.'

'What hill?'

Robert Briggs laughed and said that only proved his point.

It was two o'clock in the morning when the reception drew to an end, by which time Marcia and Phil had long ago left for their honeymoon in the Seychelles, and the villagers had gone home, exhausted, to their beds. Only relatives and close friends remained for the last waltz.

The eight-piece orchestra began to play 'Some Enchanted Evening', and Sean's girlfriend, Anita,

311

jumped to her feet and they began to dance. Sean wished with all his heart it was Jeannie he was holding in his arms. She was dancing with Lachlan, her head on his shoulders. He'd scarcely been able to take his eyes off her all day.

Elaine and Zoe remained seated, lamenting the fact they didn't have a man between them. Zoe's boyfriend had had to leave early. 'He's in a play in London and he had to be back in time for the first house.'

'I haven't got a proper boyfriend,' Elaine said. 'I'm too busy with my studies for anything serious.'

Max Flowers knew that Monica would give him hell tomorrow for getting drunk two nights in a row. Hours ago, she'd taken Gareth back to the house in a huff. He sighed. Getting plastered didn't seem such an awful thing to do, not at a wedding. Sometimes, he wished he'd tried to pay her off, as everyone had suggested, not gone and married the damn woman.

'Well, if this isn't the best wedding I've ever been to,' Kevin McDowd said to his wife. He'd danced himself silly and made himself look ridiculous, but didn't care.

'Every wedding you go to is the best ever,' Sadie remarked tartly. 'Lord knows what people thought, you turning everything, even the Twist, into an Irish jig.'

'They thought, "That fine fella drives a Rolls and manages one of the best known pop groups in the country. If he wants to dance a jig to the Twist, then hasn't he got every right in the world?"'

'Ah, go on wit'cha.' Sadie nudged him sharply.

Kevin gasped. Her nudges always turned him on. 'D'you think our Rita's clicked with that ould geezer?' he asked. His daughter was being swirled around by a spritely individual with snow-white hair. 'She's been with him all day.'

'Don't be an eejit, Kevin McDowd. That's the groom's granddaddy.' Sadie gave him another nudge.

Jaysus! If she nudged him again, he'd drag off both their clothes and give her one on the spot. *That'd* give folks something to talk about.

Chapter 11

'So, you see, Mum,' Jeannie finished, 'Max will be gutted when he finds out. It'll destroy him.'

'I think you're exaggerating, Jeannie. Our Max is a strong person. He'll survive.'

Jeannie didn't argue that Max was anything but strong. Her mother hadn't been really listening when she'd told her that Max was about to lose his place with the group that had been his life since he was fourteen. These days, she was totally preoccupied with Alex and their two little girls – Amy, three, and Eliza, who would soon be two.

It was the Monday after the wedding and the weather was still hot and stuffy. Jeannie and her mother were on a swing seat in the garden of Magnolia Cottage, a fairy-tale place, with crooked latticed windows and a red tiled roof The garden was a tumble of trailing flowers and fragrant shrubs. Climbing roses hung around the front and back doors – Lachlan complained they had been fitted with elves in mind every time he banged his head.

Inside the cottage was just as pretty. The walls and the low ceilings were criss-crossed with black beams and there was a miniature inglenook fireplace in the living room where logs were burnt when it was cold. Rose had never been allowed much say in the decoration of the house in Disraeli Terrace and had disliked the big, dark furniture that had belonged to Tom's mother. This time, she'd had free rein. Every curtain was draped and held back by a frilly tie and the cretonne three-piece suite had its own matching cushions edged in thick lace. There were flowers in the fireplace in summer and the crockery was covered with rosebuds.

Jeannie's half-sisters were splashing about in a plastic pool uttering tiny, excited cries. They were nothing like Jeannie or her brothers, the children Rose had had with Tom. Alex's girls were white-blonde, fragile creatures, like little fairies.

She was almost sorry she'd come. Her mother's lack of interest in Max worried her. It could only mean she'd be equally disinterested if she, Jeannie, had a problem. Or Gerald. She said, 'Gerald's coming home on Friday for a few days, Mum.'

'Is he, love?' She didn't add, 'Tell him to come and see me,' or ask how Gerald was getting on, living on his own in London, something he'd been doing for a year since he'd turned eighteen. Unlike Max, Gerald had realised he would never make more than a second-rate guitarist. In London, he had joined a group of like-minded youngsters, who played together for fun. By day, he worked in the advertising department of the *New Musical Express*, and was occasionally called upon to write an article or represent the magazine at a not-very-important gig. His ambition was to become a professional journalist covering the pop music scene. The few times a year he came back to Liverpool he stayed with his sister and Lachlan. Gerald wasn't important enough for Monica to make welcome at his brother's house.

'Have you seen your father lately?' her mother asked.

'Not since April. I'm not sure if he really wants to see me.' They'd more or less been abandoned by their parents, Jeannie thought ruefully. Rose preferred her new family, and Tom seemed sullen and depressed whenever she called. He was sixty-seven, still tending Colonel Corbett's garden. Various women attended to his domestic needs – possibly other needs if the frequent presence of Mrs Denning was anything to go by. She made his evening meal and stayed for hours.

'I wish he'd agree to a divorce,' her mother grumbled. 'Iris and Alex divorced quite amicably – she's already married again – but Tom positively refuses.'

'He's just being awkward.'

'He's good at that. I can't remember him being much else.'

'Never mind, Mum. You and Alex are perfectly happy as you are. A piece of paper won't make much difference.'

Rose rolled her big blue eyes and sighed. 'I suppose not, but it makes me feel like a kept woman instead of a wife. You're not going, are you, love?' she exclaimed when Jeannie got to her feet. 'You haven't had a cup of tea. Oh, aren't I a terrible hostess!'

'It's all right. I'd like to get back and make Lachlan some lunch.' Lachlan was quite capable of making his own lunch should he feel hungry, which was most unlikely. Anyway, the house had been gradually filling up with people when she left. It would be even fuller now and nobody would think twice about raiding the fridge. She just wanted to get away from the mother and the rose-covered cottage where she didn't belong.

'Marzipan Dream' was released to general acclaim. Wildly enthusiastic reviews in the music press declared it to be the best the Merseysiders had ever done. Within its first week, it shot to number four in the charts.

'Next week, it's bound to reach the top,' Lachlan said gleefully, rubbing his hands, but a few days later, the Beatles' 'Can't Buy Me Love' came out and soared to number one, where it would stay for weeks, while 'Marzipan Dream' slowly went down.

'Never mind, there's always a next time,' Jeannie said consolingly.

'We'll never do anything better than that,' Lachlan groaned.

'Of course you will. That's a defeatist way to think.' He looked so woebegone she gave him a hug, though she thought him silly to want so much when he already had more than enough.

It was late when Monica rang, almost midnight. Jeannie answered. She was about to go to bed and Lachlan was winding up in the studio downstairs.

'Do you know what your husband has done to Max?' Monica screamed.

Jeannie's heart sank. Unable to think of a suitable answer, she mumbled something incomprehensible, which didn't matter, as Monica continued with hardly a pause. 'He's only gone and given him the push. Max is bloody beside himself. He's in the bathroom, crying his eyes out. I never knew men could cry. You might like to know I'm having another baby and we're about to have an extension built on the house.'

'I'm sorry, Monica.' Now didn't seem the appropriate time to congratulate her on the baby.

'Did you know about this, Jeannie?'

'Lachlan did mention it, yes.'

'And you didn't tell Max? Fine sister you turned about to be. But then, you're all right, aren't you?' The spite in the shrill voice made Jeannie's blood run cold. 'The money just keeps rolling in. How are me and Max supposed to manage? We'll soon have two kids and the house isn't nearly big enough.'

'I'm sure something else will turn up, Monica.' The house was already three times as big as the ones in Disraeli Terrace, more than enough for four people.

'Oh, fuck off, Jeannie!' The receiver at the other end was slammed down with such force that the sound hurt Jeannie's ear.

She sat on the bed, nursing her ear and taking deep breaths, wanting to rush down to the basement to tear Lachlan off a strip for not preparing her. It would be best to wait, calm down a bit, before she faced him. He must have told Max tonight. They'd gone out to dinner earlier, Fly and Sean too, something they'd never done before. Perhaps Sean had announced he was leaving at the same time.

The phone rang again. Jeannie considered ignoring it because she knew who it would be. Let Lachlan answer. There was a phone in the basement, but he wouldn't hear if the studio door was closed.

Gritting her teeth, she picked up the receiver. 'Hello.'

'Jeannie!' It was Max, as expected, and he said her name with such reproach she wanted to weep. 'Why didn't you tell me what Lachlan was going to do?'

'Oh, Max! What difference would it have made?'

'I would have known where I stood. Did you try to talk him out of it?'

'Of course I did, Max. We had an argument, but you know Lachlan. He wouldn't be moved.'

'When was this?'

'On the way to Marcia's wedding.'

'That's more than a month ago.' His voice was sad and dejected. 'You've let me down badly, Jeannie. I'm not sure if I can ever forgive you.' The receiver was replaced, gently this time, with scarcely a click.

'Max!' Jeannie yelled, but Max had gone.

Gerald called a few days later. She'd heard no more from Monica or Max, and there was no answer whenever she tried to ring.

'Is this true about our Max being dropped and Sean McDowd leaving the Merseysiders?' Gerald asked.

'How did you find out?' Jeannie felt angry. There'd been no need to announce to the world

319

the truth about Max. Why couldn't he just 'leave', like Sean?

'It's in a press release that arrived this morning from Eddie Ford. Has Lachlan lost his marbles or something? I know he couldn't have stopped Sean from going, but he's mad to drop Max at the same time.'

'Why's that?'

'It's common sense. The Merseysiders will seem like a completely different group without Sean and Max. I'm not just saying this because Max is my brother, Jeannie,' Gerald said earnestly. 'Max may not be the best guitarist of all time, but people have got used to him. They don't like change. Tell Lachlan he's making a big mistake.'

'I will, Gerald,' Jeannie promised.

But Lachlan pooh-poohed Gerald's advice. 'What does he know? He's just a kid. He's worked on a music mag for a year and thinks he knows everything.'

'So did you when you were nineteen.'

'Yeah, I suppose.' He patted his knee. 'Come and keep me company.'

'I want to practise.' The Flower Girls had had no engagements for six weeks while Marcia and Phil were on their protracted honeymoon. Now Marcia was back and they were due to make another record and had a series of gigs lined up for the autumn.

'Am I being rejected?'

She stuck out her tongue at him. 'Yeah, I suppose.'

There was something about Sean McDowd that demanded silence from the audience. There wasn't a murmur, a cough, not even a movement from the rapt *Top of the Pops* audience, just total concentration on the tall, slight figure nursing his guitar. His voice was a husky, compelling whisper, hypnotic. There was no backing group, just Sean and his guitar.

He'd chosen an unusual number for his first solo recording, the Christmas carol, 'Silent Night'. It was released, appropriately, in December. Everyone wanted to be top of the charts at Christmas. Sean was twelfth and was quite happy about it, according to Kevin, who was now his manager. It was twice as high as the Merseysiders' latest release, which had managed only twenty-fourth before sinking into oblivion, the first time the group hadn't reached the top ten.

Lachlan had made a terrible mistake. It had all been Eddie Ford's idea, but it was Lachlan's group and there'd been no need to go along with it. He'd lost his judgement in a desperate desire to be the best. Jeannie had felt qualms when the two new members, Tod and Eric, had turned up at the house to make the recording. They were eighteen, good-looking, but only slips of kids who found the whole thing highly amusing. They would appeal to the teeny-boppers, but not the mature following the Merseysiders had built up over the years, the genuine music lovers.

Jeannie felt even more worried when she watched the group play together for the first time on *Ready, Steady Go*. Gerald was right, the change had been too drastic. The boys skitted around, laughing at each other whereas, as always, Lachlan was putting his heart and soul into his performance. There was perspiration on his brow, as if he realised, too late, he'd been seriously wrong to get rid of Max and not replace Sean with someone older.

She ran into his arms when he arrived home later that night, his face grey and drawn.

'All right, there's no need to say it. Enough people already have. I've made a major cock up.' His voice was harsh. 'I suppose it serves me right.'

'I wasn't going to say anything, darling.' She pressed her cheek against his, stroked his neck. 'Only that I love you. I always will, even when you behave like an idiot.'

The Flower Girls' next record turned out to be their last. After Christmas, Marcia announced she was pregnant and had decided to leave. Zoe immediately piped up to say she'd had an offer to host a children's programme on TV. 'I was going to turn it down, but if the group's breaking up, I'll accept.'

Kevin looked nonplussed. 'We can always get another girl in Marcia's place. We don't *have* to break up.'

'I'd sooner do the TV thing, Kevin, though I wouldn't have mentioned it if Marcia hadn't said she was leaving.'

'Then we can get two other girls.'

'Actually, Kevin, me and Lachlan are thinking of starting a family.' Monica was pregnant, so was

Stella, and now Marcia was expecting a baby. Jeannie longed for a baby of her own. She was young and healthy, only twenty-three, it shouldn't take long for her to conceive.

'What about you, luv?' Kevin asked his daughter.

'I'd like to go solo, like our Sean,' Rita said, surprising everyone.

'Jaysus!' Kevin gasped. 'It's taken just five minutes for youse lot to fall apart.'

'Nothing lasts for ever,' Jeannie said with the suggestion of a sigh. It would be a wrench, she'd always miss the Flower Girls, but time moved on. She'd made an awful lot of money in the nicest possible way and had made her mark on show business, something furthest from her mind when she'd been growing up.

No one seemed upset, not even Kevin. He had Sean's career to keep him busy and now Rita's. He was commissioned to write songs for other artists and the royalties were piling up.

Jeannie was glad they'd split without a shred of acrimony and hoped they would always remain good friends. She only wished she could say the same for Lachlan's group.

The news quickly spread that the Flower Girls intended to disband after their next record had been released. Articles appeared in the national press applauding their effect on the world of pop music. They were invited on chat shows to explain their reasons for disbanding. Marcia proudly displayed her slightly bulging stomach.

The publicity was huge. Demands for gigs

poured in. They toured Europe, playing in a different country every night for a week. Kevin said gleefully that their final record, 'Nightfall', was bound to be a hit. He was just as keen as Lachlan to get a number one under his belt.

In March 1968, 'Nightfall' reached number two. They were perfectly happy to be second.

For the first time in her married life, Jeannie became a housewife, not that there was much housework to do. A very nice woman, Connie Davies, came in three times a week to clean Noah's Ark and do the washing. Jeannie had been looking forward to, yet half dreading, a permanent return. Although it had been a relief to come back after a tour, her diary had always been crammed full with things to do – tours, gigs, appearances on television, making records. How would she feel when there was nothing? She prayed she would conceive soon. Everything would be different once she had a baby.

For the first few weeks, she went down to the basement and played the keyboard like a mad woman, hour after hour. Lachlan wanted to know if she regretted giving up her career – 'You're awfully young to retire, darling' – but Jeannie explained she was just getting things out of her system.

'What things?'

'I don't know.' When Connie wasn't there the house seemed too quiet. She was nervous the nights Lachlan was away, though she'd been alone before and it had never bothered her. They saw little of Kevin, and nothing at all of Sean or

324

Rita. Marcia lived in Wiltshire; Zoe had moved to London. The Merseysiders still used the studio, but Fly's was the only familiar face. Stella was having a difficult pregnancy and Jeannie went to see her often. She badly missed Max.

Months ago, when she'd plucked up the courage to call on him, he'd refused to speak to her.

'Do you blame him?' Monica sneered from the doorstep. Jeannie hadn't even been asked inside.

'But it wasn't *me* who dumped him!'

'It was as good as.'

'I tried to persuade Lachlan it was a bad idea.'

'Huh!' Monica slammed the door.

She knew Lachlan was suffering pangs of conscience for what he'd done to Max – and to himself – by firing him. It only made worse his constant struggle to get the Merseysiders back to the position where they'd been before. The group barely entered the charts, even though he spent hours in the studio, composing new songs, arranging the music. But he missed Sean's input. He was making himself ill, emerging in the early hours of the morning, listless and haggard.

'Hey! We're supposed to be trying for a baby,' Jeannie would remind him when he claimed he was too tired to make love.

'I'm sorry, darling. So sorry,' he would mutter before falling asleep in her arms.

Soon she would be twenty-four, still not old, but she was desperate to start a family. Stella had had a girl, Samantha, who was gorgeous, and they'd all gone to Harwood Hall for the christening of Marcia's chubby little boy, Iain. She didn't know whether Monica had had a boy or a girl.

Last time she'd passed the house, it had been up for sale.

They'd been trying for over a year and she was getting more and more upset every time a period started. She dreamt of babies, of giving birth, but always woke up before the baby was put in her arms.

Without telling Lachlan, she went to see her doctor who sent her for tests. A fortnight later, she was told she was perfectly healthy and there was nothing to stop her from conceiving.

'But it won't help if you get too anxious about it,' the doctor, an affable, grey-haired man, advised. 'How does your husband feel about things?'

'He'd like us to have a family, but he doesn't think about it as much as I do.'

'Perhaps you should be like your husband and think about it less. Try to relax. You're only young and there's plenty of time.'

Jeannie didn't think so. Marcia, Stella, Monica, even her own mother at almost forty; none had had a problem getting pregnant, so why was she? Until now, her life had always run smoothly, with few hiccups, none of which had mattered much. Jeannie wasn't used to things not going as planned.

Despite what she'd told the doctor, she wasn't sure if Lachlan cared if they had a family or not. He probably never thought about it. He was too consumed by his music. Jeannie suspected that, given the choice, he'd much prefer to be top of the charts than have a baby.

Eighteen months after he'd been so uncere-moniously dumped, Max rang and asked Jeannie if they could meet. 'Somewhere in town.'

'Why don't you come here, to Noah's Ark?' asked a surprised Jeannie, thrilled to hear from her brother at last.

'I'm not setting foot in Noah's Ark again while Lachlan Bailey lives there.'

'Lachlan's away.'

'I don't care.'

They arranged to have lunch the following day in a new restaurant in Bold Street. 'It's lovely to hear your voice at last, Max,' she said warmly. 'I've missed you terribly.'

'I didn't want to see anyone, not even my family, until I'd done something constructive with my life, had something to boast about,' Max said. Jeannie hadn't expected him to look quite so cheerful and pleased with himself. The last stressful year had apparently affected him less than it had done Lachlan.

'Come on, then, boast!' Jeannie said encourag-ingly. His answer was the last thing she expected.

'I've got three A levels.' He smiled, clearly proud of his achievement. 'The results only came yesterday. I got two A's and a B. They're the same subjects I studied at school, so I was already part of the way there. I'm amazed I could remember a thing, because I didn't listen during the lessons.'

'That's wonderful, Max.' But she didn't think it all *that* wonderful and was surprised he was so pleased.

'Guess what I'm going to do now?' His eyes twinkled.

'I've no idea, Max.'

'I'm going to college to train to be a teacher.'

'That's even more wonderful. What does Monica think?'

'Monica!' He gave a cynical laugh. 'Monica left me ages ago. You can imagine why. We're getting divorced. She's virtually cleaning me out. I'll end up with hardly a bean to show for all the years I was with the Merseysiders.'

'And Gareth?' Jeannie asked anxiously. 'I've thought about him a lot, Max, almost as much as I did you. Monica was pregnant when we last spoke, so you'll have two children by now.'

'I have a daughter, Tammy, as well as a son. Monica's met some guy who's a bit actor in films and they've moved to California, I haven't seen Gareth since he left, and I haven't seen Tammy at all.'

'That's a terrible shame.' She put her hand on his sleeve.

He looked puzzled. 'It's strange, but in a way, I don't miss them. That part of my life seems totally unreal. I can hardly believe it happened. I was nothing but a bag of nerves. Monica didn't help. She made me feel as if the whole world was against me. When Lachlan said he was letting me go, it was like the culmination of a sinister plot that had been hatching for years.'

'Lachlan's incapable of hatching a plot.'

'I know, but I still think what he did was pretty contemptible. We were friends. You know something, Jeannie,' he said ruefully, 'it's terrible to

328

discover you're no good at the thing you wanted to do more than anything else on earth. I still play the guitar, but only for myself. I'm going to be a teacher. It'll always be second best, but I was only a second best guitarist, so what the hell! I've just got to learn to live with that.'

Soon it would be another Christmas and it seemed they were going to spend it on their own. Jeannie was quite looking forward to it. The Baileys, Elaine included, were going to Harwood Hall, and Max, who wouldn't have come anyway, was going to stay with Gerald in London. Her mother would never agree to be prised away from Magnolia Cottage on Christmas Day, nor invite anyone to share it with her perfect little family.

It was years since she'd done any baking, but she could still remember how. Every day, she spent hours in the super modern kitchen turning out trays of mince pies, sausage rolls, cheese straws, and a Christmas cake that took all night to decorate. She bought a turkey so big it would have to be squeezed into the oven.

'Are you planning to feed an army?' Connie wanted to know. Every time she came into the kitchen, more food was being put in the oven or taken out.

'There's only me and Lachlan.'

Connie blinked. 'There's enough there to last the both of you till next Christmas.'

When she woke up on Christmas morning, Jeannie discovered herself alone in the bed. It often happened. If Lachlan woke up early, he went straight down to the studio.

'You think he'd have stayed, today of all days,' she grumbled.

She got up, dragged on jeans and a sweater, and went into the kitchen to prepare breakfast. Usually, they had only a piece of toast, but she wanted to do a special, Christmas breakfast for a change, a mixed grill. She put the sausages and bacon in the frying pan and went down to tell Lachlan that it would soon be ready.

Ten minutes later, everything was done, but there was no sign of Lachlan. She went down again. He was sitting in front of the bank of studio equipment staring into space.

'Breakfast's ready and it's getting cold,' she said crossly.

'I'll be there in a minute,' he murmured.

'*Now*, Lachlan.'

He looked up. There was a dark expression in his eyes, not just irritation, almost dislike. Jeannie shrank back, shocked to her bones. A moment of nothingness hung between them, until she turned on her heel and went upstairs. With shaking hands, she scraped the breakfasts into the bin and made coffee, as strong as she could take it. If Lachlan wanted some, he could get his own. There was a kettle and supplies downstairs, a toilet, a telephone. He could live there permanently if he wanted.

She sat down at the table, took a sip of the coffee, and burst into tears. What was happening to them? She prayed that Lachlan would come soon and make everything better, say he hadn't meant the look, that he couldn't remember giving her a look that wasn't anything but loving, because he loved her and always would.

But Lachlan didn't appear. She put the turkey in the oven, pushing it in with her foot and, at midday, started to peel the vegetables and steam the pudding that she'd prepared days before. She set the table in the dining room they hardly ever used.

Two o'clock, and still Lachlan didn't come. Jeannie poured a glass of wine and took it into the lounge, where she switched on the fire and the lights on the six-foot tree that had taken longer to decorate than the cake. Holly hung from the white walls and there was mistletoe over the door. Their cards, eighty-five in all, had been stuck with sellotape to the breastwork. The room looked very festive.

She sighed and went over to the window. It was snowing outside, only lightly. The flakes touched the ground and melted instantly. The garden was a lonely place, desolate. The canvas cover on the pool had sunk in the middle and contained an icy patch of water. Two birds were pecking at it furiously.

More wine! She needed more wine, In the kitchen, the cake, with its circle of red candles that she'd intended to light while they were having their Christmas dinner, stared at her balefully, each candle like a round, red, angry eye. Jeannie picked up the cake and flung it at the wall. In her entire life, she'd never done anything so outrageous. The plate broke, but the cake itself fell to the floor in one piece, landing on its bottom, not even the icing cracked.

Gosh! It must be hard. It must have the consist-

331

ency of concrete. Jeannie started to laugh. They'd have had to fetch a saw from the garage to cut it and a hammer for the icing.

The laughter swiftly turned to more tears. How could Lachlan *do* this to her?

Three o'clock. He was an hour late for dinner and six hours late for breakfast. She wondered if he would turn up for his tea?

Jeannie made a swift decision. Unless he arrived within the next five minutes, she wouldn't be there. She would go and see someone.

Who?

Everyone she knew was away. Everyone, that is, except her mother. She *needed* her mother. She needed to sink into someone's arms and cry her heart out. It was what mothers were for, and her own would just have to damn well be there for her.

'Sweetheart!' Rose cooed, holding her daughter in her slim arms. She'd turned out to be a perfect mother, after all, when Jeannie had arrived at Magnolia Cottage in a flood of tears. 'You should have come earlier. You shouldn't have stayed all day in that mausoleum of a house on your own.'

'I wouldn't have minded being on my own,' Jeannie sobbed. 'It was Lachlan being there that made it so horrible.'

'I know, love.' Jeannie's cheek was patted and her forehead kissed. 'I didn't realise you had problems.'

'Neither did I, not until today. Things have been getting worse, but I didn't notice. Or perhaps I just *pretended* not to notice.' Lachlan's total absorption with the group was unnatural. His obsession to be the best in the world even more. While these things had been stealthily building up, she'd been desperate to conceive. No one, not even Lachlan, knew how much she longed for a baby. She wouldn't have left the Flower Girls had she known how long it was going to take. She felt sure Rita McDowd would have stayed if Jeannie had wanted to. They could easily have got two girls in place of Marcia and Zoe, who'd never been the most important members of the group.

'Here we are. I've made it extra strong.' Alex came in with a tray of tea things. He was wearing a cream Arran sweater, obviously a Christmas present, and new, red plush slippers. He looked a perfectly contented, happily married man, even if there wasn't a piece of paper to prove it. 'I'll pop upstairs and make sure the girls are all right.' It was his tactful way of removing himself from the room while Jeannie continued to pour out her heart.

Amy and Eliza had been put down for their afternoon nap just after she arrived. 'They've been up since the crack of dawn, anxious to see what Santa Claus had brought them,' Rose had said smilingly. She'd used to say 'Santa Claus' when they were little, Jeannie remembered. At school, she'd wondered why the other children got their presents off someone called Father Christmas.

'Did they like the dolls from me and Lachlan?' she asked when Alex had gone.

'They loved them. Eliza's is almost as big as she is. They've taken their clothes on and off half a dozen times. I've promised to make them nightdresses for bed. Oh, and thank you, Jeannie, for the scent. It's lovely, and Alex is very pleased with his new driving gloves.'

'I haven't opened our presents yet,' Jeannie said sadly. 'We usually do it after breakfast but, well, you know what happened.'

Rose sighed and said soberly, 'I've neglected you, haven't I? The thing is, I never really looked upon you three as children. I didn't know my own mother, so I wasn't sure how I was supposed to behave. Your father always treated me like a child, then you and Max seemed to grow up so much more sensible and wiser than I was. I couldn't imagine you really needing me.'

'I needed you today, Mum.'

'I know, love.' She stroked Jeannie's arm. 'I'm just glad I was here for you as I should have been for Max. But thank goodness he's all right now. Sit up and let's have this tea before it gets cold.'

Jeannie's half-sisters came down soon afterwards, their faces pink with sleep, their pale hair tousled. She'd never really got to know them as she should, but they were pleased to find her still there and thanked her nicely for the dolls.

She watched them play on the hearth with the dolls and their other presents. The scene could well have featured on a Christmas card; two pretty little girls in front of a blazing log fire separated by a gleaming brass fireguard, a fat tree threaded with tinsel. The beamed walls were looped with paper chains. It was beautifully warm and the settee where she'd fallen into her mother's arms was soft and downy. Despite the awfulness of the day, she felt relaxed. She did her utmost to put Lachlan to the back of her mind and think about something else, such as how nice it was to find that her mother was still her mother after all. She liked being in her pretty, warm house.

Rose and Alex went to make the tea, refusing her help. 'You stay and rest, love,' her mother insisted. 'You've already made enough meals for today.'

'I've just remembered I left the turkey in the oven!'

'Lachlan's bound to surface sometime and he'll notice if it's burning.'

As long as the house didn't burn down, Jeannie didn't care what happened to the turkey. Alex shouted that tea was ready and the girls jumped to their feet and went through the door that looked as if it opened on to a small cupboard, but which led down three steps to the tiny dining room.

She discovered, after having eaten nothing all day, that she was unusually hungry, and quickly polished off a plate of cold turkey and chips. It was followed by trifle, mince pies, and Christmas cake. She thought about her own concrete cake left lying on the kitchen floor. Lachlan might notice that too when – if – he found the turkey.

After two glasses of sherry, she asked if she could ring Elaine in Harwood Hall. 'She was going to ring me this afternoon. She'll be wondering where I am.'

Jeannie didn't recognise the voice that answered when she called the Elroy-Smythe's.

She asked for Elaine Bailey, and it was a while before Elaine said, 'Hello.'

'Hello back. It's me.'

'Jeannie! Where are you? I've been trying to ring you for ages, but there was no reply.'

'I'm at my mother's. Are you having a good time down there?'

'No!' Elaine's voice dropped to a whisper. 'It's *awful*, freezing cold and deadly boring. There's nothing to do and our Marcia's driving everyone bonkers. D'you know, that poor baby's name has already been put down for Eton and he's only five months old? According to Marcia, he's a genius just because he can wave a rattle. "Look at him!" she keeps screeching, when all Iain's done is smile.'

'Oh, well. Only another three days to go,' Jeannie said sympathetically.

'There's no way I'm spending another three days in this ice house,' Elaine said bluntly. 'I've made an excuse, I said I'd been invited to a party tomorrow. Fortunately, I came in my own car, so I can leave whenever I please, but I don't know whether to go back to London or come to Liverpool. Either way, I'll be going to an empty house.'

'Liverpool! *Please*, Elaine, come to Liverpool.'

'If you're *that* keen to have me, of course, I will.' Elaine sounded pleased. 'If I set off early, I should be at your house about midday.'

'Not our house, *your* house. I'll see you in Walton Vale on the dot of twelve. Don't ask why. I'll tell you tomorrow.'

Christmas evening was spent dozing in front of

the television and drinking more sherry. She saw how Alex helped put the little girls to bed, then made turkey sandwiches and a pot of tea. She also saw her mother keep darting him little smiles and recalled that her father had never deigned to so much as put the kettle on. She probably appreciated his help more than most woman. Jeannie was glad her mother was so happy.

She slept in a cosy little bed in a warm room under a bouncy, daffodil yellow eiderdown. Although she fell asleep the minute her head touched the pillow, she woke up early, when it was pitch dark, with the memory of Lachlan's dark, unfriendly look at the forefront of her mind. She wasn't sure if they could recover from the events of yesterday.

At half past eleven, on a cold, crisp Boxing Day, she left Magnolia Cottage for Walton Vale. Her mother and Alex came to the gate to wave her off, each carrying a child in their arms. They both pressed on her that she wasn't to hesitate to come again.

'You're to think of this as your second home,' Alex said.

'I will,' Jeannie promised. 'Thank you both very much. Christmas turned out much better than I expected.' As she got in the car, she wondered how it had turned out for Lachlan?

'I rose with the birds,' Elaine said when she opened the door. 'I wanted to get here and light the fire before you came. I'm still thawing out. After yesterday, I know what it must be like to live in an igloo. I've just made some tea. Go and sit in the parlour and I'll bring it up. The fire should be well away by now.'

A coal fire crackled cheerfully in the grate and the television was on without the sound when Jeannie went into the parlour upstairs. The room was festooned with the familiar dusty Christmas decorations that were brought out every year, and the old piano on which she'd played *Minuet in G* on her very first visit still stood in exactly the same place. She'd like to bet it hadn't been tuned since. She lifted the lid, played a few notes, and grimaced. She was right!

Elaine came in with the tea. Jeannie said, 'I've been thinking about buying a proper piano.'

'Are you suggesting that one's not proper?' Elaine grinned.

'No, I meant as well as a keyboard. I miss the extra notes.'

'What'll you get, a white baby grand to go with your house?'

'No, one like this, an upright. The sort I learnt on.' She went and sat in an armchair in front of the fire, hugging her knees. 'I suppose you want to know what happened yesterday?'

'Not really. I know you and Lachlan have had a row. He rang last night to ask if you'd been in touch. He was worried about you. I'd sooner not take sides. After all, he's my brother.'

'What time did he ring?'

Elaine shrugged. 'Tennish.'

'It took him long enough to be worried.' Jeannie sniffed. 'And you're wrong, we haven't had a row. He just took it into his head to spend Christmas in the basement and to hell with me.'

338

'He's upset because Fly Fleming wants to leave the Merseysiders. He told me last night.'

'That's hardly *my* fault,' Jeannie cried angrily. 'Why should *I* have to suffer because of what Fly wants to do? It was the same with Max. He cut himself off from his family for ages and ages because of what Lachlan did to *him*.'

'Please, God, don't let me fall in love with a musician.'

'I wish I never had.'

There was silence for a while, except for the crackle of the fire and the ticking of the big clock on the mantelpiece. Then Elaine said, 'Do you really mean that, Jeannie?'

'Of course I damn well don't.' Jeannie felt, most unfairly, that it was a stupid question. 'Lachlan will always be the love of my life. We've been married nearly six years and for most of that time we've been deliriously happy...' She paused.

'But not any more?'

'Not if yesterday's anything to go by. Oh, let's talk about something else,' she said impatiently. 'How are Marcia and Iain? Your Mum and Dad? And you? Only another six months and you'll be a fully fledged doctor. Are you looking forward to it?'

Elaine pulled a face. 'I'm not exactly looking forward to working eighty hours a week on the wards, but it'll be nice to finish my training. Mum and Dad are fine, Iain's thriving, and Marcia's being a thorough pain in the bum. But when has she ever been anything else? I don't know how Phil puts up with it. By the way, she's pregnant again. Do you want more tea? I brought the pot up with me.'

They spent the next few hours chatting idly. Jeannie was struck by how uninteresting her life had become. Elaine had all sorts of experiences to relate. How Cordelia, the cadaver, had been given a proper burial and the whole class had sent flowers. The peculiar people she met on the wards where she already spent much of her time. The most peculiar of all were the consultants whose egos were a mile wide and whose arrogance had to be seen to be believed. 'The patients are usually very sweet, particularly with us students. It's horrid when someone you've grown fond of dies.'

Jeannie had little to tell in return. All she could recall doing in December was heaps of baking, which had turned out to be a complete waste of time.

'You can bring the mince pies and cheese straws to the party,' Elaine told her.

'What party?'

'The one here on New Year's Eve.'

'Lachlan has a gig somewhere, Norwich, I think.'

'That shouldn't stop you coming. It'll be quite like old times, just the two of us.' Elaine glanced at her watch. 'I won't be a minute.' She left the room.

Jeannie turned up the sound on the television when she saw Tommy Cooper was on. She had actually managed a laugh when Elaine came back.

'There's someone in the waiting room wants to see you,' she said. 'I told him to be here dead on four o'clock.'

'Lachlan!'

Elaine smiled. 'Who else?'

'I'm not sure if I want to see *him*.' She went slowly down the stairs, unsure if she would ever again feel the same about Lachlan.

He was sitting in the armchair where they'd done most of their courting, wearing the blue sweater he'd got for his twenty-first, which he refused to throw away, even though it was full of snags and holes. When she went in, he held out his arms. Jeannie ignored them, folded her own arms, and leaned against the door. He wasn't going to find making up *that* easy.

'I'm sorry,' he said abjectly.

'So'm I.'

'I had things on my mind. I forgot what day it was, where I was – everything. You should have thrown a bucket of water over me or something.'

'I asked you to come to breakfast,' Jeannie said stiffly, 'and you gave me a look as if you hated me. After that, I'd no intention of going near you again.'

'Hated you! Don't be daft, darling.' He came over, stood in front of her, and put his hands on the door beside her head. 'I adore you, you know I do.'

'You didn't yesterday.'

He rubbed his bristly chin against her forehead and this slight, not even faintly romantic gesture, affected Jeannie in a way a kiss would never have done. She knew that nothing in the world would ever stop her from loving Lachlan Bailey. She refrained from letting him know this just yet. No

341

matter how much she loved him, it didn't take away the fact that he'd completely ruined her Christmas with his thoughtlessness, though perhaps she should have made more of an effort to remove him from the basement, like empty the ruined breakfast over his head rather than in the bin.

'Fly wants to leave,' he said.

'Would you ruin his Christmas if I said I wanted to leave?'

He uttered a roar, lifted her up over his shoulder, carried her to the chair – *their* chair – flung her down, then threw himself beside her. 'If you left, I'd ruin everyone's Christmas,' he whispered in her ear.

Despite being turned on even more by this Stone Age manoeuvre, Jeannie moved her head away and said coldly, 'So, you spent the entire day in a sulk because of Fly?'

'I started off in a sulk, but the day ended on a highly constructive note.' He gave a self-satisfied smile and she wanted to punch him. 'First things first. The Merseysiders have got half a dozen gigs lined up. After that, they'll be disbanded.'

He paused expectantly for her gasp of horrified surprise, but Jeannie merely said, 'And then?'

'Then I'm starting a new group, but we won't be playing any of that psychedelic nonsense. I'm returning to my roots, to good old rock 'n' roll. There'll only be three of us – a drummer, a bass guitarist, and myself. I rang Fly yesterday and he's agreed to stay. A guy called Jimmy Cobb will be playing bass. I rang him as well and it's all been settled – I only met him recently and he's fed up with his namby-pamby group. We're calling ourselves the Survivors. Oh, and I'm ditching Ford and Firth and going with Kevin McDowd – I called him too.' He'd obviously interrupted an awful lot of people's Christmases. 'He'll be our manager from now on. He's organising a big launch at the end of March. I've already written our first number, "Rock-a-bye, Lady". Don't you think that's a great title?' He gave her a look of pained surprise. 'Yesterday, I came upstairs to tell you all this stuff, but you weren't around.'

'What time was that?'

'I dunno, Jeannie. It was dark,' he said helpfully. 'I called our Elaine and she said you were at your mother's and to leave you to cool down for some reason. By the way, the turkey's ruined. You forgot to turn the oven off and I don't know if we've got a poltergeist, but the Christmas cake was on the floor.'

'Oh, Lachlan!' Jeannie sighed. 'You've no idea, have you?'

'Darling!' He gave her a ferocious hug. 'I'm *full* of ideas, and the one uppermost in my mind at the moment is to make love to you. Shall we go home?'

'No,' Jeannie said sternly. 'We're staying with Elaine till your mum and dad come back. You'll just have to wait until tonight when we're in bed.'

'I'm not sure if I can wait so long.'

Neither did Jeannie. She would just have to accept that she was married to a fanatic, a man who would demand a guitar to play if he was on his death bed and whose wife would always take second place to his music.

It was at the New Year's party, when she was asked to play the piano, that Jeannie decided she wanted to return to show business. She was fed up being a housewife in a house that another woman cleaned, and there was no sign of the baby she longed for. If she thought about it less, as the doctor had advised, occupied her mind with other things, then she might find it easier to conceive.

The next day, she rang Kevin – she was glad the McDowds were back in their lives – and asked if she stood a chance as a pianist on her own. She didn't want to belong to another group, she said. It was too hectic and she preferred her independence.

'Well,' Kevin said thoughtfully, 'I can guarantee you some bookings purely on your name, but the days of the solo piano player ended with Winifred Attwell and Russ Conway. They were top performers in their day, but that was the fifties and now it's nineteen sixty-nine. Leave it with me, Jeannie, and I'll see what I can do.'

In March, Jeannie appeared on an afternoon programme on BBC television, *The Flower Girls, Two Years On*, with Zoe, Rita and Marcia, who insisted on bringing Iain and was proudly pregnant again. Rita was asked to sing and Jeannie to play – Kevin had made sure that she would – and gave a rendition of the Beatles' 'Can't Buy Me Love', moving seamlessly from classical style, to ragtime, then rock 'n' roll.

Following this, bookings didn't exactly pour in,

but there were a few, enough to keep her busy, while Lachlan's new group, the Survivors, got off to a rousing start. At twenty-seven, he was referred to as a 'veteran of rock', and was relieved to be back in the charts – though he still yearned to be top.

Part Four

Chapter 12

1975

Kevin McDowd had a suite of offices in Mayfair, a mews house in Knightsbridge, a mansion in Ireland, and a flat in Paris, which was hardly used as he couldn't spare the time. He also owned several cars – the favourite being a Rolls Royce Corniche – a racehorse, and a de Havilland Dove five-seater plane with a pilot always on hand to take him anywhere he wished. Kevin had built an empire, a whole stable of artists, adding to the list all the time.

The most famous person on his books was his son, who had made his name in America where he was resident for most of the year. Always a rebel, Sean's protest songs had caught the mood of the Vietnam era. Now he sang about the disillusionment of the seventies. He came home at least once a year to tour the British Isles and every venue would be packed, the tickets sold out weeks beforehand.

In her own quiet way, his daughter, Rita, was also a star, though she didn't shine as brilliantly as her brother. Rita sang ballads in her deep, thrilling voice, having no messages to deliver. Her records rarely hit the charts, but the long-term sales were excellent. After giving a concert, or one of her rare TV appearances, Rita would hurry back to the converted farmhouse on the edge of the Yorkshire dales where she lived in splendid isolation with her secretary, the stroppy Mavis, whom Kevin loathed.

It came as a total shock when his shy daughter agreed to take the leading female role in a revival of *The King and I* at a theatre in Shaftesbury Avenue.

'Mavis thinks I should do it,' she told her father.

'Does she now!' Kevin was about to add a tart remark, but realised the repulsive Mavis had done him a favour.

Rehearsals had started in August and Kevin had another shock when the news reached him that Rita was throwing her weight about, demanding, amongst other things, a dressing room as lavish as Bruce Lockeridge's, a Shakespearean actor of some repute who was playing the King.

'I bet it's that Mavis bitch egging her on,' Kevin remarked to Sadie. They were in their mews cottage in Knightsbridge and he was sitting on the corner of the bath in the black marbled bathroom while Sadie had a good old soak – she'd just returned from Knightsbridge with mountains of shopping and felt absolutely worn out. He licked his lips and eyed the enticing bits of her that peeped through a froth of bubbles. 'I wonder why we've got two such odd, peculiar children when you and me are so normal?' he mused.

Sadie flung a handful of bubbles at him. They landed on his face and smelt of strawberries. 'I wasn't always normal, was I, you eejit,' she said scathingly. 'You didn't see me when I was in the depths of despair, a broken woman, abandoned by me husband, with two kids to bring up. They raised themselves, the pair of them. If they've turned out odd and peculiar, then it's their own bloody daddy's fault.'

'Whatever, they've still done us proud, peculiar or not. Another month and it'll be Rita's first night and our Sean's coming home.' That wasn't all, the Survivors, his most successful group, had a new record out, and the others weren't doing so badly either. Jeannie Flowers – he'd suggested she stick to her maiden name – was about to start on a Christmas album, and all was well with his world. The disillusionment about which his son sang hadn't touched Kevin McDowd.

A pink toe peeped out of the bubbles. He grabbed it and gave it a tug. Sadie shrieked and, within seconds, Kevin had stripped off his clothes and joined his wife in the bath.

Jaysus! Life was good.

'Don't you think you're laying it on a bit thick, darlin'?' Mavis hissed when Rita insisted the rehearsal be stopped so she could have a drink, claiming to be parched. She'd walked off the stage, leaving the cast open-mouthed and astonished by her unprofessional behaviour.

'Laying what on?' Rita asked when they were in her sumptuous dressing room.

'*It!* I dunno what else to call it, other than it.'

'I don't know what you're talking about,' Rita said coldly.

'You'll never do another show,' Mavis warned. 'Word gets around – it already has – that you're a difficult cow. Unbiddable, as me old mum used to say.'

'It doesn't matter how arrogant I am as long as I'm good. How long is it going to take to make that tea?'

'As long as it takes for the kettle boil, unless you'd like it cold.'

The two women glared at each other in the dressing room mirror; little, insipid Rita in her neat check frock, and tall, stout, very plain Mavis Maguire, who was clad in flowing crimplene to disguise her lack of a figure. The kettle whistled, announcing that the water had boiled. They both jumped.

'It's very nice tea,' Rita said politely, taking a sip.

Mavis sat down with a groan. 'I made it strong, the way madam likes it. *I* don't want to get in madam's bad books, do I?'

They exchanged grins in the mirror. They'd met three years ago in a Ladies' toilet on Charing Cross station. Mavis was the attendant and Rita had been in a cubicle vomiting up her guts. She had no idea why, she said, when Mavis rescued her.

'Poor little lamb. You must've eaten something that disagreed with you,' Mavis crooned in her thick, creamy voice. She took Rita into her cubby-hole, sat her down, and made the first of a thousand cups of tea. 'What did you have for your breakfast?' she enquired.

'Nothing,' Rita confessed.

'It must've been something you ate last night.'

'I ate nothing last night either.' She was useless at looking after herself

'Doesn't your mum feed you?' demanded a shocked Mavis.

'Not any more. I've left home.' Rita had felt obliged to leave when it became apparent that Mam and Dad didn't want her there. Nothing had been said, but she just got the impression they would have liked to wander round the house stark naked, making love whenever the urge took them, but they couldn't because she was in the way.

She'd bought a little house in Primrose Hill, but felt desperately lonely. She'd never been any good at making friends. When invited out, she always refused, knowing the dinner or the party would be torture while she wracked her brains to think of something to say.

'You're far too young to have left home,' Mavis said reprovingly. 'Would you like a slice of bread and butter? I've brought some for me lunch with a piece of Cheddar.'

'You mean you eat in here?' It was Rita's turn to be shocked.

'It's either here or the waiting room. I'd buy a meal, but I couldn't exactly afford it on what they pay me.' She gave a big, warm smile, as if she didn't mind terribly eating in a communal toilet.

'I don't think I could eat anything, thanks. I suppose I'd better be going.' Rita was reluctant to leave. She had felt an instant rapport with the outsize woman with cheeks like cushions and bright, pea green eyes, who seemed so extraordinarily kind. She knew straight away that Mavis was the guardian angel she'd been waiting for ever since Robert Briggs had suggested at Marcia's wedding that it was exactly what she needed.

'Are you sure you feel up to it, darlin'?' Mavis regarded her with genuine concern.

'I think so.' Loads of other women had been coming in and out of the Ladies. Rita was worried Mavis was losing tips – there was a saucer on a table by the entrance containing half a dozen coppers.

'Come straight back if you feel queasy, and I'll make you another cuppa.'

'Oh, I will,' Rita promised, rather hoping she would collapse outside the door. She had a feeling Mavis hoped something the same. 'What's your name, by the way?'

'Mavis, darlin'. Mavis Maguire. What's yours?'

'Rita McDowd.' There was no spark of recognition in the green eyes.

Two days later, Rita went back to Charing Cross Ladies' toilet. Mavis was there in her white overall. She wore big, sloppy shoes and appeared to be bad on her feet. Her face lit up with her wide smile when she saw her visitor.

'Are you feeling all right now, darlin'?' she asked. 'I've been ever so worried about you. You don't look fit to be out on your own. I hope you've been eating properly,' she added sternly.

'I had cornflakes for breakfast.'

'Oh, well, they're better than nothing.' She looked wistfully at Rita. 'I don't suppose you'd like a cuppa?'

'I'd love one.'

'Are you married?' Rita enquired when they were seated in the tiny cubby-hole.

'No, darlin'. I had a fiancé once, but he was killed in Korea. His name was John. I live on me own.' She was thirty-seven, she explained – Rita had thought her much older – and her old mum had died ten years ago. They'd lived in a council flat along with her brother. 'He took over the flat, being a man, like, the rent book went to him. Not long afterwards, he got married, and he and his missus chucked me out. Now I'm on me own in this bed-sitting room in Islington.'

Rita reckoned Mavis was as lonely as herself. 'Can you type?' she asked.

Mavis blinked slightly at this odd question. 'I wouldn't be working in a Ladies' toilet, darlin', if I could type.'

'Can you cook?' Rita persisted.

'Well, I ain't an expert. Mum liked plain food, so I never learnt to make anything fancy. What's the third degree for?' she asked uneasily.

'I'd like you to work for me,' Rita stated baldly. 'I need a secretary, a cook, and a friend.'

'Do you, now.' Mavis looked even more uneasy. 'I've just told you, I can't type and I ain't much of a cook.'

'But you'd make a great friend.' Rita had never thought the day would come when she could speak so plainly, without a hint of embarrassment, to another human being.

Mavis had obviously decided to humour her. 'The thing is, darlin', I'd love to work for you, I really would, but I need to earn enough to pay

355

me rent amongst other things. As for being your friend, I'll do that for nothing. You can come and see me whenever you like.' She waved a majestic arm around the miniscule cubicle.

'I'll pay you a hundred pounds a week.'

'And where would someone your age get that sort of money? You can't be no more than sixteen.'

'I'm twenty–nine, actually. I'm a singer, and I probably earn more in a day than you do in a month. I've thousands and thousands of pounds in the bank, but I don't know what to do with them. I've bought a house, but there's hardly any furniture. I don't know anything about curtains and stuff. You can help me,' she added coaxingly.

The woman still looked dubious. And who could blame her? She probably considered Rita a lunatic. 'What time do you finish work?' Rita asked.

'Six o'clock.'

'Let's have dinner and we can discuss it properly. Where would you like to eat?'

'The Ritz,' Mavis said flippantly.

'OK, the Ritz it is. I'll book a table for half six.'

'You'll do no such thing.' Mavis sniffed indignantly. 'I ain't going near the Ritz in these old rags. I need to have a bath and get changed first – oh, I can't believe I said that. I think you're leading me way up the garden path, darlin'.'

'Just come to the Ritz at eight o'clock, ask for Miss McDowd's table, and you'll know that I'm not.'

And that's how Mavis had come to work for Rita. They trusted each other implicitly, spoke with total honesty, often resulting in blazing rows, but always ended the day the best of friends. Mavis was fiercely protective of her employer. Anyone who telephoned for Rita had to go through Mavis first, who wanted to know who was calling and precisely why. She drove Kevin insane.

'It's none of your business!' he would scream.

'Everything's my business if it's to do with Miss McDowd,' Mavis would prissily inform him.

It was Mavis's idea that Rita buy a place in the country, but keep the Primrose Hill house for when they stayed in London. 'You can get away from the rat race, darlin'. You could do with some proper fresh air, it'll bring the roses to your cheeks. You're much too pale.'

Rita suggested they buy somewhere in Ireland, but Mavis pooh-poohed the idea. 'It'd mean flying if you were needed in a hurry. I ain't pre-pared to fly meself.' She'd never actually flown, but had sworn never to set foot inside a plane. 'It ain't natural, darlin'. If God had meant us to fly, he'd have given us bloomin' wings.'

As Rita needed Mavis with her all the time, she bought a farmhouse, completely modernised, on the edge of the Yorkshire dales, only a train ride away from London, if a long one. They had enormous fun furnishing it, buying only from the very best stores, until it looked fashionably comfortable.

They both discovered an interest in gardening and acquired two stray cats. Rita had never been happier than sitting in front of a blazing fire on a winter evening, a cat or two on her knee, while

357

Mavis fetched cups of tea or cocoa. It was just as good in summer, lounging in a deckchair in the garden, watching Mavis weed.

There was a knock on the dressing room door now. 'Come in,' Mavis called.

'Have you had your drink?' the show's director demanded through gritted teeth.

'She's coming now.' The director was treated to a curt nod.

'But I haven't finished!' Rita complained when the man had closed the door.

'Then do it quickly, madam. It's time you went back. It's rude to keep people waiting. I don't know what's got into you lately, I really don't. You're usually such a mild little thing, but you've become a monster.'

A monster! Rita rather liked the idea. 'I enjoy messing people about,' she said. 'It makes me feel important.' When she'd started rehearsing for *The King and I*, she found herself in a position of enormous power, able to bring proceedings to a halt at her slightest whim. It was an odd, stirring sensation.

'You need your bumps feeling, darlin'. Now, hurry!'

Rita swallowed the remainder of the tea. 'All right, Mavis,' she said obediently.

The director gave a sigh of relief when Rita returned to the stage. If looks could have killed, the female lead would have dropped dead on the spot from the lethal glances aimed in her direction by every other member of the cast.

'We were about to do the dance scene,' he said

stiffly, 'when you decided you needed a drink. Are you ready to do it now?'

'Quite ready.'

'OK, let's begin.' The director signalled to the orchestra leader in the pit.

Rita placed herself in the arms of the King, the slightly overweight Bruce Lockeridge and began to sing, 'Shall we dance, tra, la, la...'

The director immediately forgave her everything.

What a voice! It was incredible; enchanting and immensely strong. And when the little bitch sang, her entire personality changed, as if she had become another person altogether; a much nicer, quite charming person, sparkling and incredibly pretty. Sometimes, he felt as if he could quite easily fall in love with Rita McDowd when she sang. And if he felt like that, the audience would be completely bowled over. After all, he knew what she was really like. The audience didn't.

Jeannie was sitting in the back row of the Hammersmith Odeon. Any nearer, and she was convinced her eardrums would have burst. Even at the back, she could feel the floor vibrating beneath her feet. Her body was wrapped in a blanket of noise and she could hardly move with the weight.

On the stage, three wild men were surrounded by a forest of amplifiers from where the noise came; waves and waves of thunderous, deafening noise.

The maniacal drummer played with the vigour of three normal men, his drumsticks almost invisible as they whizzed over the drums. One of the guitarists, a huge man, at least six and a half feet tall, seemed to have fallen asleep. His eyes were closed and he rocked back and forth, but still managing to play and contribute his share to the head-splitting sounds.

At the moment, the other guitarist, the lead and the best looking of the three by a mile, was striding around the stage, head arrogantly thrown back, reminding Jeannie of a jungle beast stalking its territory. He wore tight leather trousers and a leather waistcoat, leaving his chest and arms bare. A red band was tied around his forehead and he had a tattoo on his right shoulder and a gold earring in his left ear. The man returned to the microphone, his face dripping with perspiration, his body glistening, and hurled his voice at the ecstatic, rowdy audience, who responded with a roar of approval.

'Do you wanna be ma honey?' the man sang.

'Yes!' screamed the girls, and items of female clothing were flung on to the stage. Jeannie often wondered if they took off the pants they were wearing, or brought clean ones to shower their idols with.

From this distance, the singer's tattoo was just a red and blue smudge. It was in fact a heart containing a single word, a woman's name, 'Jeannie'. The wild creature was her husband, Lachlan Bailey, looking nothing remotely like the boy in the grey pullover who used to play the violin. The maniacal drummer was Fly Fleming and the sleepy guitarist Jimmy Cobb, known as 'The Cobb', a gentle giant of a man.

All three of them were stuffed to the eyeballs with drugs.

She couldn't stand the noise another minute. Jeannie went into the foyer where a middle-aged doorman regarded her sympathetically.

'Too much for you, is it, luv? I'm not surprised. That din ain't my idea of music. 'Fact, I'm not sure if it's *any* sort of music, just a jumble of noise.'

'It's called hard rock,' Jeanne said helpfully, 'though some experts claim the Survivors are heavy metal. I suppose it's a mixture of the two.'

'You sound like an expert yourself.'

Jeannie laughed. 'I think of myself more as a victim.'

She left the doorman looking bewildered and went outside. She still had her ticket if she wanted to return, though doubted that she would. Lachlan didn't know she'd come – he had no idea she was in London, so she wouldn't be missed.

After tramping the damp, foggy Hammersmith pavements until the noise that continued inside her head gradually abated, she hailed a taxi and returned to the McDowds' mews cottage in Knightsbridge where she was staying while she finished off her Christmas album, *Flowers in December*.

The cottage had been two, now knocked into one, and contained four bedrooms. The kitchens had been turned into a single long one, and the remainder of the ground floor was now a vast area with the original brick fireplaces left in the centre. The backs of the grates had been removed and the cavity contained an iron basket of mock, flickering coals, giving off no heat. There was no need, the central heating was super efficient. The big room was richly and flamboyantly furnished – too much red and gold for Jeannie's taste.

Sadie and Kevin were out and she'd been given her own key. She let herself in and took several breaths of warm air – it was unusually cold for October – and made herself a cup of hot milk. Tonight, she'd go to bed early.

The television on, she lounged on the settee and sipped the milk while she watched the news. In Bangladesh and Ethiopia, the people were starving. There was fighting in Angola, a civil war in the Lebanon, and the Khmer Rouge were still wreaking havoc in Cambodia. She got up and turned the set off. It was too depressing. Left with her own thoughts, her mind turned to Lachlan.

Soon, the concert would end and the Survivors would go back to their hotel accompanied by the roadie, the driver, the sound men, a couple of bodyguards, a crowd of hangers on, many of them girls and, inevitably, a few sensation–seeking act-resses and models, women who'd achieved a modicum of fame from merely being pretty. A party would follow, Lachlan would take more speed to keep himself awake, and when the party was over he'd take a red devil to make him sleep, then speed again the next morning to enable him to wake up. He'd need more speed for tomorrow night's concert, wherever that may be. Jeannie could understand that performing for three or more hours using a superhuman amount of energy, required some sort of stimulant, but it didn't mean she had to like it.

'It's not harmful,' Lachlan insisted. 'I won't get hooked.'

He was already hooked. At home, he needed downers and uppers to make him function. Jeannie no longer tried to make him stop. She'd learnt it was a waste of time.

'Everyone does it,' Lachlan said.

'I know, but it doesn't mean *you* have to.' Some people took drugs to experiment with mind control, to find a reason for living, a reason for dying. Lachlan had never been a philosophical sort of person. He knew his reason for living, to make music. He took drugs for practical reasons and occasionally for pleasure. He'd tried to persuade her to take LSD. 'Just once, babe. See what it's like. It's a great sensation. You feel as if there's nothing on earth you can't do.'

'No, thank you, Lachlan,' Jeannie said firmly. She occasionally smoked hash, but two puffs was her limit. The thought of messing about with her brain she found terrifying.

Elaine, now a qualified psychiatrist and working in Broadgreen hospital in Liverpool, theorised that taking drugs to make the body work beyond its natural physical capacity could only do harm in the end. 'It puts a strain on the heart. Lachlan's thirty-three. You must stop him, Jeannie.'

'I've tried, but he won't listen.'

She finished the milk, washed the cup, went upstairs and got ready for bed. She lay listening to the sound of the distant traffic in Old

Brompton Road. London never slept. There would be traffic all night long. She heard Kevin and Sadie come in. They'd been to a book launch followed by a party. She had no idea why anyone would ask Kevin to a book launch, but he was a popular man these days, invited everywhere.

Two years ago, Stella had divorced Fly, not because of the drugs, though they were bad enough, but the girls.

'I've seen his photey in the paper, Jeannie, with some woman hanging on to his arm, always a blonde.' Stella had come round to the house in Formby with her children, Samantha and Russell, to complain. Jeannie had seen the photographs in the tabloids too. So far, there'd been none of Lachlan.

'I told him,' Stella continued, 'that I wasn't interested in soiled goods. He swears that nothing happens, but can you believe that?'

'I don't know.' It was hard to believe that nothing happened when a crowd of women with sex on their minds, mixed with a crowd of virile men high on drugs.

'Anyroad, I've had enough,' Stella said bluntly. 'I'm divorcing Fly. I still love him to death, but I went to see a solicitor this morning. He can come and see the kids whenever he likes, but I want out. You're lucky, Jeannie, not having kids. It's easier breaking up when you haven't got a family.'

'It must be the only thing that it is.' Jeannie's voice was bleak and raw.

'Oh, Christ, Jeannie! I'm sorry. I know how much you want kids. That was a dead stupid thing to say.'

Now Jeannie lay in the McDowds' guest room and wondered if she should have gone to the group's hotel to see what was going on. If she found Lachlan with a girl, would she divorce him?

Never! She loved him too much, but the love was based, at least partly, on knowing her love was wholeheartedly returned. She might feel different if she discovered he was being un-faithful.

She slept fitfully and woke to another damp, London morning. Downstairs, Sadie was floating about in a black chiffon negligee trimmed with swansdown, exuding clouds of expensive per-fume, while Kevin's increasingly corpulent body was clad in a paisley silk dressing gown. His Irish accent was as strong as ever when he wished her good morning.

'It's a pity you can't come with us tonight, me darlin' girl,' he hollered. 'If I'd known you'd be here, I'd've got an extra ticket.' It was the open-ing night of *The King and I*.

'I'm going on Saturday with Marcia and Zoe, aren't I? We thought the Flower Girls should go to see Rita together, and Marcia's only just had the baby. She didn't think she could manage tonight.' With this latest birth, Marcia was now the proud mother of five boys.

'What'll you do with yourself while we're gone, luv?' Sadie asked worriedly. 'You'll be all on your own.'

'Stay in, read, have a nice rest. I have to go to the studio this morning to do some more of my album; it'll be finished tomorrow. I'll try to fit in some shopping. Christmas isn't all that far off.' She was quite looking forward to the day.

'Our Sean's arriving tomorrow,' Sadie said. 'He wanted to be here for Rita's first night, but couldn't make it.'

'I know.' Jeannie hadn't discovered Sean was coming until she'd got to the McDowds', otherwise she would have stayed in a hotel. She'd seen little of him since Marcia's wedding and would have preferred them not to be under the same roof, even if only for a few days.

Kevin announced he wouldn't go into the office today, but would work from home. He picked up the phone and began to bellow instructions to his staff, while Sadie wandered off to have a bath. Jeannie left for M&M's studio by the Embankment where the Flower Girls had auditioned for their first recording contract. The new album had eight numbers on each side, classic love songs such as 'Embraceable You' and 'Smoke Gets in Your Eyes', each linked to the next by a few bars of a carol. She played another four songs to everyone's satisfaction, including her own, then made her way back to Knightsbridge, where she decided to buy lunch rather than return to the cottage – Kevin would almost certainly have summoned a few members of staff to relay orders in person and she'd feel in the way.

It was getting dark by the time she returned, laden with Christmas presents; a lovely fluffy hat, gloves and scarf set for Elaine, Barbie dolls for her half-sisters, a necklace for her mother. Sadie had had her hair set that afternoon and was wondering what to wear for the theatre.

'I thought you'd bought a new dress specially for tonight?' Jeannie said.

'I'm not sure if I like it. It doesn't go with me hair.'

'You'd better make your mind up quick, woman,' Kevin shouted as Sadie went upstairs. 'The car's coming for us at six o'clock. I'm off to have a bath. Jeannie! Help yourself to some champagne. I opened a bottle earlier.'

Jeannie poured the champagne. Sadie came in a few minutes later in a slinky black dress that was too tight, too short, and showed far too much white bosom.

'What'd'you think?' Sadie asked. 'Is it too young for a woman of fifty-one?'

'Well,' Jeannie began cautiously, but Sadie got the message straight away.

'I'll take it back tomorrow and wear me green one. Ooh! Is that champagne?' Her eyes lit up as she helped herself to a glass. 'Me and Kevin have been drinking it all afternoon. It's not every day your daughter stars in a West End show. Things have changed a bit, haven't they, Jeannie, since you and me lived at the opposite ends of Disraeli Terrace?'

'I'll say!'

'How are all your family, luv? I don't often have time to speak to you on your own.'

'Dad's in the same house. He's seventy–three, very fit, and still works for Colonel Corbett, though only part-time. Mum, Alex, and their girls are fine, and Gerald loves being a journalist. He's with the *Record Mirror* now, and married to a girl called Helen. They've got two children.'

'That's good,' Sadie gave a little satisfied cluck. 'And how about Max? Do you see much of him?'

'Not all that much.' Max still refused to set foot in Noah's Ark. 'He teaches History and Geography at a school in Childwall. His children live in America and he misses them badly, particularly Gareth. Mind you, we all miss Gareth. He was Mum's first grandchild.'

'That's a shame,' Sadie said sympathetically. She went all misty- eyed and was bemoaning her own lack of grandchildren, when Kevin yelled it was about time she got ready. 'It takes you a couple of hours to get your bloody slap on.'

Jeannie was glad when it was six o'clock and the car arrived to take them to the theatre, Sadie encased in emerald green slipper satin and a white mink coat. She had more champagne – it would only go flat if it was left – and went upstairs to run a bath.

It was cosy in the black marble bathroom with the buzz of traffic in the distance. Jeannie didn't think Sadie would mind if she used some of her bubble bath. She relaxed and let her legs float in the scented water until it began to feel cold, then climbed out, washed her hair, and wrapped herself in the shell pink, terry towelling robe that hung behind the door of her room – she presumed it was for the use of guests.

Downstairs again, she poured the last of the champagne and looked through the McDowds' book collection for something to read as she'd forgotten to buy something that afternoon. She found a romance that hopefully wouldn't tax her rather muggy brain, and began to read but, all of a sudden, quite out of the blue, she was overwhelmed by a feeling of wretched loneliness. All over London, people were enjoying themselves and here she was, stuck in a strange house on her own.

She looked at the clock; five past eight. At the theatre, the curtain would have just gone up. Lachlan's gig would have started. She tried to remember where he was playing tonight and thought it might be Brighton, but wasn't sure. She wanted to see him, *desperately* wanted to see him. The awareness of how unsatisfactory their life had become struck her like a blow. He was away so much of the time and although she could have gone with him, a woman would have been out of place in such a male environment. Everyone would have had to watch what they said.

I've never been able to compete with rock 'n' roll, Jeannie thought sadly. It has always come first with Lachlan. She wished he were there to argue that it wasn't the case, that he'd give it up tomorrow if it would make her happy. 'Some hope,' she sighed.

Now he was abusing his body in order to play better, slowly killing himself. She sniffed and wiped her eyes on the sleeve of the robe. This was supposed to be a relaxing evening, not a morbid review of the state of her marriage.

The doorbell went – it played the first seven notes of 'When Irish Eyes are Smiling' – and she went to answer it. She hoped it was someone she knew because she quite fancied company, but when she opened the door it was to the last person on earth she wanted to see.

'I'll just pay the taxi,' said Sean McDowd. 'I asked the driver to wait in case there was no one to let me in.' He gave her the suggestion of a smile. 'Hi, Jeannie. I didn't expect to find you here.'

There was something wrong. Sean could tell straight away, see the hurt in her eyes. Her mouth was downcast. At first he thought she'd dyed her hair, it looked darker, but then he realised it was wet. The ends were beginning to dry with a slight upward curl. He noticed everything about her; her bare feet, the sheen of her creamy legs, a gleam of moisture in the smooth hollow of her throat.

'Why aren't you at the theatre with Mam and Dad?' he asked, setting his bag on the floor and removing the dark glasses that had enabled him to travel from New York to London without being recognised. He scorned minders and body-guards, who would only have intruded into his solitary life.

She explained she was in London to make an album and was going to the theatre on Saturday with Marcia and Zoe.

'How's Lachlan?'

Her blue eyes clouded over. 'Oh, he's fine.'

'Good.'

'You're early,' she said. 'Sadie wasn't expecting you till tomorrow.'

'I was supposed to go somewhere tonight in New York, a dinner, but it was cancelled.' The truth was he'd promised to attend a fund-raising event with his actress girlfriend, Melanie, but they'd had a blazing row. He wasn't committed to the relationship, she'd complained, for a reason he couldn't remember. Sean had shrugged and walked out, and caught the next plane to Heathrow. He just hoped Melanie would be gone from his apartment when he returned.

'Would you like some coffee?'

'No, ta. Is that champagne you're drinking?'

'Yes, but it's the last of the bottle.'

'I'll open more.' Champagne seemed an appropriate drink after finding Jeannie Flowers alone in his parents' house. There were usually a few bottles in the fridge.

He opened the bottle in the kitchen. He wasn't very good at it. There was a loud 'pop' and the cork thudded into the ceiling. 'More?' he asked when he went back.

She wrinkled her nose and handed him her glass. 'Why not!'

Sean filled both their glasses. He contemplated sitting next to her on the settee, but reckoned she'd prefer he kept to an armchair. 'Cheers!' He sat down.

'Cheers! Are you tired after your flight?' She was trying to make conversation. She'd wait for a while before going up to bed, so it didn't look rude. Jeannie Flowers would never deliberately hurt anyone's feelings.

'No, but I resent losing five hours of me life. But then I'll make them up when I go back, so what's the difference?'

'What's the difference?' she agreed.

371

The last time they'd been alone together he'd kissed her. Sean had thought about that kiss many times over the intervening years. How ironic it was, that a single kiss should stick in his mind, yet since then he must have made love to at least a hundred other women. It was just that the other women didn't hold a candle to Jeannie. She was superior in every possible way. For as long as he could remember, she had been his idea of absolute perfection. He looked at her furtively. She was staring moodily into the glass, her mind elsewhere, not on him.

Sean knew that Lachlan wasn't fine. He'd become a junkie, not yet a hopeless case, but he would be soon if he didn't lay off the dope. Perhaps that's why Jeannie looked so miserable, why there was hurt in her eyes. He wanted to take her in his arms and make her better, stroke her soft cheeks, kiss her ears, her eyes and feel her lashes flutter against his lips. He wondered if she was wearing anything underneath the pink robe and imagined sliding his hand inside and cupping her breast, squeezing it, gently, rubbing her nipple with his thumb. The nipple would be like the centre of a flower, a rose.

He thought of something to say that would grab her attention and hoped she wouldn't be annoyed. 'What happened to the kids you were going to have?' he asked. She'd wanted them soon, he remembered her saying. That had been eight years ago and she would be thirty in December. 'A boy and a girl, I think you said.'

She gave him a look of such anguish, he felt ashamed. 'Things don't always go according to

372

plan,' she said dully. He could have sworn she stifled a sob.

There was silence for a long while, but it was probably only seconds. During the silence, Sean could feel the tension in the air. He could actually hear it, a dull, repetitive throbbing. Perhaps it was his heart. Or Jeannie's heart. Or both their hearts beating together.

Sean stood and put the champagne carefully on the hearth, hardly touched. He could no longer help himself. He sat beside Jeannie and slipped the robe off her shoulders, then buried his head in the creamy flesh, sliding his lips along its smoothness. She was wearing nothing underneath. The robe fell back further exposing her breasts, like two flowers, as he'd thought. He bent his head and sucked greedily. Jeannie groaned, made to push him away, but instead collapsed against the back of the settee. Sean undid the robe and still she made no protest. He touched her naked body reverently until, to his intense joy, she began to respond, arching against him, gasping with delight when he slid the flat of his hand down her stomach and between her soft thighs.

While he removed his clothes, she lay, watching him, her blue eyes hazy with desire as she waited for him to take her.

At long last Jeannie Flowers was his.

Sadie found Jeannie's note when she came down very late next morning. It was by the kettle, her first port of call.

Dear Sadie and Kevin,

I apologise for being rude, but didn't want to wake you. I had a phone call last night from my mother. She's not very well and Alex has had to go away. As soon as I finish in the studio, I shall race up to Liverpool to make sure she's all right, then return to London on Saturday to see The King and I. *I'll buy the papers to read the reviews, but I don't doubt Rita gave a fantastic performance.*

Thanks for having me.
Jeannie.

When Sean heard, he was disappointed, but not terribly surprised.

Lachlan came back to Noah's Ark the week after Jeannie's stay in London, the Survivors' tour over. There wouldn't be another till the New Year, though they had a few gigs before Christmas. They were going to Eastern Europe next summer, he announced. He'd hardly been back an hour, after having had a shower and allowed Jeannie to tug a comb through his long tangle of hair, before disappearing into the studio wearing old jeans and his favourite blue sweater that she'd given up trying to repair. 'To start on some new material, babe,' he said.

Jeannie detested being called 'babe'. It had started at the same time as he'd got the earring and the tattoo. She waited a further hour, then grabbed a coat, left the house, and walked down to the shore. The tide was coming in and she watched the River Mersey lap busily to and fro at her feet, leaving behind a scum of froth that sank slowly into the sand. There wasn't another person in sight, not surprising on such a dismal October afternoon that was rapidly growing dark. The sky was a dirty grey and clouds were banked like a row of black, sinister hills on the horizon. She shuddered, pulled up her collar, stuffed her hands in her pockets, and wished she'd brought a scarf and gloves.

What were they to do, she and Lachlan? More to the point, what was *she* to do? Lachlan seemed perfectly happy to continue as he was, on the road for most of the time, buried in the basement when he was home, whereas her own career amounted to very little – a few engagements a year, the occasional record.

She hadn't realised quite how unhappy she was until last week. A happily married woman would never have allowed another man to make love to her and enjoyed it quite so much. She still felt guilty – she always would – remembering how willingly she'd surrendered herself to Sean McDowd. She'd been hypnotised by his dark eyes, the touch of his long slender fingers. Oh, Lord! She'd been so *easy!* She preferred not to think what would happen if Lachlan ever found out what she'd done.

By now, it was completely dark and the only sound was the busy rustle of the black water. The streetlights made the sky over Liverpool appear a dull orange and in Noah's Ark the brightly lit windows glowed a warm welcome. Jeannie went through the back gate and trudged up the garden, past the swimming pool, and into the house. She didn't feel particularly welcome. When they'd first looked over the house – it must be at least ten years ago – she'd thought it was a place that needed lots of people, a family. It was too big for just the two of them. She wondered if Lachlan would agree to them getting rid of it, buying something smaller, cosier, like Magnolia Cottage or the McDowds' mews house.

She went into the kitchen and was surprised to find him there, about to put the kettle on, and felt a rush of love that almost made her choke.

'I was just coming to look for you, babe,' he said. 'I think it's about time we had a talk.'

It had only just struck him that they hadn't seen each other for a fortnight, yet he'd done a disappearing act as soon as he got home. He was sorry. It was thoughtless of him. It's just that he'd had stuff in his head, music, lyrics, that he was worried he'd forget.

They both agreed that her life was very unsatisfactory. He spent so much time away and she was lonely on her own in the big, isolated house that her mother had once called a mausoleum. Jeannie waited for him to suggest they move to a smaller place and eventually he did.

'But what about the studio?' she felt bound to remind him.

'I'm the only one who uses it these days. All I do is fiddle about.' The other Survivors, Fly and Cobb, both lived in London and the final recordings were made in a studio there. 'We could buy a flat in London, as well as a house here,' Lachlan went on. 'I could hire a studio to do my fiddling about.'

Jeannie said she loved the idea of living in London for a few months of the year. 'It would be wonderful.' She could see Zoe, Rita, and Marcia when she came to town, the McDowds. 'But Lachlan,' she said, 'will it ever stop? Will the Survivors still be playing when they're old, old men?'

For a moment, he looked flummoxed, as if he hadn't understood the question. 'I reckon so, babe,' he said slowly and there was a hint of fear in his voice. 'I can't think of anything else I'd want to do. I'd die if I wasn't involved in music.'

'I see.' Jeannie sighed.

Neither of them mentioned children. Over the years, he'd said a few times how much he would like a family, but he didn't *need* one, not like her. With Lachlan, if he thought about it at all, it was a question of pride. His brothers, the terrible trio, were all grown men, all married with children. For her, it was a never-ending ache, a feeling of loss for the babies that hadn't been born.

They went to bed early, but didn't make love, falling asleep in each other's arms. When Jeannie woke, it was just gone midnight and Lachlan wasn't there. She went down to the studio and found him lying on the floor wearing only a pair of shorts. His body felt cold, but his heart was beating normally and his breathing steady. The drawer where he kept his stash of drugs was open. He must have been unable to sleep and had come to get a tablet.

Jeannie fetched a duvet, lay down beside him,

and pulled it over them both. She put her arm around his waist and felt his body gradually getting warmer. Then she fell asleep herself.

Lachlan woke first and began to touch her. They made love very slowly, leisurely, neither saying a word. It was a strange, satisfying, almost mystical experience. Afterwards, they slept for hours, until it was broad daylight, and the weak suggestion of a sun glittered over the River Mersey.

Later, he was to claim that that was the night Jeannie had conceived. 'When we were both totally relaxed, babe, not really thinking of anything but each other.'

But Jeannie knew differently.

Antony Peter Bailey, weighing 7 pounds, 11 ounces, made his first appearance on the world's stage in the middle of June, 1976. He was a perfect baby in every way apart from a complete lack of hair. Jeannie had had a trouble-free pregnancy followed by a straightforward birth. Antony slept when he was supposed to, rarely cried, and took to his mother's breast like a dream.

The Baileys declared him to be the image of his father, but the Flowers claimed he had his mother's looks. Only Jeannie could see a distinct resemblance to Sean McDowd in the neat features of her son though, naturally, she didn't mention it to a soul.

Antony was two weeks old when he and Lachlan had a photograph taken that appeared in three national newspapers and the *Liverpool*

Echo. It showed Lachlan in his leather gear, bare-chested, hair sprouting wildly from under the band around his forehead, looking like some sort of space age pirate, as he cradled his tiny, naked son next to his heart. Antony's eyes were wide open and they appeared to be looking straight into the father's tender eyes. THE SURVIVOR AND HIS SON had been one of the headlines. Jeannie had ordered half a dozen copies and they were scattered around the house.

Lachlan adored his son. Jeannie was the only person in the world who knew the truth, yet the secret didn't feel safe, not even with her. It was a terrible secret to have to keep over an entire lifetime. She was worried that one day she would blurt it out, unable to help herself.

In view of the changed circumstances, they had decided not to sell the house. Jeannie had thought it perfect for a family, and now they had one. She couldn't wait for the nurse, who stayed for two months after the birth, to leave, so she could have her son to herself

'She was very nice, but I'm glad she's gone, aren't you?' Jeannie whispered to Antony on the day the nurse left for good. Antony, sucking contentedly at her breast, looked at her wisely with his big blue eyes, and nodded. At least, Jeannie could have sworn he nodded. 'I don't care what I've done,' she told him. 'Lachlan's happy, I'm happy, and you look happy enough to me, so where's the harm?'

Chapter 13

Tom Flowers had been sent invitations to his children's weddings, his grandchildren's christenings, their birthday parties, but not once had he replied, let alone turned up. Jeannie was therefore astonished when her father arrived at the church for the christening of Antony Peter Bailey, now two and a half months old. He was accompanied by Mrs Denning, plump and grandmotherly in fuchsia silk. Tom was an erect, uncompromising figure, still with an enviable head of thick wavy hair, now completely grey. Jeannie was even more surprised when he came back to the house for refreshments. His change of heart might have been due to Jeannie having gone to the funeral of Colonel Corbett, who had died earlier in the year. The other Flower Girls had sent wreaths in appreciation of the colonel's help at the start of their careers.

'Oh, my God!' Rose Flowers gasped when she saw Tom come marching in. 'What on earth is he doing here? I don't know whether to speak to him or not.'

Perhaps because it was August and the weather so fine that every one of Jeannie's invitations had been accepted. All the Baileys were there. Marcia had left her brood in Harwood Hall and come alone. She was already heavily pregnant with her sixth child. Gerald was there with Helen and their two children, Zoe with her latest boyfriend, Stella and her new husband, and Fly and his new wife. Kevin and Sadie McDowd had stopped over on their way by plane to Ireland. Rita had brought Mavis who'd learnt to drive and chauffered her everywhere. It was a strange relationship, people thought. It was hard to know who was in charge. Sean McDowd was in America – Jeannie hadn't sent him an invitation.

There'd been a crowd waiting outside the church anxious for a glimpse of the Survivors and any other stars who might be present. Now the crowd was outside the house, being held at bay by two enormous bodyguards.

Noah's Ark was at its best in summer, but then most houses were. The French windows were thrown open, the house bright with sunshine, and the gardens in full bloom. The pool was packed with children, screaming and gleefully splashing water at each other and any unfortunate adult who happened to go near.

Jeannie and Elaine were sitting on a bench in a shady corner where they could keep an eye on things. 'Soon,' Jeannie told Antony who was fast asleep in her arms, 'you'll be doing that, splashing everyone in sight.'

'He's gorgeous,' said Elaine, 'and so good. It's a pleasure to be Godmother to such a well-behaved child. He didn't turn a hair when the vicar poured water over him.'

'That's not surprising,' Jeannie remarked. 'He hasn't got a hair to turn. Well, only a few and they're hardly visible. I hope he gets some soon.'

'He's still gorgeous, bald and gorgeous. I

wonder if his eyes will turn brown like Lachlan's?'

'We'll just have to wait and see,' Jeannie said casually.

'Can I hold him a minute?' Elaine sighed happily as she took the little boy with exaggerated care. 'I'd begun to think you two would never have a baby and, seeing as they could find nothing wrong with you, then it must be something to do with our Lachlan, a low sperm count maybe.'

'It seemed a waste of time finding out.' Jeannie shrugged. 'It never crossed his mind it could be his fault and nothing could have been done if it was – at least not yet. Imagine how he would have felt? The great sex symbol, unable to father a child.'

'I'm glad it worked out all right in the end.' Elaine regarded Antony critically. 'He's ever so like Lachlan, but I think he's got your mouth.'

'Could be.'

Lachlan came and sat on the arm of the bench. He had changed out of his formal suit into jeans and T–shirt. 'Ace is just the first of many, isn't he, babe? We're going to have at least another three, all boys,' he told his sister.

'Please don't call him Ace, Lachlan,' Jeannie groaned. 'It makes him sound like a card sharp.'

'Yeah, well he's an ace kid.'

'Elaine just said he was gorgeous, but it doesn't mean we have to call him that.'

'Actually,' Elaine said. 'I quite like the name Ace. It's unusual.'

'So's Gorgeous, except his name's Antony and

that's how it's going to stay.'

'Hello, Rose.' Tom Flowers came into the kitchen where his wife was pouring wine for her daughters to take around the guests.

'Hello, Tom.' Rose was pleased her hand didn't show the slightest tremor. 'How are things with you these days?'

'Good, Rose. Very good indeed.' He rubbed his palms together vigorously as if to prove how good things were. 'And how are you?'

'Very well. We've just heard Amy's passed the eleven-plus. Next month, she's starting at Orrell Park grammar school.'

'Just like our Jeannie.'

'Yes, just like Jeannie. But that seems an awful long time ago.'

'It's twenty years, Rose.'

'So it is! How time flies.' She couldn't believe this man used to be her husband, still was according to the law of the land. It was like talking to an old uncle she hadn't seen in ages.

'He used to be keen on you.' Tom nodded in her direction and gave a dry chuckle.

'I beg your pardon?'

'Colonel Max. He really fancied you.'

Rose realised he was nodding, not at her, but at the ruby and diamond ring on the middle finger of her right hand. The bulk of Colonel Max's estate had gone to cousins he'd hardly known. There'd been just a few bequests; Tom and Mrs Denning had been left a thousand pounds each and, to Rose's utter astonishment, the colonel had bequeathed her his mother's engagement ring.

'I'm sure that's not true, Tom,' she said uncomfortably.

'It's as true as I'm standing here. I hadn't planned on asking you to marry me until you were eighteen. After seeing the way the colonel looked at you the night of that party, I thought I'd better get a move on.'

He chuckled again and Rose felt even more uncomfortable at the idea of two middle-aged men vying for her heart. It made her feel slightly sick and she wondered if she would still have wanted to marry Tom when she was two years older?

'One of the reasons I came today,' Tom was saying pompously, 'was so I could have a word with you about a divorce. You can have one whenever you like. Just tell your solicitor to send the forms and I'll sign them.'

'Thank you, Tom.'

'Me and Nora – Mrs Denning – might tie the knot one day. I'm not sure when. We'll just have to see.'

'Don't leave it too long. You should snatch all the happiness you can out of this life.'

He gave a rather stiff smile. 'Well, you certainly did, Rose.'

'Yes, but I only wish I'd done it sooner, Tom.'

Alex came in just as Tom stomped out of the door. 'What did he want?' He wore a white suit, white tie, and a coral shirt. He still had a taste for snazzy clothes.

'To say I could have a divorce.'

'You should have told him to screw his divorce. We're perfectly happy as we are.'

'I know, but I'd like us to be married for the girls' sake.' She put her arms around his neck. 'We could have a honeymoon, somewhere romantic.'

'And take the girls?'

'Of course. Oh, kiss me, Alex. Kiss me. All of a sudden, I'm not sure if you're real.'

'I'm real all right, darling.' Alex kissed her. 'And tonight I'll show you just *how* real.'

'You know, I wouldn't mind having a few kids before I get too old,' Mavis mused.

Rita looked at her in astonishment. 'You've never said anything like that before!'

'I've never thought it before, that's why. It's just that that baby looks so bloomin' scrumptious, I could eat him.'

'You're already too old,' Rita said cruelly. 'And you're too fat and probably too unhealthy.'

'I'm forty-one. I ain't exactly ready to kick the bucket, darlin'. If the truth be known, I'm as fit as a bloomin' fiddle. When have you ever known me take to me bed with anything wrong? Not like the person who happens to be sitting next to me. See that woman over there? She ain't no chicken, but she's got two little girls. I must say, her old man's a bit of all right. I like a bloke who's a snappy dresser.'

'That's Jeannie's mother. Have you had too much to drink or something? One minute you're wanting kids, next you're eyeing up some other woman's husband.'

'I'm feeling broody,' Mavis announced. 'It's that baby, Antony, and all these other bloomin' kids. There must be at least twenty and not a single one of 'em's mine. I'm jealous.'

Not long after this conversation, Rita made her excuses and the two women left. It was the first time they'd been to a christening and Rita resolved it would be their last; weddings too. She'd had no idea Mavis nursed a desire to become a mother and it was a desire she had no intention of encouraging. She needed Mavis too much herself.

'I think I'll put him down,' said Jeannie. 'It doesn't look as if he's prepared to wake up and charm everybody.'

'I'll come with you. He's probably bored out of his mind with all these people and is staying asleep on purpose.'

'You're becoming awfully cynical in your old age, Elaine Bailey.'

'If I'm old, what about you? You're three months older than I am.'

'Yes, but I'm not cynical.'

They went into the house, passing Lachlan who was saying to Stella, 'We're hoping to have another three, all boys.'

'It's all right for him,' Elaine snorted, 'the man's part of the procedure is minimal – and highly enjoyable. It's not quite so simple for women. How do you feel about more children, Jeannie?'

'However I feel, it's easier said than done, isn't it? It took years for us to have Antony.' She kissed her son's white forehead and laid him in his cot beside the bed in their room. There'd been a nursery prepared for months, but neither she nor

Lachlan could bear to let him sleep on his own. If only she could tell Elaine the truth, that Antony wasn't Lachlan's child and there was hardly a chance in the world of her having another. 'I'd sooner he wasn't an only child,' she murmured. 'I can't imagine being without Max and Gerald when I was growing up.'

'I would have been quite happy without our Marcia, but not my brothers.'

'Your Marcia's s not so bad these days.'

'Our Marcia will never be all right until she's permanently gagged.'

'My, you *are* becoming cynical.' Jeannie stared at her friend. A few years ago, Elaine had started to wear glasses, the stern, horn-rimmed sort. Her dark hair was piled in an untidy, unflattering knot at the nape of her neck, and she wore no make-up or jewellery. The youthful prettiness was still there, but you had to look hard to see it. 'Don't you want to get married and have children of your own? It can't exactly be pleasant, spending all day delving into people's brains.'

'I find human behaviour fascinating,' Elaine said a trifle defensively.

Jeannie wrinkled her nose. 'I'd find it nauseating myself.'

'And, in order to be married, it's necessary to be asked first.'

'Is that what you're waiting for, to be asked?'

'I can't very well drag some man to the altar and marry him against his will, can I?' She sounded waspishly annoyed. 'Anyroad, there aren't many single, thirtyish men left. I haven't met one I fancy in years.'

'You will, one day,' Jeannie said, more confidently than she felt.

'Are you sure you don't mind me going, babe?' Lachlan enquired worriedly. 'I'll be gone three whole weeks.' It was his first long trip away since Antony was born.

'Of course I don't mind. I'd hate it if you didn't go and let so many people down.' The tour of Eastern Europe had been arranged since last year and was booked solid. They both knew it couldn't be cancelled at such short notice and were playing a little game of charades, sitting up in bed on Sunday morning while, beside them, their son slept soundly in his cot. A car was coming to collect him in less than an hour. His bags had been packed the night before and were waiting in the hall with three of his precious guitars.

'You won't be lonely on your own?'

'I won't be on my own, will I? I'll have Antony.' Jeannie chortled. 'I'll never be lonely again.'

'You're making me feel jealous, babe.' He grinned. 'I don't want to be jealous of our Ace.'

'Don't be daft. And don't call him Ace.'

'I'll ring every night, 'case you're pregnant again.'

'I won't be able to tell, will I? I'm still breast-feeding and I haven't had my periods back.'

'Women can get pregnant dead easy when they've just had a baby.'

'You've already told me that a dozen times, Lachlan,' Jeannie said patiently. She hoped there was a chance it might happen, but it was a very faint hope. 'We've been trying extremely hard. Let's pray it works.'

Lachlan slid down the bed and pulled her down with him. 'Let's have one more try before I leave. Today I'm feeling lucky. 'Fact, if we have another boy, that's what we'll call him – Lucky!'

Antony was gradually being weaned off breast-milk. He half-sat, half-lay in his canvas chair in the kitchen watching his mother prepare his bottle, idly kicking his bare feet. Lachlan had left two hours before.

Now that they'd had one child, he desperately wanted another, far more than he'd wanted the first. She knew he didn't care if it was a boy or girl, and that he was only joking when he said at least three, but he was anxious they have more children.

She picked up her baby and gave him a hug, then took him on to the patio to give him his bottle. It was going to be another warm day. 'I'm afraid your dad's going to be sadly disappointed,' she told him. 'He's not the only one who wants you to have a little sister or brother.'

Later, she carried him with her around the house and decided she was fed up with every-where being white. It looked too cold and clinical, particularly with wooden floors. She'd prefer warm, bright colours. 'We'll have your nursery painted, shall we? A lovely buttercup yellow. And buy a carpet. In fact, we'll get carpets for all the rooms and curtains too, blinds look too functional.' If the decor was to be so drastically altered, they'd need new furniture; scrunchy velvet armchairs and settees in dark jewel colours, lots of glowing polished wood.

She told her mother and Alex about her plans when they arrived after lunch with the girls. Amy and Eliza made straight for the pool. Jeannie wondered aloud why she suddenly wanted to completely transform the house.

'It's your nesting instinct,' Alex said. 'Ask Elaine, she'll know. You're like a bird, making the house comfortable for your young.'

'I didn't like to say it before, love, but this place always makes me feel as if I'm inside a big refrigerator,' Rose said. 'It feels warm enough, but it looks cold. I reckon you'll be improving it no end.'

'I'll ring a decorator tomorrow. Oh, it's so exciting!' Jeannie cried. Her entire world had changed with the arrival of Antony. It was a pity she'd had to wait so long for him to come.

The next few months were peaceful and uneventful, apart from the decorators who descended in their droves. Lachlan came home and refused to go on a long tour again. He was rarely away for more than one night at a time. He'd dispensed with the uppers and downers that he'd once found so essential, though Jeannie assumed he still took speed to get through the frenzied gigs that lasted three hours or more.

In September, when Antony was completely weaned, Jeannie went down to London to make an album to be released at Christmas. It would be called *A Rainbow of Flowers*, each number having a colour in the title, starting and finishing with 'White Christmas'. Although she badly missed Antony who was being looked after by Lachlan and her mother, it made a pleasant change to get away and be herself for a few days. She stayed with the McDowds, after making sure Sean wouldn't be there. When she returned, Antony was able to stand on his own and she could have sworn he'd grown an inch. Not only that, but the living room had been painted burnt orange and the new furniture had arrived. She'd only been back a day when a period started. As expected, she hadn't conceived, but was still bitterly disappointed.

That year, Christmas in Noah's Ark was like a fairy tale come true. The imitation tree stayed in the loft and they bought a real one, ten feet tall. Jeannie and Lachlan took the greatest pleasure dressing it with glittering bells and balls, tinsel garlands, and coloured lights. Antony gasped and clapped his hands with delight when the lights were switched on, his own eyes brighter than any on the tree.

'It'll be even better next year,' Lachlan sighed happily. 'Ace will really appreciate his presents. We can get him a football and his own little guitar.'

'The poor child must feel very confused,' Jeannie complained. 'You call him Ace; I call him Antony. He probably doesn't know who he is.'

'It's you who's confusing him, babe. Everyone calls him Ace. You're the only one who calls him Antony.'

'But that's his *name*,' she wailed.

'You never know,' Lachlan went on, ignoring

her. 'By next Christmas, Lucky Bailey might have appeared on the scene. Y'know, babe,' he said reflectively, 'I wouldn't mind easing off even more with the Survivors, just doing the occasional gig, so's I could spend more time at home. I'd concentrate on composing and arranging instead.'

'That would be marvellous, Lachlan.'

Nineteen seventy-seven got off to a tragic start when, early in January, Dr Bailey, apparently healthy and only in his mid-sixties, unexpectedly died after catching a particularly virulent strain of flu. He was on the verge of retirement and greatly looking forward to a more leisurely life. His shocked family were heartbroken. He had been a wonderful father, guiding his children gently and wisely through life, rarely raising his voice.

'He was always fair with us,' Lachlan said in a raw voice. 'If Dad passed an opinion, you knew he was right. I can't imagine the future without him around.'

Jeannie was struck by how unpredictable and cruel life could be. Dr Bailey was the first person close to her to die. It struck her that in the course of time other people would die, herself and Lachlan included. They discussed between them what they would do if the other died first.

'I hope I'm the first to go,' Jeannie said, 'because I don't think I could live without you.'

'I couldn't live without you, babe.'

'Then let's hope we go together.'

'It'd be pretty hard on Ace if we did.'

Jeannie gasped. 'We couldn't possibly do that to Ace. Oh, see! Now you've got *me* calling him Ace.'

'If I were you, babe, I'd give in. Stop confusing the lad and call him Ace like everyone else.'

January was slightly redeemed when, on the last day of the month, Rose Flowers married Alex Connors. Rose wore a fitted dress of blue panne velvet and a matching Greta Garbo hat with a giant cabbage rose on the brim. Not to be outdone, Alex wore a matching velvet suit and pink shirt. The bride and groom's outfits were the only grand things about the simple, registry office ceremony. Afterwards, the entire family flew to the Bahamas for the honeymoon.

The wedding was the first time Jeannie and Lachlan had met Ronnie Connors since he'd left the Merseysiders. It seemed a lifetime ago.

'Do you ever regret leaving?' Jeannie asked. 'I bet you never dreamt they'd do so well.'

'Perhaps I did,' Ronnie grinned. 'Perhaps that's why I left. If I couldn't hack it then, I'd never hack it now. I'd need a whole bottle a day of the hard stuff to calm me nerves. Anyroad, I'm dead happy working in me dad's factory. I'm assistant manager. *That* responsibility I can handle. Playing the keyboard was something else. Hey! Dad said you had a kid last year, a boy. Congratulations! We've got two, a boy and a girl. I've some photeys in me wallet.'

Lachlan's hand immediately went to the inside pocket of his suede jacket. 'I've got some of Ace...'

The small plane was being buffeted like a moth as it flew over the Irish Sea, trying to force its feeble way through the ferocious March gale. The pilot had been warned by officials at the airfield in Kent not to take off due to adverse weather conditions in the Fastnet area, but Mr McDowd had instructed him to ignore the warning.

'I'm in a hurry, Jimmy. There's this Irish singer, Donny O'Donnell, and I want to sign up before any other bastard gets to him. The guy was on TV last night,' he explained when the plane was airborne. The wind then was relatively slight. 'He sings like Engelbert Humperdinck and Tom Jones rolled into one. The programme came from Dublin, it being St Patrick's Day, like. I've already spoken to him on the phone,' he continued – Mr McDowd never stopped talking – 'and he agreed to sign a contract, but I won't feel safe till I've got his signature on the dotted line. Never trust an Irishman, boyo.' He chuckled. 'You just got that straight from the horse's mouth.'

'Yes, Mr McDowd.'

Mr McDowd rambled on. There'd been a time, he said boastfully, when he couldn't have raked together the fare to sail from dun Laoghaire to Fleetwood, let alone gone on a plane. Now he could fly to Dublin after lunch and be back in London in time for tea, and in his own aircraft too. He was a lucky man, that's for sure. Mind you, he'd worked hard. 'Luck and hard work, Jim, boy. Luck isn't enough, you need to work hard an' all. Is everything all right?' he asked when Jimmy didn't respond.

'I'm not sure, Mr McDowd. It's just that the wind's getting a bit rough.' The plane was being blown sharply to the right.

'Ah, don't take any notice, boyo. We'll be fine. The good Lord looks after his own.'

'I'm wondering if we shouldn't go back.'

'Not after coming all this far. We're nearly there.'

It was probably too late to turn back, otherwise the pilot would have done so of his own accord and to hell with Kevin McDowd. His employer stopped talking, apart from a cracked 'Jaysus Christ!' when they were suddenly jerked upwards, as if a giant puppetmaster was pulling invisible strings. Jimmy decided to continue the upward surge. If they rose high enough he could leave the gale behind and fly above it. He pulled back the joystick and the plane reared sharply. Mr McDowd made a choking sound as they continued to climb until they emerged in an entirely different world, where the air was crystal clear, the sky blue, and the sun a glaring golden ball. The pilot breathed a sigh of relief and steadied the small aircraft, but after a period of welcome calm, he noticed ice was beginning to form on the wings.

'I'll have to go down again,' he muttered. Too much ice, and he'd lose lift. They dropped as swiftly as they had risen, only to be grabbed by a particularly vicious thrust of wind that spun the plane out of control. Jimmy screamed with fear as he desperately tried to regain command, but there was nothing he could do to stop it from corkscrewing relentlessly downwards towards the angry, churning waters of the Irish Sea.

Jeannie was in the kitchen when the telephone rang. She wiped her hands and went to answer it, but the ringing stopped. Lachlan must have answered it elsewhere in the house. Minutes later, he appeared at the kitchen door. 'That was the Cobb,' he said tightly. 'Kevin's missing. He was flying to Dublin yesterday, but the plane never arrived.'

'But surely there a chance they were diverted and he's OK?'

'It doesn't seem likely. They're out searching for the wreckage. I'll ring Fly, tell him.'

'I'll put the radio on for the latest news.'

News drifted in bit by bit throughout the day. Wreckage of a plane was spotted just off the coast of Anglesey. Hours later, it was confirmed that the wreckage was the remains of a de Havilland Dove and a body had been seen some miles away. By six o'clock, another body had been sighted, and on the six o'clock news that night, it was announced that Kevin McDowd, millionaire manager of a string of successful musical acts, had died when his plane had been caught in bad weather over the Irish Sea. It went on to say that Mr McDowd was also a renowned composer, having written numerous chart successes, including the classic 'Moon Under Water'. Almost as an afterthought, it was mentioned that the pilot had also lost his life.

Sadie gave her darling Kevin a magnificent send

off. The Requiem Mass was held at Brompton Oratory in Knightsbridge and the church was packed to capacity with celebrities from all walks of life. Kevin had been the most popular and well liked of men. From the altar, Lachlan read from *Isaiah 35*. 'Let the desert and the dry lands be glad, let the wasteland rejoice and bloom; like the jonquil, let it burst into flower, let it rejoice and sing for joy.'

Zoe represented the Flower Girls. She was now a famous face on television, and she spoke movingly of the delightful man who had given her her first break. Sean McDowd appeared genuinely upset when he talked about his father. 'My dad wasn't perfect, but he made everybody laugh and he was generous to a fault. He taught me there was nothing I couldn't do. His voice and his laugh will always be with me, even if Dad won't be there himself.'

Outside the church, Lachlan gave Sean a fierce hug. 'As you know my own dad died only two months ago, so I understand how you must feel.'

'Thanks, mate.' Sean nodded curtly and turned to Jeannie. 'How are you?' he asked politely.

'Very well, thank you.' Jeannie deliberately avoided his eyes.

'I must come and meet your son one of these days.'

'Come for the weekend,' Lachlan said eagerly. 'I'll ask Fly and we can talk about old times.'

'Don't encourage him,' Jeannie whispered when Sean had gone.

'I'm sorry. I hadn't realised you didn't like him.'

'I don't *dis*like him. I'd just sooner not have him staying in our house.'

'On reflection, he's a miserable son of a bitch. I never liked him much myself either, but he's a brilliant guitarist and, after all, his dad's just died. I'm upset enough myself over Kevin.'

Marcia grabbed Jeannie's arm. She was dressed in a black bouclé suit and fur hat, and looked svelte and smart, not at all like the mother of six children. 'I suppose it'll be your dad's funeral soon,' she said in her piercing voice. 'He's by far the oldest father. By rights, he should have gone first.'

'I beg your pardon!'

'My mum's a widow, so is Sadie, so your mum's bound to be the next.'

'Your Elaine was right,' Jeannie said coldly. 'You should be permanently gagged. Also, I might remind you that my mother isn't married to my father.'

'There's no need to get on your high horse, Jeannie. Death always goes in threes.'

'I wouldn't want to see six children deprived of a mother, sis, but...' Lachlan made a face at his sister and left the remainder of the sentence unsaid. Marcia marched away in a huff.

'She's right, though,' Jeannie said. 'Death often seems to happen in threes.'

'That's just a silly superstition, babe.'

'Let's find Sadie and Rita and offer our sympathies, then go home. I'm badly missing Ace. But promise you'll drive carefully, Lachlan. I don't want either of us to be number three.'

Rita was nowhere to be found, but a white-faced Sadie, fighting to hold back the tears, told them she was doing her best to keep herself together. 'I'm setting up a trust in Kevin's name to fund aspiring musicians. I'm sure it's what he would have wanted. The Kevin McDowd Trust Fund. Doesn't that sound grand? It will keep his name alive. An accountant is going through the books at this very moment, sorting everything out.'

Jeannie was getting Ace ready for bed and combing the pale gold hair that had grown in magnificent abundance when he was six months old, when her mother rang.

'Put the television on. BBC1,' she said tersely and rang off straight away.

'Lachlan!' Jeannie yelled a few minutes later.

'What's the matter?' Lachlan rushed in. He'd just stepped out of the shower, and was clad only in a towel.

'It's Kevin McDowd.' She gestured at the television. 'His affairs were in a terrible mess. He's left behind a load of debts. Did he owe you any money?'

'No, I've been paid completely up to date. So have Fly and the Cobb, or they would have mentioned it.' Lachlan looked stunned. 'I wonder what will happen to Sadie?'

'Well, she won't be setting up the Kevin Mc-Dowd Trust Fund, that's for sure.'

Kevin had borrowed off a French bank to buy the flat in Paris, and was well behind with repayments. The bank had now started proceedings to claim the flat in lieu. The manor house in Ireland had been bought for cash, but it had been seriously run down and there was a long list of tradesmen still waiting for their money. The mews house in Knightsbridge had a mortgage, also in default, though it was in Sadie's name, something of which she was unaware. Several months' rent was owed on the Mayfair office. Wine merchants, tailors, florists, jewellers; Kevin McDowd was indebted to them all. He'd paid off a bit here, a bit there, so no one had been particularly worried. Kevin had always been an honourable man and, even now, no one doubted they would have been eventually been paid in full.

The racehorse and the plane, his most precious possessions, were the only things for which Kevin didn't owe a penny.

'Apparently,' Lachlan reported, 'Kevin had a massive life insurance policy, and the plane was insured. Sadie thinks that should wipe out at least half the debts.'

But the insurance company refused to pay. The insured, Kevin McDowd, had insisted on taking the plane up, despite advice from experts on the ground that the weather conditions made it unsafe. According to the small print, the circumstances were such they weren't liable to compensate for any subsequent loss of life or for the loss of the plane.

The wife of the pilot, Jimmy, sued Kevin's estate, demanding compensation for herself and her two small children.

'I always thought we were living way beyond

our means,' Sadie wept. '"Where's all the money coming from?" I'd ask, but you know Kevin. He just brushed me off with a wink and a smile. If he was here now, I'd kill the bloody eejit, so I would.'

The simple fact was that Kevin had over-reached himself. He was still the same person everyone had spoken so highly of at his funeral – generous, kind, big-hearted – but he'd been living in a dream world, spending money like water when the money wasn't there to spend.

The Survivors soon acquired another manager, Donald Weston, a quiet, business-like man with none of Kevin's flamboyance. Kevin had been dead for six months when the group were offered a tour of Canada and the States. Jeannie insisted that Lachlan should go.

'I'll be perfectly all right on my own,' she told him. 'It's not fair on Fly and the Cobb to turn another tour down. Neither of them are as well off as you are.'

'If you're sure you don't mind, babe.' He was obviously quite keen on going.

Lachlan was in Montreal when a letter arrived for Jeannie from Perriman & Rowe, chartered accountants, announcing there would be a preliminary meeting of Kevin McDowd's creditors in two weeks' time in their office in the Strand. She had no idea she was a creditor, but apparently she was owed the grand sum of twenty-four pounds in royalties, which had arrived after Kevin's death.

Sadie confirmed she would be attending the meeting when Jeannie rang. 'I'd feel like a coward, staying away. This is Kevin's mess. As his wife, I feel I should do all I can to help. I've already sold all me furs and jewellery and the Knightsbridge house is on the market.'

Jeannie asked her mother if she would look after Ace for the day. 'I don't give a damn about the twenty-four pounds, but I'd like to be there for Sadie's sake.'

About a dozen creditors were sitting around a long table when Jeannie entered Perriman & Rowe's conference room. With its ceiling-high, glass-fronted bookcases and dark oil paintings, the room looked as if it hadn't changed since the firm was established in the last century. Two dark-suited, accountant-like figures were seated at the head of the table. At the far end, a drawn and red-eyed Sadie sat alone. Jeannie went and sat beside her.

'I'm glad you've come, luv,' Sadie said. 'You're the only person here I know, apart from our Sean.'

'Sean's here?'

'Yes, he's just gone to find me a cup of tea from somewhere. He's flown all the way from America specially. He's a good lad, our Sean, always looked after his mam. Rita too. Her and Mavis have been staying with me on and off since Kevin died.' Sadie sniffed and, for a moment, Jeannie saw the pathetic wreck of a woman who used to live at the other end of Disraeli Terrace. But then Sadie put her hand over the younger woman's. 'I'm still holding meself together, Jeannie,' she said. 'I'm determined Jimmy's wife won't be left destitute, like I was, with two little kids to support. Once everything's been sorted, Sean's going to make sure no one's left out of pocket, even though it's not his job to clear up after his father.'

Sean appeared with a tray containing a small teapot, a jug of milk, a bowl of sugar, and a fancy mug. 'The woman in reception was dead helpful,' he said. 'She apologised for not having a saucer.'

Jeannie wasn't surprised the woman had been helpful. She was unlikely to have been asked for tea before by a world famous singer who sent shivers of desire up most female spines. She felt a little shiver herself at the sight of the tall, dour figure with the dark, smoky eyes and almost animal sex appeal. She gave him the briefest of smiles, then settled down to ignore him as the proceedings began.

They didn't last long. One of the accountants explained that the situation was dire. When everything had been sold that could be sold, it was possible creditors would receive as little as fivepence in the pound. The exact figure would be confirmed at another meeting in six months' time. There was a horrified gasp from around the table. Then Sean announced there would be no need for another meeting. He intended to clear every one of his father's debts. At that point Sadie burst into tears.

Afterwards, they went to the Savoy for a drink. 'Thank you, son. Oh, but I still felt dead ashamed,' Sadie wept. 'We shouldn't have come to a posh place like this. Under the circumstances, it seems awful ostentatious.'

Sean ordered her not to be so daft. 'You can't live like a nun for the rest of your life just because of what me dad did. Anyroad, it's me that's paying. What do you want to drink?' he asked when a waiter arrived to take their order.

'Gin and It, a double.'

Jeannie said she'd like a glass of white wine. 'Medium, please.' She wasn't sure why she was still there, having promised her mother she'd catch the train back to Liverpool the minute the meeting was over. Sadie probably appreciated having another woman's company at such an upsetting time, or so Jeannie told herself. The presence of Sean McDowd had nothing to do with delaying her journey home. 'How long are you staying?' she asked him.

'A couple of days. How about you?' He looked at her through half-closed eyes, his face expressionless.

'I'm not sure,' Jeannie answered. 'A day or two. There's a few things I have to do in London.'

'You can stay with us, luv,' Sadie said instantly. 'The house is on the market, but it hasn't been sold yet.'

'Actually, I'm booked in here, at the Savoy. Excuse me a minute.' She got up suddenly, hurried to the Ladies, and stared at her reflection in the mirror. Her eyes were pools of vivid blue and her face was white. Black always made her look pale and she was wearing the suit she'd bought for Kevin's funeral; grosgrain with a pleated satin collar and cuffs, very tight-fitting, and showing off her slim figure to perfection. She

404

renewed her coral lipstick, dabbed blusher on her cheeks, and brushed her hair away from her face until it was smooth, then took a step back and stared at herself again. It wasn't often Jeannie thought about her looks other than to thank the Lord she hadn't been born plain. Today, though, she was glad that she was beautiful.

She left the Ladies and swiftly made her way to Reception where she booked a room for that night. 'No, make it two nights,' she said to the clerk behind the desk.

'Double or single, madam?'

'Er, double. I don't want the key just yet. I have to collect my luggage.' She'd buy a toothbrush, nightdress, and a change of underclothes later.

'You're in room twenty-five on the second floor, madam.'

'Thank you.'

Her mother was perfectly happy to continue looking after Ace when Jeannie phoned to explain a couple of things had come up in London.

'You know I love having him, and the girls are off for half-term and they adore their little nephew.'

All done! Jeannie took a deep breath. Her legs were trembling when she returned to the bar. Sean was autographing the bar tariff for a flushed, star-struck young woman whose gratitude was almost embarrassing to behold.

'Thank you,' she stuttered. 'Oh, thank you. I'll keep it for always.'

'It's a pleasure.' Sean's rare smile transformed his face. Jeannie wasn't surprised that the young woman looked ready to faint when in receipt of its full power.

Sadie had drunk a second gin and It while she'd been away and asked for a third. Her voice was slurred.

'One more, Mam, then I'm taking you home. I think you need to lie down for a while.'

'All right, son,' Sadie said obediently. 'Will we be seeing you again before you go home, Jeannie? Since this business with Kevin, I've only got me old friends left. The new ones don't want to know me any more.'

'Perhaps we could have lunch tomorrow, but if you need me for anything in the meantime, give me a call.' Jeannie looked directly at Sean. 'I'm in room twenty-five.'

It was a minute past midnight when he came, knocking softly on the door. Her heart did a somersault when she went to answer it in a modest white nightdress, only slightly sheer. She'd contemplated buying something black and glamorous, but it might look too obvious and he might guess that she was deliberately trying to seduce him.

I can't do this! she thought when she opened the door to the thin, sinister figure in a long black mackintosh with the collar turned up. She laughed shakily. 'You look like a foreign spy.'

He came into the room, took off the mack, and flung it on to a chair. His eyes were burning into hers. He didn't speak, and she realised the great Sean McDowd was stuck for words.

'Come here,' she whispered, throwing caution

to the wind. She reached for his hand and pulled him over to the bed.

When she woke, it was broad daylight and Sean was leaning on his elbow, staring moodily down at her. She blinked herself properly awake and smiled. 'Good morning.'

He didn't smile back. 'Why are you doing this, Jeannie?'

'Why?' She stroked his neck, which was as taut as a rope. 'Do I have to have a reason?'

'There's a reason for everything.'

'I'm sorry, Sean, but I don't know what it is.' She pressed her breasts against him, feeling sensuous and wanton. 'What I do know,' she said softly, 'is that I badly want you to do it again.'

It was midday when he left and they arranged to meet again that night and have dinner in her room. It was too risky for them to be seen dining together in public. He'd only been gone a minute when Sadie rang to say she hoped Jeannie wouldn't mind if she cancelled the lunch date, but people were coming to view the house. Jeannie didn't mind, having forgotten all about it.

The afternoon was spent in a flurry of guilt and confusion. She was using Sean, but did she really have to enjoy it quite so much? Back in Ailsham, she'd never been one of the girls who'd fallen under his spell, but now she felt in thrall to his urgent, passionate love-making. She didn't love him. Her heart would only ever belong to Lachlan, but Sean awakened a dark side of her she'd never known existed. He made her more aware of how precious her body was. The touch of his hand, anywhere, could send her into a quiver of delight and anticipation.

She had a shower, languorously soaping herself, remembering the way Sean had touched this particular spot, and that, and how his lips had caressed the most intimate parts of her.

It was late, and the shops were almost closing, when she caught a taxi to Harrods and bought a dress. It was scarlet, of the very softest silk, with a low neck and shoe string straps. It revealed far more of her bosom than she was used to showing. The flared skirt contained yards and yards of material that rippled to and fro in tiny waves when she moved and felt as light as feathers against her legs.

Six o'clock, and the table in her room was set for two. She'd order the meal when Sean arrived. Champagne waited in a bucket of ice. Jeannie turned off the main light in favour of a cream-shaded lamp, then draped herself in the red dress seductively in an armchair. The door was unlatched and all she had to do was shout, 'Come in,' when he knocked.

Her stomach was churning pleasantly with anticipation, when it dawned on her that the room resembled a harlot's parlour and she looked nothing less than a tart. She jumped to her feet, turned off the lamp, put on the light, changed into the black suit, and was pretending to read the evening paper when Sean came.

They looked at each other across the room, neither speaking. Jeannie got to her feet and the paper fell to the floor. Sean closed his eyes briefly and gave a deep sigh, like a man facing water after a long thirst. He walked across the room and took her in his arms.

'I've thought of nothing else but you all day,' he said in a muffled voice.

It was very late by the time they ordered dinner. While they waited for the food to arrive, Sean opened the champagne. He clicked his glass against Jeannie's. 'To us,' he said with a sweet smile.

'To us.' For some reason, she wanted to cry. All she'd wanted was another baby for Lachlan. She hadn't dreamt things would get quite so out of hand.

Chapter 14

1978

'Why can't we go to the christening?' Mavis wanted to know, her little green eyes sparkling with annoyance.

'Because I don't feel like it,' Rita said, folding her arms as if that was the end of the matter, but Mavis was having none of it.

'That's not a proper excuse.'

'It's a perfect excuse. I don't feel like going and that's all there is to it.'

'But I want to see the new baby. I wouldn't mind seeing Jeannie, either, come to that. I haven't met her since your dad's funeral and then we hardly spoke. Of all your friends, I like her best. That Marcia one really gets up me nose.'

'That's just too bad. You can't go, so there.'

'I can go on me own. Jeannie addressed the invitation to us both. See!' Mavis waved the envelope in front of Rita's nose. 'Rita McDowd and Mavis Maguire, it ses here.'

'You're not using the car.'

'Then I'll go on the bloomin' train.'

'I might not allow you the time off.'

'I might remind *you*, madam, that I'm allowed time off. I'm not a bloomin' slave. Next Sunday I'm going to Jeannie's baby's christening. You can like it or lump it, I don't care.'

Rita sighed and stared out of the window of the house in Primrose Hill. The rain was coming down in buckets as it had been doing for days. 'I hate driving in the rain,' she said pathetically, realising that she'd lost. You'd never think she had in her name in lights above a theatre in Haymarket, the star of a new musical, *Dusk in the City*, that had received rave reviews. Her own performance had been described variously, as 'scintillating', 'magnificent', and 'utter perfection', yet here she was letting herself be messed about by an ex–lavatory attendant.

'I'm the one who drives, ain't I?' Mavis, knowing that she'd won, said in a softer voice. 'Anyway, the rain might've stopped by Sunday. If not, you can sit in the back and go to sleep.'

The church was packed with much the same crowd that had been at Ace's christening. Jeannie had asked the widows of Dr Bailey and Kevin McDowd to be Godmothers. 'I don't think there's any rules about that sort of thing,' she said to Lachlan. 'This time, we won't have a Godfather. A fat lot of use Fly has been to Ace.'

Chloe Rose Bailey, two months old, screamed her angry head off throughout the entire service, the screams rising to a shriek of outraged horror when the first speck of water touched her black, curly hair. Her exhausted mother wasn't the only one to feel relieved when they were able to leave the church and make their way back through the pouring rain to Noah's Ark in a procession of cars.

Jeannie virtually ran into her daughter's bed-

411

room, wanting to fling her into the cot. Instead, she gritted her teeth and laid her carefully down in her frothy christening gown. Chloe's face was bright red with rage. Her fists punched the air, her feet drummed against the mattress. She'd lost one of her white satin booties, but Jeannie didn't care.

'There you are!' Mavis came in, followed by Ace and a reluctant Rita. She bent over the cot. 'Hello, Chloe,' she cooed. 'Why are you crying, darlin'? Can I hold her a minute?'

'Help yourself.'

The minute Chloe found herself in Mavis's plump arms, she stopped crying and fell asleep. Jeannie was impressed. 'You've certainly got a way with children, Mavis.'

Ace, who would be two in June, was anxious to point out his baby sister's attributes to the stranger. 'She got a nose,' he said, 'and a mouf.'

'So she has,' Mavis agreed, 'though they're not as nice as yours.'

'She cwies all night,' Ace said importantly.

'I bet you never did, darlin'.'

Watching, Rita felt the urge to be sick. She didn't dislike babies, they were necessary for the continuance of the human race, but couldn't understand why people went all soppy over them.

'Chloe's a nice name,' she said to Jeannie in an attempt to appear interested.

'I think so. Lachlan wanted to call her Lucky, but I was having none of it.'

Rita looked jealously at Chloe, warmly en-sconced in Mavis's arms, and hoped she wasn't

412

getting ideas again about being a mother. It was why Rita hadn't wanted to come. At the last christening, Mavis had contented herself with just looking at the baby. This time, she'd actually got her rotten hands on it.

Mavis said, 'You go and look after your guests, Jeannie. Enjoy yourself. You too, Rita. I'm fine here.' She sat down on a white upholstered chair.

'Are you sure?' Jeannie looked quite keen on the idea. 'Come on, Ace.'

'Wanna stay with Mavis.'

'The more the merrier.' Mavis held out an arm and Ace tucked himself inside it. 'I'll tell you a story, shall I?'

'Please!'

Rita left the room as resentfully as she'd entered it.

'Where are our children?' Lachlan asked when he and Jeannie were about to push past each other in the packed hallway, which had an eerie appeal on a day like today with the rain bouncing off the domed glass roof.

She told him the children were with Mavis, who would make a perfect nanny. 'She's such a lovely person too. I'd love it if she came to live with us.'

'Why not ask her?'

'I would, except I don't think Rita would be very pleased.'

'Jeannie!'

'Yes, Dad?' Surprisingly, Tom had turned up again.

He gave an awkward little cough. 'I was

413

wondering if you needed any gardening done? Disraeli Terrace isn't enough to keep me busy.'

'It wouldn't feel right, Dad, employing my own father, paying him a wage.'

'It wouldn't feel right taking money off me own daughter, so you can forget about a wage. It's just that your hedge needs pruning badly, and a couple of your trees don't look so healthy. Last year, your roses had greenfly.'

'Did they?' Their present gardener frequently let them down. He doubled as a painter and decorator, and the work always took precedence over the gardening side. 'I tell you what, come and see us one day when it's quiet and we can talk about it then.'

'I'll come tomorrow,' he said with alacrity.

'Where's Mrs Denning? I thought you two were getting married.'

'I'm not sure if I want another wife at my time of life. I'm comfortable as I am. I thought it best to let things stay as they are with Nora – Mrs Denning.' He blushed ever so slightly.

'Are you feeling all right, Dad?'

'I'm fine, Jeannie. Never felt better. Why do you ask?'

'No reason. I just wondered.' It was well over a year since Marcia had made the doomladen prediction that there would be another death and it had been on her mind ever since. Even now, whenever the phone rang, she half-expected it to be the news that Tom had died.

Rose watched her daughter with the man who used to be her husband and felt sick. She reached

414

for Alex's hand and held it every tightly.

'What's the matter, sweetheart?' he asked softly. He looked rather tired, she thought.

'Nothing.' Whenever she saw Tom, she felt the need to reestablish who she was. 'I'm Mrs Rose Connors,' she told herself 'Alex is my husband and always will be. Tom's part of the past. He can never harm me again.'

'I don't know why we couldn't stay at Jeannie's like she asked,' Mavis complained. 'You're not the only one who doesn't like driving in the rain. All you have to do is sit and criticise. It's about time you learned to drive yourself.'

'I have a show to do tomorrow,' Rita said haughtily. 'I need to get back tonight.'

'We could have left in the morning at the crack of dawn. You'd've still had plenty of time, and at least it would have been daylight.' She wiped the windscreen with her sleeve and grimaced. 'I can't see proper.'

'If you must know, I couldn't wait to get away. You were driving everybody mad, the way you kept drooling over that baby. It was dead embarrassing. She had Godmothers, you know, but they didn't get a look in because of you.'

'Mrs Bailey and Sadie sat with me for ages. We had a lovely natter. Every time one of 'em took Chloe, she bawled her head off. They were only too pleased to give her back to me.'

'Mavis Maguire, the perfect mother.' Rita gave a sarcastic laugh.

'That's what Lachlan must have thought. He offered me a job as the children's live-in nanny.'

Rita felt the hairs rise on her neck. 'What did you say?'

'That I'd think about it.'

She'd die if she lost Mavis. The thought of life without her occupied Rita's horrified mind for the next twenty miles. 'What are you going to do?' she asked after the longest silence there'd ever been between them.

'I ain't sure, darlin'. It's a lovely house that Noah's Ark, ain't it? I like it better since they've had it done up. I've always fancied learning to swim,' she added casually.

'We could have a pool put in the house in Yorkshire, much bigger than the Baileys.'

'Mm' Mavis said thoughtfully. 'You'd never believe the wage Lachlan mentioned. He's not a skinflint, not like some people I know.'

'If you wanted more money, Mavis, all you had to do was ask.'

'He said I'd have a car of me own.'

'I'll buy you a car of your own.'

'A Mini? I've always fancied a red Mini.'

'I'll order one tomorrow.'

'Oh, and he said something about a mink coat for Christmas.'

Rita looked at her suspiciously. 'Are you having me on?'

Mavis burst out laughing. 'Only about the mink. Everything else is true – and I'm holding you to the pool and the Mini and the hike in wages. I'd love to look after those kids, I really would but, although you can be a nasty piece of work when you're in the mood, I'd never leave you, darlin'.'

It had been an exhausting day and Jeannie and Lachlan went to bed early. The rain continued to fall in torrents. Fly, whose second marriage was on the line, had come to the christening by himself. He'd drunk too much, even for a man who could normally hold his liquor better than most. He'd been put to bed in one of the spare rooms, incapable of driving back to London.

At midnight, dead on time, Chloe announced loudly that she was ready for a feed. Jeannie switched on the bedside lamp, staggered into her room, picked her up, and took her back to bed – there'd been no suggestion of keeping her with them as they'd done with Ace. The least sound woke Chloe and she associated waking up with food.

Jeannie climbed back into bed, undid her nightdress, and the baby greedily attached herself to her breast. Lachlan was fast asleep. Jeannie wouldn't have minded someone to talk to. It was a lonely business feeding a baby in the middle of the night. She shuffled around a bit in the hope of waking him, but it didn't work. She cursed both him and their daughter and gave an extra loud sigh, but still Lachlan slept on.

Chloe was ready for the other breast when the telephone beside the bed rang. It was on Lachlan's side, so she kicked him awake. 'Phone!' she hissed.

He grumbled something about being a famous pop idol and she had no right to kick him, before picking up the receiver.

'Hello,' he grunted. He listened for a moment,

then shot out of bed. 'Have you called a doctor?' There was a pause. 'Right,' he said crisply. 'We'll be over straight away.' He turned to Jeannie, his face stiff with shock. 'That was your mother. Alex is dead.'

'But he can't be! We only saw him this afternoon.'

'It only takes a second to die, babe. Get dressed. I'll wake up Fly. He can take care of the children.' He pulled on jeans, grabbed a sweatshirt, and left the room.

Jeannie didn't argue. She put an indignant, half-fed Chloe on the bed and threw on some clothes. A perfectly sober Fly came in. 'I'm sorry, Jeannie. Alex was a great guy. It was due to him the Merseysiders got off the ground. You don't have to worry about Chloe. I've got kids of me own. I know what to do.'

The doctor hadn't yet arrived and Alex was sitting on the settee, his head resting on the arm. He was ready for bed, in canary yellow pyjamas and a black corduroy robe. His eyes were open and his face unnaturally pale with the suggestion of a smile. He looked very peaceful.

'He died in my arms,' Rose had cried hysterically when she opened the door. She wore a blue quilted dressing gown. 'We were watching television and holding each other. After a while, I thought he seemed awfully still. I assumed he'd gone asleep. I moved away, I was going to make us some hot milk and go to bed, but he just fell on to the arm.' She ran to the settee and kissed Alex's still face, over and over. 'What am I going to do without you?' she screamed.

'Oh, Mum!' Jeannie pulled her mother away, guided her to a chair, and made her sit down. She stroked the soft brown hair. 'It must have been a terrible shock.'

Lachlan was feeling for a pulse. He shook his head slightly, passed his hand over Alex's eyes and gave a little sigh when they closed on the world for the last time. Then he went into the kitchen and returned with half a tumbler of whisky. 'Drink this, Rose.'

'I don't want a drink,' Rose shrilled. 'I want Alex!'

'Shush, Mum. You're frightening the girls.' Jeannie had only just noticed Amy and Eliza, two ashen-faced ghosts, sitting on the floor in their nightdresses in front of the dying fire. They looked terrified out of their wits.

'Shall I take the girls to Mum?' Lachlan asked. 'She'll look after them.'

'If they'll go. You'd better get their dressing gowns and slippers from upstairs.'

The terrified girls seemed relieved to be taken away from their dead father and hysterical mother. Lachlan had been gone less than a minute when the doctor arrived. He examined Alex briefly and phoned for an ambulance. 'I'll give you something for your mother,' he said to Jeannie. 'A sedative, very strong. It'll make her sleep. Try and get her to take it straight away. She'll feel better in the morning, though not much.' He smiled wryly. 'People get used to death eventually. Some take longer than others.'

'What did Alex die of?'

'I suspect a heart attack', he said in a low voice, 'but there'll have to be a postmortem. I'll wait for the ambulance, but then I'll have to go. I have another call to make. In the meantime, perhaps you could get your mother into another room, away from the body. It's not helping.'

Rose obediently took the tablet and hardly seemed to notice when Jeannie led her into the dining room. She was quieter now, resigned. She sat at the table and began to speak in a low, querulous voice. 'We were watching one of those old black and white films. Alex loved them. We'd get ready for bed and cuddle down together on the settee. It was our favourite time of the day.' She rambled on. They'd booked a holiday in Majorca in July. 'As soon as the girls broke up. But we won't be able to go now, will we?' She looked hopefully at Jeannie, as if expecting her to say, 'Why not?' and that she'd only been imagining that Alex was dead. It had merely been a bad dream.

'We'll just have to see, Mum.'

The voice got slower, became slurred. The ambulance came. Jeannie waited until Alex had left Magnolia Cottage for ever and the doctor had popped his head round the door to say he was going, before helping her mother upstairs into the bed where she'd lain with Alex for fifteen years, the best years. She sat with her until certain that the whisky and the tablet had done their work and Rose was fast asleep.

Downstairs, she made tea, and it wasn't until then that her own tears fell. She wept for Alex, now lying in a cold mortuary somewhere, for her mother and the fatherless girls. Marcia had been right, after all, but it had never crossed her mind that the cruel finger of fate would point at Alex and not Tom.

Lachlan returned. 'Mum's dead upset. She really liked Alex, but then everybody did. She's only too pleased to help by having the girls. Oh, and it's stopped raining at last.'

Jeannie threw herself into his arms and sobbed her heart out. They sat holding each other, until Jeannie's sobs subsided and she remembered Chloe had only had half her feed. 'I'd better go home,' she said. 'Or should you go and fetch her and I'll feed her here? Oh, I don't know what to do! I don't want her waking Mum up.'

'Chloe's OK,' Lachlan soothed. 'I rang Fly from Mum's. He made her a bottle. She's fast asleep. I gave him this number in case there's an emergency.'

They spent the rest of the night talking, sleeping occasionally, drinking tea, until a glimmer of light began to show through the curtains and the birds began to sing, heralding the arrival of a brilliantly sunny April day.

Alex was buried in the blue velvet suit he'd worn when he'd married Rose Flowers. Rose wore her blue matching wedding dress to the funeral. 'It's what he would have wanted,' she said. 'If he's up in heaven watching, he'll be pleased.' She was bearing up remarkably well, mainly due to Ida Bailey, who'd been a tower of strength. It wasn't all that long since she'd lost her own husband, and she knew exactly how Rose felt and which words to use in comfort. The two women had always liked each other, but from now on, they were to become the best of friends.

Life goes on. Jeannie was surprised at how quickly it returned to normal, that she was able to laugh, feel happy, think about other things. Even her mother began to smile, though the smile would never again reach her eyes and there was always something sad about it. She and Mrs Bailey – Jeannie was never able to think of her as anything other than 'Mrs' – went on the planned holiday to Majorca with the girls.

'Ida's the only person in the world I could have gone with,' Rose said. 'She's still grieving for the doctor and me for Alex. Neither of us feels embarrassed about having a little weep now and again.'

Perhaps Chloe had felt chastened by being abandoned in the middle of a feed and left with a stranger, because from that night on she cried less and slept more. She was growing to be sunny, reasonably well-behaved little girl, chocolate box pretty with her mother's summer-blue eyes, though would always be a more demanding, much noisier child than her brother.

Ace was a happy, supremely contented little boy. The Baileys continued to remark on his resemblance to Lachlan, so much so, that she began to wonder if Ace actually was his child. And, if that was the case, the same could be said for Chloe. She encouraged herself in the belief that they were Lachlan's children, deliberately ignoring the similarity to Sean in Ace's sweet, glowing smile and dark blue eyes, and that Chloe's face in repose bore the same closed expression as Sean's and her hair was the same sooty black.

Tom came almost every day to tend the garden of Noah's Ark. Alex had been dead a year, it was spring again, and Tom was on his knees, clearing the soil of weeds at the foot of the hawthorn hedge, when Jeannie's mother arrived. She often dropped in at about eleven for coffee. The Survivors were touring Australia and Lachlan wouldn't be home for another two weeks.

Usually, Rose kept out of the way of her first husband, but on that day she was in the kitchen making coffee when Tom came in for his morning cup of tea. He insisted on keeping to the kitchen when in his gardening mode, old habits dying hard.

To Jeannie's amazement, she heard them talk for a long time. Every now and then, their voices would rise, as if they were having an argument. She resisted the urge to go and see what it was about and stayed to keep an eye on Chloe, who was playing on the carpet with giant Lego. On the patio, Ace was furiously riding his bike around in circles. Connie could be heard singing while she made the beds.

When her mother came in with the coffee, she was smiling. 'Your dad's in a terrible predicament. He wants to vote Conservative, as usual, in the election, but if they win, there'll be a woman prime minister, Mrs Thatcher. He doesn't think a woman's capable of running the country.' The election was in a few weeks' time.

'So, what's he going to do?' Jeannie asked.

'I expect he'll end up voting Tory. I don't suppose you remember but, years ago, whenever there was an election, he used to tell me where to put my cross. I did as I was told, of course. The poor man nearly had a fit just now when I said I would be voting Labour.'

'Is that what Alex voted?'

'No, love. He was Liberal.' She laughed drily. 'Your dad asked the same question. It seems even you don't think I'm capable of making up my own mind about anything that matters.'

'I probably won't bother to vote. I never have before.' There'd always been far more important things to think about.

'Well, you should,' her mother said reprovingly. 'The Suffragettes went to prison and were force fed, one of them even died, to win the right for women to vote. You're letting them down.'

Sean McDowd telephoned from New York the day Lachlan was due back from the tour of Australia. It was May now, and the French windows were open for the first time to a bright, sunny morning. In the garden, Tom was giving Ace a piggy back and Chloe was impatiently waiting for her turn. Tom was softer now, far more indulgent with his grandchildren than he'd been with his children.

Jeannie had neither seen nor spoken to Sean since she'd stayed at the Savoy two years ago. He asked how she was, and she told him she was fine, and he said that he was fine too.

The formalities over, he said casually, 'I'll be in

London next week. I thought we could meet up for dinner.'

She scrambled round in her brain for a reply. 'I never get to London these days, Sean,' she said in a rush. 'I'm too busy with the children.'

'Of course, you've got two now. Last time we met you only had one.'

Her head swam. Did he *know!* Was he shrewd enough to have noticed the nine-month gaps between them making love and Ace and Chloe being born? She decided to change the subject before the silence between them became notice-ably long. 'Your mother came to stay the other week,' she said.

'Yeah, she said she had a great time. She loves your kids, Jeannie.' He paused. 'She misses having grandkids of her own.'

'Well, there's plenty of time. Sorry, I have to ring off. I can see Chloe's fallen over and she's crying.' Chloe was gleefully riding on Tom's back. ''Bye, Sean.'

Jeannie slammed down the receiver and clutched her hot face with both hands. He *did* know! But he couldn't possibly know for certain. All he could do was guess. And even if he guessed the truth, there was nothing he could do about it.

As the hours passed, she wondered if she'd seen a double meaning in Sean's words that hadn't been intended. She went over their conversation a dozen times and each time it sounded more innocent. Her fears were almost certainly the product of an over-heated imagination – or a guilty conscience. Even so, that she had come so close to thinking he might have guessed the truth was disturbing.

At half past five, Lachlan rang from Heathrow. He was just about to catch a taxi to London where he would pick up his new Ferrari and drive home. 'See you around tennish, babe. I can't wait.' He'd been away six whole weeks.

'Me neither.' She asked him not to eat anything. 'I'm making dinner. And drive carefully, please.'

'You always say that, babe.'

She visualised him grinning at the other end of the line and grinned back. 'It always needs saying, otherwise you'd drive like a maniac.'

Chloe was put to bed and Ace followed an hour later, after being allowed to stay up for *Top of the Pops*, on which he occasionally saw his daddy, something he took in his stride. Tonight, Daddy would be there for real, Jeannie promised. 'He'll come and kiss you goodnight, like he always does, once he's home.'

'Will I be awake?'

'You might, you might not. Who knows?'

She set a little table in front of the window in the living room, rather than use the vast one in the dining room that could take twenty at a pinch, spreading a lace cloth over it and putting a red candle in the centre. She wasn't a very adventurous cook and there was only chicken casserole in the oven and prawn cocktails in the fridge for starters. They'd have ice cream for a sweet. The wine was being chilled.

After a bath, she searched through her wardrobe for something special to wear. She hadn't bought anything new in ages, spending most of her time nowadays in jeans and cotton tops. The few forays she made into town were too rushed to search for the latest fashions. Next time she went, she'd spend a whole day replenishing her wardrobe. Lachlan would be glad to look after Ace and Chloe once he was home. She could even go to London for the day, she thought idly.

And meet Sean McDowd?

No!

She paused in her search, furious with herself for allowing such a thought to even enter her head. How could she possibly consider such a thing when she and Lachlan were so blissfully happy? It didn't help when she spied a glimpse of something scarlet at the back of the wardrobe and realised it was the dress she'd bought in London when she'd stayed at the Savoy. It hadn't been worn for more than half an hour. She recalled sitting in the chair, wearing the dress, and waiting for Sean to come. He made her feel uniquely desirable and quite different to the woman other people knew, including her husband.

There was the crunch of wheels on the gravel drive. Lachlan! Earlier than expected. He must have driven like a maniac, after all. She ran to the door in her bathrobe. He was just getting out of the car; a tall, familiar figure, shabbily dressed as always. She felt a thrust of love that took her breath away.

'I was just about to put on something incredibly glamorous,' she cried. 'I'm not even wearing lipstick.'

He scooped her up in his arms and carried her

into the bedroom. 'Right now, babe, I don't want you wearing anything.'

An hour later, they sat down to dinner. Jeannie had forgotten all about Sean McDowd until Lachlan poured the wine, raised his glass, and said. 'To us!'

'To us!' It was the same toast Sean had made before the only meal they'd ever had together. Jeannie took a vow never to see him again, not even to think about him, to banish him from her mind for ever.

'I thought about you all the time while I was away, Jeannie, you and our kids,' Lachlan said huskily. He reached across the table for her hand. 'I got to realising what a lucky guy I was, the luckiest guy on earth. Everything I want is in this house.' He grinned. 'Including the studio. You, Ace and Chloe, and rock 'n' roll. They're all I'll ever want in this world.'

Thousands of miles away across the Atlantic, in New York, where it was only early evening, Sean McDowd was sitting on the balcony of his fifteenth-floor apartment overlooking Central Park, still smarting from the phone call he'd made to Jeannie earlier in the day. He'd had a date that night, but had cancelled it, not in the mood to conduct trivial conversation with a woman he hardly knew and had no wish to know better.

He would have sworn on his life there was something between him and Jeannie. The first time they'd made love, he'd taken her by surprise, though she hadn't objected and gave the impression of having enjoyed it as much as he had. The second occasion, she'd actively encouraged him. Sensitive to every nuance where Jeannie Flowers was concerned, he recalled how she'd given his mother her room number, glancing at him to make sure he'd heard. For two nights, she had welcomed him into her bed, two nights that he would never forget.

It was a year before he was in England again – he would have flown there every week had he thought he could see Jeannie. She'd not long had a baby, Chloe, and Alex Connors had just died. It was the wrong time to suggest that they meet. He'd thought about going to Alex's funeral. Alex was a decent guy and he'd liked him, but cringed at the thought of seeing Jeannie and Lachlan together and being reminded that, however eagerly she'd seemed to want *him*, she belonged to someone else.

Another year passed. In two weeks' time, he would be home again for a series of concerts and had expected Jeannie to jump at the chance of them meeting again. Instead, he'd been given the brush off. It hurt, badly. He didn't believe that Chloe had fallen over. It was just an excuse for her mother to put down the phone. If only he could see her, touch her, get her alone. Sean was convinced it would take very little for him to seduce her again.

Below him, the traffic edged slowly and noisily around Central Park, The Americans had a habit of crazily honking their horns if they were unable to drive at full pelt, as if the car in front would get a move on if it was honked at enough by the car behind. At this time of day, at most times of day, the traffic was a solid, stationery mass. Perhaps the horn sounding was just a way of getting rid of their frustration.

The noise was getting on his nerves. Sean got up and went into his apartment, where the walls were covered with brown hessian and the furniture a mixture of ebony and stainless steel, reflecting, although he didn't know it, his dark, brooding personality. He turned on the television to CNN for the latest world news and learnt that Margaret Thatcher would almost certainly be Prime Minister of Great Britain by tomorrow morning. The polls had closed and initial predictions were looking good for the Tories. He turned the set off in disgust. He had no truck with politicians from whatever party. All they did was make a mess of the world.

The telephone rang, but he ignored it. It might be his date wanting him to change his mind about tonight. Picking up his guitar, he played a few notes of 'Moon Under Water'.

'I was just wondering,' Jeannie had said, 'if it was a scene like this that inspired your dad to write that song.' That had been many years ago, at Marcia's wedding. He'd followed her to the lake where the moon was reflected in the still, black water. He'd kissed her but, first of all, they'd talked. He was about to leave the Merseysiders. 'I want to be in charge of my own destiny,' he'd told her.

She'd said she didn't think of show business as her destiny – she was in the Flower Girls then –

she wanted children, at least two, 'soon'.

It wasn't long after that, that the Flower Girls had broken up. Marcia was having a baby, and his mother had told him Jeannie was also hoping for a baby soon. Why had she waited so long, he wondered idly, another seven or eight years, when she was past thirty, before she'd had Ace?

Sean put down the guitar and went to pour himself a Jack Daniels on the rocks. The drink had barely touched his lips, when he put down the glass with a crash and began to walk agitatedly up and down the room, working out dates, times, counting out months, coming to the inevitable conclusion that he, not Lachlan, was the father of Jeannie's children. The first time had been an accident, the second time she'd used him, quite ruthlessly set him up.

'Jaysus!' His mind was a cauldron of simmering emotions; anger, amazement, incredulity. He couldn't believe that the saintly Jeannie Flowers could stoop so low. He seized the whisky and tossed it into his mouth. Now that he'd served his purpose, he thought cynically, he wasn't needed any more. He refilled the glass, sank into a chair, and burst out laughing. Jaysus! He certainly admired her nerve!

The next few years went exceptionally well for the Survivors who had reached cult status and were highly regarded by the critics. Their fan base continued to grow. They were genuine survivors, one of the few groups, like the Rolling Stones and The Who, still playing to packed venues since the heady days of the sixties. The

431

Beatles had long ago disbanded and gone their separate ways. Other groups came, shone briefly, then disappeared, never to be seen nor heard of again.

Lachlan wrote a couple of songs that were so successful they were taken up by other bands and solo artistes: 'Cabbage Soup', a thumping, rollicking, rock 'n' roll number that sent feet tapping with the first few bars, and 'Wayward Woman', angry, haunting and sad.

Sadie McDowd got married again to another extrovert Irishman with the gift of the gab called Paddy Rafferty. She went to live in Limerick where Paddy ran his own import-export agency.

It was about this time that Fly Fleming divorced his second wife and remarried Stella, also divorced. The reception was a riotous affair that lasted three days.

When Ace was ready to start school, Jeannie and Lachlan decided to educate him privately, rather than in the state sector. He was enrolled in a small school in Southport. Jeannie expected shrieks of horror from her mother, who disapproved of people who educated their children privately, but Rose was too worried about Amy, who had got engaged at the age of seventeen to a most unsuitable boy. 'If only Alex was still alive, he'd talk sense into her. She takes no notice of me.'

In March 1982, Tom Flowers turned eighty. He refused a party, condescending only to a birthday tea with his grandchildren in the kitchen of Noah's Ark. Jeannie invited Max, knowing he would refuse, but feeling it necessary to make the gesture. Max reminded her that he had vowed never to set foot in the house again while Lachlan was there. He sent Tom a card. As far as the bitterly unforgiving Max was concerned, his father was second only to Lachlan in his list of sworn enemies. Gerald sent a video of his children singing 'Happy Birthday' to their grandad, giving Jeannie the perfect excuse to get the video recorder she'd been meaning to buy for ages.

Watching it, Tom was enthralled. 'And you can actually see films on it?' he gasped in amazement.

'Yes, Dad. You hire them from a shop. I'm sure there'll soon be a video shop in Ailsham.'

'There already is.'

She gave him the recorder for a birthday present. He drove away in the elderly Morris Minor, the man who'd once refused to have a television in his house, with the very latest in media equipment on the back seat. Rose thought it hilarious.

A few months later, in August, Lachlan turned forty. He also refused a party, preferring instead a short holiday in Paris with Jeannie, his wife of nineteen years. 'Our mums can look after the children.'

It was an utterly perfect, headily romantic few days, the first time since their honeymoon that they'd been away, just the two of them, together. Hand in hand, they roamed the sweltering streets of Paris, sampling the tiny, exotic restaurants; climbed the Eiffel Tower until they could climb no further and caught the lift for the rest of the way; lit candles in Notre Dame where, to Lachlan's embarrassment, he was recognised by a crowd of screaming schoolgirls who surrounded him, demanding his autograph. He'd long grown used to this sort of thing, but it hadn't happened before in a church.

Each night, after a leisurely meal, they strolled along the Champs-Elysées to their hotel, exhausted after their busy day. On the final night, they were too tired to make love, but they weren't as young as they used to be and it didn't matter. They had the rest of their lives to make love whenever they pleased, and promised each other they would return to Paris to celebrate Jeannie's fortieth birthday in three years' time.

Back in Noah's Ark, they were so glad to see the children, they wondered how they could have brought themselves to go away, despite it having been the most wonderful holiday. Presents were distributed; a remote-controlled Ferrari for Ace, and for Chloe a hand-embroidered frock as she always preferred clothes to toys. Lachlan had bought his mother a marcasite brooch in the shape of a four-leafed clover, and Jeannie had got Rose, who had recently decided she would no longer wear leather or eat meat, a tapestry handbag.

'Oh, by the way, Lachlan,' Mrs Bailey said. 'Your manager, rang last night, Donald Weston, and again this morning. He said to get in touch the minute you get home. It's urgent.'

'I'll have a cup of coffee first. It can't be all *that* urgent.' It was half an hour before Lachlan made the phone call that was to change all their lives.

Chapter 15

Lachlan went down to the studio to make the phone call. Ace and Chloe curled up in an armchair with their mother and demanded she tell them about Paris while the two older woman made dinner. Half an hour later, the meal was ready, but Lachlan was still downstairs.

'That's some marathon phone call,' Rose remarked.

Jeannie sent the children to wash their hands and went to fetch him. She found him in the studio with the receiver still in his hand. His face was ashen. She had never seen him look so shattered. She could feel goosepimples rise on her arms. 'What's wrong?'

'Christ, Jeannie! It's terrible. Some kid, a girl, she's only fourteen, claims I'm the father of her baby.' His voice was slow and quivery, like an old man's.

'But you can't possibly be!'

'Thanks for the vote of confidence, babe. I'm not sure the general public will be so easily convinced.'

She ran and sat on his knee, hugged him, and could feel his body trembling. 'You can have tests, Lachlan, blood tests. They'll prove you're not the father.' Even as she said it, Jeannie had the feeling that everything was about to fall apart.

'That's what I told Donald, but he said it's not always a sure fire thing. Me and this girl could share the same blood type or something. Or it could be me and the baby, I'm not sure. A test mightn't prove anything.'

'It's not the first time this sort of accusation has been made against someone like you, darling, a pop star or an actor. This girl's just trying it on. Don't let it worry you.' She gave him a little comforting shake. 'It happened to Max with Monica, remember?'

'Yeah, but with one big difference. No two. First, it didn't get into the papers. Second, Max admitted he'd had sex with Monica. There's another difference. Monica was an adult, this girl was only thirteen when it happened. She's a minor. That's what really gets to me, Jeannie, people thinking I've had it off with a kid young enough to be my daughter. It's a crime in itself, even without the fucking baby. I could have stood it otherwise. I might even have laughed it off.' He hardly ever swore in front of her and his face crumpled, as if he was about to cry.

'Oh, Lachlan.' She cradled his head in her arms. 'What did you mean, Max and Monica didn't get into the papers?' she asked, suddenly scared herself

'One of the tabloids has got the story this time, babe, the *Mirror*. It's not surprising that's where the girl went first. Now the other papers have got hold of it. Donald's been inundated with calls.' He rubbed his eyes tiredly. 'He's sending a lawyer to help me deal with things.'

436

There was an awful lot going on in the world at the moment. The newspapers were still concerned with the aftermath of the war in the Falklands, the Israeli invasion of the Lebanon, the conflict raging between Iran and Iraq, to make much of the suspected behaviour of a pop star. Apart from the *Mirror*, who made quite a feature of the affair, the news was buried in the inside pages. Even so, next morning, it didn't stop half a dozen reporters from camping outside the house, demanding a statement from Lachlan. The stony-faced lawyer, who had arrived before it was light, went out to advise them that the charges were comprehensively denied. He also dealt with the sudden rush of phone calls from people who had somehow managed to get hold of their unlisted number.

When Ace came home from school, he wanted to know what Daddy had done. 'Some boys said he'd done something very bad. It said so in a newspaper.'

'You tell these boys it's not true,' Jeannie said fiercely. 'Daddy's done nothing wrong.'

Fly and the Cobb were one hundred per cent supportive, as were the Survivors' loyal fans. The group played two gigs and the subject wasn't an issue. No one so much as mentioned it. Fly rang frequently to assure Jeannie it was all a big con. 'The girl's just after money,' he said one day. 'All it needs is a few thousand quid for her to say it was a mistake, she was confused, and the charges will be withdrawn. But Lachlan won't hear of it. Not that I blame him. It would be an admission of guilt.'

437

'What charges?'

'The police are considering pressing charges, Jeannie. Sex with a minor. Didn't he tell you?'

'He refuses to talk about it any more,' she said helplessly. 'Fly, this girl's awfully young, only fourteen, to come up with such a story on her own initiative. There must be someone behind her.'

'I guess there must be. I'll do a bit of digging, Jeannie,' he promised, 'See what I can find out.'

He rang again a few days later to say the girl came from Liverpool and it was her mother who'd gone to the *Mirror*.

'Do you know her name?' Jeannie asked eagerly. An idea was forming in her mind. Could *she* pay the girl off? Was it possible Lachlan would find out if she did?

'No. Y'know what, Jeannie, it don't half stink,' Fly said indignantly. 'Because she's underage, the girl's got anonymity. It's not right, the little bitch can throw accusations right, left, and centre, yet nobody knows who she is. By the way, the mother claims the incident happened in Manchester. We did a gig there about fifteen months ago, which would make the baby about six months old.'

'Lachlan always comes straight home if it's a local gig.'

'I know, luv. He's never looked at a girl since the kids came along. Mind you, these days I don't either, not since me and Stella got hitched again. Tell you what, why don't you ask your brother what he can find out? I know Gerald's only a music journalist, but he's bound to have contacts in the press.'

Some of what Fly had just said, inadvertently Jeannie felt sure, she tucked away in a little corner of her mind to think about another time. He asked to speak to Lachlan and she told him he'd gone to London to see Donald Weston and wouldn't be back until tomorrow.

'I wonder why? He didn't say anything to me about going.'

Gerald was only too pleased to do a bit of proper investigative journalism for a change. He called Jeannie back next morning. Ace had gone to school, Chloe to playgroup. Lachlan was still in London and she was in the house alone. 'Does the name Pearson mean anything to you, sis?' he asked. 'I got it off this guy I know on the *Mirror*.'

'No,' Jeannie conceded.

'The guy didn't have an address. Anyway, sis, if you knew where the girl lived, you'd be crazy to go anywhere near her. You could end up making things much worse. How's Lachlan coping, by the way?'

'It's hard to say. He's drawn into himself and hardly speaks.' When home, he spent most of his time in the basement, writing songs – or pretending to. There was a nightmarish atmosphere in the house. The children had noticed and were unnaturally quiet. Jeannie couldn't concentrate on a book or watch television. She spent hours on the phone to her mother, Lachlan's mother, Stella, Elaine, because she found it helped to talk. Lachlan's friends rang, but he would only speak to Fly or the Cobb, and then not about the subject that haunted him.

439

When Gerald rang off, she looked through the Liverpool telephone directory and found almost an entire page of Pearsons covering the length and breadth of the city and its environs. She began to go through them with her finger, but stopped when she reached 'Pearson, B.' What point was there? In one of these houses a young girl lived who had turned Lachlan's life, all their lives, upside down. Jeannie didn't have second sight. She removed her finger and was about to snap the book shut, when an address leapt out from exactly the spot where her finger had been. She caught her breath; Pearson, B. Mrs, 29 Grenville Street, Bootle. The house where Benedicta Lucas used to live – *still* lived. Of that, Jeannie suddenly felt quite sure.

'I'll never forgive you for this, Jeannie Flowers,' Benny had said the last time they'd met. *'Never! Not for as long as I live.'*

It was too much of a coincidence. In some way or other, Benny Lucas was behind Lachlan's nightmare. She would go and see her straight away, sort it out.

She felt it was important to look her best, to appear calm and in control when she confronted Benny. After a quick shower, she put on one of the dresses she'd bought for Paris, which was turquoise, sleeveless, very plain. For the first time, she noticed how dull it was outside, so added a dark green velvet jacket. She brushed back her hair and tied it in a knot on the nape of her neck, then rang her mother and asked if she'd pick Chloe up from playgroup. 'There's something important I've got to do. I'll be back by half past three in time for Ace.' Then she got her car out of the garage and drove to Bootle.

Grenville Street had hardly changed. The houses, squashed so closely together, were a bit smarter, the curtains fancier, the front doors and windows painted brighter colours. There were far more cars, Jeannie discovered, when she tried to park her own.

The last time she'd been here, the Flower Girls had been about to launch themselves on to the world. It had been August, the day had been very hot, she recalled, and she had brought a letter asking Benny to meet them that night in Colonel Corbett's barn. This time, more than twenty years later, it was September and, not only dull, but cold as well, heralding the end of the fine summer and the start of autumn.

The door of number twenty-nine was an attractive navy blue and the brass letter box and matching knocker gleamed. Jeannie was about to use the knocker when she noticed a bell. She pressed it and it tinkled gently inside. Seconds later, Benny Lucas opened the door. Younger than Jeannie by six months, she now looked ten, fifteen years older. Her thin, fly away hair was grey, her face almost the same colour, except for the clouds of tiny red veins on her cheeks, hundreds of them. She wore jeans, an over-sized T-shirt, and plastic flip-flops on her long, narrow feet.

'*Jeannie!*' She would always have been surprised at her old friend turning up out of the blue after such a long time, but the surprise was nothing compared to the look of terror in the pale eyes. Her entire body seemed to shrink and her face flushed an ugly red, leaving Jeannie without a shred of doubt of the woman's guilt.

'Benny!' she said brightly. 'May I come in?'

'What do you want?' Benny stuttered.

'I think we need to talk, don't you?'

'No!' Benny violently shook her head.

Jeannie had no intention of taking no for an answer. She stepped into the hall, unintentionally pushing Benny against the wall. Perhaps conscious that a neighbour might be watching, Benny slammed the door behind them and, from somewhere within the house, a baby began to cry.

'I'll see to her, luv. Don't worry, yer mam'll get her.' A small, stooped woman in a candlewick dressing gown hurried out of the living room at the back and clambered up the stairs like a monkey. Jeannie recognised the strange figure as Mrs Lucas.

'Is that your baby crying, Benny?' she enquired lightly.

Benny uttered a long, hoarse sigh. Her shoulders drooped. 'She's me granddaughter.'

'What's she called?'

'Saffron.'

'That's a pretty name! How old is she, about six months?'

'Six and a half.'

'Would you mind if we sat down?' They were still standing in the narrow hallway. Upstairs, Mrs Lucas could be heard making cooing noises. The baby stopped crying.

'In here.' Benny led the way into the small parlour that Jeannie remembered had been a dark, gloomy room, never used, but was now nicely decorated and furnished with a moquette three-piece suite and a modern teak sideboard on which stood half a dozen photographs, one of a wedding. She picked it up. It showed Benny in an elegant white lace dress standing next to a tall, well-built man. Both were smiling joyfully at the camera.

'Your husband's very handsome,' Jeannie said.

'*Ex*-husband.'

'I'm sorry. What happened?' Jeannie made a face. She replaced the photograph and sat on a moquette armchair. 'Sorry again. I asked automatically. It's just that we used to be such good friends and tell each other everything.'

Benny scowled. 'No, you and Elaine used to tell each other everything. Me, I was only thrown the scraps.'

'We were just kids. Elaine and I couldn't help feeling close to each other. We still are, though not quite so much.'

'Oh, what the hell does it matter after all this time?' She shrugged wearily. 'As to me husband, he had a brainstorm or something and just walked out when Paula, that's me daughter, was two. He's never been seen again. Even the police couldn't find him. John was a policeman himself, a sergeant. We had a lovely police house in Kirkby, but I had to leave once he'd gone. That's when I came back to live with me mam.'

'You've made the place look very pretty,' Jeannie said encouragingly. Secretly, she wanted to tear the woman's throat out for what she'd done to Lachlan. 'Where is Paula?'

'At school.'

'And your mother looks after her baby?'

Benny stuck out her jaw pugnaciously. 'Who said Paula had a baby?'

'*You* did. You said Saffron was your grand-daughter, and you've only mentioned having one child. Have you got more?'

'No.'

'Your mother must have her work cut out, looking after a baby at her age.'

'Except she doesn't. *I* do. I had to leave work – I'd gone back to the Inland Revenue. Me mam's lost her mind a bit. She's not up to it.'

There was a slithering, shuffling noise as Mrs Lucas came down the stairs. She entered the room; tiny, hunched, and almost completely bald.

'Hello, luv.' She smiled at Jeannie. Several of her teeth were missing. 'I know you, you're our Benny's mate from school. Where's the other one, the doctor's girl?'

'She remembers the past, not the present,' Benny muttered.

'You mean Elaine? She's a doctor herself now.'

But Mrs Lucas didn't appear to understand. She announced she was going to make a cup of tea and left.

Jeannie watched her go, then turned and looked hard at the woman who'd used to be her friend. She went for the kill. 'So, Benny, you're claiming that my husband made your daughter pregnant at a gig in Manchester fifteen months ago?'

444

Benny went red again. She blinked furiously, as if she'd thought Jeannie had merely come on a social visit, despite her visible collapse when she'd opened the door. 'Why shouldn't he be?' she blustered. 'Lachlan screwed a whole load of girls after the gigs were over. There's no reason why our Paula shouldn't have been one. *Someone* put her up the stick. It could well have been Lachlan.'

'You don't know anything about Lachlan,' Jeannie said coldly, though Benny's words had badly shaken her composure.

'No, but me husband did,' Benny countered. 'John was into rock 'n' roll. He used to go to the Cavern and the Taj Mahal, same as us. That's how we got together, 'cos he remembered me from way back. He knew Fly Fleming slightly and he'd follow the Merseysiders around, go backstage when the gigs were over and they'd be as stoned as crows. There were girls everywhere, John said, begging for a shag with any tenth-rate musician who happened to be around. They all took advantage, your husband included. There's no reason for John to have made it up.'

'I always knew stuff like that went on,' Jeannie lied. She clasped her hands together tightly until the knuckles showed white, feeling as if she was losing her grip of the situation. The room felt very small and claustrophobic. She could hardly breathe. 'Lachlan was only young and things used to get quite wild. They're different now. We've got a family. He wouldn't dream of touching another woman, and certainly not a thirteen-year old girl.' She decided to go on the

445

attack, 'I'm surprised at you, Benny. What sort of mother allows a young girl, hardly more than a child, to go all the way to Manchester for a gig?'

Benny didn't answer. She stared at Jeannie, her light eyes frantic, as she tried to think of a reply.

Jeannie didn't care how much the woman was hurt. *'That* part won't look very good when it gets in the papers, will it? Nor will the fact that you used to be a Flower Girl, but left because you weren't prepared to take a risk. The rest of us went on to make a fortune, but you're still here, in the house where you born. I bet a day doesn't pass that you don't regret not taking the chance.' She pressed on remorselessly. 'It will look as if you were using Lachlan to get at me. That it was nothing but sheer spite...' Jeannie paused and uttered a little cry as comprehension dawned. 'That's it, isn't it! You were getting at me through Lachlan.'

'Do you blame me?' Benny snarled. 'I'd've risked everything to be a Flower Girl, but you, you didn't give me the chance. You just wanted to be shot of me.'

'I put a note through your door, but you ignored it. Then, when you found how well we were doing, you pretended you didn't get it.'

'You're nothing but a bloody liar,' Benny screamed. 'I never got any note.'

Mrs Lacey chose that moment to bring in the tea. She must have caught remnants of the conversation. She looked severely at Jeannie. 'You're upsetting her again. It was you who brought that daft letter asking her to give up her nice, safe job and go singing. She's a respectable girl, my Benny. She wouldn't be seen dead on the stage. All she ever wanted was to work in the Civil Service. She had to pass an exam to get in,' she finished proudly.

Benny's face collapsed. 'What happened to the letter, Mam?'

'I flushed it down the lavvy. Wasn't that right, luv?'

'No, Mam,' Benny whispered, 'no, that was very wrong. It ruined me life. It ruined everything.'

Mrs Lucas laughed. 'Don't talk soft, Benedicta. We're dead happy, the four of us together; you, me, Paula and – what's the baby's name?'

'Saffron.'

'Saffron. Well, you'd both better drink that tea before it gets cold.'

'She never gets dressed,' Benny said in a dull voice when her mother gone. 'She refuses to go out, so can't get her teeth fixed or something done about her hair. I love her, but she's driving us insane. Since Paula had Saffron, it's even worse. She won't leave the baby alone and I'm scared she'll harm her.' She stood and went over to the window, where she folded her arms and looked out onto the narrow street. 'I'm desperate for us to have a place of our own.' She turned and her eyes flicked over her old friend's smart outfit. 'You've never known what it's like to be hard up, have you? You've had the best of everything, looks an' all.' She made a face. 'Anyroad, that's why I did it, to make a few bob. You often hear about it on the news. It was worth a try and any old singer would have done. Then I thought, why not say it was Lachlan? I'd had it from the horse's mouth the way he used to behave, and I'd be getting back at you an' all. I remembered the Survivors had done a gig in Manchester at just the right time, it was in the *Echo*. I thought he'd pay just to keep it out of the papers.'

'Then you shouldn't have gone to the papers first.'

'I know that now. When I read about it, I got scared. It had all got out of hand. The man at the *Mirror* said the same as you: "What sort of mother lets a thirteen-year-old girl go all that way to a gig on her own?" I felt dead ashamed.'

'Aren't you ashamed of encouraging the same girl to lie about the father of her baby?' Jeannie said contemptuously.

'Yes,' Benny whispered. 'But I was desperate, like I said.'

'Not half as desperate as Lachlan's been over the last few weeks. It's knocked all the stuffing out of him.'

'I'm sorry.'

'Out of interest, who is the baby's father?'

'Some kid at school. Paula won't tell us his name.'

Jeannie picked up the tea, she needed it. 'While I'm here,' she said curtly, 'would you kindly ring the *Mirror* and tell them Paula was fantasising. She was never at the gig. She's never even laid eyes on Lachlan. It was all a big mistake.' She put the tea down when she saw the surface was full of black dust.

Benny smiled wryly. 'That's Mam. She doesn't understand tea bags. She tears them open and empties them in the pot.' She sighed. 'I'll make that phone call now.'

What was it Fly had said? *He's never looked at a girl since the kids came along?*
Lachlan screwed a whole load of girls after the gigs were over, Benny had just claimed.
Did it matter that it was years ago? Perhaps not as much as if it happened now, but all the same... The nights he'd been away, when she was in the house on her own, missing him so much, he'd been making love to other women. When she'd toured with the Flower Girls, she'd never so much as looked at another man. Marcia and Zoe had had a whale of a time, but Jeannie had always gone back to their hotel with Rita, wishing that Lachlan was there, missing him, always missing him.
Can we get over this? she asked herself.
Yes, they could, she decided – they'd have to, not just for the sake of the children, but for each other. She was positive that, despite everything, he loved her as much as she did him.
The car turned into the drive of Noah's Ark and skewed to a halt on the gravel. She'd driven home much too fast. To her surprise, Lachlan's black Ferrari was parked crookedly only a few feet away from the door. He was usually very careful to put it away in the garage. She looked at her watch; just gone two. Time to have it out with him before the children came home.
She called his name when she went in, but there was no reply. He must be in the studio, but when she went to look, the studio was empty. She

found him in the kitchen, sitting at the table with an empty mug in front of him, twisting it round and round so that it made a grating sound on the wood. It was something she'd seen him do before when he was upset. His eyes were red, as if he hadn't slept all night.

'I've been calling you,' she said accusingly.

He shrugged. 'I didn't hear.'

'You'll be pleased to know,' she said in an icy voice, 'that all the charges have been withdrawn. Benny Lucas was behind the whole thing. I've just been to see her.'

'I know what's happened. Donald just rang. The *Mirror* called him.'

'Aren't you pleased? I thought you'd be delighted.'

He shrugged again and said nothing.

'I've been hearing an awful lot of unpleasant things about you lately, Lachlan.' 'Unpleasant' wasn't the right word, but she couldn't think of anything stronger. She sat opposite him at the table and said threateningly. 'If you shrug again, I'll scream.'

'What sort of unpleasant things, babe?' He gave the ghost of a smile.

'That you were in the habit of making love to the girls, the groupies, the hangers on...' She stopped, unable to go on, unable to find the proper words. 'How could you?' she cried.

'You're the only woman I've ever made love to, babe,' he replied steadily. He didn't seem the least upset that she'd found out. 'I had sex with the others. We were as high as kites and they were *there*. It meant nothing. I couldn't remember

450

their faces by next morning.'

'Is that supposed to make me feel better? You were *unfaithful* to me, Lachlan, over and over again. How many times? Hundreds?'

'I think you're exaggerating a bit, Jeannie. I haven't a clue how many times. I didn't count. I was hardly aware of what I was doing. I told you, I was stoned.' To her intense irritation, he shrugged yet again. 'Anyroad, it was a long time ago. I was younger then. These days, I behave like a monk – except with you, my wife.'

'You don't seem a bit ashamed,' she said indignantly.

'Oh, I am, babe.' He laughed, but it came out more like a snort. 'I'm dead ashamed.'

It struck her that he was behaving very strangely. He clearly didn't give a damn if she'd discovered he'd murdered the girls, not just had sex with them. 'Is something wrong?' she asked. 'Why did you go to see Donald? Fly didn't know anything about it.'

'That's because I didn't see Donald but, at his suggestion, I went to Harley Street to see a doctor for tests.'

'Tests?'

'A blood test, for one. Until an hour ago, I was being accused of making a girl pregnant, remember? The doctor thought it advisable to investigate every possibility – oh, and he gave me a thorough medical at the same time. You'll be pleased to know I'm in perfect health. There's just one thing wrong, only small, and it can easily be put right. I have an obstruction in my epididymis.'

'What does that mean?'

'It means the tubes that transport fertile sperm are blocked. In other words, babe, I am unable to father children.' He smiled at her gently, but his eyes were bitterly accusing. 'Ever since, I've been wondering, where did our two come from?'

Jeannie felt herself blanch. The blood turned cold in her veins and her heart began to beat much too fast. She put her hand to her breast and could feel its loud, rapid thump. 'Oh, Lachlan!' she said in a hushed voice.

'Yes, babe?'

'I never wanted you to find out.' It seemed useless to deny it.

'I'm sure you didn't, just as I hoped you wouldn't find out about the girls. But my crimes, if you could call them that, pale into insignificance compared to yours.' He suddenly stood and flung the mug he was nursing against the wall. Jeannie uttered a little, frightened cry. 'Whose are they, Jeannie?' he roared. 'Who gave you the children that you've been pretending all this time were mine?'

'It doesn't matter who. And I wasn't pretending. They *are* yours. I've never thought of them as anything but yours.'

'They're *not* mine. They're some other guy's. *Who*, Jeannie, *who?*' He seized her arm and yanked her to her feet, pressed his face against hers.

'I said, it doesn't matter,' she protested weakly.

'And I say it does. It matters to me, very much. I'd like to know just who the lucky bastard is who's been fucking my wife.' He shook her hard. *'Tell me.'*

Jeannie let out a long, slow breath. 'Sean McDowd.'

Lachlan recoiled as if he'd been shot. 'Sean!' His eyes narrowed. 'He's always fancied you... I didn't notice, but Fly did. He used to laugh about it. We both decided you wouldn't give him the time of day. But we were wrong, weren't we, Fly and me?' He shook her again. 'How long has it been going on? Is it *still* going on?'

'Are you going to kill me, Lachlan?'

He released her arm. 'I'm sorry,' he muttered, sinking back into the chair.

'Nothing went on,' she told him. 'Not in the way you mean. Sean and I didn't have an affair. The first time we made...' She paused and started again. 'The first time it happened was in Kevin's house in Knightsbridge. I think you had a gig in Brighton that night, and I was imagining you having a great time afterwards – it turns out that you were having an even better time than I thought. Anyway, I was feeling very unhappy, very lonely. Sean made a move.' She swallowed awkwardly. 'I know I should have stopped him, but I didn't. Not long afterwards, I found I was expecting Ace, and I realised Sean must be the father.' She looked at Lachlan pleadingly. 'I'd been wanting a baby for so long. I never thought of it as *his*. It was *our* baby, Lachlan.' She put her hand on his arm. *'Ours!'*

'Why didn't we talk about this before, babe?' His face was puzzled. 'I knew you wanted a baby, but I never dreamt it was my fault we never had one.'

'I didn't know anything could be done about it,

453

that's why,' she cried. 'It was years and years ago and perhaps then nothing could. I didn't want you knowing it was your fault. I thought it would upset you.'

'That's awfully nice of you, Jeannie, but it wouldn't have upset me half as much as much as knowing you've had it off with Sean McDowd,' he said brutally. He shook her hand away. 'And what happened with Chloe? Did Sean make another move you couldn't resist, and you found yourself pregnant again?'

'No.'

'So, what did happen?' he pressed.

Jeannie knew she had no alternative but to tell the absolute truth. The air had to be cleared so they could continue with their lives, if not quite the same as before. 'The second time, it was me who made the move,' she said in a small voice.

'That's strange,' Lachlan said lightly. 'For the life of me, I can't imagine you making a move on a guy.'

'I did it for you. Oh, does that sound daft?'

'Yes.'

'Well, it's true. This time it was you wanting a baby, a brother or sister for Ace. Sean and I just happened to come across each other in London. He came to my room – I was staying at the Savoy. You were in Canada.'

He rolled his eyes. 'The sacrifices some women make for their husbands! I bet you hated every minute. How long did you stay at the Savoy?'

'Two nights.'

'Two nights of sheer torture, all on my behalf.'

'It wasn't torture.'

'What was it then?' He banged his fist on the table.

She shrank from the look in his eyes, the bitter, sarcastic tone of his voice. Suddenly, she resented being treated like a whore for sleeping with one man, when he'd slept with God knows how many women. Anger surged in her breast and she replied in a way she would always regret. 'It was wonderful,' she said. 'Quite wonderful.'

Lachlan stared at her blankly, then got up and vomited in the sink. He ran the tap and neither spoke nor moved for a long time. Lachlan stared into the sink and Jeannie at the table, both contemplating the wreckage of their lives.

Without looking at her, Lachlan asked, 'Does Sean know about the children?'

'No, of course not.'

The front door opened and Jeannie's mother shouted, 'It's me,' and a few seconds later she and Chloe came into the kitchen.

Jeannie got to her feet and remarked she should have left ten minutes ago to fetch Ace. Rose said while she was gone she'd prepare the children's tea. 'Are you all right, Lachlan?' she added. 'You don't look a bit well.'

Jeannie didn't hear his reply. She could never remember driving to Southport. Ace complained she was late when she eventually arrived outside the school. He chatted excitedly about something or other all the way home, but Jeannie didn't hear a word. This was the worst day of her life.

When she drew up outside the house, Lachlan was throwing a suitcase into the boot of the Ferrari. She leapt out of her car. 'Where are you

455

going?' she cried.

'Away. I've said goodbye to Chloe, now I want to do the same to Ace. Then I'll be off.'

'But where to?'

'Dunno, babe.' His mouth twisted non-chalantly. 'Somewhere or other.'

'But Lachlan!' She was frantic now. 'Oh, darling, we can sort this all out. I love you. I don't care what you've done. If there'd been a thousand women, it wouldn't matter. Please let's forgive and forget.'

'Can't, babe,' he said abruptly. 'I might've forgiven you for Ace, but never for Chloe. I'll never forget, either.' His face set hard. 'Never!'

She stamped her foot angrily. Ace had got out of the car and was looking at them anxiously. 'Then you mustn't love me, not the way I love you.'

'Trouble is, Jeannie, I love you too much. Now, if you wouldn't mind going inside,' he gave her a dismissive nod, 'I'd like a last word with my...' His voice broke. 'With my son.'

No one could understand it. Why had Lachlan left? The *Mirror* printed an apology next day. They'd been taken in by a delusional young girl, who'd been egged on by her mother. The identity of the pair wasn't revealed. Lachlan was completely in the clear, not that anyone who knew him had believed the allegation in the first place.

'What happened?' Jeannie's shocked mother wanted to know. She'd heard him say goodbye to Chloe, and it sounded as if he was going for good.

'When's Daddy coming back?' Ace and Chloe asked frequently.

'What on earth have you done to him, Jeannie?' Fly demanded when he rang from London a few days later. 'He's in a terrible state.'

'Nothing,' Jeannie said weakly. 'We had a row, that's all.'

'It must have been one helluva row!' Fly snorted. 'The guy's virtually suicidal. I keep telling him to go home, but he won't.'

'Where's he living?'

'He kipped down with me and Stella for a couple of nights, now he's in some crap hotel. Don't ask me the name, Jeannie, because he ses I've not to tell you.'

'I'll come straight away if I'm needed, Fly,' she promised.

'Yeah! I'll tell him that.' He rang off.

Elaine came to Noah's Ark, looking purposeful, as if she was determined to get to the bottom of things. 'What exactly is going on, Jeannie? Mum's terribly upset. You know she hasn't been very well lately, and your mum thinks it's a permanent split.'

'We had a row,' Jeannie admitted for the umpteenth time.

'What about?'

'I think that's between me and Lachlan, don't you?'

'Lachlan is my brother. I've a right to know what it's about.'

'No, you haven't,' Jeannie said stubbornly.

'Are you getting divorced?'

'I don't know.' The deadly word struck Jeannie

457

like a blow. Please, God, she prayed. Please don't let it come to that.

'Is it to do with that girl and her bloody baby? It wasn't actually true, was it, and Lachlan paid her off?'

'No!'

'Don't sound so indignant. Some girls of thirteen can look like adults with the right clothes and make-up. Lachlan wouldn't exactly have been guilty of child abuse, though I could understand you being as mad as hell if he'd done it.'

'He didn't touch the girl. He never even met her.' Jeannie saw a way of distracting her friend from her mission to unearth the truth. 'If I tell you something, will you promise not to breathe a word to a soul?'

'Cross my heart and hope to die.'

'Benny Lucas was behind the whole thing.' She described her visit to Grenville Street in detail. 'All I wanted was to throttle the woman, but I have to admit the situation in the house is dire. Under different circumstances, I'd have felt sorry for Benny. I'd have wanted to help.'

'I feel like going round and breaking all her windows.'

'That's why I'd sooner no one else knows, in case they do.'

The following day Max came. He hadn't been to the house since around the time of Marcia's wedding. Now Lachlan had gone he was willing to set foot in the place again. Jeannie saw little of her brother these days. It was hard to believe that this Max, with the lace-up shoes, pressed trousers, and sensible pullover, now Deputy Head of

458

a comprehensive school in Aigburth, had once been a wild rock 'n' roller. Jeannie noticed the beginnings of a paunch and could have sworn his hair was receding. He'd never remarried and these days didn't give a damn about his height.

'What I can't understand,' Max said, 'is how Lachlan can bring himself to walk out on his kids. If I hadn't wound myself up into such a state when she dumped me, I'd never have let Monica take my two to America. Gareth's seventeen and I've seen hardly anything of him, and even less of Tammy.' He visited them once a year in the summer holidays, but Monica didn't make him very welcome.

If only she could tell him, tell *someone*. She would have valued another man's judgement. She would have liked his opinion, to know if what she'd done had been so truly awful that Lachlan was justified in walking out on their marriage. Perhaps Max, any man, would have done the same. She wondered if her unwillingness to tell a soul, not even Elaine, with whom she'd once shared all her secrets, meant that in her heart she recognised the enormity of her crime – Lachlan had called it a crime. She'd always thought of herself as a highly moral person, yet she'd acted in a way that only now she saw as quite outrageously wicked.

Jeannie was perplexed. Perhaps Elaine could have explained it to her. She was an expert at understanding people's minds. Right now, Jeannie didn't understand anything.

She'd got used to him not being there for a lot of

459

the time, but now she had to accept he wouldn't be coming back. In the house alone, she played his records at their very loudest, so his voice followed her everywhere. Each time a car drew up on the gravel path, she rushed to the door in case it was him. Ace and Chloe did the same. She told him this in the letters that she wrote every week, saying how much they missed him, how sorry she was about everything. She sent the letters care of Fly. He had no idea if they were read.

'I give them to him, Jeannie. Whether he opens them or not, I wouldn't know.'

Christmas came and she tried to make it as normal as possible for the children, inviting loads of people to dinner. They were inundated with gifts, but the present they most wanted was their daddy.

Didn't he realise, Jeannie thought fretfully, that he *was* their daddy? Why was he being so perverse? Was it pride? He was making them all of suffer because of his stupid pride, himself most of all.

He'd rented a flat in Fulham, a dump, according to Fly, who'd been told not to let her have the address. Now he was back on drugs again – heroin, this time, as well as the uppers and downers.

'He looks awful,' Fly said darkly. He had become the bearer of bad news. Was he trying to make her feel guilty? If so, he was succeeding. She felt more guilty with each phone call. 'Yet the strange thing is, his music has never been so brilliant. He plays the guitar like a man possessed.'

460

Another New Year, 1983. Jeannie braced herself to face it alone.

Money was becoming a problem. For tax purposes, she and Lachlan had always had their own personal bank accounts, with a separate, joint one, for household expenses, into which Lachlan transferred a large sum every month. Her own account was pathetic. She received occasional royalties when a Flower Girls record was played, which didn't happen often nowadays. The group had become merely history in the annals of rock 'n' roll.

She guessed what had happened. Lachlan had transferred his account to a London branch and hadn't thought to re-establish the monthly transfer. She felt sure he wouldn't be so small-minded as to cancel it.

It wasn't something she was prepared to mention in the letters she still sent. Somehow, she'd have to manage on her own. Noah's Ark couldn't be sold. It belonged to them both, and she wanted it to be there for when Lachlan came back. He *would* come back, one day, she tried to convince herself

Managing on her own wouldn't be easy. All she could do was play the piano. She wondered if she could get a job as a pianist in a club or a hotel? It might still be possible to trade on her name, even if the Flower Girls were now history.

Every day, she went down into the basement and practised for a few hours, but when the bank statements arrived at the beginning of February, she discovered there was no need for her to work.

A huge sum, twice as much as before, had been transferred into her personal account.

'Thank you, darling,' she whispered. 'I knew you wouldn't let us down.'

Two weeks later, Fly called to say Lachlan had disappeared.

'Where to?' Jeannie shrieked.

'If I knew that, Jeannie, he wouldn't have disappeared. He didn't turn up for a rehearsal. When I went round to the flat, his guitar and his clothes were gone. There was a note: "Sorry, but I can't carry on any more".' Fly's voice broke. 'I love that guy, Jeannie. I don't know what I'll do without Lachlan.'

On a Monday morning in April, Tom Flowers was found dead in his bed. The cleaner had last been there the Thursday before, Mrs Denning had been away that weekend, and Tom had been dead for three days. He was 81 and had seemed in the best of health.

'Oh, it's a terrible end for a man like him,' Rose wailed. 'Dying all alone!'

'No, Mum, it was the best sort of end,' Jeannie said sadly. 'He was still doing our garden till last week. He would have hated being ill. Anyway, in the end, we all die alone.'

The funeral was attended by a surprising number of people. Tom hadn't exactly been a popular figure in Ailsham, but he'd been a familiar one. Jeannie found it strange to see so many faces she recognised, all much older now. Mrs Denning was the only person to cry. Rose sniffed a bit, Gerald was upset, but Jeannie remained dry-eyed and Max's face was cold throughout the whole service. He didn't come to the cemetery with the rest of the family. Both Max's enemies had now gone – his father and his sister's husband. Jeannie wondered if it had made him any happier.

A few days later, Tom's bank rang to say they were holding his will. It had been drawn up shortly after his marriage to Rose, who'd been entirely unaware of its existence. All his worldly possessions, including the house in Disraeli Terrace, had been left to his ex-wife.

'He must never have got round to making another,' Rose marvelled. 'Do you think I should let Mrs Denning have the house?'

'Don't be daft, Mum, she's got a perfectly good house of her own,' Jeannie said sternly. 'Sell it. The money would come in useful.'

Surprisingly, Rose decided she would sooner sell Magnolia Cottage and move back to Disraeli Terrace. 'The cottage is damp and draughty in the winter, and it costs a fortune to keep up.'

'But it's full of memories of Alex!' Jeannie exclaimed. 'How can you move to a place where you were so unhappy?'

'I wasn't always unhappy, love. When you three were little was one of the best times of my life. And my memories of Alex are in my heart and in my head, not in bricks and mortar – or lath and plaster where the cottage is concerned. Amy won't like it, but she's getting married soon to that useless young man. I've talked it over with Eliza and she doesn't mind a bit. 'Oh, and I've decided to take piano lessons,' she said, even more surprisingly. 'It's something I've always wanted to do.'

And so it was that, when summer came, Jeannie would visit her mother and lie on the grass in the garden of the house where she was born. Another cat, Patch, had taken the place of Spencer, who'd gone to cat heaven many years before. As she lay, eating her father's strawberries, it was easy to believe that the intervening years had never occurred.

The children were in bed. Jeannie waited until she was certain they were asleep before inserting the video into the machine. It had arrived that morning, sent by Fly. The door closed, she sat crosslegged on the floor in front of the television and pressed Play.

Lachlan's face was the first to appear on the screen. Jeannie gasped. He was wearing a black leather outfit and looked terrible. There were lines on his face, deeply etched, running from his cheeks to his jawbone. He was wearing eyeliner, something that he had contemptuously refused to do in the past. It was a tragic face, the face of a man who had suffered, a man who had been betrayed by the woman he loved most in the world.

She began to cry. She cried all the way through. The video was of the Survivors' final gig in Leeds, the one before Lachlan has disappeared, to no one knew where.

Fly was right. Lachlan was playing as if possessed. He roamed the stage like a mad man, throwing back his head until the muscles were taut in his neck. He made sounds that she hadn't thought possible from a single guitar. They were too fast, too complicated, too clever. Yet an inspired, distraught, totally crazy Lachlan somehow managed to play them. He came to the microphone and sang in a hoarse, angry voice,

Are you gonna leave?
Or are you gonna stay?
Are you gonna be my baby?
Or are you gonna be a low down wanton woman.

Later, he sang 'Moon Under Water', and another of the Flower Girls' songs, 'Red for Danger'. They were strange choices for a heavy metal band.

The audience were getting rowdier. It was Lachlan's fault. He was winding them up, communicating his rage, his despair, and his frustration on to them, so that they responded with their own rage and feelings of despair.

It was like watching someone die on stage, Jeannie thought, despairing herself. She was worried the gig would end up a riot.

The eyeliner was beginning to run and Lachlan's face and neck gleamed with perspiration. He removed his leather jacket and flung it towards the wings, exposing the tattooed heart on his arm that contained her name. The girls in the audience screamed in ecstasy.

And so it went on, the video, for hours. Instead of tiring, Lachlan's playing became even more inspired, his voice angrier. His energy would have shamed a twenty-year-old. He must have taken enough speed for a dozen men.

At last, it was over. Lachlan gave a flamboyant bow, the Cobb too, though he'd been merely a shadow throughout the whole performance. Fly laid down his drumsticks and mopped his brow. The crowd screamed for more, but Fly shook his head, exhausted.

Then Lachlan stepped forward and the audience fell quiet. He clutched the microphone with both hands and began to sing.

'I dream,' he crooned in a soft, sad voice,

of Jeannie with the light brown hair,
Floating like a shadow in the soft summer air.
I see her tripping where the bright streams play,
Happy as the daisies that dance on her way.

Behind him, the Cobb shrugged. Fly looked bemused. Some of the crowd were getting restless. There were murmurs of annoyance, but just as many irritable 'Shushes'.

To Jeannie's surprise, when Lachlan reached the chorus, at least half the audience joined in, though faltered after the first few lines.

When he'd finished, Lachlan stared straight into the camera, right into Jeannie's eyes. She leaned forward and laid her forehead against his on the screen. There was a series of flashes and dots, then the screen went blank.

Jeannie turned the set off and resolved never to watch the video again.

She sat for ages in front of the television, seeing her blurred reflection in the empty screen. Caverns opened up her mind, empty until now, but gradually filling to their depths with her bitter grief Never before had she known such unhappiness. Now she knew how her mother had felt when she'd lost Alex. But at least Alex had died in her mother's arms. She knew where she was, had been able to draw a line.

'But I know nothing,' she whispered. Lachlan had left her in a cruel limbo. She would never be able to draw a line. And it would go on like that, year after year, not knowing where he was, how he was. Jeannie shivered and hugged her knees. If it wasn't for the children, the rest of her life would hardly be worth living.

Chapter 16

1985

At the beginning of July, Jeannie was surprised to get a phone call from Marcia whom she hadn't spoken to in ages.

'What are you doing on the thirteenth, it's a Saturday?' Marcia asked in her usual peremptory fashion.

'I've no idea.'

'In that case, it can't be anything much. I've got four tickets for the Live Aid concert in Wembley. D'you fancy coming? I thought it'd be nice for all four Flower Girls to go, but Rita's got a matinée, so I've asked our Elaine instead.'

'Elaine won't go,' Jeannie said with conviction.

'You're wrong, wise guy, she just said, "yes".'

'In that case, I'll go too. Mum'll look after the children.'

'Good! Dress casually,' Marcia commanded, as if Jeannie was likely to turn up in a ball gown. 'I'll ring Zoe, see if she'll come. I'll be in touch later and we can arrange where to meet.' She rang off without so much as goodbye.

The Live Aid rock concert was being organised by Bob Geldof of the Boomtown Rats to raise funds for famine victims in Africa. An all-day event, it would be broadcast to 152 countries and a concert was being held simultaneously in Philadelphia. Everyone who was anyone in the world of rock and pop was lined up to perform.

Jeannie began to look forward to attending the largest, longest, and most distinguished gig ever held with her old friends. It was a while since she'd had a day out and the last gig she'd been to was at the Hammersmith Odeon, she remembered with a sigh, the same night Sean McDowd had turned up at his parents' house in Knightsbridge...

Ace, now nine, and Chloe, seven, kept well abreast of the pop music scene and pestered to come with her. She was glad to have a legitimate excuse to refuse.

'I've only got one ticket,' she told them. 'They're like gold dust and I can't get any more. You can watch it on television.' She promised to buy them T-shirts.

'Will Daddy be playing?' Ace enquired.

'No, sweetheart.' The Survivors had been unable to survive without Lachlan. They didn't bother to get a replacement for the man who'd been the inspiration and the star. A downhearted Fly still rang occasionally. He was making a decent living as a session musician, but it didn't compare with belonging to one of the foremost groups in the country. The Cobb had been seen busking on the London Underground.

She and Elaine decided to catch an early train rather than drive – parking in London was difficult anyway, and it would be madness to go anywhere near Wembley with a car. They would meet in Zoe's house in Islington, then take a taxi to the stadium.

469

Zoe now presented a holiday programme, *Chocks Away*, on ITV. She had never married and was often in the press, flitting from one highly publicised affair to another, the most recent with a well-known footballer. She lived alone in her smart, four-storey house.

Age had treated her kindly, Jeannie thought when Zoe opened the door on the day of the concert. She was as beautiful as ever, her elegantly moulded cheekbones prominent in her thin, lively face, her black eyes huge. Like Jeannie and Elaine, she was wearing jeans and a T-shirt.

'Marcia isn't here yet.' She grinned widely. 'Oh, I'm really looking forward to today.'

Marcia arrived shortly afterwards in a taxi. She'd commanded the driver to wait, she announced. She had on cream trousers with fiercely pressed creases and a short–sleeved cashmere sweater, which Jeannie supposed was her idea of dressing casually. Her blonde hair had been set and lacquered to stiff perfection. Elaine remarked she looked like Mrs Thatcher at which Marcia seemed inordinately pleased.

Jeannie knew that coming had been a mistake as soon as the first group, Status Quo, far away on the distant stage, struck up with 'Rockin' All Over The World'. It reminded her too much of Lachlan, who would have been there if she hadn't made such a mess of their lives. *Where is he?* she fretted. He seemed to have vanished off the face of the earth.

Another disturbing thing was that, even though it was eighteen years since the Flower Girls had last played together, it seemed unnatural on such a grand occasion to be a member of the audience and not part of the show. 'I never realised till now how much I miss performing,' she lamented.

'Me neither,' Zoe cried, 'I want to be on stage or in the wings, waiting our turn to go on.'

'I feel completely out of things,' Marcia wailed. 'Not only that, I look like everybody's grandmother. Whose idea was it to come?'

'Yours!' the others chorused.

'Stop being such prima donnas,' Elaine chided.

The stadium was a sea of people, few of them over twenty; bright-eyed, excited young people, enjoying the electric atmosphere and conscious they were present at a unique event. For some, it was the first time they'd realised how lucky they were to live in a country where they led comfortable lives and had enough to eat. It was a gratifying sensation to know that by buying a ticket they were helping people less fortunate than themselves.

The next group was the Style Council, followed by the Boomtown Rats with, 'I Don't Like Mondays'. A deafening cheer went up for Bob Geldof, who'd already become something of a saint. INXS performed on a giant screen via satellite from Melbourne, then Ultravox and Spandau Ballet. With each group, the ex-Flower Girls became more and more loudly depressed. Why had they given up? they moaned.

'You'd've looked daft, prancing around the stage at your age,' Elaine said caustically. 'You, Marcia, are forty-five and have six children. Where's your pride?'

471

'Men prance around the stage,' Marcia argued. 'The Rolling Stones are on later. Mick Jagger's got dozens of children, and he's about the same age as us.'

'It's different for men.'

'What about Tina Turner? She's on too. And Joan Baez.'

'Tina Turner doesn't even vaguely look like everybody's grandmother and Joan Baez is a folk singer. She can get away with growing old.'

Growing old! The Flower Girls shuddered.

'What shall we do?' Zoe asked. 'I can't stand much more of this. I keep telling myself that *Chocks Away* is far superior to being a Flower Girl, but I'm not sure if I believe it. I'm beginning to think my life is crap.'

'It *is* crap,' Marcia informed her. 'It's about time you got married, settled down, and had some children. But you'd better hurry up before it's too late. Oh, come on, let's go,' she urged. 'Let's find a pub and drown our sorrows. Lord! What a disaster this has turned out to be. Look at all the happy faces everywhere! Ours are the only sour ones.'

'My face isn't sour,' Elaine heatedly pointed out. 'I'd be enjoying myself no end if it weren't for you lot.'

Jeannie was all for leaving, but Elaine insisted she wanted to see Sting and Queen. She was mad about Freddy Mercury, she claimed. 'And Sean McDowd will be on later from Philadelphia. I haven't seen him since he left the Merseysiders.' They agreed to wait for Sting who would be on soon, but not Queen or Sean McDowd, who weren't performing until the evening.

Elaine tossed her head derisively. 'That's nice of you, I must say. I'm never coming to a gig with you again.'

'Don't worry, sis,' Marcia sneered. 'You'll never get the opportunity. Anyroad, I'd've thought you'd be the first who'd want to leave. At least us three have got a decent head of hair. Yours is almost completely grey and have you never thought of giving it a comb? You look far more like a grandmother than I do.'

It was past midnight when Jeannie arrived home. 'Did you have a nice time,' her mother asked.

'No,' Jeannie said bluntly. 'We all felt as old as the hills. I kept thinking about the Cavern and Lachlan and how wonderful things used to be. Oh, Mum! Why does everything have to change?'

'We'd all like the best times of our lives back, love. I know I would. But it's not possible. Time moves on, things *do* change, and you'll just have to be happy with what you've got – Ace and Chloe and this lovely house.'

Two months later, on a humid, airless evening in September, the phone in Sean McDowd's New York apartment rang. It was the desk downstairs to tell him he had a visitor. 'It's a guy, name of Lachlan Bailey. Shall I send him up?'

Sean hesitated a few seconds before answering. 'Yeah, OK.'

What the hell did Lachlan want? He went outside and prowled the corridor, listening to the mechanism of the lift shift into gear at the bottom of the shaft. It was three years since Lachlan and Jeannie had split up. Sean's normally iron self-control faltered slightly. Did Lachlan know that Sean had made love to his wife? If so, surely he hadn't come round to make a scene after all this time? The split had come directly after some girl had claimed she'd had Lachlan's baby. Although the allegation had been withdrawn, Sean had always assumed it was the reason why the pair had broken up and his involvement in their lives had had nothing to do with it. He'd rung Jeannie a few times. She'd been polite, but distant.

The lift whirred, clanged to a halt, and the doors slid open. Sean turned to greet his visitor. 'Hi! Great to see you after all this time. How's things?' He was aware of the tone of false joviality in his voice.

'Hi.'

The two men stared at each other. The first thing Sean noticed was that Lachlan had lost a considerable amount of weight. When last they'd met, he'd still been recognisable as the boy who'd introduced him to rock 'n' roll in the Flowers' garden shed. Now the skin sagged on his neck and there were deep lines on his gaunt, deeply tanned face. His eyes, which had always been soft, were hard. The guy had been through a tough time. He was dressed like a tramp, in a shabby suede jacket and tattered jeans.

'You haven't changed, Sean,' he said without a smile.

'I could say the same for you,' Sean lied. 'Come on inside.'

They went into the vast living area of the apartment overlooking Central Park. 'Would you like a drink?'

'Something cold. A coke or a pepsi. New York always gives me a thirst, though it's cool in here.'

'I've got air conditioning. You're sure you want nothing harder?'

'No, thanks. I'm on the wagon. Had a bit too much of the drink and drugs for a while.' Lachlan wandered over to the window and looked out on to the traffic that never stopped. 'I like the view. Do you ever use the balcony?'

'Occasionally. The noise can get too much, even from this far up. Sit down, why don't you.'

Lachlan threw himself into a brown corduroy armchair on a stainless steel frame. He looked around the room, at the dark, hessian-covered walls and sparse, plain furniture, and chuckled. 'Jeannie would have some fun with this place. She'd have it painted orange within a week and hung pictures everywhere.'

'I was sorry to hear you two had broken up,' Sean felt obliged to say.

'Were you?' Lachlan gave him a keen look.

'Sure thing,' Sean said with all the sincerity he could muster. He wished the guy hadn't come, that he would quickly go, and searched his mind for something to say in the meantime. 'Why did you leave the Survivors? It was one of the best rock bands in the country – in the world, come to that.'

'Why did you leave the Merseysiders?' Lachlan countered.

'To do my own thing.'

'Me too. I've been doing it for the last couple of years; seeing the world, how the other half live, realising there's more to life than rock 'n' roll, that showbiz people are basically shallow and don't see any further than the ends of their noses, me included, and that you, Sean, me old mate, are nothing but a fucking hypocrite.' Lachlan grinned and became immediately recognisable as the boy from the Flowers' shed.

Despite the grin, Sean braced himself for a 'How dare you screw my wife' routine, but Lachlan had other things on his mind.

'I watched you on the Live Aid concert – I was in Africa at the time, Somalia – and I thought to myself, "That guy's nothing but a fake, singing about peace and love, and all that crap." Your entire career has been based on that sort of stuff; anti-war, anti-poverty, brotherly love, yet since when have you ever given a shit about anyone apart from yourself?'

'They're songs, not statements of belief,' Sean said stiffly.

'Yeah, 'cos you don't believe in anything except number one.' Lachlan's face was contemptuous.

Sean managed a croaky laugh. Lachlan's words had shaken him. He had the sickening feeling they might be true. 'Is this why you've come, to tell me I'm a hypocrite? If so, you're wasting your time. I don't give a damn what you or anyone thinks.'

Lachlan shrugged. 'That figures. You don't give a damn about anything. I feel sorry for you, Sean. You're the best guitarist I've ever known, but you lost your soul a long time ago. Now, you play with

476

one eye on your bank balance.' He laughed. 'All that money, but nothing to spend it on except things, not people. The only person you've ever loved is yourself.' He got to his feet just as Sean had been about to suggest it was time he left. It seemed the short visit had merely been to point out a few home truths. 'Thanks for the drink,' Lachlan said. 'I'm off to California in the morning. Don't bother to wish me luck.'

Sean went towards the door, opened it. 'Don't worry, I won't.'

They were in the corridor. Lachlan pressed the button for the lift. 'Oh, there's just one more thing before I go.' He swung his fist and caught Sean a mighty punch on the jaw. 'That's for fucking my wife.'

Sean staggered backwards, nursing his face, while Lachlan stood there, waiting honourably for his response. But Sean had no intention of engaging in a fight. 'You're wrong about only loving myself,' he said slowly. 'I love her, Jeannie. I always will.'

'Lachlan and I had planned on going to Paris on my fortieth birthday,' Jeannie said sadly.

'If you tell me that again, I'll throw something at you,' Elaine said threateningly. 'This jug of cream, perhaps. That'll make a fine mess of your new frock.' Jeannie's frock was misty blue, very plain, with long tight sleeves, the skirt flaring into soft folds from the hips.

'Sorry. I'm not being very good company, am I?'

'The worst. I take my best friend out to dinner

on her birthday to the most expensive Chinese restaurant in Southport, and all she does is complain she's not with someone else.'

'I wonder where he is, what he's doing?' Jeannie sighed. 'I bet he's not having as good a time as me,' she added quickly when Elaine picked up the cream. She'd gone through a startling transformation since Jeannie had last seen her. Her bird's nest of hair had been ruthlessly cut and framed her face in little curly spikes and she wore a red velvet frock with a low neck and cap sleeves, exposing an unusual amount of bosom. Her skin was smooth and creamy. They'd actually finished eating when Jeannie became aware she wasn't wearing glasses.

'Ah, so you've noticed at last!' Elaine exclaimed. 'I've got contact lenses. They feel dead uncomfortable, but the optician said I'll get used to them.'

'You remind me of someone I used to know when I was young. Her name was Elaine too, and she was very pretty, just like you.'

They smiled at each other, and Elaine said, 'I didn't want to give our Marcia the opportunity to make any more rude remarks about my appearance. Remember what she said at that Live Aid concert?'

'We're not likely to meet Marcia tonight, are we?'

'No, no, of course, not.' Elaine went pink for some reason. 'I was just speaking generally. Would you like more wine?'

'One more glass, then I think we'd better go. The children were in a funny old mood tonight.

I'm worried they might be giving Mum a hard time.'

'I'm sure she'll be able to cope. She coped with you, Max, and Gerald. I bet your Max was a handful, wasn't he?'

'Not until he began wanting things, like televisions and guitars.' She frowned suspiciously. 'Are you trying to keep me here for some reason, Elaine? I've a feeling you're just making conversation. I'm sure you're not interested in whether Max was a handful.'

'I used to be quite keen on your Max.'

'You've never mentioned that before because it isn't true. You're playing for time, I can't think why.' Jeannie looked around the darkly lit restaurant, already lavishly decorated for Christmas. 'I half expect the staff to come in with a giant cake and a male stripper will leap out and wish me Happy Birthday.'

'No such luck, I'm afraid.' Elaine glanced at her watch. 'Eight o'clock. Come on, let's go. I'm obviously boring you, and you're stuck with me until you get home, seeing as we came in my car.'

They linked arms on the way to the car park. Specks of ice were being blown to and fro by the arctic wind that penetrated their thick, winter coats and cardigans. They laughed and began to run. 'Thank you for the lovely meal,' Jeannie gasped when they reached the car. 'I adore fried seaweed, though Lachlan used to say...' She broke off. 'Sorry.'

'You can mention his name, idiot. Our Lachlan used to say what about fried seaweed? Tell me in

479

the car. I'm freezing to death out here.'

'That it tasted like starched grass. Oh, Elaine!' she cried, collapsing into the passenger seat. 'This will be our fourth Christmas without him and each one is worse than the one before.'

Elaine squeezed her arm. 'He'll come back one day, Jeannie,' she said gently. 'I can feel it in my bones. He loves you every bit as much as you love him. Whatever it was he did, or you did. I'm sure it will all work out all right in the end.'

They drove back in silence. The ice turned to snow and began to collect in little heaps at the bottom of the windscreen.

'There's no lights on inside,' Jeannie said anxiously when the car drew to a halt outside Noah's Ark. 'I hope everything's all right.'

She felt even more anxious when she unlocked the door and went inside. The house was un-naturally quiet; no children making their usual din, no television. 'Mum,' Jeannie shouted, 'Ace, Chloe. I'm home.' She reached for the light switch, but before she could touch it, the lights went on, and a thousand voices, at least it sounded like a thousand, screamed, 'Surprise!'

'Oh, my God!' She clutched her throat with a trembling hand. Everyone was there; Mrs Bailey, very old now and unable to walk without a stick, Marcia and her husband, Phil, Fly and Stella, Rita and Mavis, Sadie, all the way from Ireland, Zoe with a man Jeannie had never seen before, Max, her other brother, Gerald and Helen, his wife, Amy and her useless husband, Eliza, a few faces she had yet to recognise, Benny – what the hell was Benny doing there? And, of course, her

480

mother, beaming happily, and her own lovely children.

Chloe came dancing up. 'I've known for *days*, Mummy, but I promised not to tell. And I didn't, did I?'

'No, sweetheart,' Jeannie said emotionally, 'you never breathed a word. This is the biggest surprise of my life. The cars must be parked miles away, there's none outside. And you've put the Christmas decorations up! No wonder Elaine tried to keep me in the restaurant. You've all been working very hard.'

'The tree's done, Mummy. Come and see.' As Chloe began to drag her into the living room, Jeannie turned and looked beseechingly at Elaine, who understood the message in her eyes.

She shook her head. 'No, Lachlan isn't here,' she whispered. 'Max tried his utmost to find him, but he had no joy, I'm afraid. Please don't let it spoil the party,' she implored. 'It's taken months to organise. Max and I did it between us, your mother's made some wonderful food, the champagne's waiting, and every single person we asked said it would be a pleasure to come.'

'It's a pleasure to have them. Nothing could spoil a party like this.'

The guests dispersed into other rooms, though some stayed in the magnificent hall where they could see the snow dropping silently on to the green tinted glass roof It was like being inside a spaceship circling the world.

Ace was in charge of the music. The first record he played was a Flower Girls LP. 'Will you still

481

love me tomorrow?' Rita McDowd crooned, backed up by his mother on piano and the voices of Zoe and Marcia. 'Tomorrow, tomorrow, tomorrow,' they chanted.

Jeannie began to circulate, to thank everyone for coming, agreeing that, yes, it was the biggest surprise of her life. 'I'm also surprised that you could come,' she said to Rita. 'I thought you were still on the West End.'

'I finished last Saturday,' Rita explained. 'Someone else took over my part. Rehearsals start next week for *Anna*, based on Tolstoy's novel, *Anna Karenina*. After six months, we're transferring to Broadway.'

'I expect you're playing Anna?'

'Well, yes,' Rita said modestly.

'How are you getting to America, Mavis?' Mavis's aversion to flying was well-known.

'She's being a real pain,' Rita complained.

'I'm going by ship, Jeannie. Flying ain't natural. If the good Lord had meant us to fly...'

'I know, I know, he'd have given us wings.' Rita made a face. 'She must have said that a million times. I've offered to stuff her with gin and Valium, but she won't hear of it.'

'I don't want to become a drug addict, darlin'.'

Max came up and asked if she had the key to the studio. 'I just tried to get in, but the door's locked.'

'That's because I'm worried the children might damage something. Why do you want to get in?' He followed her into the kitchen where she kept the key. The table was full of savoury bites and she could smell mince pies warming in the oven.

A giant cake was covered with forty pink candles. She hoped she wasn't expected to blow all of them out.

'We're doing a pantomime at school, *Aladdin*. I wrote the words and music, and I thought it'd be nice to make a few records for the parents. I was wondering if I can still find my way around the equipment. It's Elaine's idea. It's strange,' he mused, his face softening, 'I knew Elaine for all those years, yet it's only over the last few weeks I've got to know her properly. Arranging this party could be compared to organising a vast military operation. We ended up meeting every night.'

Jeannie didn't show her delight in case it was premature. She said, 'Does that mean I can expect the entire cast of *Aladdin* any day soon?'

'You don't mind, do you, sis?' he said anxiously.

'I'd welcome it, Max. Though don't forget, the studio is very old-fashioned. These days, studios are all digital.'

'That doesn't worry me. I'm an old-fashioned kind of guy.' Max disappeared into the basement.

'What's Max up to?' Fly wanted to know.

Jeannie explained what her brother had in mind and Fly said he'd go and help. 'I often think about the great times we used to have down there. Y'know,' he said thoughtfully. 'Max wasn't too bad a guitarist, it's just that Lachlan was a perfectionist. Everything had to be just right.'

'I know, Fly.'

'I don't suppose you've heard anything from him?'

'Not a word. I'd've told you if I had.'

'Of course you would, Jeannie.' He went down to join Max. He was a wan, downcast figure, who missed Lachlan almost as much as she did.

Having exhausted his mother's records, Ace had now started on his daddy's. 'See you later, Alligator,' promised Lachlan and Sean's youthful voices. It was the first number on the very first record the Merseysiders had made, bringing back a whole host of memories, both wonderful and sad.

Nearby, Mrs Bailey said in a wistful voice, 'I *do* wish our Lachlan were here, Rose,' and Jeannie's mother answered, 'So do I, Ida. Oh, so do I.'

'Would you like more champagne?' Chloe asked her grandmas. She was enjoying her role as waitress for the night.

Across the room, the usually restrained Elaine danced a few exuberant steps in time to the music, and Jeannie wondered if she realised why she was so happy.

'I'll be leaving in a minute,' a voice said in her ear. Jeannie winced. It was Benny Lucas whom she had so far managed to avoid. 'Thank you for the lovely party.'

'I didn't invite you, Benny,' she stiffly pointed out. 'To tell the truth, I don't know why you're here.'

'Elaine asked me,' Benny said humbly. She looked considerably better than when Jeannie had last seen her. Her greying hair had been tinted blonde and she wore a smart, black suit. 'She came to see me, years ago, just after that business ... well, you know. She arranged to get Mam in a home. It's a nice place, she's happy

484

there. I visit her every Sunday.'

'Elaine never told me.'

'She's been incredibly kind.' The thin, sad face shone with gratitude. 'I'm back with the Inland Revenue, only part-time, while Saffron's at playgroup.'

Jeannie had no idea what to say. She made a sort of strangled noise in her throat, and Benny went on. 'You two were always doing things for me at school. I didn't realise then. I was jealous of your friendship and felt left out, yet you were trying to include me. I should have realised you wouldn't drop me from the Flower Girls.' She put her hand on Jeannie's arm. 'I'm sorry, Jeannie, for everything. I'm sorry too that Lachlan's gone. I didn't know until the other week when Elaine invited me. She thought it would give me the opportunity to apologise. I don't expect we can be friends again, not after what I did, not after all this time, but I'd like to think you don't bear me any ill will.' The pale eyes searched Jeannie's face for a sign of forgiveness, the absolution of her sins.

If it hadn't been for Benny and her monstrous scheme, there'd have been no need for Lachlan to see a doctor for tests. He would have never discovered he couldn't have children. If it hadn't been for Benny, right now she and Lachlan would be in Paris, together, having a nightcap before they went to bed, and the last three years would have been very different.

But Jeannie and Lachlan had both committed sins of their own that were nothing to do with Benny, who had merely been the catalyst that tore their marriage apart. The only thing left was Lachlan's voice, filling the room with its hoarse passion, asking them if they wanted to be his honey.

Benny turned away after what had been a long silence. 'It doesn't matter,' she said dully. 'I understand. I'd find it hard to forgive if it was the other way around.' She glanced around the big, cheerful room, full of people. 'I'll be forty in a few months, but I won't be having a party. There's no one to ask.'

'Benny!'

The pale eyes shone hopefully. 'What?'

'On your birthday, let's go out to dinner – you, Elaine, and me. We'll get dressed up, make it a special occasion.'

'That'd be very nice, Jeannie. I'll look forward to it.' Benny nodded gravely and was gone.

'I'm glad you said that.' Elaine appeared at her side a few minutes later.

'Said what?'

Whatever it was you just said to Benny. It must have been something nice because she went home looking happy.'

'You're nothing but an interfering busybody, Elaine Bailey. I said we'd take Benny to dinner on her birthday. If you don't come, I'll never speak to you again,' she threatened.

'I'll come, don't worry.'

Jeannie's mother entered the room bearing the cake with all forty candles lit, and Lachlan's voice was smothered by the sound of everyone joyfully singing 'Happy Birthday'. Ace and Chloe were summoned to help blow out the candles as their mother didn't have enough breath to do it on her own. The song finished with a loud cheer and Jeannie was showered with hugs and kisses. She found it hard not to burst into tears.

'I love you,' she cried. 'I love all of you. You're the best friends in the world.'

She didn't hear the doorbell ring. She hadn't known another guest had arrived, until Gerald came in and announced excitedly, 'Guess who's here!'

Lachlan! It could only be Lachlan. She stood, transfixed, in the centre of the room, heart racing, waiting for him to appear, but instead of Lachlan, it was Sean McDowd who entered the room after Gerald.

Sean saw the disappointment in her eyes. She'd been expecting someone else and it could only be Lachlan, which meant he wasn't here. Not that Sean cared if he was or not. Lachlan was unlikely to throw a punch in front of the guests and have them wondering why. As for Jeannie, he'd given up on her years ago. Sean had come for one reason only, to see the children that were almost certainly his.

His mother had told him about the party and Sean had decided to just turn up. Apart from Jeannie, everyone else would be glad to see him. They surrounded him, shaking his hand, thumping his shoulder. People who would once have turned away in disgust from the young Sean McDowd were now his greatest fans. His mother flung her arms around his neck and kissed him and Sean kissed her back with real affection.

How dare Lachlan Bailey suggest he loved no one but himself when he loved his mother with all his heart. His sister too. He hugged Rita fiercely. 'Hiya, sis.'

'I'm coming to New York next year, Sean,' she told him. 'I'm going to be on Broadway.'

By God, they'd made it, the McDowds. They were top of the tree. Stars! People paid a fortune to see them.

'Are you really *the* Sean McDowd?' It was a little boy who asked. He was very handsome and had Sean's lean face and dark blue eyes, though his hair was blond. 'You're on records with my daddy.'

'Are you *the* Ace Bailey?' Sean was aware his eyes were twinkling at the child who was undoubtedly his. Emotions, never felt before, flooded his body; a gush of tenderness, an urge to protect, the awareness that he would kill anybody who dared lay a hand on his son.

The little boy blushed shyly. 'You mean you've heard of me?'

Was I ever so naive? Sean wondered. If anyone had asked him the same question when he was the same age, he would have told them to get lost. 'I hear you're a very smart kid,' he said.

'I can play the guitar, but not as good as Daddy. Or you,' the child added sadly. 'Uncle Max is teaching me. Daddy used to, but he's away. He's been gone an awful long while.'

'There's plenty of time for you to learn,' Sean said encouragingly. 'I'd never even seen a guitar when I was nine.'

'How did you know I was nine?'

'I just did. Is your Uncle Max here?' He and Max had never got on all that well, but he quite fancied seeing him for old times' sake.

'He's in the studio with Fly.'

Sean fancied seeing Fly even more. 'Shall we find out what they're up to?'

'OK.'

Fly was sitting behind the set of drums that had been a permanent fixture downstairs, while Max idly strummed a guitar. They were talking, but jumped to their feet in astonishment when Sean came in. An incredibly middle-aged, hardly recognisable Max looked quite pleased, and Fly, who was merely an older version of his younger self ecstatically pumped Sean's hand. 'Sean, me old mate. Shit, it's good to see you!'

'You, too, Fly.' Sean genuinely meant it. He felt different tonight, looser and more at ease, among people he knew – he glanced at Ace – and his son. Somewhere upstairs was his daughter. He noticed half a dozen guitar cases leaning against the wall. The hard case with the scratches had belonged to him, and he wondered if it still held the electric guitar he'd bought for the Merseysiders' first gig at the Taj Mahal. It had cost twenty-five pounds, which had seemed a fortune in those days. The others watched as he opened the case and found the black instrument nestling inside. Smiling, he lifted it out, plugged it into an amplifier, and played the first few bars of 'Wake Up Little Susie'. He smiled again when Max joined in. Fly picked up the drum sticks, and the studio began to rock in a way it hadn't done in a long time.

'That takes me back,' Sean said when they'd

finished. Lachlan had been right. He'd lost his soul. It was a while since he'd felt such a tingle in his veins when he played the guitar. 'Another?'

'Half a mo.' Max put a guitar in a wide-eyed Ace's arms, and Sean wished he'd thought to do it himself. 'Do your best, kiddo. Tomorrow, you can tell your mates at school that you played a jam session with the famous Sean McDowd and Fly Fleming.'

'They'll never believe him,' said Fly.

Max laughed. 'Maybe not, but he'll know it's true.' His hand was poised over the strings of his guitar. '"The Great Pretender"? I'm stuck in the past. I only know the old tunes.'

'"The Great Pretender" it is.' Sean played the first few bars and the others took their cue. He saw that Ace was frowning seriously as he tried to keep up.

'Hey, we could do with a few beers down here.' Fly laid down the sticks when the number ended.

'Shall I fetch some?' Ace offered. 'Nana's got beer in tins.'

'The wish is father to the thought,' Max remarked, when a little girl entered the studio with half a dozen tins on a tray. 'Hello, Chloe. Have you been reading minds?'

'Nana sent these, Uncle Max, but she wouldn't let me bring glasses in case I dropped them,' the child said importantly. 'You'll have to drink out of the tin. I'd like to drink out of a tin, but the lemonade's in bottles. Does it taste different?' she enquired curiously when the men snapped open the beers.

'Nicer,' Sean assured her.

'Can I have a sip?'

He gave her the tin and she pulled a face. 'It's horrible!'

'I'd stick to lemonade if I were you.' Their fingers touched when she returned the beer and Sean realised with painful sadness it was the closest he would ever get to his little girl. She had his chin – small, determined, neatly round – and the same black hair, but the similarity to himself wasn't as marked as it was with Ace. He wondered if anyone had noticed – apart from Jeannie – but thought it unlikely. It wouldn't enter people's heads, not even Lachlan's, that he wasn't the father of these children. He wondered what had prevented him from telling Lachlan this when he'd punched him in New York, and realised he'd been protecting Jeannie.

'I have to go.' He got to his feet, unable to stand being in the house another minute. He didn't belong.

'Ah, do you really have to, Sean?' Fly looked disappointed. 'I thought we were having a great time.'

'We were. It's been great, but I've an appointment in London in the morning. The roads were bad when I arrived and it's a long drive.' It was a lie. He was meeting no one.

There was a shout from upstairs. 'Are the children down there?' It was Jeannie.

'I'm here, Mummy.' Chloe scampered across to the door. 'Ace is here too.'

'Aren't you supposed to be a waitress? And isn't Ace in charge of the music?'

Sean followed the little girl up the stairs. The

skirt of her frilly frock bounced against her thin, brown legs. Jeannie was waiting at the top. There was a look, almost of fear, on her lovely face, when Sean followed her daughter – *their* daughter – through the door.

'I'm off now, Jeannie.'

'But you've hardly been here five minutes!'

He lied again. 'I've an appointment in London tomorrow.'

'Couldn't you cancel it? It's a terrible night outside.' She looked worried, despite it being obvious she'd sooner he was gone. 'Stay the night. There's loads of people staying,' she added quickly. 'You might have to sleep on the floor, but it's better than driving in such awful weather.'

'Thanks, but I'd sooner not.' He *had* to get away. 'I'll just say tara to mam and our Rita. 'Bye, Chloe.' He ruffled the black hair.

''Bye, Sean.' She looked at him cheekily.

His mother looked desperately sad to see him go. Her new husband had been too busy to come. She must be missing Kevin, who wouldn't have turned down a party for anything on earth. Sean wished with all his heart that his dad was there, making his usual outrageous show of himself.

'Tara, sis.' He kissed his sister's smooth, un-wrinkled cheek. She too would soon be forty, but could have passed for half that age. As far as he knew, Rita had never been in love. She had never born a child. Apart from the death of their father, she had never known tragedy. Life had passed by, leaving her untouched. How strange they were, Sean thought, the children of Sadie and Kevin McDowd.

Jeannie showed him to the door. 'I do wish you'd stay,' she said, her face creased with concern when she saw the snow which was falling heavily now and already inches thick on the ground. In the short time he'd been in Noah's Ark, the world had been transformed into a white, ghostly grotto.

'Sorry, Jeannie. No can do.' They were standing very close and he noticed there were fine lines under her eyes and on her forehead. He had the strongest feeling he would never see her, or his children, again. Never before had he experienced a feeling of such aching loneliness. He was a man who had everything, yet he owned nothing of real value.

'Goodbye, Sean.' Unexpectedly, she cupped his face in her hands. 'Thank you.' She kissed him softly on the lips. 'Thank you for everything.'

He ran to his car, a hired Mercedes, hardly visible in the snow. When he got inside, he could see nothing. He turned on the engine, the radiator, and the windscreen wipers, front and back. The snow disappeared, the car slid forward and, through the rear-view mirror, he could see Jeannie framed in the brightly lit doorway. Perhaps he should have told her he'd met Lachlan in New York. At least she would have known he was still alive. He could still feel the touch of her soft fingers on his face, and his lips tingled from her kiss. She waved and was still waving when he manoeuvred the car around a curve. When he looked again Jeannie, and the house, were gone.

Neither Jeannie or Sean had seen the other car,

the black Ferrari, hidden behind the trees in front of Noah's Ark. Lachlan had just witnessed his wife embrace Sean McDowd. It hadn't been a passionate embrace, more like a farewell to an old friend.

While the door was open, the still night air had been invaded by the sound of the Survivors and Lachlan heard his own voice singing one of his own songs. Lights were on in every room. He suspected a party but, if so, why weren't there more cars? Now that the Mercedes had gone, there was only Elaine's rusty old Fiesta.

He was brooding over this, when the front door opened again and Max Flowers came out. Wrapped up warmly, he began to hurry down the drive, his footsteps crisply sharp on the frozen gravel. A few minutes later, Max returned, this time in a Cortina, which he parked as close as possible to the front door. He went inside and a few minutes later, Lachlan's mother came out. He groaned. She was walking with a stick, being helped by Max on one side, and Elaine on the other. With great difficulty, she got into the back seat of the car. Max slammed the door. Elaine was about to get in the front, she must be leaving her own car behind, when Max grabbed her waist and nuzzled his face in her neck.

Elaine shrieked. 'Stoppit! You're freezing.' She punched him playfully.

At least someone's happy, Lachlan thought as the Cortina drove away.

It was much later that an incongruous figure emerged; a man in a black overcoat and a monstrous Russian-style fur hat, who began to walk stiffly down the drive. It took Lachlan a while to recognise Philip Elroy-Smith, Marcia's husband. It was hard to believe this man had once played the drums in a rock 'n' roll band. These days, he was something important in the city.

Philip returned in a Rolls Royce. Marcia came out of the house wearing an ankle-length fur coat. She began to chastise Philip for something, her penetrating voice carrying as sharp as knives through the trees, laden with snow. 'Why didn't you think to offer my mother a lift? Our car's so much more comfortable than Max's.'

'Why didn't you think of it, darling?'

They got in the car, still arguing. Lachlan could see their faces – Marcia's angry, Philip's patient – as it glided away.

It dawned on him that all this toing and froing with cars indicated the party had been a surprise. Elaine had taken Jeannie somewhere in the Fiesta and the guests had arrived while they were away, parking their cars out of sight. He wondered who else was in there? Fly? The Cobb? If so, they'd probably stay the night. It would be crazy to travel far on a night like this. Marcia and Philip must be staying with his mother in the house in Walton Vale.

He thought tenderly of the house where he'd first met Jeannie. She'd told him she'd fallen in love with him at first sight. 'But my love just grew and grew,' he'd told her, 'Until you became so much part of my life I realised I couldn't live without you.'

The day of their first kiss came back to him as

clearly as if it were yesterday, yet it was exactly twenty-four years ago today. Her sixteenth birthday. They'd met on the stairs and he couldn't resist her flushed face, her starry eyes. He'd known then that they would marry – and be happy ever after?

Lachlan groaned again. He clutched the steering wheel and buried his head in his arms and the question returned for the millionth time.

How could she do it?

He hadn't even thought she could tell a lie. She was the most open and honest person he'd ever known, yet she'd betrayed him in the foulest possible way. It wasn't just that she'd slept with Sean, though that was bad enough, or that she'd deliberately sought Sean out, seduced him, which was even worse, but she'd allowed him to believe that Sean's children were his! And she would have let him go on believing the same monstrous lie for the rest of her life, all their lives, if circumstances hadn't led to the truth.

Why had Sean been there tonight? He loved her. He had told Lachlan that to his face when they'd met in New York. Jeannie was still Lachlan's wife, they'd never divorced, but for more than three years she'd been free to do whatever she wanted with her life. He wondered why she and Sean hadn't got together? He was, after all, the perfect choice for a partner. They already had a ready-made family. He imagined Ace and Chloe calling another man 'Daddy', and his heart twisted. He wanted to rush into the house, pick up his children, hug them.

My children. *My* children. *They're mine.*

He saw now what he should have done three years ago; torn up the test results, never mentioned them, just gone on living as they had done before. It would have nagged him for ever, wanting to know who the father was, but it would have been better than walking out, cutting himself off from the three people he loved most in the world.

Jeannie would have forgiven him his own betrayals, the star-crazed girls he had taken in a fog of drugs. God! That was a lousy thing to do. Fifty, sixty, a hundred deceits. Jeannie's one affair was mild by comparison.

But the children, the children! How could he possibly forgive her that?

Why had he come? Why was he sheltering under the trees outside his own house, slowly freezing to death? Had he just wanted to be near Jeannie on her birthday? He'd left California two days ago and flown to London where he'd unearthed the Ferrari from the garage where it had been stored, then just driven, nowhere in mind, crisscrossing the country, getting nearer and nearer to Liverpool, as if Noah's Ark was a magnet, drawing him inexorably closer to the woman he loved, but could never forgive.

More people were leaving the party, but Lachlan didn't bother to look to see who they were. He envied their shrill laughter and wondered if he would ever laugh again. After they'd gone, he started up the car, backed out of the trees, and zoomed away into the snowy night.

Chapter 17

Jeannie woke, sensing that someone was in the room with her. She wasn't afraid. The house was full of people and sometimes Ace crept in if he couldn't sleep, or Chloe if she'd had a nightmare.

Before going to bed, she'd drawn back the curtains so she could watch the snow falling while she fell asleep. It was a peaceful sight, though it was a long time before she'd dropped off. Perhaps it was because she'd drunk too much champagne that such strange, dislocated thoughts kept drifting into her mind, then drifting out again, forgotten. She couldn't remember a single one. A cold, white light shone into the room and she could see a dark figure sitting at the foot of the bed. It was an adult, not a child.

'Who is it?' she asked.

'It's me.'

'*Lachlan!*' She sat up too quickly and her head swam. Fumbling for the bedside lamp, she switched it on, and there he was, Lachlan Bailey, sitting on the bed, as if he'd never been away.

'You've had your hair cut,' was all she could think of to say. It was cropped close to his head, giving his face a naked look. She wondered why he was so brown and thought how ordinary he looked, nothing like the handsome, charismatic Lachlan Bailey she'd always known. He was wearing a khaki anorak and thick trousers and his eyes were bloodshot and red-rimmed, as if he had been weeping. His shoulders were hunched with weariness. She could tell from the bleak expression on his face that something terrible had happened.

'Sean's dead,' he said in a tired voice. 'I was driving along the East Lancashire Road when I came across an accident. The police were there, an ambulance. A Mercedes had skidded off the road and crashed straight into a wall.'

'Sean – *dead!*' She shook her head in shocked disbelief 'No. No, that can't be.'

'I'm afraid it is, Jeannie. I held his hand in the ambulance when he was dying. They weren't going to let me, but I told them he was my friend. I stroked his face. I even cried.' For the first time since she'd known him, Lachlan burst into tears. 'Jesus Christ! It was horrible. He was smashed to pieces.' He looked down at his hands. They were covered in blood.

'Darling!' Jeanne scrambled out of bed and sat beside him, cradling his exhausted body in her arms. 'Oh, my darling Lachlan.' She tried, feverishly, to get her head around the fact that what he'd said was true, that Sean was dead. 'I'm glad you were with him, that he didn't die alone.' She imagined the long, lithe body, all broken and crushed, the perfect face ruined.

Lachlan shivered and continued to weep in her arms. She ran her fingers through his strange, short hair, kissed his forehead, trying to make him better.

'I thought I hated him,' Lachlan whispered,

'but all I felt was pity.' He looked at Jeannie, bemused.

'Did he recognise you? Did he know you were there? Oh, I hope he realised it was you holding his hand!'

'Yes, he smiled.' Lachlan smiled too at the memory. 'He even spoke. He said, "You're a lucky guy, Lachlan," and then he died.'

'Poor Sean.' She remembered thinking how sad he'd looked when he left the party and her eyes filled with tears.

'Poor Sean.' Lachlan's mouth twisted drily. 'Lucky Lachlan. Oh, Jeannie!' He pulled her against him, holding her so tightly she could hardly breathe. 'I've missed you,' he said gruffly. 'I've missed you so much. The things we did, you and me, they seem trivial when you come face to face with death.'

'I know, darling,' Jeannie soothed. She didn't ask why he'd been driving away from Liverpool – he must have, if he'd come across the accident. Or how he'd known Sean had a Mercedes. If he hadn't known, he wouldn't have stopped. She suspected that, if it hadn't been for Sean, Lachlan would be miles and miles away by now, driving to who knows where.

He was still shivering and she realised his clothes were damp. She gently removed herself from his arms and fetched dry ones from the wardrobe where they'd been kept in the hope one day he would return. 'I'll make coffee. Come into the kitchen when you're ready. It's warmer there.'

The kitchen gave no sign of there having been a party. Her mother had tidied up. The leftover

500

food had been put in the fridge, the tins and bottles were outside to be collected, the surfaces gleamed.

She was plugging in the kettle when Lachlan came in wearing the jeans and thick sweater she'd given him, looking more his old self. She noticed the jeans were too big, that he'd lost weight.

'By the way,' he said. 'The police asked me about Sean's next-of-kin, but I couldn't remember Sadie's new name, or where she lived in Ireland.'

'Sadie's here. Rita too. I'll tell them later, let them sleep in peace a little while longer.'

'We'll tell them together.'

Jeanie nodded, grateful. 'Yes, I think that would be best. Mavis is here as well, Fly and Stella, Zoe and her boyfriend. The house is full.'

'Fly's here!' His face brightened. 'I wonder...' He stopped.

'Wonder what?'

'Nothing. It doesn't matter.' He shook his head irritably. 'I was thinking about the future, but it doesn't seem right, not yet, not when Sean no longer has one.'

The door opened and a drowsy Chloe came in sucking her thumb. 'Had a bad dream, Daddy.' She climbed on to Lachlan's knee and immediately fell asleep. He gazed at Jeannie in astonishment. 'You'd think I'd never been away.'

'She'll remember in the morning when she's properly awake.'

The kettle boiled and she made coffee. They drank it in silence, Chloe's dark head tucked in the curve of Lachlan's neck. Jeannie felt as if death was in the room with them. Sean was the first member of the gang to die. He was part of that exhilarating time when they were young and the only thing that mattered was rock 'n' roll. With his death, that dazzling era had finally ended.

'It seems wrong,' Lachlan said soberly, 'that I've got his kids. That he never knew he was a father.'

'I would have thought you'd be pleased.'

He sighed. 'I am, but it still seems wrong. I'm glad we can talk about him like this, but there's one thing, Jeannie.' His eyes glistened. 'That day, the day I left, when we had the row, you said being with Sean was wonderful. Did you mean it? Or did you just want to wind me up?'

'I just wanted to wind you up.' The years ahead would be made much easier with that one, last lie. 'Are you back for good, Lachlan?'

His lips twisted in a wry smile. 'If you'll have me.'

'You know I will.' Her voice broke. 'You left a great big hole in all our lives.'

'It seems daft to stay away, make everyone miserable, including myself. We only have one life. Until a few years ago, it was perfect. Only a fool would expect it to stay like that for ever.'

'I never claimed to be perfect, Lachlan.'

'I know, Jeannie. The trouble was, I thought you were.' He got carefully to his feet, trying not to disturb the child in his arms. 'I'll put Chloe down, take a look at Ace, then I think we'd better wake Sadie and Rita.'

'We'll wake everyone. They'll all want to know.'

She heard him say, 'Shush, sweetheart,' as he carried Chloe back to bed. A minute later, the door to Ace's room opened. From now on, she thought, their marriage would be very different and she prayed it would be for the better, not the worse. They'd grown up, learnt some very harsh lessons, acquired an awful lot of baggage over the last three years. There was more to life than rock 'n' roll.

He was back, standing in the doorway, holding out his hand; older, wiser, but still the man she loved with all her heart. His face was grim. It was an awful thing they had to do.

'Are you ready, Jeannie?'

'Yes, Lachlan.' She got up and took his outstretched hand. With this simple gesture, she had the strongest feeling that, once they'd got over this terrible, tragic period, everything was going to be all right.

MOON UNDER WATER!

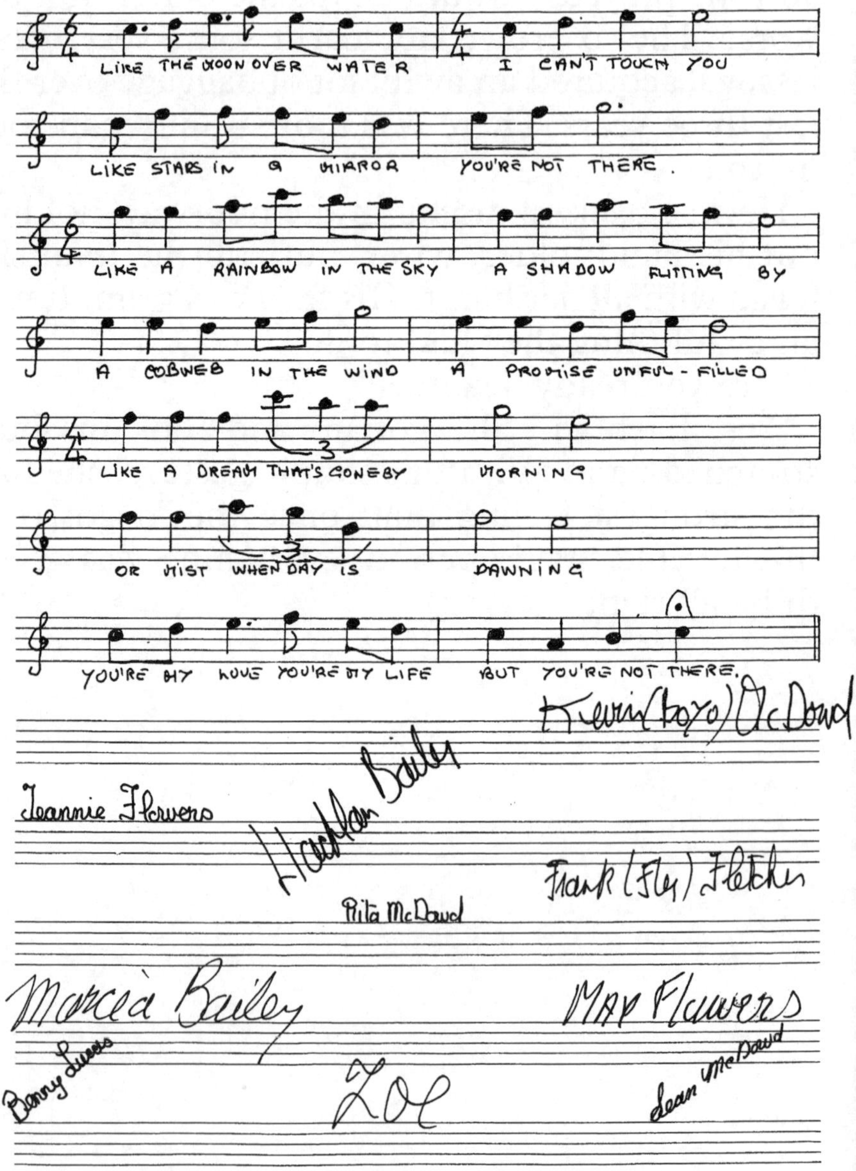

The publishers hope that this book has given you enjoyable reading. Large Print Books are especially designed to be as easy to see and hold as possible. If you wish a complete list of our books please ask at your local library or write directly to:

Magna Large Print Books
Magna House, Long Preston,
Skipton, North Yorkshire.
BD23 4ND

This Large Print Book for the partially sighted, who cannot read normal print, is published under the auspices of

THE ULVERSCROFT FOUNDATION

Other MAGNA Titles
In Large Print

LYN ANDREWS
Angels Of Mercy

HELEN CANNAM
Spy For Cromwell

EMMA DARCY
The Velvet Tiger

SUE DYSON
Fairfield Rose

J. M. GREGSON
To Kill A Wife

MEG HUTCHINSON
A Promise Given

TIM WILSON
A Singing Grave

RICHARD WOODMAN
The Cruise Of The Commissioner